Cherokee Afternoon

Cherokee Afternoon

Bryan D. Jackson

Gadugi Media

This book is a work of fiction. While the author has attempted to stay true to some events as they occurred, historical situations, real people, or real locales are used fictitiously. Other names, characters, places, or incidents are products of the author's imagination, and any resemblances to persons living or dead, are coincidental and unintentional.

For Mary, Annie, Emma, and Estelle,
for showing up when you did.
I did the best I could with what I had.
My hope is that I never disgraced you.

Content Warning

The following material contains graphic content including profanity, derogatory racial language, sexual violence and its explicit description; teen sexual activity, physical and verbal abuse, suicide, and murder, most of the aforementioned in the context of Indigenous women, past and present.

Reader discretion is advised.

Foreword

During our time on earth, we meet many people from different walks of life. Have you ever met someone and it was as if you had known them for a long time, maybe in another realm? When I met the author, Bryan Jackson, that is how I felt. According to Bryan, it was mutual. Bryan and his wife Penny call me "Auntie." Bryan and I have a connection in that we are both Cherokee, but the connection runs deeper than that. That connection is like we have known each other through numerous lifetimes. It is inexplicable.

When people say that we are standing on the shoulders of those who preceded us, it is true. They have paved the way for us. And if there was any trauma that our ancestors experienced, it was passed on to each one of us. Our ancestors speak to us when we are open to them. We hear artists speak of this when creating new work—music, dance, writing, art—the artist channels their new creation. People will ask them, "How did you get that idea?" And the artist will respond that it just came through. This was true for Bryan as he wrote the book. As an artist from a different art form, I choreographed a wealth of material in ballet and modern dance. So many times, I would go into the dance studio, and the choreography would pipe through me.

When COVID-19 hit the world and everything shut down, we relied on Zoom or other digital platforms to communicate with each other. The Cherokee Nation and our Washington State Cherokee Community of Puget Sound (CCPS) were early leaders in reaching out to the regional Cherokees via these platforms. That is how I met Bryan. During the early days of COVID, CCPS started a two-hour meeting every Wednesday evening for the Northwest Cherokees to share and talk with each other. That is where my connection with Bryan deepened.

The first book I read that Bryan wrote was *Chattahoochee Rain*, which is a middle-grade historical fiction novella that centers on a thirteen-year-old Cherokee girl before the Cherokee Removal and the Trail of Tears. Because of my enjoyment of *Chattahoochee Rain*, I looked forward to *Cherokee Afternoon*. This past January, I read the draft of the manuscript for this book. It takes place in two worlds. One world is the present day in the Cherokee Nation in Oklahoma. The second is the 1838-1839 journey of a family on the Trail of Tears Bell route. The sojourn begins at Fort Cass in the Old Cherokee Nation. It ends at the Vineyard Post Office, near today's Evansville, Arkansas.

Cherokee Afternoon is like a woven blanket where Bryan weaves the stories of two different time periods, where the characters experience many trials but whose lives are nevertheless occasionally peppered with joy and humor. In the present day, the story portrays Molly and her sister Emmy, who live in the Cherokee Nation. At the same time, the author leads us back to 1838, where Mary McNair and her family are forced to leave the Old Cherokee Nation and travel on the Trail of Tears to Indian Territory. Mary's spirit voice speaks to Molly in her challenging life journey with her family. That same voice was with Bryan as he wrote this book.

Cherokee Afternoon is a perfect title. At the end of the book, Mary and her family arrive in Indian Territory, while one hundred and eighty-six years later, Molly and Emmy are sitting in rocking chairs on the front porch of a favorite getaway spot.

The two related families from different time periods celebrate a sense of calm in the end. They begin anew in the warm sun on a Cherokee afternoon.

Mary Price Boday
Cherokee Nation

Heritage Statement

Bryan D. Jackson shares a heritage relationship with the Cherokee Nation and belongs to a Cherokee Nation community. His lineal ancestors populated Cherokee rolls from 1817 to 1909.

Documented Cherokee Lineage

"Susannah" Sonicooie (Cordery) [m. Thomas Cordery, Reservation Roll, 1817]

Sarah Cordery (Rogers) [m. John Rogers, Jr., Reservation Roll 1817, Henderson Roll, 1835]

Ann Chappell Rogers (Lenoir) Siler Roll, 1851 (#1712); Chapman Roll, 1852 (#1822); Hester Roll, 1883 (#2222); Dawes Roll, 1900 (#13055, stricken due to death) Migrated to Indian Territory (later Oklahoma) Township 24 North, Range 18 East, Chelsea Cooweescoowee District, 28 June 1900

Emma Elizabeth Lenoir (Roberts) Hester Roll, 1883 (#2236)

Estelle Corinne Roberts (Wiggins) Guion Miller Roll, 1909 (#2991)

Aileen Wiggins (Jackson) (Farrell) Cherokee descendant, (Unregistered)

Walter Coburn Jackson Cherokee descendant, (Unregistered)

Bryan Douglas Jackson, Cherokee descendant, First Families of the Cherokee Nation, 2011 (#931/Sonicooie), Cherokee Community of Puget Sound (Cherokee Nation), Mt. Hood Cherokees (Cherokee Nation)

Mary Rogers McNair, a co-protagonist in this book, was the oldest sister of Bryan's third great-grandmother, Annie Rogers Lenoir. Mary and her husband, Nicholas Byers McNair, can be found on the Cherokee Drennen Roll of 1852 in family group #476, Saline District, Indian Territory.

Unless Mr. Bell on his arrival shall be able to infuse a more reasonable spirit into many of the Emigrants composing this party, I am entirely of the opinion that nothing but Force will be able to make them consult their own interest and proceed quietly upon the Route to the West.

—Lieutenant Edward Deas, October 18, 1838, on the Trail of Tears

I never saw any of the daughters except Mary, the oldest. I remember her well when she was just growing up and was just from school. She was a beautiful girl with a lily complexion, glossy black hair and beautiful black eyes. I think she was educated in North Carolina and, to my young mind, was one of the most lovely women I ever saw. The memory of her sweet face haunts me still after these forty long years...

—Judge Richard D. Winn, 1872, *History of Gwinnett County, Georgia: 1818-1943, Volume 1,* regarding his recollection of Mary Rogers [later McNair] during the early 1800s

1

Indian Time

Present Day, Late January
Late Afternoon
McNair House
Muskogee, Oklahoma
District Four, Cherokee Nation

Molly heaved the hardcover book across the room and against the wall, breaking the second hand on her Cherokee Nation seal clock.

"Oh, my God, what a load of hokum horseshit!"

Lying on her bed, she slid her hands to her face and rubbed her forehead with her palms. She was coming to terms with what it meant to be a Cherokee. The book, a serious account of the history of the Cherokee Trail of Tears, was open on the floor to some obscure page which pointed, like all the others, to a somber and sometimes gruesome history.

"What's going on in there, Peewee?"

"Nothing, Mom. Everything's chill," she responded. But nothing was chill. Why did she have to find out about this stuff? She could feel her heart racing. Do people have chest pains at seventeen? When she had gotten to the part about how they herded her ancestors like cattle along buffalo trails, goaded by white men with bayonets and guns, that's when she had flung the book. She stared at it, then glanced up to the clock. Oh, well, she thought. Damn thing never worked right anyway. That's Indian time for you.

She reflected on her reading. Her people. The marching and sickness. The beatings. The rapes. Being seen as subhuman. How could people treat others this way? Tears dribbled down her pale face. She grabbed strands of her long, chestnut hair and put them in her mouth. She gnawed on the end, a habit she developed at fourteen. She realized what she was doing, raised her head, and flicked her hair back.

She wiped away the tears with her cotton bedspread. "What *is* it about this country that despises the people who were here in the first place?" Molly considered herself knowledgeable about indigenous culture and the national dialogue regarding Native rights. Since the beginning of her senior year, she had become more cognizant than ever of her people's challenges in a society where many considered Cherokees obscure relics of the past. She knew she had ancestors who made the Trail of Tears journey during the harsh autumn and winter of 1838. She knew her fourth great-grandfather was a guy named McNair, her surname. He married a Cherokee woman named Mary Rogers. Molly closed her eyes, ruminating.

"I'm sorry," she heard herself say. "So very sorry," she repeated as she thought of her forebears and the pain they endured. No wonder they called them warriors. Molly found it all eye-opening. She had read about the Trail of Tears in school before, but most of what she knew was from family oral tradition, which was vague. An outside cloud hovered, eclipsing her personal space, and the room was quiet.

It wasn't *your* fault.

"What?"

"What?" said her mother, Sandra, who was putting clean sheets in the hall closet. Molly noticed beneath her closed door that her mom had turned on the hall light to see. "Did you say something?" her mom shouted.

"Nothing," she said. "I didn't say anything," she shouted back. She listened to her footsteps as they disappeared into the kitchen.

"Dang," she lamented quietly. "Losing my damn mind."

No, you're not.

Molly bolted upright. "What—what did you say?"

Silence.

She sat in frustration, looking through the blinds of her bedroom window. Things were favoring an unusually warm and early spring. She shook her head. People didn't go crazy until they got older, she assured herself. She crossed her arms over her chest, locking herself in a secure embrace. The heat pump was doing its job, though she felt a chill.

She rocked, lost in thought. Her wide eyebrows felt strained. She smiled as she thought of them, slightly darker than her hair, and moved them up and down twice. Her mom and sis, as well as some of her girlfriends, always said she had stunning eyebrows. And Devon. She knew he liked them. He blabbed to Chris Swimmer, who told Linda Adair, who of course told Tara Longbranch, who told Molly.

She turned her head and grabbed her nail file. She went after her middle toenail, which seemed uneven and ugly to her. She admired her hot pink polish, though, as she filed the nail.

Such pretty feet. I walked in the snow. Snow so cold you can't imagine. Mine bled. You're about to face some serious challenges, so remember that. Remember my walk.

"Okay," whispered Molly without thinking.

Atta girl.

Molly looked up, startled. "What? Wait, no—what the hell!" The cloud passed over and the sun streamed through her window, the blinds reflecting on the wall beside her full-length mirror.

Gotta go.

The conversation turned telepathic: No! Not yet, please!

Be sweet.

Who *are* you?

The one who will be with you on this journey.

What journey?

The one coming up, of course. Always a journey, always a lesson.

The ride?

Sort of.

Sort of? What the hell does that mean?

Don't raise your voice to *me*, young lady.

Oh . . . sorry.

Nah! I'm just yanking your chain!

You're Mary, aren't you? *You're* the one who's been talking to me!

Bingo.

My Trail of Tears ancestor, she communed in wonderment, her thoughts returning to the book as she finished her nail.

Again, circle gets the square.

Very funny. Look, I gotta know some things.

You will—later.

Later? Seriously? Know what? Screw it. You're not really here.

If you say so.

People are gonna think I'm a banana, they ever catch me doing this.

Hmm. Amelia Earhart, Rosa Parks, Chief Mankiller—you're in good company.

I still say you're not actually here.

Uh-huh.

Sigh.

Silence.

Heavy sigh.

Impressive. You practice those a lot?

Next time, I'm *absolutely* pretending you're not here.

Good luck with that.

What am I supposed to do?

Thanks for tuning in.

Wait—

Until we meet again.

Don't—

Be sweet.

"Shit!"

The room was silent. The sunshine created a comfort that Molly cherished, but she felt chilled.

2

Just Another Savage

Saturday, October 6, 1838
Main Trail to Fort Cass
McMinn County, Tennessee Line
Aquohee District
Old Cherokee Nation

"**S**ir! Look at that!"

The soldier pointed to a scene unfolding in a grove of trees on private property, about fifteen or twenty yards away. A pack of red wolves had an elderly Cherokee man on the ground and were lunging at him. The old man was weak and unable to fend for himself. The snarls and growling were horrific and echoing, exceeded only by the man's growing screams. "Permission to fire, sir?" the soldier asked as he pulled his musket from its pouch and raised it to his shoulder.

"Negative," came the response. "Keep moving, Corporal."

"But, *sir*, they're killing him, sir!" He had lowered the weapon in response to the major, but hoisted it again and took aim.

"Goddamn it, boy. I said keep moving!"

The attack worsened, the screams intensified, and the corporal could see blood on the ground. He noticed it oozing from the man's right hand and side. "Yah! Yah!" he yelled in the wolves' direction, to no avail.

"This ain't our fight, soldier. Let's go!" yelled the major. When the corporal hesitated, the major hurried his horse over to the soldier. "Corporal, this is a direct order: put that damn rifle back in the case and move your ass along! We ain't got time for this shit." The corporal turned to object and the major held up his hand. "Shut it, boy, right now. One more word and I'll have your ass up on charges, we clear?" The rest of the soldiers looked on.

"Yes, sir," came the reply.

"I understand your feelin', son, but this ain't no goodwill mission. Far from it. We need every cap and ball and powder horn we got. Can't afford to waste no resources."

How can he ignore those *screams?* the soldier wondered.

"It's just another savage, son, and, by the looks of it, that problem will soon take care of itself." The young soldier resigned himself to securing his weapon. The sweet smell of the tall pines and the smoke of a remote fire mingled in the air. The Cherokee elder's screams faded into the late afternoon air. The melancholy reverberation ended. A crow from a nearby dogwood cawed. The wolves battled one another for their fare amid the ripping and tearing of muscle and bone. The major turned to address the other men in the company. A private vomited.

"Understand somethin', people. We got an executive charge to carry out this here Indian removal, and we won't have the time nor capital to be the saviors of mankind. Leave that to the goddamn missionaries. Be men. Toughen up. Got it?"

The men hesitated, blandly staring at him.

"GOT IT?"

"Yes, sir!" came the unified response.

"All right then. Let's move out!"

The corporal, a mere teen, reluctantly fell in line with the others. He prayed no one noticed the tear streaming down the left side of his face as they headed northwest to the Cherokee Agency. Soon they would begin assembling the Indians for the migration west. The crow cawed once more, readied itself for flight, launched into a circular pattern, and headed down to compete with the wolves.

3

How Hard Can It Be?

Present Day
The next day
Nancy Ward High School
Muskogee, Oklahoma

"**D**id you just fart?"

Rebecca eyed her best friend with suspicion.

"No, I *did not* fart, you crazy grandma over-reacher," said Molly. She looked away, suppressing a laugh. But Rebecca knew her friend, and no amount of denial could stem the rank reality.

"You *did* cut one! You're disgusting, Molly McNair! You wouldn't have done that if Devon was here. I'm texting him right now. I'm telling him you're a walking, talking, fart factory." She typed rapidly and Molly realized she was serious.

"No!" Molly lunged for her friend's smartphone, but Rebecca was quick. She was on her feet, with Molly close behind and screaming.

"Don't you dare, Becks! Give me that! Rebecca . . . please?"

She overtook her friend and snatched the phone from her hands. She breathed a sigh of relief as she realized Rebecca hadn't hit "Send" before Molly seized the phone. She looked down at the text.

OMG! Devon! Molly thinks U R a gorgeous hunk of Tsalagi manhood! She awaits her kiss and daydreams of U! She also farts

Molly pressed the backspace button until the text was gone.

"You're such an ass, Rebecca Taylor!"

Rebecca grinned as she responded.

"You know, he hasn't asked me yet." Molly looked dejected.

"Asked you out?"

"Yeah."

"He will."

"How do you know?"

"I just know."

"But *how* do you know, Chief?" Rebecca bore an uncanny resemblance to a young Wilma Mankiller, former Principal Chief of the Cherokee Nation, hence the "Chief" moniker. "We've known each other since we were little kids. All those on-and-off crushes we had on each other over the years, and now he won't ask me out. You should see me trying to get my fat ass in shape for this ride." Molly had applied and been selected for the annual Remember the Removal Ride, an event held since 1984 for Cherokees to retrace the Trail of Tears by bike. It was sponsored by the Cherokee Nation and included enrolled members of the Cherokee Nation as well as the Eastern Band of Cherokee Indians. "So, what makes you so sure?"

"I just know."

"What*ever*."

Rebecca eyed her friend's Fuji Absolute as Molly turned the tumblers on the combination lock. Molly hoisted the bicycle from its steel stall and Rebecca smiled.

"How's the training coming?"

"Okay," said Molly with a shrug. "Up to twenty-five miles a stretch now. I've met some of the other riders and it looks like a great group. We'll be doing training rides soon, I hope."

"Wow, that's great, Molly. I'm exhausted just thinking about it." Rebecca studied Molly. "What's wrong?"

Molly stared at her. Her best friend knew her well. She shrugged once more. "I wouldn't say anything is wrong, really. . . maybe a little weird."

"Whatcha mean?"

Well, Molly thought, if I can trust anyone, it's Rebecca. They had grown up together and shared everything—like sisters. She took a deep breath and exhaled. Here goes.

"I dunno. Ever since they accepted me to do the ride I get the feeling Mary is trying to tell me something . . . like . . . she talks to me . . . " She looked down at her bike, afraid to see Rebecca's reaction.

"Mary? Oh! Your four times great-grandmother who was on the Trail of Tears. How cool is that, Molly!"

Molly looked up with relief. "Think so? It's really strange. I keep getting this sense that she's there somehow; I mean, even more so than they teach us about our ancestors. It's freaky. The other day I was doing my online family tree and some important stuff came through that was amazing. And it's like, like she's talking to me through it all. And yesterday she just, like, appeared." She was hesitant to look at Rebecca after saying that.

"I think it's awesome, Molly. My dad's mom used to say the same thing about our ancestors."

"Really?"

"Seriously. She believed her great grandfather spoke to her every morning—had breakfast with her and shit, seriously."

"Wow," Molly replied with obvious relief.

"Yeah. And you know . . . I think there really is something to the whole seven generations thing. Grandma used to talk about that a lot, too. She said we are to live our lives so that seven generations from now will reap the benefits of what we've done."

"Right . . ." Molly seemed lost in thought as she propped her bike against the rack so she could ready her backpack.

"Hey, Molly," said Rebecca with an odd expression, "what *would* you say to Devon if you could say anything you wanted?"

Molly thought about it. "I don't know. I guess I would tell him how cute he was, maybe. That he's got a sweet smile, that he's buff as hell and has totally awesome legs!" She giggled as she lightly slapped her own behind through her sweats. "I don't know. Why? Where are you going?" Rebecca was backing away, a wry smile on her face. Molly sensed someone behind her.

"'Siyo, Molly. How goes it?"

No. She did not just do this to me. *Holy shit.* She abruptly turned.

Flustered and embarrassed, she said, "Devon! *Why* are you sneaking up on people?"

"I didn't. I mean, ah, sorry?"

"Well," said Rebecca, clutching her books to her chest, "gotta go. Bye, Devon. Bye, Molly!" She winked as she backed away faster, giving Molly the signal to text her later. She turned toward the parking lot and scurried away.

"Rebecca!" yelled Molly, her arms in the air, exasperated. "Becks, what the hell?!" She turned again, forcing a smile. "Siyo, Devon. How are you?"

"Fine."

"Just got done with my day classes at State," he said, rolling his shoulders. Devon's parents were divorced. Devon lived with his dad, who didn't make much money. He had been living with his mom, but when Devon turned eighteen, he chose to stay with his dad because it was closer to the local community college and his dad wanted to bond with him. Because Devon loved wrestling, he chose the community college which had a decent wrestling team. "Got a couple of night classes, too."

"Devon, I'm really late. I gotta go." She pulled the bike to her.

"Late for what?"

"None of your business."

"Oh."

Molly was annoyed, but immediately regretted her words. She stared at Devon. "Well?" she said, as she put on her helmet and positioned her bike. She watched him checking her out. There he goes again, she thought, loving my eyebrows—and my ass, for heaven's sake. She sighed. He was never going to ask her out on a real date. How hard can it be, for God's sake? She yanked the helmet down and fastened the strap. "See ya," she said, her right foot on a pedal, hands grasping the handlebars.

"Wait! Well . . . um . . . ya wanna go to a movie sometime?"

Later that day

ThunderClap Ultimate Fighting Championship (UFC) gym

Muskogee County, Oklahoma

Molly's sister finished pulling her RDX sparring glove over her wrist with her teeth. She bounced on her toes as Tina "Trouble in Paradise" Gallager, a top MMA contender, approached.

"Don't try any of that Indian shit on me, bitch, else I send you cryin' to your boyfriend!" Gallager chided, tightening her headgear.

Emmy blew her an air-kiss through her mouthpiece as they circled each other. They moved in and tapped gloves, then Emmy bounced forward and landed two short punches to Tina's gut, sending her into the ropes. She backed Emmy up with three rapid-fire jabs, then caught her off guard with a right oblique kick to the thigh. Emmy winced. The next minute or so was a mixture of kicks and punches as each felt the other out.

Tina tried tying Emmy up by shooting on her, lunging for her waist. Emmy threw her off and made a big circle back to the center. I'm an octopus, Emmy thought. A flaming hot octopus, and sooner or later, girlfriend, I'm gonna get that position and choke you down. They clinched, and Emmy struggled more than usual. She was having a hard time handling Tina's strength, which was unusual for Emmy. How hard can it be? she thought. Emmy felt weaker, not quite up to her norm. Breathing was a little more difficult. Finally, she saw her opening and went for it. She snaked behind Trouble in Paradise, seized her neck, and began to close in. She positioned Tina for the fall, bringing her backward so they would hit the mat as one, Emmy slamming them both onto her own back, Tina snug in her abdomen, ready for the choke-out.

You're mine now, Trouble. It's all over for—

Before she knew what was happening, Emmy found herself airborne. She saw the "We fight like bitches here because we *are* bitches" sign on the upper wall of the gym on her way over. Strangely, the sign appeared to be moving rather than her. Tina had deflected Emmy's attempt just in the nick of time, stepped out and back, put her in a gorgeous shoulder throw, and dropped Emmy to the mat like load of bricks. Oh, fuck, Emmy thought, slapping out of the throw. She knew what was coming. Tina was the regional queen of the arm bar. She snared Emmy's left arm as she fell to the mat and slapped both legs across her neck and chest. Arching her back, she pinned Emmy within three seconds. Emmy tried resisting, but to no avail.

Tina yelled, "Give it up, bitch!" Emmy winced. Just like every dedicated warrior woman, she tried not to tap out. She moaned.

"Seriously, Em, don't make me do this. It's okay, girlfriend," Tina mumbled through her mouth guard. Emmy felt Tina ease the stress on her elbow but increase the pressure on her face and chest with her legs. They felt like railroad ties pushing in on her. Emmy tapped, hating herself for it.

Emmy lay there for a second, wondering what the hell had happened. She moaned again as Tina sprang to her feet and pulled out her mouthpiece. "Warned ya 'bout those Indian tricks, bitch! Best getcha sexy ass in here on a daily basis, else I hafta pancake ya more often!" She bounced on her toes and threw a rapid left-right-left into the air. She smiled and climbed through the ropes, laughed, and headed for the showers. Emmy could hear Tina snickering as she walked away.

Eddie Standingcloud, Emmy's manager and trainer, made his way through the ropes and patted Emmy's back before wrapping her in a towel. "We'll get her next time, Emmy," he said with a smile. Yeah, right, Emmy thought. Tina was a top contender for a reason.

Back in the locker room, Tina emerged from the shower and smiled at Emmy.

"Wanna join me in here, princess?" she said, beaming.

"Nah," Emmy laughed. "I think I'm good."

After exiting the shower, Tina slapped Emmy on the butt as she walked past. Knowing full well that Emmy was straight, she loved goosing her nonetheless. "What a *magnificent* ass!" she once told Emmy. "I'd fight Conor McGregor for that tush!" She opened her locker and watched as Emmy struggled to put on her T-shirt.

"Hey, you okay?"

Tina listened as she put on her street clothes. Emmy admired Tina's slim waist yet muscular build. The product of an African-American father and a Latino/Caucasian mother, her lighter-skinned figure betrayed her black and Latino speech patterns. Kind to the core, Tina was a great friend and confidant. She reminded Emmy of a young Halle Berry crossed with a young J Lo.

"Dunno. Something's not right. Can't put my finger on it. I'm just not myself. Like, we all know you're Tina, right? Respect. But I'm, well, if I do say so myself, I'm fucking amazing with the rear naked. Should've had you. I mean, how hard can it be, really?"

"Shoulda coulda woulda. Not your day. So what? You know fightin' as well as any. All up for grabs every time you step in that cage." She shut her locker and approached Emmy, who had a good two inches in height on her. She studied Emmy's eyes. "God, girl. Those are the most beautiful eyes I've ever seen. Sure I can't turn ya?" she grinned.

Emmy smiled and looked down, shaking her head.

"Ah, I'm just fuckin' with ya. You know, you do look tired. How's classes? Grad school stuff, right?"

Emmy nodded. "Okay, I suppose. Pretty heavy load this semester." Emmy sniff-tested her sports bra.

"Hey," Tina said. "Got mad respect for you, being of service to your people like that. That's some Mankiller shit, for real." She held up her palm, then closed her fist and bumped Emmy's own fist. "Gotta split, hot stuff. Got a kid to feed."

"Okay. Wado, Tina," replied Emmy, saying "Thank you" in Cherokee and emphasizing the *doh* in wah-doh.

"Sure thang," Tina said, and turned to leave. She stopped as if remembering something. "Hey, Storm, maybe you should get checked out, huh?" She slid a ratty, thinning flannel shirt over her tank top.

"Yeah," Emmy replied, lost in thought. "Maybe."

"Gotta keep you in the stable, bitch! You goin' places!" Tina shouted, slapping Emmy's arm. She left the locker room, leaving Emily "The Cherokee Storm" McNair to ponder her future.

She was twenty-four and knew she shouldn't be this fatigued. She was climbing the ladder. Emmy was undefeated, and the fighters she had encountered thus far had a healthy respect for her. She was aware of several who had managed to duck her on the card because they didn't want to face her in the cage, a fact that Eddie Standingcloud found hilarious.

Emmy walked over to the full-length mirror. Her beauty was exceptional, but that didn't matter much to her. Her focus of late had been her graduate studies and the UFC. She thought about the past five years. She turned her head to the side, then faced her image head-on again. She smiled, then grimaced. Something made her pound her right fist into her left palm. She inhaled deeply, closed her eyes, then exhaled and opened them.

Reflecting on her "Grams"— her mother's mother and her mother's sister, Aunt Lisa—Emmy recalled the traditions and customs passed down by unassailable Cherokee women and smiled. She muttered a breath prayer to the Creator, walked back to her locker, grabbed her bag, and shut the door.

4

Preparation for Hostilities

Sunday, October 7, 1838
McNair Farm, Hiwassee River
McMinn County, Tennessee
Aquohee District
Old Cherokee Nation

Impending death was in the air. Mary could feel it. She held Martha to her chest and kissed her cheek.

"Let's get ready for the Creator's day," she whispered. The toddler grinned and drooled. As she dressed her daughter for church, her hands shook and her breathing was labored.

"There we are," said Mary as she stood Martha on the edge of the small bed and pulled the child's red handmade dress over her face. "Pretty as a picture." She kissed the girl's forehead. Now Mary's whole body shook.

Mary had dark eyes and hair, and a complexion that revealed her blended Caucasian and Native American ancestry. Today her face betrayed anxiety. She was a Cherokee with much to lose. Her body shook. The United States Army, that terrifying mass of angry men with hateful eyes and booming voices, was about to force her family to leave their farm and travel to a faraway land.

It was a cloudy morning and distant thunder echoed through the mountainside as fog rolled through the crisp Appalachian trees. The Hiwassee River—known to the Cherokee as *Hit-chit-ee*, or copperhead long man—was visible from the window and flowed by a hill below their home and snaked around the side of the mountain, its rocks brown and solid along the curve of the bank. Augustine, an English Mastiff that shared residence at the McNair farm, rolled in the lush grass beside their cabin. Mary felt Nick's arms envelop her waist as he kissed her wet cheek.

"We are going to be fine," said her husband. "I promise." Also a Cherokee, Nick projected strength in his words.

Although she smiled at his encouragement, she still shook. The hostile Cherokee relocation was more than enough reason to shudder. But there was another reason: Mary was pregnant. She rested her head on Nick's shoulder as Martha grinned at them. Mary closed her eyes, her husband wiping the tears from her face.

The McNairs exceeded most Cherokees in wealth. Both Mary and Nick possessed what was a good education for the day. Their respective parents had worked hard to match their children's learning with that of the white community. They were well-to-do "mixed bloods," products of a combination of Cherokee and European ancestors. They owned a vast property, a nice cabin, slaves, many wagons, and goods. But they were losing it all. They were about to be marched with the rest of their Cherokee brothers and sisters to the Indian Territory west of the Mississippi River.

Monday, October 8, 1838
McNair Farm
Aquohee District
Old Cherokee Nation

"Nick, Captain Ambrose is here to see you again." Mary left the cabin door open as her husband walked through the kitchen and out the front door to greet the army officer.

"Good to see you again, McNair," said Captain Ambrose with a smile. They shook hands. Nick wondered how friendly the soldier would be if the McNairs were not well-off and in possession of wagons that would prove beneficial, if not essential, for the journey. Many of their neighbors and friends were confined to stockades.

"All right, Captain, let's get on with it."

"Well, the main thing I need from you right now is your say-so on them five wagons. How 'bout it?"

"Of course. But if I said no, you would requisition them anyway, wouldn't you?"

"I'd have to, McNair. The army is in short supply and we need all we can get."

"Is it that, or is it that the army wants to humiliate us by making us use our own equipment to move us out of here?"

"I'm not gonna stand here and argue with you, McNair. Let's just get the paperwork done, shall we? Now the Fourth Artillery—that is, the U.S. government—is willing to pay you a pretty penny for them wagons. You wanna talk about *that*?"

As they spoke, Nick could hear Mary gathering her clay pots and dishes. He pictured her laying them out on the table, trying to figure out how to wrap them for the pilgrimage. He knew she would be protective of the ones her grandmother had made, fired over the open flame and hand-painted. Martha cried. A raven lighted in the maple tree by the dirt road and squawked in the sunshine, as if protesting the soldier's presence.

The captain produced the papers for Nick to sign.

As Nick signed for the wagons, he was reflective. Chief John Ross had asked the government for permission to lead the various detachments of Cherokees once forced removal became a reality. The Treaty Party, led by Major Ridge and some of Mary's brothers, ceded the Cherokee lands to Washington City for a sum of five million dollars during the Christmas holidays of 1835. Considered a supreme act of treason by most of the Cherokees, it was a source of great tension in Mary's clan.

Chief Ross divided up the Cherokee detachments into groups of roughly one thousand persons each and began moving them out in June, over two years since the signing of the Treaty of New Echota. The exceptional heat caused such misery and death that the government agreed to halt the removal until the weather cooperated. This was fortuitous considering that many whites, government and non-government alike, subscribed to the adage, "The only good Indian is a dead Indian."

A Negro in his mid-thirties appeared with a large ax. He held it out with both hands and looked at Nick with a questioning expression.

"Just drop it on the buckboard for now, Enoch."

"Yezsir," Enoch replied, letting the weighted end of the ax flip over in his arms before setting it on the flat wooden wagon. His prematurely gray beard and lined face suggested a life of hardship and a weathered disposition. As Enoch walked away, Ambrose noticed something in the back pocket of his trousers.

"What's he got there?"

"Book."

"What kind of book?"

"Shakespeare."

"Say again?"

"The man reads Shakespeare—all the time."

"Don't see too many Negroes reading Shakespeare."

"This one does."

At times, when Enoch spoke, the words flowed in such a graceful structure and rhythm, they rivaled the great orators of the New York stage.

"How many slaves you own?"

"Six."

"Houses for 'em?"

"Two."

"So noted. We're lookin' at a total of fifty-six wagons and more than three hundred horses for this here detachment. I need your signature for the wagons you're puttin' forth. Sign here," he said, handing Nick a sheet of paper and a leather notebook. Nick signed the paper.

"Good enough?" he inquired. Ambrose nodded.

"What about Mother Rabbit? She going with you, or in a separate detachment?" Ambrose asked.

"She's going with us."

"Fine."

Mother Rabbit, now an old woman, had been a fixture at the McNair home, helping Mary with the baby, cooking, and helping with the house. She was a popular elder, but she had no one to look after her, so the McNairs had adopted her as family. Nick heard more pottery clanking in the kitchen. Mary came to the door holding her favorite cup.

"I just don't know how we're going to pack all this," she said, one hand on her belly.

Before her husband could respond, Captain Ambrose squinted at her in the sunlight and said, "Oh, there won't be room for any of that stuff on the trip, Mrs. McNair. Gotta get rid of it."

Captain Ambrose turned around and walked away, leaving Mary to stare at her husband.

5

News That Should Never Be News

Present Day
McNair House
Muskogee, Oklahoma
District Four, Cherokee Nation

Molly grinned. The thought of a movie—an actual "date-date"—with Devon Farmer was just too much. She pulled her hair into a short ponytail and hopped aboard her mother's stationary bike. Today's goal was forty-five minutes. She usually got bored on the machine and found she had to read or watch TV while she worked out.

Molly incorporated the stationary cycle into her training routine. She had placed it strategically by the den window, and now the springtime sun was streaming in through the white curtains. She felt the warmth of the sun on her face, the open window allowing the breeze to bathe her body as she pedaled.

She grew bored and reached for her book. She held the handle in her right hand, flipping open *The Catcher in the Rye* with her left and picking up where she left off. Her bookmark had a unique Cherokee design of many colors, hand painted by a Cherokee Nation artist.

Holden Caulfield was a smart-ass and she appreciated that. She couldn't wait to see what he had to say next. He should have been a Cherokee, she thought.

She chuckled as she read Holden's description of his younger sister, Phoebe. Molly could relate. She knew she was often a source of aggravation to her older sister. Her mom was spending time with Emmy this weekend, and Molly was enjoying the solitude. As she giggled at J.D. Salinger's sense of humor, she thought she heard a small, disappointed voice.

Now *I'm* the one who's sorry, truly.

Molly slowed her pedaling, focusing on what she thought she had heard. Her cell phone rang, startling her. She saw that it was her mom and answered.

"Osiyo, Mom."

"What are you doing right now?"

"Ridin' the bike. What's goin' on?"

"I have something to tell you, Molly, and I need your attention."

"Pa-leeze, Mom. I can listen and pedal at the same time, ya know?" she said, laughing. "Hello? Mom? You there?" She heard her mother sobbing. "Mom?"

After a moment, her mother spoke. "I was at the doctor yesterday afternoon with Emmy."

"Is something wrong? Is Emmy okay?"

"They found a tumor, sweetie. It's malignant."

She halted her peddling. "What does that mean?"

"Emmy has breast cancer, Molly."

Molly steered her Fuji along the curvature of the asphalt pathway through the park. Warmer than usual, the temps were in the low fifties. She fought back tears while thinking about Emmy and her diagnosis. Emmy was an MMA fighter; professional athletes shouldn't be getting cancer. Emmy had become a regional celebrity since beginning her fight career.

And she was smart, going for a master's degree in public health. She had so much to live for. Molly held her sister close to her heart as she raced around the lake, making record time.

Molly had applied and been selected for the annual Remember the Removal Ride, an event held since 1984 for Cherokees to retrace the Trail of Tears by bike. She had successfully passed her physical, background check, and drug screen. She had been doing the required home exercises they devised to help prepare the riders for the event, which was to be held in June, five months away, getting in better and better shape as time went by. She couldn't imagine, though, what it took to get in the kind of shape Emmy was in. Her sister seemed superhuman to her. She reached under her shades and wiped another tear from her eye.

As Molly leaned into the slight breeze, she tried recalling what she had heard just before her mom called. Something like "Now I'm sorry" or "I'm the one who's sorry now"? She tried to recapture what she thought she heard. *Damn.* Guess not. Falling behind, she thought. With that, she leaned forward and used her thigh muscles to propel her. As she did, the left pedal reached its apex and she pushed forward to gain momentum around a curve of the lake. As she did, she felt a pop in her left knee, which gave out on her. She lost control and rode off the pathway and into a nearby public trash receptacle. The bike came out from under her and forced her to roll onto her side, before she and the bike landed in a pile together.

As she tried to get up, she found she could barely stand. An older couple who had been walking saw the whole thing and came to her aid.

"Are you okay, dear?" the woman asked.

"Yes, I'm fine. Thank you."

"I don't think you are," the man observed. "We should call an ambulance for you." The woman nodded.

"No, please," said Molly. "I'll be okay, really."

"My dear, you can barely walk!" said the woman.

"I have a friend who will come and get me. It's okay, really," said Molly.

"Well, all right," said the man, "if you insist. We sit out here and feed the ducks a couple days a week. We'll just be right over here if you need us, okay?" Molly thanked them and texted Rebecca. She carefully shifted her weight to her strong leg and rested on it.

> Can u help me? Fell off my bike in the park and messed up my knee.

She placed her bike against the trash barrel, which the man had kindly picked up. After about three minutes, Rebecca called her.

"Omigod, girlfriend! Yes! Lemme get the truck and I'll be right there. You at Civitan Park?"

"Yes."

"You okay? Need me to bring anything?"

"No. Just want to get back home and ice this knee." She put her phone back in her riding pants. She pulled them up to examine her knee. It didn't hurt, but it did have a numb, tingling feeling to it, with a mild throbbing beneath what appeared to be swelling.

Soon, Rebecca arrived in the parking lot adjacent to where Molly and her bike were waiting. Becks had brought her family's spare vehicle, an old Chevy truck that looked as if it had been run through a giant meat grinder. A typical Indian pickup, as Rebecca called it. The couple came over to help them put the bike in the back. Molly thanked them and got in with Rebecca. Molly pulled up her pant leg to reexamine the knee.

"Damn, girl!" said Rebecca. "Look at your knee! Shit, Molly, you tryin' to make pancakes out there or what?" Molly lightly touched her knee and flinched. "Damn, girl. That ain't good. Want me to take you to Indian Health Service—get it looked at?"

"Oh, hell no, girlfriend. Just get me home. I think it just needs ice." She cried to Rebecca about Emmy on the way home, which only made her knee hurt more. Rebecca hugged her friend when they got to Molly's house, comforting her as best she could. They agreed to talk later.

Over the next twenty-four hours, Molly watched her knee swell and her mother worry. Finally her mom said, "Get dressed. We're taking you in." And that was that.

The IHS doctor diagnosed it as patellar tendonitis, which usually resolved on its own within six weeks. Six weeks. Six damn weeks, really? Molly began to feel the threat of losing her seat for the ride, which required consistent, serious training. Only time would tell, but she was worried, and her mom— obviously preoccupied with Emmy's diagnosis—told her to take it one day at a time. She hated that shit.

6

Embarkation

I fought through the Civil War and have seen men shot to pieces and slaughtered by the thousands, but the Cherokee removal was the cruelest work I ever knew.

—Georgia volunteer

Wednesday, October 10, 1838
Fort Cass, Calhoun, Tennessee
Old Cherokee Nation

The journey down to Fort Cass, one of the army's holding facilities and embarking stations, was laborious and frustrating. The McNairs had to leave most of their belongings behind, not knowing if they would be able to return for any of them. It made little sense to Mary and Nick that they had to cross Chickamauga Lake before the official beginning of their immigration process. The small ferry that Captain Ambrose paid for was unstable, and Enoch's wife, Annabelle, nearly fell overboard. Their party had to travel some miles southeast, the opposite direction of removal, to reach Fort Cass. From there, the plan was to head southwest for Ross's Landing.

During an overnight camp on some white people's farmland, things became rowdy and unseemly. Mary was making her way back from a narrow stream at dusk when she spotted what appeared to be a large hog or some other type of animal behind a rail fence, just on the inside of some nearby woods. It appeared to be rooting, moving to and fro on top of something that sounded as if it were crying or squealing. As she got closer, however, she realized to her horror that it was a man—a white bearded mountain man atop a little Cherokee girl who couldn't have been more than nine or ten. He was raping her, grunting and growling at her to "shut up and be still!" The child was completely helpless and alone. Her dress was hanging sadly from a branch of a nearby tree. A small, beautiful corn husk doll lay strewn to the side.

Mary froze. For some reason, everything seemed to be in slow motion. She tried moving forward, but couldn't. It wasn't until she heard the girl scream for her mother in Cherokee that Mary came out of her frozen place and charged the man, screaming, "No! No no no no!"

She heaved her pail of water on the man, soaking both him and the child. As she climbed the rail fence, the man, shocked at being caught in the act, got up and bolted. Mary launched the empty pail after him as she landed on the other side of the fence. She took the crying girl in her arms. She held her briefly before convincing the girl to let her retrieve her dress. Mary was so enraged she had to stop, forcing her brain to shift from the English language to Cherokee so that the child could understand her. She stayed with her for a few minutes before taking her back to camp, fearing the man's return.

After finding Nick and reporting the incident to Captain Ambrose, Mary was shocked to learn there was nothing he could really do. The man was gone, it was a local matter for the county sheriff, and it was proving difficult to find the girl's family.

"Hell, Mr. McNair!" Ambrose said, "We don't even know if she's part of this detachment. We got Indians running all over the goddamn place, if you'll excuse me," he said impatiently.

"No," said Mary with disappointment and disgust, "I will *not* forgive you for that. We need to find this child's mother, Captain!"

"I know that. Don't you think I know that?" he said. "It's just complete chaos at the moment, folks. I'm helpless to do much of anything."

The child stayed with the McNairs during the night and a doctor of some sort came by to evaluate her, permitting Mary to clean the child up and get her as prepared as possible to be moved once her parents were located. The next morning, a soldier and the doctor stopped by with a young Cherokee woman of the Wolf clan, who talked to Mary and said the parents had been located. She would take the child to her mother. Mary rushed to prepare for the day's journey—things were moving fast and the army was enforcing forward movement.

Captain Ambrose had seemed cordial during the previous days at the McNair farm when the army needed their wagons, but once at Fort Cass, the McNairs realized things were horribly different. Soldiers were parading about, barking orders and shoving the Indians around. Mary put her hands to her face when she saw a corporal slap a Cherokee man for dropping his belongings. Augustine growled. Nick thrust his hand in Mary's. Many of the Indians looked diseased; some were soaked in perspiration, others vomiting. Still others had a gaunt appearance, a result of starvation and poor treatment from their time in the stockades. A large soldier stepped on a corn husk doll that had fallen from the arms of a little girl trailing behind her parents. It was pressed into the mud from the recent rains. A tall and proud-looking Cherokee elder strode by and vomited as he passed, bright red blood spewing from his nostrils.

Nick and Mary were grief-stricken about leaving their farm and most of their belongings behind. Also, Mother Rabbit, Enoch, Annabelle, and their two children, Deborah and Thad, all watched the frightening events unfolding before them. The other two adult slaves, Micah and Clara, were sold out from under the McNairs in an illegal auction that Nick had been unaware of. By the time he found out, Micah and Clara were on their way to Virginia.

Caty Walking Stick stopped to hug Mary. She was sobbing and pale and told Mary of her time in the stockade. Mary held her friend and wept with her. Mary felt a primal rage. Caty told them the army herded the Cherokee together, "like many cows," and overcrowding became a problem early. If any Cherokee resisted, the wagon masters or soldiers struck them with riding sticks, jabbed them with bayonets, or horsewhipped them.

Caty said a great fever ravaged the camps and many Indians died. Diana McClendon, a missionary about age thirty sent by the Baptists, walked up and encircled Caty and Mary in her arms, praying for them.

"You there!"

An angry sergeant was pointing at Diana. "No mixing with the Indians."

Diana looked at him, her arms still around the women. "Are you denying me the opportunity to pray for the souls of others, sir?"

"No, ma'am," said the sergeant. "But I most certainly am telling you to heed our warnings about Indian stink."

"What do you mean, 'Indian stink'?"

"They can be filthy, ma'am. They got the lice, pox, what-have-you." He sneered. "You know— that special kinda shit smell only Injuns have." He roared with laughter.

"How dare you! Such words are profoundly cruel."

"Preachin' lady, you best put a cork in it and fall in with the rest of 'em if you're comin'."

An unseasonable chill in the air had the Cherokees swaddling their clothes as tightly as possible. The chaos was overwhelming. People and animals ran amuck; the lack of order on all sides and the stench of sickness everywhere were almost more than Mary could bear. She had to look deep within for new strength. How did things become so bad so fast?

One little boy, who couldn't have been more than five, walked around in a daze with signs of delirium. His eyes were covered by a red bandanna wrapped precariously around his small head. He was barefoot and carried a spear that seemed too big for him. Mucous dribbled from his nose. The little boy caught up with his parents and his mother put her arm around him and ushered him along.

Mary felt for the child as she watched him pad along behind his mother. Nick put his arm around his wife and escorted her back to the family buckboard, a haven unavailable to so many others. Most of the Cherokee would be walking this trip.

The government had appointed John Bell, a close friend of Mary's father and a signer of the Treaty of New Echota, to conduct this trip. He worked in conjunction with Captain Ambrose. Bell, like Nick and Mary, was a mixed-race Cherokee, and the tribal members on this route counted on him for successful passage to Indian Territory. Nick had voiced his suspicions to Mary that Bell chose this particular route to avoid confrontation with Chief John Ross's party, which was making the journey on different avenues.

The two factions became known as the "Ross Party" and the "Ridge Party," or "Treaty Party." The Treaty Party and its followers were convinced that the Cherokee needed to sign a treaty or the government would eventually allow their extermination. In December of 1835, members of the Treaty Party met at the Cherokee capitol in New Echota and signed a treaty to sell their lands for five million dollars, and Mary was remembering that this enraged the chief and the majority of Cherokees who did not authorize the agreement, and the Ridge people and Ross people had been at odds ever since.

As Nick and Enoch worked to get their families' things in order, Captain Ambrose approached. He pointed to a section of the stockade. "Time to get inside. Let's move, now."

Nick was stunned. "I just gave the army my wagons. You couldn't make this trip without people like me, Cornsilk, and John Hicks. We're not criminals."

"Didn't say you were. Policy. Gotta lock you up. Incidentally, you didn't *give* us your wagons; you leased them to us. Big difference. In any case, get your family together and step inside—now."

"I don't think you're understanding what I'm saying."

"I do understand. And it don't matter, McNair. Gotta follow policy. Now get in there."

"Captain, we've got a baby here. We need to—"

"Don't make a difference, McNair! I know back home you're an important man. Not so much here. Get into that jail, now. *Right now.*"

Mary tugged at her husband's sleeve. "Please, Nicholas; do as he says."

"That'd be wise, ma'am," said Captain Ambrose.

"You're a bastard, Ambrose," spewed Nick.

Ambrose drew his sidearm. "Be that as it may, I'm bound by orders, sir. Now, for the last goddamn time, get your ass in that cage, posthaste!" A corporal and a private jumped to Ambrose's assistance with rifles, flanking the McNair clan. Enoch stepped between them, hands raised.

"Sirs, please!"

"*Move!*" yelled Ambrose.

"All right, all right," Nick said, raising his own arms in surrender. "We'll go."

Nick and Enoch managed to get some of their things together and the families filed into the stockade. Mary observed the previously jailed Cherokees who watched with a heavy sense of grief. She averted her eyes and looked down.

As Captain Ambrose locked the door to their section of the stockade, Nick turned around and stared at him. Ambrose shook his head and approached the wooden slats that separated them. "Probably be no more than twenty-four hours, tops," he said, as if to encourage the McNairs. "Besides," he continued after giving it some thought, "you're Treaty Party folk. Might be advantageous for you to keep in mind that you're not apt to have a lot of friends where you're gonna be going. Best be on your best behavior facing forward," he added with a nod. "If you're not careful, the full-bloods are liable to chew you up and spit you out in the Indian Territory."

Nick motioned for Captain Ambrose to come closer to the slats. Ambrose obliged, with caution, holstering his weapon, but keeping his hand on it. The men glared at each other, face to face. Nick rubbed his dark mustache once.

"Yes?" Ambrose inquired with a sigh.

"Kiss my white, Cherokee *ass*, you horse-humping son of a bitch!" Nick said with all the nastiness he could muster. Ambrose grunted. Amos Deer Skin, a young Cherokee neighbor of the McNairs who was watching the exchange, roared with laughter.

"Nicholas!" Mary scolded. "Enough! In the name of God, have a care for your family, please." She pulled him away from Ambrose, who walked away with the other soldiers. After they left, Mary moved in, hugging Nick and putting her head on his shoulder. He held her in the now quiet of the prison camp.

As predicted, the McNairs had the fortune to come in on the tail end of the confinement process. Within thirty-six hours, they were released, and the Bell Detachment was being set in motion for immigration to the west. It appeared that the soldiers had managed to get the Cherokees more or less in order. After a long, quiet, and painful talk with Mary, Nick had calmed down and resigned himself to the inevitable. When the fateful day was upon them and the morning unfolded, a long, lonely train of people and wagons formed. They all slowly became quiet. Nick's entourage came to attention as they heard a relay of cold, harsh voices shimmering down from what was probably the front of the line.

"Head 'em up! Move 'em out!"

"Head 'em up! Move 'em out!"

"Head 'em up! Move 'em out!"

7

Staying Sacred

Present Day
February, Late Saturday Afternoon
Open Country Cinemas
Muskogee, Oklahoma

Molly wondered if she was up to this. Yet she knew she needed to get out of the house. The news of Emmy's cancer had hit her like a spear in the heart, and she was grieving.

He picked her up at her house, and they headed into town. The weather had mellowed during the week, but the weekend temps were up into the low sixties, the climate being somewhat out of whack. She wore an elastic brace on her knee, and with pain medication she had managed to move from a full-on limp to just a slight hitch in her stride. The doctor's orders were no biking until further notice. Life sucked, big time. Devon was being polite, but she could tell he had no real clue. She had always liked Devon, but if pressed she would admit he wasn't the sharpest knife in the drawer. Rebecca was in Tulsa for the day. Molly's mom, a hospital paralegal, was on call and would not return until late. Tara Longbranch was home studying for a big test. Molly had no one she could really talk to.

Devon picked the 4:30 afternoon showing and they had a quick meal of fast food before getting to the theater. Molly would have walked right out of there if Devon hadn't bought her the meal. The least he could have done was take her to a buffet or some kind of real sit-down, she thought. She was in no mood for crap. They were seeing a new indigenous film so she knew she could hang. She told Devon about Emmy, and although he was polite about it, he seemed distracted. For some reason, she wasn't surprised when she heard it:

Pay attention. Take care of *you*.

Okay.

Seriously.

The voice seemed to come from within her and yet it didn't. It was ancient, yet relevant. Friendly, yet distant. Kind, yet authoritative. Feminine to the core, the voice beckoned her. Molly wondered if she *was* going crazy. The voice brought with it a power, a blurry, undefined boundary that seemed just on the other side of Molly's consciousness. A woman named Mary. A lovely woman, Molly decided, who had likely been through more in a few hours than Molly had ever known.

Devon wanted to sit in the rear corner. She wanted to be in the middle, closer to the front, but after a bit of banter she gave in. He was smothered in cologne, and she figured he must have raided his father's collection. It just had that kind of smell. She didn't even notice the previews; her mind was on her sister. Cancer: what a shitty word.

Soon she found herself crying in the dark corner. She appreciated that Devon wiped a tear from her eye as the movie got underway. They had been there less than ten minutes when Devon leaned to his left and kissed her aggressively. She put her hand to his shoulder, prying herself away.

"Wow," she said. "What was that?"

He grinned. "You know . . ."

Molly shook her head. "Not exactly. Take it easy, okay?"

He nodded and turned back to the screen, but she felt his hand moving across her leg.

"Devon, I've just gotten some really bad news. Can we just watch for a while?"

"C'mon, Molly," he said, leaning in again. "I really want you." He kissed her softly this time and she kissed back. She pulled away again, though, and tried to focus on the film. She had removed her sweater and her purple tank top revealed her supple upper arms. Devon kept rubbing her opposite shoulder. He seemed preoccupied, agitated.

"C'mon," he repeated, kissing her ear. Something was different about him, but what? He was aggressive in tone and touch, and she wasn't used to that. They had kissed once on Molly's front porch, but that was different; a different time, different place.

"No. I wanna chill for a bit." She felt her underarms sweating. Should she be scared? He was in college now, which to her seemed years away, even though she knew that they were only separated by a year. She envied him being out of high school, the world's most boring place.

He wrapped his left arm around her neck and yanked her to him, overpowering her, and rammed his tongue into her mouth.

No means no.

"Stop it!" she exclaimed, still whispering and pushing him back.

"I gotta have you, Molly. For real. You know that. I've wanted you forever." She felt his right hand on her left breast as he moved in for more. He squeezed and it hurt. He was like one big hormone with no control. He thrust his hand between her legs and rubbed hard, tugging on the zipper of her denim shorts. She managed to grab his hand, stopping him. He moved from his seat and climbed on top of her. Stretching his muscular body over hers, his legs and feet dangling in the aisle, he trapped her and prevented her knees from bending. In addition to everything else, this put stress on her injury. "You want it as much as I do, I can tell," he breathed. They were in a dark corner and there weren't enough people in the theater to even notice. The theater had reclining chairs and Devon pushed hard to get the seat down. "I wanna be inside you," he whispered in a strange way, his father's cheap-ass cologne drowning her. He pinned her shoulders to the chair so that she couldn't move her arms, which was painful.

No means no, and don't forget our cry: stay sacred!

"No," she said in a tone she thought more forceful.

"Yes," he responded, trapping her on the seat. "I want it, Molly, and I think after all these years, I've earned it." He bit into her neck. He pressed her arms into the armrests of the seat and began dry humping her. He seized her zipper again, simultaneously popping the button open as if he had rehearsed his move. He kept her right arm pinned with his shoulder and managed to get her shorts below her hips. It was then she realized that somewhere along the line he had lowered his own shorts. And to think she had always liked him in those shorts, thinking they highlighted his thighs in a sexy way. Now, none of this was sexy.

"You want it. I want it. Now give it up." She felt the tip of his penis against her panties, trying to find a way in. He started removing her underwear. "Give it to me," he groaned. It was so dark and unpopulated in their corner that Molly knew no one was on to what was happening. She panicked and found herself unable to say more. She had never thought she would freeze this way.

This is bullshit, Pretty Feet. Absolute bullshit. You should fight before it's too late.

He squeezed her left boob again. Maybe it was something symbolic about her breast and the thought of Emmy. When he leaned in again, she responded with a quick nip of his upper lip.

"Ow, fuck!" he yelled.

The reaction caused him to move his right arm to his mouth. Molly looked down.

Grab it.

Molly seized Devon's penis and twisted it the way Standingcloud, Emmy's trainer, had once told her to should she ever be in a situation like this.

"Ahhh! Son of a bitch!" Devon roared.

Several people looked around, wondering what was going on. Molly summoned all her strength and shoved him back, then struggled to stand, pain shooting through her kneecap.

"Jesus, Devon! Haven't you heard a word I've said?" she shouted as she got to her feet, securing her shorts. "You're a selfish bastard!" She snatched Devon's sixteen-ounce soda from its holder and poured it directly into his lap. He shot to his feet like a jack-in-the-box clown.

"Whoa, shit!"

Molly turned and limped for the exit. Now everyone was turning around and staring, one man asking what was going on over there. Devon tried to wipe the syrupy mess from his shorts with a single napkin, yanking them back up.

"We'll talk later, Molly. You can *count* on it!" he hollered as he watched her move through the door to the lobby. He told the man to mind his own business when the gentleman inquired a second time. Devon left to find Molly, but when he got to the lobby she was gone.

What kind of bastard tries to attack you in a theater? she wondered. Molly hobbled the two blocks to the coffee shop and called Tara Longbranch to tell her what happened. While waiting for Tara, Molly tried to decide what she should do. She sat at a table, biting her nails. When she saw Devon on the sidewalk looking for her, she found a seat hidden from view until he was gone. Though she had prevented Devon from going any further, she felt dirty, violated. She kept a low profile while waiting. Luckily, the theater wasn't far from Tara's house.

"Look at your fucking arm, Molly!" Tara said when she arrived. Tara pulled Molly to her and hugged her. A huge bruise had surfaced and Molly hadn't even realized it. She rubbed her arm and felt a singe of pain. Her friend's eyes welled with tears. "Oh . . . and your poor knee—goddamn it! Where is that son of a bitch?" Molly managed to calm her friend, who was usually the calmest among the three of them, and insisted that she was fine. She just needed a ride.

Although furious at Devon, Tara thought it was hilarious that Molly had yanked his pickle and dumped her drink in his lap. Instead of driving her straight home, Tara bought Molly a latte and they talked until about 6:00 pm because Molly wanted to rest, taking another dose of Dilaudid. Tara ensured they sat close to other patrons and in sight of the manager behind the counter. At one point, Tara held Molly while she cried about Emmy. She told Tara that Devon scared her, that he was so unlike himself. It was as if he was becoming someone else.

"I thought for a minute he might rape me, Tara," she admitted, her lip quivering. "I mean, he was like, you know, trying his best to make it happen. I just wasn't ready. And in a damn theater, really? I think he threatened me." She told Tara what Devon had said as she left, and Tara became angrier. She was scared for her friend. "Like, what exactly did he mean by that? 'We'll talk later—you can count on it?'" Tara, having moved back to her seat, stretched her arms across the table and held her friend's hands in hers. The chat was helpful for Molly— it took her mind off Emmy for a while.

"I think he's been roiding, Molly. I saw him and some of the other wrestling guys from the college at Lisa Lamar's party with little bags of pills—like, like big pills, though. Glandulars, I think they call 'em? I heard one of those gorilla guys calling them 'Arnolds.'"

Molly considered this.

"You know, he was one of our best wrestlers when he was still in high school, and I think he let that crap go to his head. No surprise that he's doing more of it at college. Well, cro-mun-ity college anyway," Tara said with a condescending look.

"Hey," said Molly. "Come on now. It was all he could afford, ya know?"

"Okay. Sorry. But don't go defending him, Molly. What he did was wrong—period."

"I know."

"C'mon," said Tara. "Let's get you home."

When she got back, the house was quiet. For the first time in a long time, she longed for her mother. And she ached for Emmy. Having finished her homework for Monday, she flung herself onto the bed, taking care to protect her aching knee, and dozed until her mother came in around midnight. She checked in with her mom about Emmy, but she felt strange about telling her what had happened and chose not to. She felt safe now that she was home, and she just wanted to forget about everything. Devon just got a little out of hand, she convinced herself.

8

The Dying and the Innocent

Friday, October 12, 1838
South, along the Hiwassee River
Old Cherokee Nation

Mother Rabbit coughed. She was sickly due to the stockades. Mary put her arm around her friend as the wagon creaked along. Augustine hopped upon the buckboard, lay there, and started licking Mother Rabbit's hand. She rubbed the great dog's head. Mostly black, he sported a broad, white chest and flecks of white facial fur despite his young age. Captain Ambrose circled the wagons and came upon the McNair's. He and Nick glared at each other as Ambrose trotted along. Captain Ambrose averted his eyes and moved ahead.

"Bastards," said Nick under his breath as he shook his head.

Despite moving south, the wagons and walkers negotiated numerous hills that intersected with the lush trees and rolling plateaus of the Tennessee valley. Standing Over Hill twisted his ankle and fell down a steep embankment and had to be retrieved by the army. Not long after Captain Ambrose moved up the line, John Bell followed. Although he was moving his own family forward in wagons, he opted to ride his horse alone and check in with the Cherokees as they lumbered down the trail.

As Bell came alongside the McNairs, he tipped his hat to Mary and Mother Rabbit.

"Afternoon, ladies. How are we making out here?"

Mother Rabbit nodded as Mary spoke. "Fine, John. What is our stopping point for the evening? Mother Rabbit is very tired." Mary placed her hand over her own growing belly and Bell could see the fatigue taking its toll.

"There's a place called 'Cleveland.' Heard of it?"

Mary nodded. "Yes, a few hundred folks there, I believe. We've traveled there and the people are friendly."

"My thoughts exactly, Mary. That's the target. Came up this-a-way with your father once. Had quite a steak there at the Shiloh Hotel. Ever been?"

Mary shook her head.

"I have," said Nick. "And you ain't kiddin' about the steak. Wish I had one now, that's for sure."

"Nick, please," said Mary. "How can you talk about food?"

"Hungry's all I'm saying," said Nick. He nodded at Bell.

Bell looked at Martha, who was sitting in her mother's lap. She stared at him. He winked and she smiled. Augustine scrutinized him.

Enoch spoke up as the wagon bounced along. "Sir, would there be a decent formulation of water for the proper ablutions of the soul at this destination?"

"Better than most, I should say," said Bell as he squinted into the late afternoon sun. "We should arrive around sunset." He rode on ahead.

Mother Rabbit hacked. Augustine licked her hand again.

A long, difficult day gave way to a rainy, humid night. Several Cherokees tried to escape the roundup by running away during breaks or disappearing near the back of the wagon train and were captured by the soldiers. Much to Mary's relief, none were beaten, but a few—particularly two young men—were threatened.

After stopping for the night, Nick set up a tent and Mary tried to keep Mother Rabbit comfortable in the wagon. Little cover from the rain didn't help those who were sick. Dr. Kurt Arbogast volunteered his services for the Bell Detachment. He had two assistants along for the journey, but he maintained supervision over the more pressing and serious medical matters. He was a prematurely balding man of twenty-nine. His grim expression seldom permitted a smile, but when it did it usually had something to do with children or animals.

He moved from person to person, examining the Cherokees with exceptional care. He approached Mother Rabbit next.

"Does this hurt?" he asked. She shook her head.

"What about here?" He gently poked her side. Again, she shook her head.

"Here?" She flinched.

"Uh-huh."

Dr. Arbogast palpated her abdomen. His grim expression increased as he prodded her. He reached inside his jacket and pulled out a device similar to a small telescope. He placed it on Mother Rabbit's chest and put his ear to the opposite end.

"What's that for?" asked Annabelle.

"Stethoscope," said Diana McClendon. The missionary appeared at the door of the makeshift tent Nick had created for his family. Diana and another missionary, Simon Rhodes, had been charged by their respective churches to accompany the detachment.

"Wazzat mean?"

"Well," said Diana, walking up and putting her arm around Annabelle while looking down at Mother Rabbit, now lying on a small blanket, "it's so Doc Arbogast can listen to her heart and lungs."

"Oh."

Dr. Arbogast glanced at Nick, frowned, and shook his head. A tear formed in Mary's left eye as Mother Rabbit coughed again.

The Rabbit didn't miss much. "Ain't got long, have I?"

"It's hard to say, Mother Rabbit. I'm not good at predicting the future," said the doctor.

She patted his cheek and managed a smile. "You good liar, Doc." Dr. Arbogast tried to smile, but could not. He bent forward and looked her in the eye.

"I'll look in on you regular, hear me?"

She nodded. Nick placed his hand on the doctor's shoulder and thanked him. Augustine, lying nearby, whined.

9

Main Event

Present Day
Monday afternoon, late February
Eddie Standingcloud's Main Office
Broken Arrow, OK
Indian Country

"No." Eddie was emphatic.

"Yes," Emmy countered.

"No," said Eddie, shaking his head.

"Yes, dammit."

"No."

"Why not? I've been cleared. The doc says I'm good to go. In fact, he said if I'm going to fight, I had better do it now. I want this fight."

"No, dreamboat. No way."

"Eddie, *please*. I'm cleared on everything—blood work, EKG, all the shit fighters don't even have to have yet in this state. Give me a break here."

"I wouldn't be able to live with myself if anything happened to you."

"I've seen your place. I don't know how you live with yourself now."

"Ha. Good one. But no deal."

Emmy stared at her manager. "It hasn't changed anything fundamental about me or my abilities. I'm good to go. I can take this bitch."

"Never doubted that."

"Then let me do this."

"It's a crazy idea."

"I do crazy pretty well, ya know?"

Eddie leaned back in his chair, hands on his head, elbows out, as if to think about it. He sighed.

"Look," he said. "You've already noticed a difference in your wind—your strength. You need to be the best you can be. I'm worried you've lost your edge. This woman is dangerous."

"I've been working harder on that; you know I have. I've gained the needed ground. I'm in fighting shape—still got that edge. And by the way, *I'm* dangerous!"

"True," he admitted. "But cancer is serious shit."

"It's very early stage. Won't matter."

"Says you."

"Says the doc, for crying out loud."

He shook his head again. "I don't like this. I think it'd be a huge mistake."

"You don't have to like it. Just go with it, big boy." Emmy stood, hands on Eddie's desk, and leaned forward, letting her freshly blow-dried hair, which she purposely wore down today, fall slowly over her shoulders. She flexed her muscles as she leaned closer, giving Eddie the best possible view of her cleavage. She wore his favorite shirt, a white cotton button-down which fell open at the top to her advantage. And his favorite perfume. She knew he loved the Black Rose scent she had on. She winked at him.

"Cut the shit, girl. That doesn't work with me." He looked away, but glanced back as she continued to stand there, poised and determined. She closed her eyes three-quarters of the way and pursed her lips.

"Pretty please?" she said enticingly.

"Emmy—"

"I *promise* I won't get hurt."

But Eddie was reflective, thinking of the possible consequences. "You know damn well that's a promise you can't keep. Who the hell you think you're talkin' to? You're putting me in a bad position, girl."

She halted the sex appeal and looked down at his desk, keeping her hands planted. "When we formed this relationship," she began, "you promised me you would support me all the way, so long as I didn't go rogue, didn't dope out, didn't fail to give it my all." She looked up at him. "I kept my end of the bargain, Eddie. What if this is it for me? Then I never get a title shot, never get to go out on any kind of positive note. Besides, this woman needs beating. She's bad for our business; you said so yourself. It's *my* life, Eddie, *my* fight."

"Our fight," he said.

"Kay-den, our fight. Be there with me, Eddie. Don't make me go to someone else."

Eddie looked hard at her. "You threatening me, dreamboat?"

"No. But you know I'll do what I gotta do. I've come too far to stop. You brought me all this way, Eddie. Native women need a voice and a fist to go with it. For God's sake, don't drop me in the shitter now. Please." She teared up as she looked at him, not breaking eye contact.

Eddie stared at the ceiling and sighed. Clearly reaching, she tried spreading a little manure. "Think of the headlines: 'Eddie Standingcloud, trainer for the Storm . . .'" she said as she spread her hands and fingers out, as if presenting a major headline. "Your handsome face featured above the piece, revealing all that hyper-masculinity . . . umm, yum . . ." Then she grinned the grin that had broken men's hearts from Tulsa to Tacoma.

Eddie threw his legs up on his desk and rapidly wiped his jeans. "Whoa, nasty stuff never mind," he said with concern, finishing with his boots.

"What?" asked Emmy, puzzled.

"The bullshit in here, gettin' high and thick," he said without cracking a smile.

She smiled and looked down, then back up at her boss.

"Please, Eddie? Don't leave me this way . . ."

"Didn't Thelma Houston or somebody sing that?"

Emmy sighed. She arched her eyebrows, pleading with her mocha-chocolate-mocha eyes.

Eddie caved. "All right, Em. All right. There's nothing saying you can't actually get in that ring." He sighed and shook his head. "You're my girl. It's my job to see you don't get hurt. This one makes me nervous, you need to understand that."

"So noted," she said.

Eddie stood and extended his hand, making direct eye contact. "Don't make me regret this, Emily." She knew Eddie meant business when he called her that.

She beamed. He smiled back. She thrust her hand into his and they shook.

"Love you, asshole," she said, grinning and wiping a tear with her left hand.

"Love you back, bitch. Now get the hell out of my office. You're stinking up the place with that perfume. Like you better salty."

"Yeah, right!" she said and winked. As she reached the door, Emmy turned. "Thanks, Standingcloud," she said, her voice cracking.

"Go on. Get outta here."

She grinned again and left.

Eddie sat down, leaned back in his chair, and wondered if he had made a fatal mistake.

Friday Night, Early March
Sequoyah Center
Tulsa County, Oklahoma
District Thirteen, Cherokee Nation

LaToya Ortiz was the dirtiest fighter in the league. She once "did a Tyson" by biting into an opponent's ear. Though she hadn't ripped it off, the other fighter had to have plastic surgery, lost confidence, and never fought again. On another occasion, Ortiz spit in Natalie "The Grateful Dead" Robinson's face, then took a knee to the bridge of Robinson's nose, flattening her on the mat, and pummeled her face for thirty seconds before the referee and Robinson's corner help could pull her off, sending Robinson to the hospital. Ortiz was disqualified both times, but she managed to avoid being kicked out of the UFC. LaToya "The Black Mamba" Ortiz was of Spanish, African-American, and Cheyenne descent. And she was Emmy's next fight.

Emmy was looking forward to it. She was pretty sure she could take Ortiz, but she also knew she would have to be careful, as Standingcloud reminded her. At the weigh-in, which had been held the morning before in front of a few cameras and a small crowd, Ortiz had pushed Emmy back in an effort to intimidate her as they posed for the obligatory photo shoot. "Gonna make you wish you was never born, you skank!" Ortiz whispered as they flexed, nose-to-nose, for the photographers, holding up their arms in the typical biceps pose.

Emmy knew the best way to get under Ortiz's skin was to embarrass her, so she kept standing on her tiptoes, looking down at Ortiz, making her look smaller. She followed up by caressing LaToya's nappy hair with her index finger, saying, "How's the view down there, short shit?"

Ortiz was livid, and had lunged for Emmy, yelling, "I'ma kill you, bitch!" Though it was great publicity, Emmy hated the weigh-ins. She considered herself a professional and abhorred the monkey business.

Something about Ortiz told her Emmy needed to finish her early; the woman clearly hated people in general and Emmy in particular. There was more to it than just typical fighter trash talk. Emmy sensed a darkness behind Ortiz's eyes. Maybe it was a Cheyenne versus Cherokee thing.

As Emmy sat on the bench in the locker room at Sequoyah Center, focusing on her breathing, she tried to meditate. She had just gotten her breathing rate down when she heard a voice behind her.

"Break that skank bitch's nose for me, Storm!" It was Tina. "She once called my mom the C word. Hate that ass clown." Tina smiled at her friend.

Emmy nodded and raised her right arm in the classic bicep pose. "Will do." She grinned.

Tina shook her head in wonderment. "Sure I can't turn ya, babe? I'll make it worth your while." She winked.

Emmy laughed. "Thanks, Trouble, but I think I'm good here."

"You can say that again, sweet thing," Tina said. "Seriously, put that dog down, girlfriend. She's bad news. Bad for the business. Go get her!" She threw a few rapid punches in the air and turned to give Emmy back her privacy. Emmy returned to her meditation.

Soon enough, Eddie appeared at the door. "It's time, Emmy. Ready for this?"

"Been ready," she responded. She could hear the fans getting more rowdy, having been primed by a couple of under-card bouts. With that, she and Standingcloud left for the fight of Emmy's career.

The announcer stood between Ortiz and Emmy, holding a microphone and grinning, doing his best to calm an unusually rowdy crowd. He made the usual statements and remarks, then moved to the "without further ado" portion as the fans went wild with anticipation.

"Laaaadies and GENtelmen! Welcome to the magnificent Sequoyah Center, and welcome to tonight's main UFC event in the women's featherweight division!" The crowd roared their approval. "We've got a special treat for you this evening. In *this* corner, wearing black trunks, standing five feet, six inches and weighing in at 137 lbs., LaToya 'The Black Mamba' Orteeeeeeeeeeeeeeeeeeeez!" Ortiz made a big show of hopping around, pointing to herself, nodding, and carrying on.

The crowd applauded mildly, and several people shouted "boooooo!" showing their familiarity with Ortiz.

"And in this corner, wearing orange and green trunks—the colors of her beloved Cherokee Nation flag—at five feet nine inches and weighing 144 lbs., Emily 'The Cherokee Storm' McNaaaaaaaaaaaaaaaaair!" The crowd went apeshit. They waved their arms, and the women tried to avoid being drowned out by the men, most of whom were fist-pumping and high-fiving, and more than a few whistled. It was a regional event, and Emmy was a crowd favorite. Emmy turned to every section and waved to show her respect, unleashing a barrage of applause. One man held a giant sign that read, "Marry me, Storm!" The announcer continued with his instructions while the two women bounced in place, staring each other down. When the ref signaled them to the center of the cage, the crowd calmed. Ortiz got up in Emmy's face and snarled, trying to inch her back. Emmy was all business now. She ignored Ortiz's attempts to throw her off and nodded at the ref as he quickly reviewed the rules. She maintained her focus, keeping eye contact with Ortiz while occasionally giving the ref his due respect.

As they were about to return to their respective corners, Ortiz grimaced, yanked out her mouthpiece, and spewed, "I snagged your man last night, trailer trash. He *still* callin' my name!"

Emmy stepped within an inch of her face, rose to her tiptoes, and stared downward. Quickly pulling out her own mouth guard, Emmy snapped, "Yours told me the night before the only thing he throttled weaker than you was some white dude's Pomeranian." She grinned and overwhelmed Ortiz's personal space.

Ortiz pushed her back and screamed, "Gonna wipe you, girl!" and went after Emmy, but the ref ordered them to their corners. Emmy grinned and backed toward her corner, re-inserted her mouthpiece, rolled her shoulders, and bounced in place.

Ortiz made a show of thumbing to herself, forewarning the world of her certain victory. Emmy paid no mind. The crowd heckled Ortiz and there were shouts of "Storm! Storm! Storm!" Emmy glanced over at the front row, where Molly, Rebecca, and Tara sat, and winked before trotting to center cage. Her mom, Sandra refused to go to these events.

"I just cannot bring myself to watch you get beaten to a pulp, Em. You're my firstborn and I love you dearly but *please* don't ask me to come," she had said. Emmy understood, though Molly was annoyed by it and tried to explain to their mom that the referees would never allow Emmy to get seriously hurt. She hoped.

"GO, SIS!" screamed Molly.

"Kick her ass, Em!" yelled Rebecca.

As they approached each other, Emmy knew there would be no tapping of the gloves or any other semblance of respect, so she didn't bother. The bell rang and Ortiz blitzed her early. She threw a volley of punches at Emmy and followed with a knee to Emmy's groin. The crowd booed. Emmy pushed Ortiz's face back with her glove, knocking her feet out from under her by dropping her with an inner reap. She went for a ground and pound, but Ortiz looped Emmy's leg with her own and flipped Emmy over. Ortiz was famous for using the classic Jon Jones–style "hellbows," digging her elbows in at the most sensitive places. She jammed her powerful right elbow into Emmy's shoulder, producing a yell. Ortiz dug in.

"You flea-bitten whore!" yelled Rebecca from the seats.

"Becks, please!" said Molly, trying to calm her. "Seriously? Are you high again?" Tara laughed and eyed Rebecca with admiration.

Emmy reared up and wrapped her right leg around Ortiz's neck. She took her down in a modified triangle choke, but Ortiz escaped quickly, getting to her feet and trying to rouse the crowd. She paraded around the cage, thumbing to herself again and performing what had become the "Ortiz strut" as Emmy recovered from the elbow and got to her feet. Another minute or so of attempted takedowns, punches, and kicks, and then the bell rang, sending both fighters back to their corners.

"She's fuckin' with you, you know that, right?" Eddie asked after half a minute.

Emmy nodded and let Bo, her other corner man, squeeze water into her mouth from a bottle. Eddie wiped her down with towels.

"You're a smokin' hot, flaming octopus, girl," said Eddie amid the deafening crowd. "You're the Cherokee Storm! Put that ugly woman in her place!" Emmy nodded again, taking long, deep breaths. "You the woman, hear me? Men love ya. Women love ya. Kids love ya. Ya gotta octopus that flake, you hearin' me?"

"I'm the woman," Emmy repeated, "I'm the woman. Gonna snake her for sure, gonna snake her," she recited, gasping.

"And protect that left knocker, understand? Those boob guards only work so well against somebody like this, hear me?" Emmy nodded. "All right-den, dreamboat. Go mess that bitch up!"

"Gonna mess 'er up, mess 'er up," Emmy repeated.

When the bell rang for the second round, Ortiz sprinted across the ring and caught Emmy with a flying tackle. They hit the mat violently. Ortiz headbutted Emmy and spat in her face.

Eddie raised hell with the ref, to no avail. Emmy smacked Ortiz in the throat when the ref wasn't looking, which stunned her long enough that Emmy could get back up.

Ortiz was fairly well-versed in tae kwon do, and she caught Emmy with a hard side kick to the sternum. The other thing Ortiz was known for, and what Eddie had been so worried about, was a powerful spear kick to the liver, which had dropped many opponents. They would either not get up afterward or Ortiz would instantly drop on top of them and beat them mercilessly until the ref stopped the fight. She had hospitalized three fighters that way. But Eddie had a secret. He had a spy in Ortiz's camp who told him that she would involuntarily raise her right eyebrow and flare her nostrils just before launching the spear kick. So Emmy knew to be on the lookout.

Emmy charged Ortiz with short, powerful lefts and rights, bending Ortiz over with her last right hook to the ribs. She was moving in again when Ortiz straightened. Emmy noticed the telltale eyebrow arch and nostril flare and, sure enough, in came the spear kick. It was lightning fast and powerful, but Emmy moved forward and to the left, catching LaToya's leg and kicking her outer thigh as hard as she could with her left foot. Ortiz yelled and Emmy was trying to follow with a takedown when Ortiz caught her hard with an elbow to the jaw. It didn't feel broken, but it stunned Emmy. Ortiz quickly followed with a punishing sidekick that knocked Emmy to the mat.

"Oh, no," Molly said. She stood, grasping Rebecca's hand. Please don't hurt my sister, Molly prayed.

At that, Ortiz dropped atop Emmy's rigid body and dug her elbow in again, trying for the same spot in the shoulder. Suddenly, Ortiz leaned in and said, "Hope ya like dis one, bitch!" She raised up and struck Emmy as hard as she could in the breast twice with an inverted elbow strike—despite Emmy's blocking attempts—digging the last one in for good measure. Emmy shrieked in agony.

"All right, Ortiz, up, up, up," the ref said, moving her away.

"Oh, my God," exclaimed Molly. She put her hands to her face and Rebecca hugged her friend. Eddie was going insane from the corner and tried to enter the ring. The ref sent him back. Emmy looked at him and waved him away. Ortiz strutted inside the cage again, trying to get the fans hyped up. She bent over and showed them her ass, swatting it provocatively, which sent a broil of lewd comments and boos from the crowd. She proudly posed her right arm and kissed her bicep. The place sounded as if it were coming apart as the ref made Ortiz return to her corner.

"You're a miserable rotten skank bitch!" yelled Rebecca, who hid when Ortiz turned in her direction on the way to her corner. Molly slugged her friend's arm and reminded her to calm down.

Ortiz maximized the strutting, stopping now and again to eye someone in the crowd, yelling, "Ima get you, too!" and "Step inside dis cage, boy, I'll beat yo' ass!" to a heavyset man in the front row wearing a ball cap with a tractor on it.

Emmy closed her eyes as she struggled to get to one knee, focusing on her breathing. How could she know? she wondered. Did they have a spy, too, who knew about this tumor? Sharp pain radiated from her breast to her shoulder. Her lip was bloody now from the elbow to the jaw. Maybe she should have listened to Eddie. After all, that's what he's there for. People were on their feet, yelling "STORMY! STORMY! STORMY!"

It was at that moment that Emmy recalled something her grandmother used to say. She would sit, with Emmy in her lap, and read classic children's stories to her. She would say, as she finished the story, "When all else fails, sweetie, just remember where you came from and the journey our people made." She always made sure Emmy nodded or acknowledged it in some way. Emmy figured that was where she got her love for reading and books. She glanced up at Ortiz, who was back to engaging the crowd, egging them on. Ortiz pointed her hands together over her head, hands and arms forming a triangle, and bobbed in place, swaying her body like an Egyptian dancer.

Soon enough, Ortiz turned, gestured toward Emmy, and pounded her fists together. She pushed the ref out of the way, moving closer to Emmy and looking down at her. Profoundly smug, she mouthed "I own you, I own you!" pointing to Emmy with her glove. "You *and* your trailer-trash family!" She eyed Emmy, yelling "Kiss 'em, bitch! Kiss my feet! Do it now, trailer park!" as the ref fought to keep her back.

In two seconds flat, Emmy was across the ring and in the air, planting her left foot deep into Ortiz's right hip, right foot high on her left shoulder, clutching her tank top strap with her left hand.

Having effectively tree-climbed her opponent, Emmy seized Ortiz's braid with her left hand and, with a straight vertical downward punch, shattered her nose, spewing blood in all directions. It sprayed some fans in the front row. Emmy followed with three more rapid-fire rights, tenderizing Ortiz's face. The arena exploded. Molly and Rebecca's jaws dropped simultaneously. Somehow, Ortiz managed to stay on her feet— powerful as usual—but stunned and wobbling, and Emmy twisted around Ortiz's shoulders like a chimpanzee. She swaddled her neck with her high-octane thighs, shifted her weight, and, arching her back like a gold medal Olympian gymnast, slapped her palms on the canvas and flipped Ortiz over by her head and piledrived her to the mat.

A highly respected Cherokee elder and devout Methodist, Elias Pumpkin—seated directly behind Molly—rocketed to his feet and roared, "Jesus Christ! Did you fucking *see* that?"

Pumpkin owned a sizable ranch and was an important Emmy backer. His foreman and best friend, an elderly black man named Woody, said, "Man, I ain' never seen *nothin'* like that befo'!" and high-fived his boss. He cupped his hands to his face and hollered, "Beautiful, girl! Beauty-ful!"

Tara, drops of Ortiz's blood on her arm, stood, put her hands to her head, yelled, "Oh, shit, I think I'm gonna be sick!" and lost her pizza right then and there. The people next to her jumped back to avoid Tara's partially digested tomato sauce, anchovies, mushrooms, green peppers, cheese, and sliced onions. Molly squealed and ran into Rebecca's arms, then realized Tara was freaking out and helped her to sit. Rebecca gave Tara, still bent over, her napkins and gently pulled her hair back in case she hurled again. She gave her a kiss on the head and comforted her.

People threw beer cans, food containers, programs, whatever they could get their hands on. Fans were pushing one another, caught up in the moment, and the Native women's typical "Ley-ley-ley-ley-ley-ley-ley-ley-ley!" victory call was so loud as to be piercing. Their girl was making good.

Blending in with the crowd in a center seat was Tina "Trouble in Paradise." She stood and thundered, "Fuck that bitch *up*, girlfriend!" thrusting her left fist in the air. Back in the cage, Emmy reversed her position on the mat and, getting behind her opponent in a seated position and backing herself to the cage for support, pulled a squirming Ortiz to her chest and applied her version of the rear naked choke. It was, simply, punishing. The fans were screaming, some crying, and Eddie and Bo jumped up and down in an embrace.

Predictably, Ortiz refused to submit. Emmy applied the needed pressure, her triceps muscle flexing. Ortiz went limp, her eyes becoming vacant and arms collapsing at her side, and the ref called it. Molly thought the roof was going to come off the place. For a moment, she feared for her safety. Cherokee fans, especially, were in a state of utter riot. Even the cops, there for security, looked nervous. Fans in the middle were raining popcorn, peanuts, and Junior Mints onto those in front, and Rebecca hugged Molly tightly as they ducked to avoid the flying debris.

"Jesus, Molly, that was out of this world, like, literally," Rebecca yelled, a handful of Skittles just missing her forehead. "Are you sure your sister isn't some kind of Area 51 alien or something?" Molly grinned and kissed her friend's cheek.

When Emmy stood, the ref grabbed her arm and held it high. The fans flipped out, Emmy flashed her irresistible grin, and Molly screamed in delight for her big sister. Ortiz's corner people helped her to her feet, her trainer lightly slapping her face to rouse her. Within a minute or so, the crowd calmed down. The ref held an arm of each fighter and made the announcement: "Winner by submission via rear naked choke, Emily 'The Cherokee Storm' uh, McNaaaaaaaaaaaaaaaaaaaair!" He hoisted Emmy's arm into the air as the fans screamed and cheered. Emmy received a sixty-second standing ovation, and as the corner men and women gathered to shake hands, Emmy walked over to Ortiz and forced a hug.

She could tell Ortiz wanted to get out as fast as possible, but she didn't care. As she hugged her, Emmy said, "Good fight. Just so you know, I would never have done what you did to me in there. Get past yourself or go straight to hell." With that, she turned and waved to the crowd, offering a modest bow as she usually did to each crowd section, blowing a kiss with each one. The people went berserk and yelled even louder, giving her another ovation. It never seemed theatrical; something about Emmy made the fans know she was genuine. They were crazy about her. She waved again and made her way out of the cage.

"Let's get back outside and wait for Emmy," said Molly. "This place is in crazy overload." They helped Tara maneuver through the crowd. One of the cops knew the McNairs and Molly asked him to escort them to a place where they could wait for Emmy. He took them back to Emmy's dressing room and let them wait.

10

Trying to Move On

Present Day
Saturday afternoon
McNair House
Muskogee, Oklahoma
District Four, Cherokee Nation

Molly picked at her food. She pondered Emmy's predicament, which reminded her of other unpleasant times. Her father had died of a heart attack when she was eleven. She just couldn't take another loss. Emmy's biopsy had revealed something called invasive ductal carcinoma. The doctor had suggested surgery right away, but Emmy was hesitant. She was a health-conscious Cherokee and professional athlete. The thought made Molly smile, especially in light of her sister's victory over Ortiz. She was proud of her big sis. After extended discussion with Dr. Prescott, her oncologist, Emmy convinced the doctor to opt for a "watch and wait" protocol while she investigated her options.

"Try and finish, Molly; you're not looking so good," her mother said.

Molly's parents were Cherokee. They came from a long line of "mixed-blood" Cherokees—those who had intermarried with whites—and, although Molly was Native American by birth and citizenship, her skin tone was white. Both her mom and Emmy had darker complexions. Molly favored her father's side. In fact, Molly knew that even Mary, though distant in history, was also a mixed-blood Cherokee.

"Whatever," said Molly.

"Don't 'whatever' me, Peewee. Eat!" She playfully thumped Molly's forehead, something Molly despised. She dug her fork into what was left of the dumplings and fry bread on her plate. I am going to get so damn fat on this, she thought as she took a bite. My ass is gonna be the size of Oklahoma City. I won't even be able to sit on that bicycle seat.

She could sense Mary standing in the corner of the kitchen, in a stunning red tear dress, snickering.

"It's not funny," said Molly without thinking.

"Well, pardon me all over the place," her mom said with a sigh.

"No, I didn't mean you. I just, oh, never mind."

"Are you getting weird on me, Peewee?" her mom asked.

"No more than usual," Molly replied with a smile.

Their conversation turned to Emmy. They talked about her and what having cancer could mean, pondering the future.

Given that Molly couldn't ride, Sandra encouraged Molly to walk. She felt things should be as "normal" as possible after Emmy's diagnosis. It was the weekend, which helped Molly relax, and she took to the neighborhood for a walk to strengthen her knee. She thought of her big sister alone in her house and how difficult all this must be. Since getting the news, she had gone online, doing extensive research on invasive ductal carcinoma. The information was mixed. Women usually got this when they were older. The prognosis was good if the cancer was caught early, yet it wasn't clear how early Emmy had discovered hers.

She put her head down into the slight drizzle. Breast cancer: what a load of crap! Then she started thinking about Devon and couldn't get her mind around the whole thing. How had she misjudged him all these years? What if she hadn't said something? Correction, she thought: What if Mary had not said something? *No means no.* In spite of the increasing rain, she felt warmth from the memory of Mary's intervention, or whatever one might call it.

Molly's awareness of Native women's rights was sharp. She was familiar with the national dialogue among indigenous communities regarding sexual assault and the mistreatment of women in general and Native women in particular. Her mother, sister, and aunts reinforced dealing with the problem head-on, which no doubt accounted, she thought, for her wrenching Devon's pecker and dumping his drink in his lap. She winced as she replayed the scene in her mind. This recollection gave way to a somber frustration. She had had high hopes for the movie night. After all these years, she had thought Devon would be a gentleman.

Like a lot of girls her age, she had previous experience. A year and a half ago, when she turned sixteen, she let Chris Jones—who had made his rounds with some of the girls—get in her pants and regretted it. The sex was awkward and didn't last long, and she swore she wouldn't do it again until she was ready. Rebecca convinced Molly to get tested, and that's when Sandra found out about it. Because of the backlash she received from her mom about Chris, she didn't want to tell her about Devon.

After Rebecca got back from Tulsa, they finally had some chat time. Molly told her about the movie date. She told her everything she could remember about how the date unfolded and the things Devon said to her.

"I'm going to kick him in the balls," Rebecca said.

"No, Chief, there's no point. I just want to forget about it and move on."

"Yes," said Rebecca, "moving on is good. But first, I'm gonna kick him in his little gopher nads."

"No," said Molly.

"Yes," Rebecca fired back.

"Why? Why now? Just forget it. It's over and I'm over it. He's not a bad guy, Becks. He's never acted like that in all the years I've known him. We grew up together. Tara thinks he's on something."

"What he did took balls, Molly, and they must be throttled to the max. Did you tell Emmy?"

"No, and I don't want to. It's none of her business. Besides, I don't need her to protect me."

"Maybe you do."

"I don't."

"But maybe you do."

"Fuck it, Rebecca! It's not important anymore!" she had roared.

Now Molly was able to laugh at her friend's protective nature. She gave thanks for Rebecca's friendship. She walked as far as she could before turning back toward home. The IHS doc had said it was a particularly bad case of tendinitis and might take longer than usual to heal. She shook her head as the rain increased. What next? She just wanted to curl up in bed and hide.

She thought of Emmy again, and the tears returned, mixing with the rain on her cheeks.

Wednesday Evening, 7:30 pm
Emmy's Bungalow
Muskogee, Oklahoma

A knock at the door interrupted Emmy's effort to get through her required reading of a graduate-level anthropology text.

She rubbed her temples and put down her one cup of coffee for the day. Still nursing wounds from the fight, she slowly stood and shuffled toward the door. She was stiff and sore. She checked the peep hole to find Molly's best friend standing with her arms crossed. When she opened the door, she noticed that Rebecca was teary.

"What's wrong, Chief?" She opened the main door and offered the flimsy screen door to Rebecca so she could come in.

Rebecca was succinct. She told Emmy about Devon's assault on Molly and demanded to know what they should do about it. Waving her arms now and then, her voice rose with each new gesture. She recited most of what Molly told her, including what Devon had said at the end.

Emmy leaned against the wall impassively, hands in the pockets of her gray sweatpants, saying nothing. As she rubbed her head, her thick, dark hair fell past her green Cherokee Nation T-shirt to her full, powerful torso. She shook her head and sighed, jiggling her gold, feather-style earrings. Finally, she spoke.

"Rebecca, I know you're upset, but I don't know that I can really do anything to help Molly. She's becoming her own person and I don't think I should be getting involved in her private life."

Rebecca's jaw dropped. "You're *shitting* me, Emmy! You've got to be fucking kidding me!"

Emmy held up her hand. "Look, don't yell at me, Chief. I can't come to Molly's rescue anymore like she's a ten-year-old. She just told me not three days ago to mind my own damn business about something, and I thought, hey, you know, she's probably right. She should handle her own problems. She's basically an adult now."

"What about the bruise, Em? What about that damn bruise he left on her?"

Emmy shrugged. "Honestly, she's probably fine, Chief. She's pretty tough; she's been a tomboy rough-and-tumble since she was little. She's my sister and I love her, but nothing I do can change what happened, and she'll wind up resenting me more if I stick my nose in this. You know—and if not, you will find this out—sometimes there's just no helping people."

Rebecca couldn't decide if Emmy was just being hard to get along with or if she and Molly were having some kind of conflict. She quickly recalled Emmy's diagnosis, though, and felt like a shit for yelling at her. Emmy had been like a big sister to her, too. She hugged Emmy, who seemed almost catatonic. She departed unsure of what to do. She speculated that her understanding of the human race in general and Emmy in particular had somehow been totally fucked up from the beginning.

Since Emmy wasn't going to do anything, Rebecca wondered what she should try next. Should she go to the police? She knew that Devon had recently turned eighteen, meaning he could be charged as an adult. But was that an overreaction? Was Devon really evil, or just out-of-control horny? She hadn't known him as long as Molly and she couldn't recall him ever doing anything like that. Still, he had done it. He had hurt her best friend. She thought about going to Mrs. McNair, but something didn't feel right about that. She had been taught to always tell someone. Christ, she just fucking did that. The one person she knew would take most offense. Now what? She felt cheated. She was also afraid for her friend.

11

Move or Die

Thursday, October 18, 1838
Ross's Landing
Aquoah District
Old Cherokee Nation

John Bell was nowhere to be found. The Cherokees were agitated and depressed after almost a week of cold corn fodder and dried bacon. They seemed less apt to move on their own power without their Cherokee conductor present.

"Ain't inclined to move just now," said one Cherokee man. A younger, more outspoken Indian, Tobacco Bill, dropped his trousers at the small campfire that three soldiers had built to heat their food. Drunk from the whiskey with which they had enticed him, Tobacco Bill belched loudly and urinated directly on the flames. Pointing his penis in the soldiers' general direction, he showered a private's lap and boots and was beaten for it.

Captain Ambrose was starting to panic. He wrote a letter to General Scott which said, in part:

> *After crossing the Tennessee River, many would not proceed in the absence of their Conductor Mr. John Bell... If Mr. Bell cannot convince them to move on, it appears the Army will have no choice but to use force.*

Ambrose's hand trembled as he put away his notes. His preference was a peaceful journey without resistance. Although Bell's whereabouts were a mystery at the moment, Ambrose knew he had to act. He addressed the Cherokees in six groups of about a hundred each, shouting the same thing each time.

"It has come to my attention that many of you are not 'inclined' to move just now. Well, let me assure you, you *will* move or by God, we will incline you! I can't speak for Mr. Bell at the moment, but I have my orders. Any Indian not moving on their own by this afternoon will be shot. Is that clear? Move or die, people!"

The Cherokees got the message. Nick was furious, but he also knew that Ambrose was sworn to keep order. That afternoon Captain Ambrose paid a Mr. Samuel Hamill fifty dollars to ferry the crowd across the Tennessee River at Ross's Landing. The Cherokees were exhausted after their second crossing of the Tennessee River. The river flowed around Ross's Landing, weaving in and out of the land mass like a massive snake. This necessitated more than one crossing.

It was around this time that Mary befriended a young woman called Pretty Water in the Morning. She had no husband, but was on the verge of giving birth on the river. Mary had since left the wagon and helped Pretty Water every step of the way. She was furious with the soldiers, some of whom were young and impatient and prodding the women forward with bayonets or swords. They sometimes fell behind the McNair wagons and Nick had to stop, pull out of line, and wait. The army was not keen on waiting. Mary had empathy for the woman and knew it was only a matter of days or hours before Pretty Water gave birth.

A few hours down the line, Tobacco Bill got rowdy again and was beaten a second time for peeing on the boots of a sergeant who was walking directly in front of him. An older Cherokee, Buzzard Flopper, pulled Tobacco Bill aside and tried to explain that the more antics, the more beatings, plain and simple. But Tobacco Bill was resolute. Because he drank so much alcohol, his urge to urinate was frequent and he protested the entire removal in the most personal, direct way he knew. Buzzard Flopper tried to be firm with him, but ultimately walked on ahead, shaking his head and mumbling.

Mother Rabbit vomited blood four times in the late afternoon. When they rested for the evening, Mary used a wet cloth to pat Rabbit's forehead and keep her clean. She talked to Mother Rabbit and encouraged her, but the older woman was growing weaker by the hour. She had dysentery, or what they sometimes called "the flux." Mary called on her Methodist faith and prayers as quietly and effectively as she knew how. Nick joined her in prayer and they each took one of Rabbit's hands. Despite her condition, she squeezed their hands in appreciation. "Wado" she whispered.

When the McNairs awoke with the morning light, Mother Rabbit was dead.

12

Soothsaying

Present Day
Meg & Mike's Gifts and Food
Muskogee, Oklahoma

"**H**ey, who's shrungry?" shouted Rebecca, slurring her speech.

Molly, Rebecca, and Tara were shopping for nothing in particular. Tara had her mom's SUV and a full tank. Molly smelled weed and suspected Rebecca of getting high before they got together.

They stopped at Meg & Mike's for something cold. Molly's suspicions were reinforced as Rebecca stumbled getting out of the car, giggling. As they entered the shop, a short bar of Native American flute music provided a customer alert for the owners. Rebecca spotted the new fortune-telling machine she had heard about. She held her hand up to the shiny glass cabinet that contained a Native American–type Zoltar, complete with shoulder-length hair, choker, Cherokee bracelet, the whole deal.

"Guys, check this shit out! Looks like Elder Downing!"

"Honestly, Becks." Molly laughed, shaking her head.

"Whoa, no kidding, Chief," said Tara, grabbing two Snickers bars. "Elder Downing with sexy eyes. Kinda like yours, actually." Molly turned and glanced at Tara, then kept walking.

"'Si-yooo in theeere," Rebecca teased, waving and making faces at the machine. She studied the fortune teller, wobbling a little as she cocked her head, her rich black hair falling over one eye. While Molly and Tara browsed, she decided to take a chance. She pushed the black button.

"Please deposit seventy-five cents," said the Zoltar. Rebecca sighed. "Hey," she shouted over to Meg, who was behind the counter. "Got change for a dollar?"

"Sure, Chief," said Meg.

Rebecca returned to the machine with her loot. She deposited the coins, which was a challenge.

"'SIYO, young warrior!" came the report in typical Native American inflection. The Zoltar moved its head up and down and its eyes rolled from side to side. The arms moved in conjunction with the eyes over a crystal ball with a Native American design.

"Yeah, yeah," said Rebecca, her shitty mood transparent, the marijuana fueling a sense of rising paranoia.

"You are going to do very well for yourself, O fair one! But you must remember to breathe and trust those who hold your ideals in the crux of their bosom for you." Several multi-colored lights flashed, and Rebecca thought she heard a train whistle in there somewhere. She looked around and realized Tara and Molly were in the far corners of the store. Molly was reading from a magazine and Tara was texting someone. "You will need the wisdom of the elders and the hands of an auto mechanic for your next challenge," the machine continued.

"Fucking seriously?" Rebecca managed to say, garbling her words.

"Hey," said Meg from behind the counter, "I heard that." Rebecca shrugged and turned her attention back to Elder Downing. He was beginning to blur as she returned to his voice.

"The raven will awaken you with new ideas and the coyote will guide you to trails beyond your wildest imagination. Do not hesitate to follow them, young champion. I will now tell you how to get there. Please deposit another seventy-five cents for your answer."

"Asshole!" said Rebecca, putting her face to the glass. She thought she heard Meg snickering. Molly was engrossed in whatever she was reading and Tara was still texting. Thanks to the weed, her friends looked as if they were on a huge, flat scale in the middle of the room, their respective corner positions balancing the nonexistent device. Rebecca pulled back, her forehead leaving a smudge on the glass. The Elder Downing stopped moving, his eyes came to a halt in the middle, and a card ejected from the slot at the bottom.

> You are a lovely person with possible Indigiqueer leanings and an eye for injustice. Fight well, young warrior!

"Indigiqueer? Don't think so, old man," Rebecca mumbled. "I'm a guy-humper through and through," she added, marble-mouthed. Though I'd probably jump Amber Midthunder if given the chance, she reflected. She's pretty hot. She scratched her head and approached the counter. "I need change again," she said emphatically. "Here are two more ones," she added, slurring the word "more" and slapping the bills on the counter. Meg smiled, her red hair and crow's feet highlighting a hard but happy life.

Meg was no fool. She smelled the weed and could spot the signs. "Go easy there, Chief. Elder Downing is just getting his feet wet here," she said with a silly expression. "He came in with the last delivery. Like him?" She gave Rebecca the coins she needed.

"I'll be sure and let you know," said Rebecca sarcastically, almost falling as she spun around to seek her fortune again.

She returned to the Elder Downing Zoltar with the sexy eyes and dropped in another seventy-five cents of her hard-earned babysitting money. Once again, the contraption came to life, complete with flashing lights and locomotive whistle. The eyes darted side-to-side again, hands hovering over the fake Indian crystal ball. Out of the corner of her eye, Rebecca swore she saw one of the Little People lobbing a hatchet at her from the candy isle. "Oh, crap!" she managed to say as she shut her eyes and ducked. When she opened them again, nothing was there. She looked behind her for the tomahawk; nothing. She blinked several times and turned back to Elder Downing.

"Zay-hey, young champion! You're back!"

"That's right, jerk-off. You were saying?"

"You have a trail to follow and a destiny to unlock. Wish to hear about it?"

"Yes, goddamn it! Like, if it's not too much trouble?" This time she heard Meg laughing, no doubt about it.

"Do not fear the rattlesnake, for she is your sister. The path you seek may be fraught with danger. You must follow your heart above all else, for it is the path of light and fewer calories."

"Crap! You're worse than my calculus teacher! Make sense, will you!" Rebecca exclaimed, throwing up her hands. Meg looked in her direction again. Molly and Tara realized the problem looming on the horizon. They glanced at each other and headed toward Rebecca and Elder Downing.

"The snow-capped hills of the plains will provide a respite for you when your car stalls in the middle of nowhere. Never leave your prized possessions in the hands of the white man, for he will charge you five times their worth to return them. Give yourself time to understand that which you do not understand. Please deposit another seventy-five cents for greater clarity," said the Zoltar in his classic Indian drawl.

"Oh, you can bet your ass I will, Tonto," Rebecca mumbled. The machine kicked out another card.

> It is the will of Creator that you follow your path, unless you get arrested by the Lighthorse Brigade on the way there. Then it was just a dumb idea of your own doing.

Rebecca sensed Molly and Tara inching toward her, as if cautiously approaching a bomb technician with a dangerous device.

"This fucker is some white man's idea of a joke," she told them, shaking her head.

"What's going on, Becks?" asked Molly.

Rebecca hastily filled the machine again, dropping a quarter in the process.

"Damn it!"

She retrieved it and dropped it in, nearly falling backward as she did. The medicine man and his flashing lights and choo-choo whistle fired up again. His eyes, Rebecca was sure, were drilling into her gray matter. She thought she saw an armadillo hobble out of his mouth and she backed up, shaken. Molly put her hand on her friend's arm, then glanced at Tara, who shrugged, gazing compassionately at Rebeccca.

"You are currently in the sunrise of your awakening!" Elder Downing exclaimed. "You have but little time to discover the true meaning of your existence. Do not forget to follow the scream of the hawk and the cry of the chipmunk on the way to fortune and fame. Loving those who love you and keeping your friends close is the way to perfect freedom and happiness. Please deposit another seventy-five cents for the guidance you seek." As her friends slid beside her, Rebecca stared at the machine and sighed. Another card shot out from his naval.

> There are no real yesterdays or tomorrows, young champion! You must persevere in all that you do today. I will now go back to my horse and wait for your response in solemn expectation. Aho!

Molly took the card from Rebecca. She and Tara read it and they all stood in front of Elder Downing and pondered. Rebecca looked first at Molly, then at Tara. She snatched the card back and banged on the glass.

"No yesterdays or tomorrows? What the hell kind of advice is that?" she yelled. Molly glanced back at the counter and realized thankfully that Meg had gone to the storeroom.

"Becks, chill out, okay?' She tugged on her arm.

"No, Molly, no. I damn well wanna know what kind of coyote-following, raven-shitting crap I'm supposed to do for my two dollars and twenty-five cents. Seriously!"

"Take it easy, Chief," said Tara. Molly nodded to Tara and they tried pulling Rebecca away from Elder Downing. But Rebecca broke free and pounded on the glass again.

"Hey, old man! Screw *you and the horse you rode in on,* you phony pretendian wannabe cock holster!" Rebecca shouted. "All men suck! And that goes for you, too, Devon Farmer! You shit bird!"

"Okay, girlfriend," Molly said. "We're outta here."

Rebecca's marijuana-induced psychosis reached its peak. Her eyes widened and she pointed to the medicine man. "Holy shit, he's got a fucking gun! Everybody run! Active shooter, active shooter! Lock it down!" she yelled as she turned from the Zoltar, stumbled over Molly's feet, and fell to the floor, her remaining quarters rolling in all directions. They pulled Rebecca up and ushered her to the counter, where Molly threw down a ten and a five to cover the drinks and candy bars.

"Later, Meg!" she shouted toward the storeroom. They ran through the door to the car, setting off the flute music again and dragging along Rebecca, who was now singing a song about Elder Downing.

Meg charged out of the storeroom waving an over/under double-barreled shotgun and yelling, "What shooter? Where? Where the hell is he? Nobody move!"

As Tara backed the SUV out of its parking space, Rebecca hung her head out the window and sang to the tune of "Oh, My Darling, Clementine."

Elder Downing, Elder Downing,

with the dark and sexy eyes!

You fucked us over

with your bullshit

wasted my money

on your lies!

Ohh, Elder Downing, Elder Downing,

grabbed my boobs

and didn't like 'em—

Some people who had just pulled in were getting out of an old Toyota Tacoma and staring. Tara frantically pushed the button to roll up the rear window while Rebecca fought to keep her head out. Finally, she fell back into her seat, giggling.

"Hey!" she shouted. "We should get Emmy to go in there and fuck that guy up! Bet she could kick his ass all the way down the street to the Chevron. You see the size of that gun? Lousy, smousy, shigar store brooger man!"

Molly, sitting up front in the passenger seat, had put her head down and her hands over her ears. As Tara picked up speed, Molly sat up. "Oh, my God. How embarrassing." Looking over at Tara, she said, "Shit, Tara, what if the *real* Elder Downing hears about this? How crazy would that be?"

Tara checked the rearview mirror and sped up. "Let's get her to my house, Molly. I've got the place to myself for the weekend. We'll let her sleep it off there. She got into some seriously bad medicine today!"

"Sleep it off with Elder Downing, bitches! Ha, haaaaaaaaa!" cackled Rebecca. She mumbled a few more times, then became quiet and crashed. She snored like a bulldog as Molly and Tara talked about Devon.

"Heard that asshole smashed some nerdy guy's jaw at the bowling alley the other night," Tara said, looking both ways while making a left turn. "Asshole just pounded some poor skinny geek with glasses over space at an air hockey table."

"Please don't call him that, Tara. I need time to think about this."

"What's there to think about, girl?"

"Just need time, Tara," she repeated, her voice cracking and tears in her eyes.

Tara nodded. She reached over and held her friend's hand, thinking about all that Molly was dealing with. "Okay, Molly," she said. She glanced in the back seat. "Jesus Christ," she said. "Did you know she snores like that?"

13

Hell Visits Cumberland Plateau

Saturday, October 20, 1838
Beyond Brown's Ferry
Old Cherokee Nation

Mary and Nick were still reeling from Mother Rabbit's death. Mary appealed to the army to let Rabbit be returned to her home so that she could be buried with her ancestors. Enoch became upset when Captain Ambrose told Nick that such a thing was impossible, that Mother Rabbit would have to be buried now—along the trail.

"But, sir," Enoch staunchly pointed out, "such a thing is sacred, a traditional right for the Cherokee people." Captain Ambrose apologized for the McNair's loss, but he was steadfast in his resolve.

"I'm afraid it's just impossible, folks. She must be left here and now." Corporal King, who seemed to be acting as assistant to Captain Ambrose, had just sauntered up, guiding his horse by hand. Enoch spoke again on behalf of Mother Rabbit, but the corporal cut him off.

"We've heard enough outta you. Keep your mouth shut and get back there and get ready to move out. Ya hear me, boy?" Enoch lowered his head and quietly returned to his duties of preparing the McNair family and his own for the day's journey.

"You have an hour to get that woman in the ground, McNair, and I'll give you an additional ten minutes for prayers or what have you. Long day ahead, so let's move out," grumbled Captain Ambrose.

For the next hour, Nick, Enoch, and some helpers cut two large pieces of cottonwood from a nearby tree. Roughly measured at seven feet by four feet, they became a bark-encrusted makeshift casket. Mother Rabbit's body was carefully but hurriedly placed between them. They laced up the sides with rope and tree twine. The team dug the best grave they could manage, but the hard ground made it difficult. The tomb was shallow by any real standard of comparison. Mother Rabbit was placed in the cursory hole and covered with dirt, leaves, and small branches. Nick took the lead in prayer, followed by the missionary Diana.

During the noon hour, several soldiers and civilian wagon masters hired for the use of their equipment—all white men—built a fire in a clearing not far off the trail. The Indians grieved for Mother Rabbit, who had been especially well-respected. Tobacco Bill was no exception. When he discovered she had been buried in a shallow hole along the trail, he showed his disdain by marching directly up to the fire in the clearing and pissing vigorously into the flames. Corporal King had just placed his freezing hands over the fire when Tobacco Bill gave it his best arc while simultaneously shouting maniacally in Cherokee.

Corporal King and two of the civilians beat Tobacco Bill so severely he walked with a limp thereafter. Captain Ambrose ordered Corporal King to arrest the young Cherokee, and for the next three days, Tobacco Bill made the journey with bound hands and feet, giving him just enough slack to walk.

The group moved slowly but steadily across the autumn terrain. The people and animals struggled on increasingly steep hills. The nights turned colder. Trees shed their leaves, offering a tapestry of brilliance in the wake of the moving party. With Mary's help, Pretty Water in the Morning gave birth behind a large oak tree near the river. Captain Ambrose halted that section of the party just long enough for the birth to take place.

The brutality of birthing a child outside, amid the elements, was evident to all.

With Mary acting as midwife, Pretty Water was luckier than many other women on the journey. Most were obliged to have their baby alone. Mary used comfrey root and taheebo to sterilize the knife she used to sever Pretty Water's umbilical cord. It was a straightforward, uncomplicated delivery, and Mary was pleased that she could both help the mother and contribute to life itself.

The Week of Monday, October 22, 1838
Kelly's Ferry, Jasper, Tennessee
Moving Toward the Cumberland Plateau
Old Cherokee Nation

John Bell had returned, yet none of the Cherokee seemed to know where he had gone. He spent most of his time near the front of the detachment, oblivious to many of the things going on near the middle and rear, such as soldiers misbehaving and women giving birth. The party crossed the Tennessee River for the third time at Kelly's Ferry landing. Captain Ambrose and John Kelly initially argued about the fee due to the unusually large number of people, but Mr. Kelly finally agreed after Captain Ambrose increased the payment. This angered Nick because some of that money came from the till that was promised the Cherokees whenever they were to arrive in Indian Territory.

As they journeyed onward, the winds became harsh and the cool autumn air turned frigid. At one point, Corporal King slowed to let Tobacco Bill relieve himself. Because he was bound, hands in front, this proved difficult. Afterward, the corporal got in the Cherokee's face and snapped, "This oughta teach ya not to act like a savage in this camp. Bet you think twice about ever doing that again, am I right, Indian?" Tobacco Bill stared at him blankly, looked down at King's feet, then spit on the corporal's boot. King was too exhausted to make anything of it. He sighed and shook his head. "All right, people. Shit!" he roared. "Let's keep moving."

Tuesday and Wednesday they negotiated the headwaters of Battle Creek at the toe of the great Cumberland Plateau. Natives wept as they watched each other struggle along the trails, their feet bare. Dysentery was widespread, and many people were soiling themselves uncontrollably. The detachment sustained its next two deaths while ascending the Cumberland Plateau. Two elderly Cherokee, a man and a woman, gave in to fatigue and sickness. Whooping cough and a strange, unidentified illness that caused much of the dysentery gripped the people.

While traveling up the mountain through Coffee County near Battle Creek, Pretty Water's baby, a boy, cried constantly. The soldiers and white wagon masters grew impatient. Pretty Water would alternate her speed so as not to disturb any one section of the party more than necessary. Yet the child cried almost constantly; only his mother's breast would assuage him.

"Keep that kid quiet!" said one especially mean corporal.

"Yes, sir," came Pretty Water's soft response. She continued to move at a sporadic pace in the hope of avoiding the wrath of the soldiers. The Cherokees, on the other hand, showed no signs of annoyance or frustration at her baby's discomfort. The autumn leaves blew and were plastered to the walkers and riders as they pressed on. When one Cherokee named Sap Sucker dropped his meager bag of belongings, a private on horseback jabbed him between the shoulder blades with a sword.

"Move your filthy ass, Squanto."

Sap Sucker nodded and hastily picked up his things, then dropped them again because he was so intimidated. "I said move it, you little corn nigger," the private said, jabbing Sap Sucker again. The private teased the ends of Sap Sucker's hair, which extended beyond his shoulders, with the tip of the sword. "Hey, Billy," said the private, turning to one of his fellow soldiers, "look at this—he's a pretty one, ain't he? All we gotta do is pull his hair back, blindfold ourselves, yank them drawers down and we wouldn't be able to tell the difference!" The other soldier roared with laughter. Sergeant Thomas pulled up behind them, slowed his horse, and stared at the two soldiers. The other private quickly moved on.

"Private," he said calmly, "put that sword back." He glanced at Sap Sucker. "You—go on, now. It's okay. Keep moving—go ahead," he said, motioning him forward. Sap Sucker finished gathering his things and nodded.

"Wado," he said, thanking the sergeant. Sergeant Thomas nodded in return, then looked at the private.

"Private, I catch you doing anything like that again, I'm gonna dismount, see? Then I'm gonna walk over there real calm-like, see? Then I'm gonna yank you off that Quarter Horse and beat the living shit out of you. Then your mother— assuming you got one—is gonna be writin' me, asking why I scatter-assed her son on some backwoods trail in the middle of nowhere. I don't need the headache. So, here's what you do: You keep this party moving, and you keep your damned opinions to yourself, and save us both a lot of trouble, okay? Anything about that not clear to you, private?" The private shook his head. Sergeant Thomas nodded, told him to move out, and the journey continued.

Down the line, as the McNair wagon made its way past the Ryder Place, the baby screamed relentlessly in spite of Pretty Water's attempts to placate him. She tucked him to her chest, covering him with a shawl she had made back home for her new baby. She tried hiding him from the rest of humanity, such as it was. This attempt to smuggle him up the trail in secrecy came to a halt when a shout from one wagon master to another brought bloodcurdling screams from the child.

"SHUT THAT BASTARD CHILD UP!" roared the same corporal who had admonished her before.

"Sir," said an elderly Cherokee, "he's just hungry and tired."

"Well, so am I!" the soldier retorted.

Pretty Water did not want them to see her cry; she hung her head and pressed on. She veered in and out of the long caravan, farther from Mary's watchful eye, until she was out of sight and gone. She had been up and down the line enough for most to be familiar with her. The faster she went, the louder the infant screamed. Other Cherokee bowed their heads as she passed. Children placed their hands over their own ears to muffle the sound of the poor infant's cries. Pretty Water struggled to gain ground. The child's wailing grew until it seemed the only sound in the countryside.

Mary wondered what happened to her new friend. She prayed as she walked, relinquishing her wagon seat to alternating Cherokees who expressed appreciation. Nick, whose skill and strength in driving a team required he stay aboard the wagon, kept a watchful eye on his wife as she crept up the mountain. She held her belly with her left hand and a blanketed Martha occupied her right arm.

Down the line, Pretty Water found relief in a brief period of silence until the boy started up again. This time, his bawling reached a new high in pitch and duration. The young mother scurried, hoping that would help. When it did not, she pulled him closer to her breast and moved even faster, almost running now. Her people compassionately watched as she climbed as best she could. They neared the top of the mountain and the newborn shrieked with all its might. Pretty Water tried valiantly to hide her tears.

Up ahead, a wagon rolled to a stop. A bearded, dingy-looking man driving a team of oxen dismounted and approached Pretty Water. Without saying a word, he slapped her face, seized the infant, ripped him from his holder and shawl, grabbed him by the legs and swung him round three times before hurling him against the base of a large, lone pine tree. The boy's head exploded upon impact, his brain matter spraying the ground, the tree, and his terror-stricken mother. The man calmly returned to the wagon and climbed aboard.

An appalled, dumb, sickening silence followed. The people and animals seemed frozen in time. A pristine, glistening rain descended, lightly covering the fallen autumn leaves.

14

Punked

I am the punishment of God. If you had not committed great sins, God would not have sent a punishment like me upon you.

—Genghis Khan

Present Day
Friday Night, Mid-March
Eagle Feather Shopping Center
Muskogee, Oklahoma

Devon's evening shift at Crunch Time was over. Exhausted, he reeked of toasted bread, onions, peppers, and ammonia-drenched counter cleaner. Life: one big pile of shit after another.

He loathed making sandwiches for people. He hated the complaints ("My bread isn't quite done"—yeah, no shit, moron), didn't like his boss, abhorred repeating "Welcome to Crunch Time! What can I get for you this evening? Will that be whole wheat, white, or rye?" and despised working at night, absent hotties like Molly McNair. Most of all, he felt like somebody's bitch. He vowed that he would *not* be life's eternal punk. He suffered crappy moods and prayed that someone, anyone, try to make something of it.

He stretched his sore body, turning the corner of Crunch Time, a decaying gray building that smelled like piss and vape on the outside. Flexing his barbell-acquired muscles, he headed for the parking lot in the rear, adjacent to the strip mall sidewalk where people occasionally strolled by with their post-colonial grab shit. He smiled about the nerd he clobbered at the bowling alley. What a geek!

He morphed his walk into an arrogant strut, thinking scornfully about the world and its nonstop, apple-red nonsense. He hocked up a good one and blew the snot rocket onto the trunk of a nearby Kia, which he knew belonged to his boss, Melanie. He grinned. *Bitch in a box, my gift to you.* He was fed up hearing, "Now, Devon, coming to work late won't gain you any points in the real world, young man!" and watching her wag her bony finger in his face. *Cheers, you moon-faced, flat-ass, librarian-looking, honky colonizer.* Women pissed him off no end. And what was *Molly's* problem, anyway? Were they all puritans and she-dogs? *A wench is a wench is a wench,* he concluded.

In truth, Devon never saw it coming. The worst part, he later decided, was not so much the dizziness and embarrassment, but the definitive inability to breathe that a panic attack invokes. In the enveloping haze he spotted a brown upper arm from the bottom corner of his right eye. It had his neck in the firmest, most powerful grip he'd ever known.

"O-see-yo, *GI Joe.*"

He caught the sarcasm of the Cherokee greeting and instantly recognized the voice: *Emmy.* An annoying thing about Emmy was that, half the time, she didn't sound like an Indian at all. She talked like a goddamn English teacher.

"I truly hope I'm not interrupting anything important in what must be quite the fulfilling life," she intoned, squeezing harder.

"Em . . . Emmy . . . ca—, can't *breathe!*" he squeaked as he dropped the drink he had stolen from Crunch Time's drink station. It splattered Melanie's fender.

"I know; wild, isn't it? Trust me, it's the gift that just keeps on taking."

She sounded as if she was at the bank cashing a check or ordering a drink somewhere. He could tell she had just come from the gym. He smelled her funk and her arm was salty with sweat. He also detected a hint of her perfume, a subtle "I'm a woman, but I can beat the ever-loving shit out of you blindfolded" kind of sweet.

"Over here, you punk ass bitch," Emmy said, dragging Devon away from the light, but still close to the parked cars.

"I have a few things I want to say to you, Devon," she said, "and I have not the slightest doubt that I'll have your undivided attention." He desperately tapped her powerful forearm. "Oh, no, no, dearest Devon! This is real life—no tapping out here, sport!" She glanced around. "Nope, don't see a referee anywhere, Studly. All things considered, I'd say you're screwed."

He sensed himself passing out. "Now," she added, "number one: The judo term for this—*pay attention*! Are you paying attention?" Devon managed to grunt as his eyes slowly narrowed, like the curtain closing on a final act.

Emmy eased her grip to keep him conscious. "As I was saying before you so rudely interrupted, this is what they call a 'Hadaka-jime' in judo. It's a rear naked choke, only different from that wrestling horseshit they're teaching you girls over there at Screw U. Gotta say, I hate the damn things. Once I got to go to fight camp with 'Ambush' Jones and she octopused me like this and I scorched my pants. I mean, right there in the ring. Humiliating, to say the least." Devon flailed his arms. "Seriously, after I limped to the locker room it looked like I shit a 3 Musketeers Bar in my bloomers. Didn't walk right for two days."

"Emmy . . . back off me—"

"Shut the *fuck* up."

He did. He had never known fear like this.

"Six seconds, pissant; that's all it would take for me to put you out. Be grateful I'm generous. So, the thing about the Hadaka-jime is that if I shift my weight even the slightest, you'll

sing like a canary from now on. So you best be very, very still."
He froze, trying to think of a way out of her merciless grip, but
then quickly blacked out again. "Second—*pay attention*, I
said—I know Molly has a soft spot for you because you two go
all the way back to elementary school and kindergarten
together. And I can respect that, ya know? Ya know?" She
nodded from the side so he could get a glimpse with his
peripheral vision.

He offered a slight acknowledgment—more with his
eyebrows than anything—as Emmy spoke as if she were talking
to an eight-week-old puppy. Her dark, silken braid came to rest
on her mighty arm near his cheek. "Like, that's quite the
commitment when ya think about it, ya know? Ya know?"
Puppy-dog talk again. "And you *are* committed to Molly, aren't
you? I mean, from a friendship perspective, no? Like, friends
honor friends and shit like that."

Devon groaned again. Angry, he tried squeezing Emmy's
brick-like arm. When that didn't help, he dug his fingers in—
anything to get some relief—though he didn't dare try to bite
her. That failed, so he went for an elbow to her ribs, which she
expertly avoided. He collapsed further into her hold. He
couldn't believe a woman could be this damn strong. Panic and
the inability to relax only made a choke harder to escape. He
sensed her forearm tighten against the left side of his neck, her
bicep pressing the right. He thought his eyes would blow their
sockets. She let up on him and spoke again.

"Last but certainly not least, Dev my man," she began,
easing the choke and moving her head to the side so Devon
could see her face. Once again her braid, which extended to her
waist, swirled around and landed across his red cheek. Her
mocha coffee eyes seemed on the one hand demonic and on the
other almost glorious.

"If you *ever* disrespect my little sister again, I'll
motherfuck you so bad the EMTs will be prying hoagies out of
your ass with the fucking Jaws of Life, understood?" Emmy
tightened the screws and leaned in close to Devon's right ear.
"Understood?" she demanded, her muscles twisting like an

anaconda. He whispered something that resembled agreement. "And frankly," she added venomously, "I think I will have *earned* it." Devon's eyes flashed with recognition, his own words echoing in his mind. She took a whiff of his Crunch Time polo shirt. "Jesus Christ, boy, what the fuck is that—onions or cat piss?" He desperately tapped again, pleading for air.

"Excellent!" she roared, releasing him. "I knew we would see eye-to-eye, well, eye-to-blackout, about this. Yeah, yeah?" Again with the nodding and puppy speak. Devon nodded.

Two women with bags from Wanda's Bath Works walked by on their way down the alley between the stores. Devon flexed his arms and it looked as if his temper might flare as he puffed out his chest, a little vein in his neck pulsing. Emmy flashed her dazzling smile, held her arms out wide for Devon, and exclaimed, "Oh, come here, you! Give me a hug. It was *so* good to see you, brother-cousin-nephew!" She pulled Devon forcefully to her in a happy bear hug. The women smiled and just kept going, though they were still in earshot.

"You come and see me again; it's been just too long!" Emmy declared for effect. A few more folks strolled by, mesmerized by Emmy's "loving" energy. Still embracing Devon, she whispered in his ear, "I suppose you know I'm sick, right?" Gasping, he nodded slowly, not knowing what to say or do.

"Well, that doesn't mean jack shit." The last of the observers began to filter away. She trapped his arms with a front bear hug, continuing to whisper. "When it comes to family, I'm not afraid of doing time. And no pussy cancer is gonna keep me from snapping your goddamn neck like one of those pathetic Crunch Time toothpicks. I'll ground and pound you so hard your fucking *ancestors* are gonna need plastic surgery. Just something for you to reflect on. Molly deserves better and you chose to shit on her. I'm contemplating putting you in intensive care for that, but I'm restraining myself, see? See? Yeah," she added in her puppy voice.

He nodded as she rocked him from side to side, then she eased her hold on him. Suddenly, he pushed back on her, breaking her grip and trying to tie up her arms. He grinned nastily, knowing this was his opening to drop her with a single-leg takedown. She deflected his effort, shaking her head. She dug her thumbs into his mastoid process, producing the intended gag response and a yell, then bitch-slapped him, which shocked him into a standstill.

"I'm really disappointed, Devon," she said calmly. "Seems as though you're one of those last-century guys who doubts the value and capabilities of women. Permit me to put those motherfucking doubts to rest."

She seized him by his lapels and flung him over her hip onto the hood of Melanie's Kia with a loud thump. She plastered his back to the car, his Crunch Time shirt partially covering his shocked expression. She wrenched it down, exposing the rest of his face. She leaned over him menacingly and snarled, "You mushroomed Molly's arm, did you know that? DID YOU FUCKING KNOW THAT?" She shook him roughly. "You blackened her, you little shit-ass!"

"No!" he yelped, like a cartoon mouse staring up at a cat seconds before being squashed. "I-I-I'm sorry. I didn't know! Really!"

"Plus, you scared the hell out of her, leaving her with doubts about men. That's even more unforgivable."

"I didn't mean to, Emmy, honest!"

"Bullshit!"

"No really!"

"You doping?"

"Fuck no."

"NO?"

"I swear!"

"I think you've been tasting that gym candy, you little piss-pot," she barked.

"No."

"The hell you say. I smell Oxy on you, bitch!" She jerked him, drilling his eyes with hers.

"No-no-no, seriously. I haven't!"

"Don't. The only thing it will do for that tiny dick of yours is shrink it even more. Plus, it ruins your life in ways that you can't even imagine yet, capiche?"

"Yes, ma'am."

"Don't 'ma'am' me, you little chooch. Just listen for once in your life. You knew she had a knee trauma and you pressed on—just couldn't help yourself, right?" she thundered, jerking him again by the shirt. "Just another little hottie to you. If I find out you permanently injured her, I'm gonna splatter your thick skull on the roadway and kick your barren brains under a fucking transit bus!" She smacked him again.

Though Devon had a good two inches on Emmy, she dwarfed him in the moment, dominating the situation. He nodded and looked away, ashamed. His eyes found an old Ford F-150 two spaces over on which to focus. An older Cherokee man strolled by just as Emmy slapped Devon. He looked at Emmy, his eyes widening, and she nodded briefly at him. The man held up his hands as if to say, "I don't even want to know what this is," and kept walking. Emmy looked back down at Devon.

"Sorry I scared her and hurt her, really," he cried, chirping like a parakeet. He'd realized by the man's response that no one was coming to his aid.

"You're sorry all right. So we apparently agree on something, no?"

"Yes," he whispered, looking back up again and wincing, frightened she might use her fists. Emmy studied him before speaking again, looming inches from his face.

"Apology tulips."

"Huh?"

"She loves them."

"What?"

"The *flowers*, motherfucker! The flowers!" She wrenched him up and slammed him back down on the hard car, pancaking him on the hood again, his feet flying upward from the impact.

His face belied sheer terror. "Yeah-yeah-yeah! The flowers! What about 'em?"

Emmy sighed, shaking her head. "My sister loves tulips, you double-digit, *fucking* caveman moron."

"Yeah-yeah-yeah—tulips, got it!"

"Say it again: tulips."

"Tulips."

"SAY WHAT?"

"Tulips! Tulips!"

"Kay-den," she answered. Still maintaining a nasty grip on his shirt, she dug her elbows into his chest. He groaned. He felt like a Prius being crushed at the auto junkyard. This time her braid swung around and popped him lightly on his right jaw. Again, he winced. "Clark's," she added, "that'd be a good start."

"Huh?"

"Clark's, *asshole*, Clark's! That pretty-boy gay guy that owns the flower shop over on Fourth Street behind the dry cleaners—he's got Angelique tulips—white man's flowers at a good price. And understand something, dipshit: I'm not talking romantic flowers here—these are *apology* blooms, am I right?" Devon nodded rapidly. "Or you can go to Old McDonald's fucking farm and dig 'em up with your shriveled nards for all I care, got it?" She squashed him against Melanie's spit-laced car and once more pressed in with her elbows. "We on the same page here, Mighty Mouse?"

"Same page, same page! I'll make good on it, Emmy, I swear to God," he moaned. She studied him, then nodded once.

"And they're what kind of flowers?"

"Uh, tulips?"

"Fucking apology flowers, bitch!"

"Fucking apology flowers—got it!"

"Osda," she replied in Cherokee.

Despite his earlier attempt at bravado, Devon trembled as she pressed into him. She yanked him to his feet and released him. Devon stumbled and half landed back in Emmy's arms. She straightened him and put her hands on his shoulders, lightly this time.

Then her demeanor changed again. "You make sure to tell your parents I said siyo, and that I'll try to stop by soon, yeah, yeah?" She was grinning and nodding with the puppy talk, her ponytail braid bobbing up and down, inducing Devon to repeat the action. "I would *love* to chat with them again!" She poked her head toward Devon's rattled face and quietly added, "About the doing time thing—just think, maybe by then they'll have coed facilities and we could be cellmates. And you can bet you'll be doing my damn laundry, sport."

"Sick . . . to my stomach," he managed to say in a quaking voice, holding his left hand to his throat and his right over his belly.

"Well, goddamn it," she calmly replied, pushing him back. "Don't you slosh up my fifteen-dollar Walmart shoes. Just washed the damn things." She steadied Devon and smiled. "Dizzy, like you're gonna pass out?" He nodded. "Yeah, that's the blood rushing back to your carotids. You'll feel like you've been high for the next couple of hours, but you'll manage." She lightly slapped his cheeks. He flinched in response. "Snap to, man. Can ya drive?"

"Yes, dammit," he managed to say, rubbing his neck and pushing her away. "I know how to fucking drive, okay?"

She studied him one last time. She reached over and cupped his chin between her thumb and fingers. He pulled back and frowned. "Having known you since you were a tyke, I know you're a good man at heart, Devon," she said. "I can't imagine you *not* doing the right thing hereafter, yeah?" She nodded again, releasing his chin. "I'm sure the whole thing was just a big brain fart. If you were anybody else, you'd be dead. Something's clearly wrong with you and I'm not your damn counselor. But I want you to think about how long you've known Molly, what she means to me, and what you thought you were getting away with. *Think hard.* You and me—we have to have this little rap session again, it won't be a rap session. I'll just deliver your fucking marbles to your mama in a jar."

"Yeah, yeah, got it, got it!"

"They have programs for guys like you, Dev. Meetings for dudes with anger and impulse control issues. Better get your ass in one soon before somebody like me beats you to death in a piss-stained parking lot in front of a bunch of clueless white people. I happen to know there's a meeting next Tuesday at the Baptist church on Seventh Street. Seven o'clock. Be there, Devon; be at that fucking meeting." He nodded rapidly again and she stepped back, then moved closer a final time. "*So* good to just run into you like this, little brother! Whodathunkit?" Patting his left cheek, her biceps and triceps shimmering in the light from above the parking lot, she smiled and added, "You have a thoughtful and productive evening, Devon. Good night."

"Yeah, uh, night, Emmy," he managed to say, shaking the cobwebs out of his head. He looked up. "Hey, I'm sorry you're sick and—" And just like that, she had vanished into the night.

Now *this*, he thought, this is just the kind of bullshit I don't need: fuckin' Gina Carano–Ronda Rousey Deer Woman shit. He rubbed his throat and vigorously shook his head once more. Actually, he didn't hate Emmy or anything. Like most guys his age, he was in awe of her. After all, she beat the hell out of people in her spare time legally and for money. It dawned on him as he got to his car: He just got punked. Big time. So much for my grand fucking ideas, he thought. Punked by a sexy MMA fighter with cancer; god*damn* it. An image from a greeting card he had once seen at the pharmacy came to mind. It showed a grizzly bear in the woods wiping his ass with a rabbit. He definitely felt like that rabbit.

Something occurred to him and he looked down. Fucking unbelievable! She had made him shit his pants.

15

Family

Present Day
McNair House
Muskogee, Oklahoma
District Four, Cherokee Nation

Emmy was home. Not due back in classes until Wednesday, she felt shelter from this particular storm. She and Sandra had spent the morning consulting with her oncologist in Tulsa. They were having an early afternoon meal. Molly brought the salad to the table and glanced at her older sister.

"I love you, Em," she said.

Her sister, seated at the table, managed a smile. "I love you, too, Nine-Speed." Molly's first adult bike had been a nine-speed, and she loved that Emmy still called her that. Emmy seemed tired. Molly, too, offered up a faint smile. She put the salad down and studied her sibling. Despite the fatigue, Emmy felt good; one would never know she might be seriously ill. She was, after all, The Cherokee Storm.

They all sat now, and Molly asked to say grace. She thanked the Great Spirit for another day, and for Sandra and Emmy, and prayed for good results on Emmy's upcoming tests. A tear dribbled down Emmy's cheek as she managed a smile for Molly and patted her hand. Sandra talked about the weather, slowly bringing the day's events into the conversation. She explained to Molly that the recent biopsy, in this case known as a fine needle aspiration, had revealed cancerous tissue and that today's conversation with the doctor centered on the need for imaging. A PET scan was scheduled for first thing Monday morning. This was to determine if the cancer had spread.

Molly's chin quivered. Her mother placed her hand in Molly's and said, "Let's not get ahead of ourselves." As they finished supper, Emmy took a swig of iced tea and stared out the kitchen window while their mother gave Molly more details about what had transpired and what was to come. Emmy faced the unknown. The breadth of what was happening was extensive, and the depth of it diminished her ability to maintain perspective. She had always been protective of her younger sister and now having cancer made her feel protective of nothing. She considered herself strong, able to take a beating and keep standing. But she wondered about cancer. Would she bounce back? Would she be permanently disfigured? Would she die? No—she refused to go down that road.

But what if she did die? Who would miss her? What would become of her mom and Molly? She often told Molly about the importance of being a fair and balanced warrior woman. She gazed at her younger sister, reflecting on earlier times. She felt like she had let Molly down along the way. Her thoughts were interrupted when the doorbell rang. Sandra got up to answer it.

"Molly McNair?"

"That's my daughter," they heard Sandra answer. "Oh, my. Those are stunning!"

"Best wishes from Clark's!" the voice boomed.

Their mother shut the door and came around the dining room corner with a huge bouquet of rainbow tulips. Molly's eyes widened. Emmy belched, then farted.

"Honestly, girl!" Sandra exclaimed.

Emmy grabbed a toothpick from the holder on the table and began chomping it.

"There's a card," Sandra said, handing the flowers to Molly, then studying her oldest and trying to ascertain what her problem was.

After Molly examined the card, she seemed lost in thought, and a little sad. She was, though, also admiring the tulips.

"Well?" Sandra inquired. "Do tell!"

Molly shrugged. "Just some guy from school," she murmured.

Emmy's hands were folded in front of her. She unfolded them and cracked her knuckles.

"What ... the ... *hell*?" said Sandra, turning her head toward Emmy and picking up on the innuendos.

"What?" Emmy replied, feigning ignorance.

"Something you wish to say?" her mother asked.

"Not really."

"Jealous much?" Sandra chided.

"Oh, yeah, Mom," Emmy replied with scathing sarcasm. "Uproariously covetous, for sure."

"Uh-huh." Sandra turned her attention back to Molly and her tulips. "They really are beautiful, aren't they?" Molly couldn't help it. She grinned.

"Yes!" Molly replied.

Sandra caught an ever-so-slight smile forming on Emmy's face.

"Ha!" she shouted. "You know something about this, don't you?"

"No, why would I?" Emmy responded.

"Hogwash. You forget that I knew you before you knew you," said Sandra. Molly eyed her sister with suspicion.

"Jesus, Mom. I'm just here eating dinner. Molly got flowers. I'm jazzed already, okay? And that 'I knew you before you knew you' stuff ... honestly, Mom. Makes you sound like Mother Superior or somebody."

Sandra laughed and shook her head. She knew something was up, but given Emmy's circumstances, she dropped the matter. She told Molly she was impressed with the tulips. "I sure would like to know who sent those," she added with a wink.

Wanna bet? Emmy thought.

"I suppose you'll tell me if you want me to know," said Sandra. "So," she said, turning her attention back to Emmy. "What are your thoughts about what the doctor said?" Molly pushed the flowers aside, grasping her face in the palms of her hands, focusing on her sister.

"Look," Emmy began, wondering what her mother's reaction was going to be, "a woman in Tulsa, a naturopathic doctor, has some ideas about cancer. I want to meet with her and hear what she has to say."

Sandra considered this.

"Like, like a natural healer person?" said Molly.

"Kinda. She's a doctor. I saw her speak when I was an undergrad. Herbs, homeopathy, Native American healing practices, that kind of thing."

"Does she treat people with cancer?" Sandra asked.

"Yes, so long as you've consulted with an oncologist—that's the law right now."

"Right. It seems like I read that in a brief once," their mother answered. "But this is *serious*, Emmy. I mean, this is your life we're talking about." Emmy looked at her mother.

"So what the hell's your point, Ma?"

Sandra knew there was no point in arguing this. She sighed, but smiled at her daughter. "So, when do you want to do this?"

"I'll reach out to her. In many states, ND docs are not yet recognized as licensed healthcare practitioners, so insurance coverage is out of the question. Strictly out-of-pocket because Oklahoma is dragging its ass."

Sandra sighed. "Well—"

"I got this, Mom," Emmy interjected. "It's cool."

"No," Sandra said. "It's *not* cool. I'll help you."

"No, I'm good."

"No, you're not. I'll help, I said."

"I heard you. I *got* this, Ma."

Molly was into this exchange. Her eyes darted from her sister to her mother.

Sandra slammed her fist on the table. "I'm helping, period," she insisted. "I knew you before you knew you and all that," she said, glaring playfully at her oldest.

Molly laughed. She watched them both. It was the ultimate staring contest: Mother vs. daughter; paralegal vs. MMA fighter. Her mother, now forty-five, still had it "going on." She was lean and had dark, flyaway hair and her family's piercing charcoal eyes. Her silken skin revealed the mixture of Scots-Irish and Cherokee Indian, blended through the generations. Molly noticed that men sometimes did a double take when they saw her mom in the market or places like the Walmart Supercenter, which was weird because it was, well, her mom.

Emmy stared back. Today her thick hair was in a ponytail, her own dark eyes setting off her round, unfinished wooden earrings, forged into the shape of small tree stumps. Her full black eyebrows were arched, as if challenging their mom to a three-round match at Sequoyah Center. Her rounded mouth was set in her typical "I'm a badass and I'll pay my own way, thank you very much" posture. It was a face Molly wished wasn't regularly pummeled and kicked by some of the world's toughest women.

"Fine," said Emmy, giving in with a sigh. It occurred to her that it might be good for her mother emotionally to help out.

"Fine," Sandra repeated.

"*Fine.*"

"Fine!"

"Well damn, fine already!" Emmy stressed with exaggerated frustration.

"All right, y'all, dang!" Molly shouted. She snickered and grabbed her sister's hand and guided it to her mother's. She tried connecting them. They resisted, both doing their level best not to smile or laugh. But love won out, and Emmy laughed first, taking their mother's hand.

"Wado, Mom," she whispered, a tear in her left eye.

Their mom nodded. End of discussion.

After dinner, Emmy and Molly helped with the dishes and cleanup. They played Scrabble, Molly's favorite since childhood. Later, during a quiet moment, when Molly was in the bathroom and Sandra was changing out Emmy's laundry because Emmy's washer was getting repaired, Emmy peeked at the card that came with the flowers.

"I apalogize" was scribbled on the card, the misspelling irritating Emmy. Had to be Devon. Clark Roberts, an intelligent and sensitive man, clearly hadn't signed it for Devon. At least the kid gave it a shot, Emmy thought. She shook her head.

Be at that meeting, Devon, she thought as she put the card back in the bouquet. *Be at that fucking meeting.*

16

Learning What Was Always There

Present Day
Saturday, following their visit to Meg & Mike's
Tara Longbranch's House
Muskogee, Oklahoma

Tara and Rebecca reclined on the family's sectional sofa, slurping Coke and watching TV while they finished off their BBQ wings. They had split a "Hit Man" medium pizza from Goodfella's. Rebecca had always liked that Tara loved Hollywood movies from the early twentieth century. Tara's parents left her some money for meals, even though she had her own part-time job at the Go Mart.

"Hey," Rebecca said as Tara finished, "you got a little somethin' on your mouth," and wiped it away with her own napkin.

"Wado," said Tara, double-checking with her own. Tara watched Rebecca watching the program, which she wasn't really into that day because her mind was preoccupied. They talked about school, their jobs, college or not college, and Molly and Devon.

"He is *such* an asshole!" Rebecca exclaimed.

"She doesn't want us calling him that," Tara said, turning her head from the TV and making a face.

"The hell I won't," said Rebecca. "Asshole, asshole, asshole, asshole, asshole, asshole!" They laughed.

"You've known them both a lot longer than I have. Whad'ya think is up with that shit?"

Rebecca shook her head. "Not really sure. He was always the sweetest kid when we were young. It's like he's gone through some kinda jock bullshit metamorphosis or something. He's like, Steroid Steve now or something. Hey, I'm so glad you were there for Molly while I was over in Tulsa. I know she really appreciated it." She placed her hand in Tara's and squeezed. Tara tried to hold onto it as she was pulling away. She glanced at her friend, who was staring at her. Tara was a white Cherokee—more like Molly, with pretty, blondish-brown hair that was almost down to her shoulders this year. She wore red feathered earrings and a white pocket-T with light red trim that she'd been wearing all day as they hung around the house.

Rebecca felt strange in her gut, and a tingling made its way up and down her inner forearms. She looked back at the TV, which Tara had muted while they were talking. "Hey!" she said laughingly, "how about that crazy cigar store medicine man! What a hokey thing for Meg to order, huh? Seen them before, but that one was wild. I guess my being high as a kite didn't help anything, huh?" She laughed, noticing Tara's slow nod. She rested her head back on the sofa again, looking at Rebecca with her penetrating gray-green eyes. Rebecca looked back at the TV, shaking her head again. "Crazy Indian Country shit, huh?" she said, catching herself squirming. "Calling me 'Indigiqueer' and pretending like he knows me ... what a cheese dick white man's joke, right? Trickster shit!" Tara just gave her slow, methodical nod again.

"Oh, hey," Tara said, suddenly sitting up. "Hold that thought. Gotta pee. Be back."

"Roger that, captain," said Rebecca, grabbing the remote and turning up the volume again, as if nothing had just happened. She realized while Tara was gone, though, that she wasn't watching anything at all. Not at all. She heard the water running after the commode flushed, and thought she heard Tara quietly gargling. Tara returned and resumed her posture.

"You were saying?" she asked politely.

"Oh, nothing, really. Just crazy coming off that high. I'd *swear* that Zoltar had a gun. I know I should curb that stuff. Getcha into some bad medicine, girlfriend."

"Becks?"

"Yeah?" Rebecca answered, using the hand sanitizer that Tara's mom always had in the living room and some paper towels to clean her hands.

"Remember the night of Emmy's fight?"

"Yeah, 'course. What about it?"

"You know how you held my hair back for me?"

Rebecca nodded.

"That was sweet. Thank you."

"Hey, you'da done the same for me, girlfriend, right?" she responded, briskly rubbing in the sanitizer and wondering where this was going.

Tara leaned forward and hung her head. "How'd you do that again? I mean, like what method did you use?"

"Method? Jesus, girl, are you shittin' me? Just did like this," she said, sweeping Tara's hair back and away from her face. "You know, can't have shit face on top of being shit-faced!" she said and giggled as she let go. Tara sat up, shook her head so that her hair fell in an enticing way, and put her left arm delicately behind Rebecca's neck.

"You mean like this?" she asked, inching toward Rebecca, who felt the tingling magnify, this time between her thighs. They locked eyes as Tara moved Rebecca's thick, black hair away from her face.

"Yeah," said Rebecca quietly, "something like that—yeah." Tara closed her eyes and leaned in and kissed her friend. She locked her lower lip against Rebecca's upper and brought her right hand up to Rebecca's face, still holding the opposite side with her left. She hung on, then separated her lips from Rebecca's. She rubbed her friend's nose with her own. Her breath was minty, hiding most of the BBQ wings and pizza. It was the most amazing kiss Rebecca had ever experienced, which had been limited to guys.

"Hold my hair again, Becks," she whispered. "Hold it again like that," she added with an undercurrent of force in her voice. Rebecca grabbed her friend's hair, pulled it aside again, and squeezed.

"Like this?" she asked, feeling like her chest was going to cave.

"Yeah, but squeeze it harder, Becks. Do it." Rebecca did and then kissed Tara aggressively. When she pulled away, Tara pleaded, "Lay on top of me, Rebecca, lay on me." She tugged her friend down on top of her. Rebecca found herself staring down at Tara's considerable chest. Though she wore a bra, Rebecca could see what was underneath and she felt charged, like the biggest car battery in the window at AutoZone. Suddenly, she jerked upright, wiping her mouth and gasping.

"Whoa, whoa, what the hell, girl? What're we doing?"

"I think you know what we're doing, Chief. Lay with me, Rebecca, *please*. Just do it." She used her pleading eyes to find her friend's core, her soul. She wrapped her legs around Rebecca and squeezed her hips with her knees. "Hold me, Becks," she whispered again, touching her own breasts with Rebecca's right hand. "Make me feel *good* inside, please," she added, lifting her head from the sofa, her perfect mouth half-open, moaning, hair falling straight back, tickling the cushion.

Rebecca looked down at her, only inches away. "Oh, *shit*," she whispered, her voice catching, and she collapsed onto Tara again and kissed her passionately, almost violently. She pulled back and up and away, gazing at Tara. "Oh, my God. Oh, good Lord." She kissed her friend again softly, then placed her head on Tara's chest. "Oh, my God," she said again. Rebecca Taylor and Tara Longbranch had come to one of life's curious but revealing intersections. They spent the evening loving each other, as they somehow knew they always had.

Tara and Rebecca lay embracing on the sofa. The morning sun peeked through the curtains. Tara's bra was on the back of the sofa, while Rebecca's jeans had been flung across the coffee table. Tara awoke to see her French bulldog, Dumbledore, sitting and staring at them.

"Oh, dear," she said.

"What's wrong?" asked Rebecca, blinking herself awake and looking around. "What the hell?" she said, rubbing her eyes and seeing Dumbledore. "Does he always stare like that?" Dumbledore looked as if he had a hundred questions to ask.

"Only after I hump my girlfriend, apparently," Tara said with a smile. "C'mon, Dumbly," she said, and got up and fed the dog. After both of them were up and around, Tara asked Rebecca if she wanted breakfast. She said no and they both returned to the sofa, their haven for the weekend. They sat in silence, avoiding awkward conversation until it was no longer avoidable. Eventually, Rebecca gave in and spoke.

"What do we do, Tara? I mean, what was this?" She shook her head. Tara seemed disappointed.

"I hope it was special, is what," she replied with a frightened look.

Rebecca looked at her friend, then held her hand. "Of course it was," she whispered. She pulled Tara's hand to her face and kissed it. "I just don't know how to . . . what I think of . . . what to do or say, Jesus Christ." She leaned back and stared at the ceiling. She suddenly looked at Tara. "When did you know? I mean, *how* did you know? Like, *I* didn't even know, really . . ."

Holding Rebecca's hand, Tara replied, "I think I've always known, sort of. I just know I've always wanted you." They gazed into each other's eyes. Rebecca rubbed her head.

"Oh, shit," she said, looking back at the ceiling. "Jesus please-us, Tara, do we tell anybody? How do we hide this?"

"I don't *want* to hide this, Becks. I want people to know. My parents—well, I don't know. They've just always known you as Rebecca, ya know? They've known you as my friend, not my lover."

"Oh, hell no, Tara. Not our parents. You know my dad. God almighty damn, girl. No way. You know how he is. He just won't get it. No fucking—"

"Hey, hey," Tara said quietly, squeezing her love's hand, "we don't have to say anything to our parents." Rebecca gave a profound sigh of relief.

"Good," she said. "Thank God." They looked at each other.

"Molly!" they said in unison.

Rebecca ran around, trying to get ready to leave, multitasking by brushing her hair with Tara's brush and helping clean up some of the weekend mess they had made. They had run by Rebecca's house on Saturday afternoon before getting the pizza to pick up the truck and a couple of personal items, but a hair brush hadn't been one of them. She handed Tara the brush and kissed her cheek. "Wado," she quickly said, looking for her wallet. Tara calmly leaned against the frame of the doorway between the kitchen and living room.

"Here it is," she said, holding the wallet. Rebecca shook her head and took the wallet.

"Right in front of my big nose, never mind," she said, flustered. She was clearly nervous. "Okay okay okay," she rattled, "think I have everything. So, wild, right? Come to your place to come down off some bad medicine and end up getting laid." She looked up at Tara, who smiled her soft, calming smile. Her arms were crossed and she looked like a maiden from Sherwood Forest as she melted into the woodwork of the doorway. God, she's beautiful, Rebecca thought as she tried to get her shit together. "Okay okay okay," she mumbled once more, "guess I'll see you in the cafeteria tomorrow—then AP Lit, right? Yeah? Our last few months of high school, girl!"

Tara, arms still crossed, did her slow nod thing again, hexing Rebecca once more with those gray-green eyes.

"Hey," said Rebecca, throwing up her hands, "don't start that shit again, please. Like, it's just makin' me nuts, okay?" Tara just kept nodding, ever so slowly, giving Rebecca her best smoky-eyed Lauren Bacall-in-Casablanca look. Rebecca couldn't cope. Another embrace, another long kiss. They pressed their foreheads together, just standing and gazing.

Reluctantly, Tara pulled away and said, "Yeah, you better go. My folks will be home soon. And if they come back while you're here tonight, I won't be able to hide my feelings for you, seriously." Rebecca nodded and glanced out the kitchen window.

"Crap, raining now."

"Here," said Tara, moving from the doorway, "take my rain jacket."

She pulled it from the back of a chair that faced a small desk in the living room. Rebecca put on the jacket and dished her hair out from under it, looking down toward the doorway. Dumbledore was there, again, sitting and staring. Rebecca grinned.

"Goodnight, Dumbly, see you later," she said with a grin and blew him a kiss. He wandered over to her for a pet, to which she happily obliged. "O-KAY," she said forcefully to convince herself to leave. "Going now. Text you later." She turned toward the kitchen.

"Becks," said Tara softly.

"Yeah?"

"Love you."

"Yeah, love you, too." With that, she forced herself to walk through the kitchen, open the door, and leave.

Nancy Ward High School
Mr. Wolfe's AP Lit Class
Muskogee, Oklahoma

Mr. Wolfe's students loved and respected him. He had passion for the subject matter and an ease of communicating it. Plus, he was just one of those teachers that you knew was on your side.

"All right, people, people, people," he began as usual. They all smiled. "We've spent some time this year analyzing a couple of the classics. And, can I just say, by the way, I'm so damn proud of all of you." His eyes got big and he looked around conspiratorially. "Whoooah. Did daddy just use a curse word?" he said with mock surprise, covering his mouth with his left hand. They giggled. He scurried around, looking through the window in the door as if checking for the tribal cops, then stopped. "Ah," he said, waving his arm, "you're all about to graduate—screw it." The class erupted in laughter. "Nah, nah," he said, getting serious again. "You titans have done well. You're young warriors. Proud of you," he added in his Native drawl. Molly thought she saw a tear in his eye. "You guys, really," he said, patting his heart, "I'm so glad *you* were my AP kids this year. Wado."

Some of the students teared up and they all applauded their teacher. Billy Daugherty and a couple of the other guys gave Cherokee whoops, then the class calmed down. Mr. Wolfe returned to the front and continued. Molly leaned forward and tapped Tara on the shoulder.

"Got any more paper?" she whispered. Tara nodded and gave her some. Rebecca was seated to Tara's left.

"So," Mr. Wolfe said, "we talked about having you analyze something more contemporary during these last few months before you go on to college." He looked up. "You're *all* going to college, yes?" A few of them nodded, a raised hand here and there. "You're *all* going to college, yes?" he repeated, his Wolfe family eyes on the rise again. "Yes," came several responses. He sighed. "You're ALL *going to college, yes*?" he cajoled. He cupped his right hand to his ear and leaned forward. "I can't *hear* you," he said in a full-on army way.

"Yes, Mr. Wolfe!" came the unanimous reply, followed by more giggles.

"Kay-den!" he said, followed by laughter. "So, several months back I passed out copies of Louis Sachar's *Holes*. Everybody still have theirs? It's okay if you don't have it with you today. If you haven't read it, and I know you have, get on with it. We don't have much time, even if it's Indian time never mind." More laughter. "I want you to do me yet another favor. I want you to pretend that you're in college, let's say it's your sophomore year, and you've been asked to do an analysis on *Holes*." He placed dramatic emphasis on the title.

Rebecca giggled.

Oh, no, Molly thought, high again—really? But she wasn't high. Molly could see a sparkle in her friend's eye. Something was different about Becks. She demonstrated an alertness and energy that she hadn't had in a while. Rebecca glanced at Tara, who also snickered. Mr. Wolfe caught it but continued.

"You've been tasked with providing an overview for a high school freshman class assigned to read *Holes*," unintentionally emphasizing the title again. This time it was Tara. She seemed to find the book's title hysterical. She giggled uncontrollably. Rebecca soon joined in.

Mr. Wolfe looked at Molly for some kind of explanation. She shrugged her shoulders with a "beats me" expression. "Ladies," Mr. Wolfe pleaded, "my dear, sweet, wonderful, and *mature* students—what is so funny?" Tara couldn't look at Mr. Wolfe and buried her head in her hands. He looked at Rebecca. "Chief! Pray tell, what is so entertaining about *Holes*?" Rebecca snorted and laughed even harder. Mr. Wolfe stretched out his arms. "For God's sake, girl!" Others in the class laughed without knowing why, Molly shrugged again, and Mr. Wolfe shook his head as the girls managed to quiet down. "Continuing on, you are in the position of mentor and you want to help guide these poor, inexperienced high school students to a better understanding of *Holes*."

Again with the cackling.

"What?" he said, nearing the limits of his patience. "What is so funny about that word? Are you two going Beavis and Butthead on me?" The class laughed again. "*Holes* is just the name of the book never mind!" Rebecca pulled her hair over her face and giggled again, setting Tara off once more. Mr. Wolfe just stood there, hands on hips, and said, "*Never* have I had trouble with you two. I'm assuming you got white man's spring fever, so I'm gonna let it slide. But if you don't let me get through this, off to the principal you go. Now, you want that?"

"No sir," they both said. Molly balled up the piece of paper that Tara had given her and tossed it at her. Tara turned to look at her friend.

"*Stop* it already," said Molly, with exaggerated frustration.

"I'm sorry, Mr. Wolfe," said Rebecca.

"Me, too, Mr. Wolfe," said Tara. "Sorry." Mr. Wolfe nodded and continued. The girls managed to control themselves for the rest of the class.

The bell rang and everyone piled out. It was their last class of the day and Tara had her mom's SUV again, so Molly hitched a ride with her friends. Molly got her things from her locker and headed down the hall toward the parking lot.

"So what was *that* all about?" she inquired. Rebecca glanced at Tara, but just kept walking. The three of them reached the parking lot. "Seriously," Molly said and stopped, "what was so damn funny about Mr. Wolfe saying *Holes*?" Rebecca snickered again and Tara just looked up at the sun, putting on her shades.

"Dunno," she said nonchalantly, "just struck me as funny, I guess." She smiled her soft smile.

"Bullshit," said Molly. "Besides, Becks is the one who went off first. Honestly, guys, we're women now. That seemed so immature, really." Tara unlocked the SUV with her remote.

Rebecca opened the back door and bowed low. "Oh, you're quite right, Missy," she said dramatically, "you of the upper and more mature class would certainly know best, I suppose," finishing her bow. Then she curtsied to Molly. Molly flipped her the bird and got in front while Tara laughed. As Tara backed up, stopping to look behind her, Molly saw her glance at Rebecca. Molly turned just enough to see Rebecca nod to Tara. What was up with that? Molly wondered.

As they drove along, Tara started a conversation. "So Molly, how was the rest of your weekend?"

"Okay, I suppose, nothing special. How was yours? Oh, hey, did you sleep things off okay, Becks? You were really winding down the last time I saw you." Rebecca looked at Tara in the rearview mirror. "What's wrong?" said Molly. "Did something happen?"

"You could say that," Rebecca said, with what sounded like guilt in her voice. Tara stared at her friend in the mirror, then resumed her focus on the road. Rebecca gazed out the side window. Molly thought she seemed unusually at peace. Rebecca looked to the front again and pulled her hair back over her left ear. Molly noticed that Tara was watching her friend again, but with a strange look. Empathetic, maybe.

"All right," Molly said, "enough already. What the hell did you two do? I mean, you didn't set fire to anything, did you?"

"Kinda," said Tara, looking over at Molly through her shades, then back to the road again.

"What does that mean? Tara! You guys didn't kill anybody or anything, did you?" Her mouth was wide open, her own sunglasses about to fall from her face. She straightened them. Tara put her hand on Molly's knee, then spoke.

"Remember that I was taking Becks home to sleep it off?"

Molly nodded. "Yeah."

"Well, I did. I mean, she did. I mean, *we* did." Molly looked at them both. Rebecca looked nervous.

"Well, good. I mean, I'm glad you got to sleep it off, Chief," said Molly, still clueless. "That was the safe thing to do," she said with an affirming nod, as if she were the mom of the bunch in that moment.

"We spent the weekend together," said Rebecca, trying to get the point across.

"Yeah, I remember," said Molly, nodding again. "And, again, I think that's cool. Glad you were there for her, Tara. I mean, after that medicine man debacle, she *needed* to sleep it off, for sure," she added, laughing.

"Molly," said Tara, turning her way with a sigh, "Becks didn't sleep it off by herself, if you get my meaning," then looked ahead again.

"Oh," said Molly. "OH!" She looked back at Rebecca, then quickly at Tara, then back at Rebecca, and then at Tara. "OH, oh, my God!" she exclaimed, putting her hands to her face. "Oh, holy *fuck*!"

"Ah, yeah, pretty much," said Tara with her usual understatement. Rebecca moved forward in her seat, putting her elbows on the back of the driver's seat and resting her chin on the right side, on Tara's shoulder. She began slowly caressing Tara's arm.

"Oh, oh, yeah. I mean, okay. Omigod. Oh, my God," Molly repeated as she put her right hand to her forehead. "Oh, oh—this," she said, shaking her head as if remembering something monumental from the past. "This, oh, yeah—dang! This explains *so* much!"

"Really?" said Tara. "How so?"

Rebecca looked at Molly with great interest, placing high value on her friend's opinion. She continued to rub Tara's arm.

"Well," said Molly, hands to her face again. "Well, just, going back, I . . . oh, my God." She shook her head again, then slapped her forehead and yelled "Duh!"

"What's the 'duh,' Molly? What did you see? I really wanna know," Tara asked again.

Molly settled and took a breath. "You just always—I don't know—really seemed to admire Becks, like, in a *different* way. Almost like you swooned over her, sort of. Like, I would catch you gazing at her, like, in class, at assembly, at the mall—holy smokes. And that was a really gentle kiss on her forehead when you held her hair at the fight, Becks; I mean, now that I think about it. I mean, I guess I just didn't realize . . . holy cow. What kind of friend was I, guys, completely missing all that?"

As they reached Molly's neighborhood, Tara just smiled at her. "You've been a *great* friend, Molly."

Rebecca looked at Molly. "It kinda surprised me, too." She glanced in the rearview mirror at Tara's shades and smiled. "Actually, Molly, she seduced me. I'm an innocent party in all this. I was overcome by her estrogenic properties. Did my best to run away."

"*Bullshit,*" said Tara, glancing back at her from the mirror. "You were on me like a fly on shit."

Molly laughed.

They were all quiet as the SUV pulled into Molly's driveway. Molly turned to examine her friends. She shook her head in wonderment again and smiled. Then she had an epiphany. "Oh! *Holes!* Omigod, omigod! Holes, holes, holes— *seriously,* you two? Jesus!" All three of them laughed hysterically, thinking about Mr. Wolfe.

"We good?" said Rebecca.

"Yeah," said Tara, "we cool?" They both looked concerned.

"Why wouldn't we be?" said Molly with genuine surprise. "I love you guys." They both smiled, Rebecca especially showing signs of relief. Molly looked at Tara. "Shut off the car for a sec."

"What?"

"Just turn it off. Have something I wanna say." Tara switched off the ignition, resting her left arm on the steering wheel and looking at Molly. "Listen, you two. I recently got the worst news of my goddamn life." They both touched Molly's arm. "Then, Devon turns out to be a major disappointment." Rebecca squeezed Molly's hand. "I don't know if I'm gonna be able to do the ride—probably not—and it's just frustrating. Now, on top of everything else, I don't know if we're gonna have enough money for me to go to college, and Mom has to help Emmy out some—which is way more important than my damn education any day. Ya know, it's just been a collection of bad vibes lately. But, watching you two—wow. I think it's great." She looked at them. "Are you in love?"

"Yes," said Tara without hesitation. Molly checked Rebecca, who nodded her affirmation.

"Well then," said Molly, staring through the windshield and taking a long, slow breath and letting it out, "That's it, then, isn't it? I mean, that's all that matters in this shitty motherfucking world, isn't it?" Tara began to cry, angry at what Devon did, and Rebecca pushed forward and hugged Molly tightly. They all hugged briefly before Molly got out, and Rebecca walked around to the front passenger seat while Tara wiped her face with her shirt. Rebecca held the door for Molly as she hauled her backpack out. "By the way," she said to Rebecca, "you snore like a damn banshee."

"That's what Tara said! I don't believe it," Rebecca protested.

"Oh, no; it's true," said Molly with a laugh as she wrapped the backpack around one shoulder.

"She snores louder than Dumbledore!" Tara added before Rebecca shut the door. Molly laughed and waved to her friends. They watched Molly walk to the door. "Well," said Tara, "we did it. I knew she'd be fine with it. You worry too much." Rebecca stared at the dash. "What's wrong? Did I hurt your feelings about the snoring?" Rebecca shook her head and waved it off. She looked back at Molly going through the front door.

"Asshole cheese dick cock holster!"

"Who?"

Rebecca looked at her and rolled her eyes.

"Oh," said Tara as she backed out of the drive.

"Don't know where he's been hiding, but I'm gonna throttle his balls till they come out of his mouth when I see him," Rebecca said bitterly.

Tara patted her girlfriend's knee as she put the car in drive and started moving forward.

"Easy, Chief," she said. "Take it easy." They drove away.

17

People Are Dying

October 28, 1838
Rattlesnake Springs Branch
Beans Creek
Old Salem, Tennessee
Old Cherokee Nation

"**P**eople are dying, Captain," said Nick.

The group had set up camp on Beans Creek at Rattlesnake Springs Branch. Nick's contempt for Captain Ambrose and the army had reached a point where it was becoming something different. A bargaining attitude, perhaps. Or maybe just resignation, a grasp of things as they were, not as Nick and Mary preferred them to be. He didn't know. There had been talk of another rape of a Cherokee named Lizzy, a twenty-year-old from Georgia. Mary heard it from a friend whose family was in the back third of the detachment. Apparently, a wagon master and what was rumored to be a soldier attacked her by the creek in a thicket, but no one could prove anything.

Ambrose looked around at the closest group and sighed. He gave Nick a sympathetic look. Joshua Sanders, a cousin of Mary and Nick's, stood on the bank of the stream and plopped, face down, into the cold water. He began to drift away.

Nick jumped to his feet, rushed to the bank, and dove in after his cousin-uncle-friend. "Whoa, Joshua! Get back here!" he shouted, swimming after Joshua as he floated away. But the closer Nick got, the faster Joshua glided in the water. Eventually Nick caught up with him and seized his shirt, which was old, dirty, and ripped in numerous places. He seized his cousin by the neck and hauled him in.

"Let me go, cousin," said Joshua weakly. "Can't . . . can't do this any longer. Hell awaits me, my friend. Let what will be, be."

"No, dammit!" Nick declared. "And no hell awaits you, Joshua. You are one of the godliest men I've ever had the pleasure to know. It's heaven that awaits you, my friend, not hell."

"But I cannot . . ." Joshua garbled at the water's edge. "I cannot do well by Him. I have hatred in my heart, cousin. I now wish to kill the white man. I wasn't like that before," he said as he tried to free himself, to no avail. Nick was younger and stronger. Joshua Sanders's fate was sealed. He was born to live.

"Look," Nick said as they reached the shallow bank section, "I have hate in my heart, too. You know why?"

Joshua shook his head. "No," he said in a sad, resigned voice.

"Because they're all a bunch of assholes, that's why." They floated in the calmer water near an isolated edge of the large stream and looked at each other. They felt a man-to-man kind of love and respect. "I say let's set fire to their goddamn shoes tonight," Nick added, bobbing in the water with a weak smile. They laughed, putting their heads together. Joshua nodded, and they began to climb out.

"All right, cousin-nephew; all right, then. It is as you say. I will try to make another few good miles," Joshua said, and smiled at his cousin and thanked him.

"Good man," said Nick, patting his cousin's shoulders. "Let's get you near a fire."

Many Cherokees were vomiting and soiling themselves. Bloody diarrhea, a horrific by-product of the flux, made it extremely difficult for the afflicted to maintain any sense of daily hygiene and was an assault on human dignity. The handsome little boy that Mary had seen earlier in the journey waddled by their campsite with blood and waste running down his ankles.

"Oh, sweet Jesus," said Mary, grabbing Nick's hand and squeezing until it was painful for Nick. The boy seemed lost and confused. Mary struggled to her feet, holding her belly and telling Nick to see after Martha. Augustine, lying near the fire, raised his head, tilted it to the right, and whined. Mary motioned to Annabelle for help and grabbed the boy before he got too far away. "Come with me," she said in Cherokee. She took his hand and they walked down to the water to clean him up. Nick did his best to entertain Martha, who watched yet again as Mary mothered other children. She sucked her thumb as Nick sang softly to her, cradling her in his arms. Enoch and Annabelle's daughter, Deborah, tickled her and tried to get her to smile.

Second Lieutenant Ross Whitworth approached the encampment and saluted Captain Ambrose. "Lieutenant Whitworth reporting as ordered." The entry guard turned to Ambrose, who, studying a map with Sergeant Thomas, nodded and waved him in. Whitworth stood at attention. Ambrose mumbled something to Sergeant Thomas, then shook his head and massaged his temples.

"At ease, Lieutenant. Come over here, Ross. What the hell kind of map is this, anyway?" He handed it to Lieutenant Whitworth, who squinted at it under torchlight. Whitworth was considered an expert map reader, the main reason for his assignment to this detachment.

"Well, it's older, sir, that's for sure." Captain Ambrose handed him a magnifier to help him see the details. "It's . . . I don't know, pre-1830, maybe? Shit." He looked up. "Ah, sorry, sir." Ambrose brushed off his officer's comment, placing a hand on his shoulder.

"Look," Ambrose said, speaking equally to Whitworth and Thomas, "We've gotta get this right. General Scott must think we're some kinda engineering or surveying unit or something. I mean, this bullshit is costing us days here, am I right?"

"Yes, sir," came the quiet but unified response.

"You see this?" he said, pointing to the area marked between Savannah and their current location of Old Salem. "This area is discolored. See it? I can't tell what the hell is a trail and what is a river and what is a state or federal road." He shook his head. Whitworth looked even closer.

"Wait a minute, sir. See this area here? Looks like somebody spilled something at one point on the map. Maybe a coffee stain . . . yes, look closer, sir. Damn liquid stain of some sort. We just need to go straight through the heavier forested section . . . right there—at the tip of my finger." He tapped the map with authority.

"Ah, you sure?" asked Ambrose, scratching his head.

"Positive, sir. No question." He smiled. "Believe it or not, sir, one of the main obstacles in the advanced map-reading conference was discerning liquid spills on older maps!" Sergeant Thomas looked at him.

"You're *joking*, sir."

"Not at all, Sergeant." He looked at his captain. "Seriously, we're good to go, sir. I'm certain of it. Let's just cut through that middle section. It's dense, but there are trails that should permit us to move with some precision. Should save us two, three days."

Ambrose slapped Whitworth on the shoulder.

"Well done, Lieutenant. Well done."

The next day, the soldiers and John Bell got the group moving again. Bell was doing his best to accelerate his people, but he often deferred to the army because Captain Ambrose had made these trips before and, though navigation was difficult in places and maps sometimes hard to read, Ambrose was familiar with the removal process and how long it should take.

"Pretty near to Alabama, aren't we, sir?" Sergeant Thomas rode alongside Lieutenant Whitworth as Whitworth checked the map for accuracy. He had to stop his horse. The map was thick and difficult to fold over, and it was being worn away from constant use on this trip. Sergeant Thomas slowed his horse, then guided it over to Lieutenant Whitworth. He held the end of the map for the lieutenant.

"We're good, Sergeant, we're making good time. Yeah, we're dippin' down a ways toward that state line, but we'll curve back up here, see?" he said, pointing to the area that approached Fayetteville, Tennessee. Sergeant Thomas nodded and helped Lieutenant Whitworth fold the coarse parchment over. Soon they journeyed onward, regaining ground and passing many of the wagons and walkers.

The detachment made good time through Fayetteville, then camped in the Boonshill community. Four fights broke out in Boonshill. One was due to two drunk privates arguing over a card game. The larger private broke the smaller private's nose, which had to be tended by Doc Arbogast. The second fight was between two Cherokee women over a Cherokee man. Tribal members settled that one. The third was between two Cherokee boys over a hatchet that didn't belong to either one of them. A black eye arose from that encounter, the one boy also having to see Doc Arbogast. The last one involved, to no one's surprise, Tobacco Bill. He bribed a private for some whiskey. When the detachment slowed to a crawl, he chose to make his mark again by peeing on the boots of another private who had dismounted to check his horse's shoe.

The private yelled at Tobacco Bill, "Hey, what do you think you're doing? Back away from me!"

Tobacco Bill just nodded and said, "Oh, oh, yessir, sorr-*ie!*" and turned to his right and peed on the boots of Sergeant Hollingsworth, who had himself just dismounted to repack his saddle roll. The soldiers had to pull Sergeant Hollingsworth off of Tobacco Bill for that one. The sergeant, an ill-tempered man, had beaten him severely and called him filthy names.

The detachment made its way west in the direction of Pulaski. Pretty Water in the Morning had been suffering with depression—as one would expect—since the murder of her child. Mary found her and kept her company. Nick swore to Captain Ambrose that he was going to press charges against the man that did it. Ambrose said, "McNair, I understand your frustration. That man is a civilian; technically he's not under my control. And murder is a state charge, not federal. Best you can do is report it to the county sheriff where it took place, and I ain't even sure exactly where we were. You can always try finding a state judge that will listen, or get a message to the governor. Otherwise, I'm afraid there's not much can be done."

This didn't sit well with the McNairs nor any of the Cherokees. In the old country, they would have killed that wagon master flat out. Instead, Pretty Water tried to kill herself by using a Case knife that Old Stomper gave her. Mary made sure that the Cherokees understood that Pretty Water was not to have access to sharp tools or a gun. She counseled and consoled Pretty Water day and night for four days. At last Pretty Water showed signs of coming back around and wanting to be among the living. Mary tended Pretty Water's wounds from the Case knife, and had Doc Arbogast treat the main cut, which posed the greatest threat.

Mary, when alone with her family, took time to reflect. Pretty Water's situation was an extreme example of the many injustices for Native Americans. The Indians could find a reprieve, certainly, in almost any adverse condition, but no real relief. The United States of America had set itself against a race of people who were the land's original inhabitants. The so-called "truths" that were supposed to be "self-evident," that all "were created equal," had proven nonexistent for Mary's people. The noble idea of "life, liberty, and the pursuit of happiness," as set out in the Declaration of Independence, was an empty one, as this forced journey to the west made clear.

They arrived in Pulaski on time and set up camp under stormy, windy, and dangerous conditions.

October 30, 1838
Bell Detachment Camp
Pulaski, Tennessee
Old Cherokee Nation

Exhaustion was evident, fear obvious. Uncertainty everywhere. The detachment was having a number of wagon axle and wheel breakdowns. The affected group would stop, make repairs, and get moving again, only to come across another section of the detachment broken down a few miles later.

One Cherokee named Lucinda Halfmoon was walking along a narrow section of the trail when a mountain lion burst from the brush and tried to take her as a meal. Two Cherokee men and an army private with a bayonet managed to free her. When the desperate animal tried again with one of the men, Sergeant Hollingsworth shot him from horseback, after which the private managed to finish the animal with his sword. On another occasion, the winds picked up dramatically and another Cherokee, Tadpole, happened to walk under a large oak tree when one of its older and, unhappily, larger, branches snapped and came straight down, killing him instantly. He was nineteen.

The windy conditions abated, though showers continued for a few days before the detachment got a reprieve from the rain.

The camp was quiet. Martha was asleep, as were Enoch, Annabelle, and their family. Nick had apparently gotten up, perhaps to relieve himself. Mary quietly made her way down the path toward the stream. She needed to rinse off. On the way, the baby kicked. Despite her circumstances, she managed a short-lived smile. What kind of world would this child be born to? Chaos? Peace? Would there be enough food and shelter where they were going? The government had promised them there would be, but events were proving that questionable at best.

Mary rinsed at the stream and dried herself as best she could. Several soldiers milled about, but all were polite and seemed serious about guarding the camp. On the way back, Mary thought she heard something behind an enormous rock in some woods beside the trail. She heard groans and what sounded like heavy breathing, moaning of a carnal nature. Oh, no. Dear Lord, thought Mary, please not again. We've had enough of this on this horrible journey. The sounds grew louder, but they also seemed purposely muffled. She decided, baby or not, family or not, she couldn't ignore such a thing. To be Christian meant to do more than simply nothing, and she knew she had to act.

Summoning her will, Mary walked behind the rock, which was against a large tree, and peeked around the edge while planning how she would respond. Should she bash his head in with a rock? Gouge out his eyes? With the exception of deer and other food animals, killing was foreign to her, but she knew this might be a life-changing moment. To her shock, she found Nannie Cold Weather and George Wildcat, two Cherokees from her home district of Aquoah, making passionate love.

"Pleeease, Georgie, more. More. *More!*" Nannie moaned, but at a volume so as to not alert anyone. They were plastered together in the cool end-of-October air, her arms wrapped around him from below, her legs squeezing George's waist, her fingers digging into his back.

Mary put her palm over her mouth. Oh, dear! she thought to herself. *Oh, my goodness.* She backed away. Just as she was turning, she ran right into Nick, who had been looking for her. She almost screamed. Nick had heard the sounds as well.

"Oh, thank goodness it's you. I was worried! What is that? Is someone forcing themselves on someone, Mary? I'm *not* tolerating this again. I will kill someone this time—"

She put her hand over his mouth, motioning for him to move on.

"Go!" she whispered.

"What?" he said.

"Shhhh! Just go!" she said again in a low voice.

As they made their way back up the path, she told him no one was being raped or forced.

"No one is being forced. Um, in point of fact, she seemed to be quite enjoying herself, actually," Mary said, touching herself on the neck and chest. She looked at her husband with a "you know what I mean" expression.

"*Oh!*" Nick managed to say. "Well, then, ah . . . my gosh."

"You know," Mary said upon reflection, "they were talking about getting married during the next Green Corn Ceremony." She seemed lost in thought.

"Hmm," said Nick. "I didn't know that."

Mary looked at her husband and tears came to her eyes. "They never had a chance; oh, my God, Nicholas, they never had a chance!" She cried as she rested her head on his shoulder. He stroked her hair and rubbed her back. She lifted her head and looked at him. "For God's sake, Nick! Think of it: to conceive a child here—of all places. To bear a child as a result of *all of this*! It's almost unspeakable."

Nick pondered. "Well," he said, trying to offer comfort, "better a child from here than not at all, right?" He looked at her and offered the warmest smile he could muster. She seemed so tired to him, so worn.

"I suppose," she said with resignation.

"Think about the birth of Jesus," he reminded her. She smiled and nodded, then rested her weary head on her husband's shoulder again. As he held his wife, his belly to hers, Nick thought he felt the baby kick.

It was dark and quiet, excepting distant snores and the sound of oxen and horses eating grass. Part of Nick's section of the detachment was in a grassy area, others were in the open, some sought refuge underneath a wagon, and some found sequestered areas of brush. Each Cherokee in this detachment had been issued one blanket, which did little against the elements. This evening, the McNairs were surrounded by some sizable flora, their clothing draped in various ways and places to provide some privacy and meager shelter. Nick had been in a light sleep cycle for what he guessed was about an hour, and as he awoke, he felt his steady, rhythmic breathing working in concert with his heartbeat. He opened his eyes and could see the stars, some slowly becoming brighter than others. Despite their forced relocation, he felt at peace with himself for the first time in weeks. He closed his eyes again, breathing deeply.

Suddenly, he felt a hand over his mouth and something on top of him. He opened his eyes to find Mary sitting over him, trying to pull her blanket so that it covered them both. She had let her hair down to her waist. She smelled of the countryside. But he noticed the always present sweetness about her, the kind that seemed to come from mother and child in the same body. She removed her hand from his mouth and pulled back her saddle dress.

"What is it?" he mumbled, still feeling disoriented from a light sleep.

"Shhhhhhh," she whispered. "Everyone is asleep. Martha is asleep." She straddled her husband and began to rub him gently, slowly. "Nannie and George," she whispered again. "That was very exciting to watch, Nicholas."

"What?"

"I said it was exciting, Nicholas. *Very* exciting." With that, after a few moments having manipulated her husband's body to suit her needs, she mounted him.

"Oh . . . well, all right."

"Yes," she said softly, "yes, oh . . . yes!" She sat straight up, as if reaching for those stars.

Sometimes, Nick thought, even during a living hell, you just go with what life gives you. And he could definitely go with this. He stroked his wife's hair. As he looked up at her, he thought about how, back home, she would sometimes go down to the Hiwassee River to wash her long, luxurious black hair with Castile soap. He loved how it smelled when she was done. She would let it dry in the sun, and he would admire her as she walked the property, doing her chores, her tall, slim figure capturing the farm, pasture, and hills—not the other way around. He suddenly missed his home more than before. He could still see her, when she was very young, in his mind's eye. He knew he had lassoed the most beautiful woman in the Georgia Cherokee valley, before moving north to Tennessee.

Mary moved her hips up, then down Nick's abdomen with precision. Her pregnant belly was more alluring than he had remembered. He let her have her way with him. Nick knew from experience that when Mary reached this term in her pregnancy she would get, well, a little out of hand. She yanked his hair forcefully a few times—even slapped him once—then grew calmer. Better bruised than unloved, he thought with a smile as she leaned in and passionately kissed his chest, her hand around his throat.

She kept moving up and down, grunting occasionally and breathing heavily through her pursed lips. She yelled out briefly, then collapsed onto his chest, hugging him with all her might. He held onto her and told her he loved her. He recalled her father, John Rogers, saying, "She's my eldest girl—take care of her, son." Then he heard the unmistakable sound of a mother grieving. He felt her tears, true Cherokee tears, trickle down his neck onto his back, then onto the ground that was, according to current mapping and understanding, still Cherokee land. He rubbed her back and told her they would make it. They would survive this.

In spite of dire circumstances, Nick and Mary McNair slept uncommonly well that night.

18

Native Healing

Present Day
Gadugi Center for the Healing Arts
Tulsa County, Oklahoma
District Thirteen, Cherokee Nation

Sandra and Emmy pulled into an available parking space five minutes before Emmy's appointment. The Gadugi Center was on North Harvard, and the drive wasn't too bad with light traffic.

"Nervous?" asked Sandra.

"Nah, not really," Emmy assured her mother.

"Well, I'm a little nervous, frankly. Can't help it, I suppose."

"It will all work out, Mom. What will be will be."

Sandra sighed. "I suppose you're right. It's just a consult, right?"

Emmy smiled and nodded. She kissed her mom on the cheek.

"Thanks for coming, Ma. I got this. Let's rock and roll." Her mother smiled and they got out and walked in. Emmy approached the front desk.

"Emmy McNair. I have a ten o'clock appointment."

"Right!" said the receptionist, who reminded Emmy of a young Martina McBride. "We got your paperwork through the portal; thank you for that. She'll be with you shortly if you want

~ 126 ~

to have a seat." Emmy joined Sandra on a roomy love seat against the wall facing the door.

After a few minutes, an attractive woman with a shock of short black hair and remarkable posture emerged from the side room and came forward.

"Emily?" she asked with a smile.

Emmy stood and shook her hand. "It's Emmy. And this is my mother, Sandra."

"Okay, Emmy," the doctor said, "and Ms. McNair. Nice to meet you both."

"Please," said Emmy's mom, "call me Sandra."

The doctor smiled and nodded, then escorted them to her office and shut the door behind her. "Please have a seat," she said, sweeping her arm out to another love seat like a game show hostess. Emmy couldn't get over the woman's amazing posture. Every move was methodical, dance-like. She moved like a martial artist. Emmy and Sandra sat. The woman pulled what looked like a new file from her desk and sat in a swivel chair, then faced them, putting the file in her lap.

"Welcome," she said. "If it's okay, let me introduce myself, so that you can get to know me a little better and decide if this is a good fit for you. After all, you're in the driver's seat, Emmy, and I want you to be comfortable." Emmy smiled and nodded. Sandra was dumbfounded, clearly making mental notes.

"I'm Paisley. Paisley Walkingstick. I've been in practice for eleven years as a chiropractic physician, nineteen as a naturopathic doctor. I will not lie to you. Naturopathic medicine is my first love and my true calling, but I made the difficult decision to return to school for chiropractic while living in Arizona. I did this because, as you probably know, a number of states, like Oklahoma, still refuse to recognize ND docs as primary care providers, which makes it challenging not only to run an effective business as one, but keeps us from being able to make the living we deserve. Chiropractic adds to that nicely. The two professions blend well due to many educational and standard of practice applications. For example, I do spinal manipulation for some of my naturopathic patients, and I use methods such as kinesiology, homeopathy, and Native American herbal formulas for some of my chiropractic patients, so the two really do go hand-in-hand in my case. I am a citizen of the Cherokee Nation and advocate for better food choices for our people. And that's one of the places I would like to start with you, Emmy, if that sounds reasonable."

Emmy smiled again and said, "Yeah, ah, sure." Considering the threat of chemotherapy, radiation, and disfiguring surgery, what she was really thinking after listening to all of that was, *this chick rocks.*

"Great!" said Paisley. "Emmy, the reason for the extensive dietary questionnaire was my theory on food as medicine. I have no doubt that, as a professional fighter, you want to embrace the best diet you can. Are you familiar with the whole food, plant-based lifestyle?"

"I've heard of it, you know—read some things here and there."

"And what did you think?"

"Well, it's really about becoming vegan, isn't it?" Sandra shifted in her seat.

"Not exactly," said Paisley. "You can call it that, but it's really more accurate to use the long, boring term 'whole food, plant-based.' You see, a lot of vegans eat things that are not seriously whole food or plant-centered. I'm talking about planning your meals around starch-based foods such as beans, peas, potatoes, corn, rice, and leafy greens. You don't have to eliminate meat altogether, but your weekly consumption should be no more than ten to fifteen percent. If you ate this way regularly, consistently, your chances of getting another cancer down the road decrease dramatically and your chances of heart disease even more so, despite your father having died of an infarction.

One problem is that we are all—especially here in Indian Country—fighting the food companies, the cattle industry, the dairy industry, and so forth. Our hospitals—conventional and Indian—are still not in the habit of pointing patients to what is truly good for them. Instead we submit to the politics of these giant industries that have enormous financial interest. Long story short, here at Gadugi, I do my best to point you in the direction of the healthiest possible nutritional options for your needs. And yes, there are studies that show retardation or reversal of breast cancer through a whole food, plant-based diet that is starch-centered, high carb, and low fat. That would be my number one tool of choice for addressing your cancer and staving off heart disease. And the second and third are going to sound even stranger. You ready?"

"Yes," said Emmy, smiling and liking what she was hearing. She glanced at her mom, who was listening with more skeptical ears.

When the appointment was over, Sandra and Emmy drove to lunch. Paisley suggested several places they might try, and they settled on her first suggestion, which was closer to I-44 and the ride home. Though on the expensive side, the restaurant had excellent food and Emmy and her mom were impressed. Paisley pointed out that Emmy would be preparing most of her own food, and she offered a number of tips to help her cope with food on the road—usually the biggest challenge—as well as ideas for snacks and meals.

After lunch, they ordered hot tea for Emmy, coffee for her mom. Emmy pulled a modified prescription list from her shoulder bag.

- Whole food, plant-based nutrition (as discussed)

- Homeopathic Carcinosin 200c, 4 pellets, 4 times a week at bedtime

- Turska formula, one tsp. Twice daily

- Berberine capsules - 1000mg twice daily

- Pau de Arco (taheebo) tea - 3 cups daily

Follow-up appt. in one month

Paisley had discussed alterations down the road, but believed this to be a good start in Emmy's particular case. The foods she was to concentrate on were a high volume of cruciferous vegetables, mushrooms, onions, beans, whole grains, and the like. The greens, if not eaten immediately after being cut, were to be dressed—especially when heated—with mustard powder, which would stimulate the sulforaphane, an effective cancer fighter, in the kale, broccoli, or cauliflower. She provided links to studies showing the effectiveness of each of the items listed, something that impressed both Emmy and Sandra.

"Well," said Sandra, "that has to be the most interesting prescription I've ever seen." Emmy nodded in agreement. "Her take on food is *very* interesting. Our people just aren't used to something like this. It's not part of our tradition, you know?"

"Whoa, whoa, Ma. Really?" Emmy said, holding up her left hand as if to stop her mom at a red light. "Just go back a few generations—especially to Tennessee and Georgia and the rest of the old country. Most of what our people ate were vegetables and fruit; nuts, acorns, pumpkin, squash, beans, corn—and of course apples, persimmons, all that kinda stuff. Sure, we hunted and ate meat, but because of the difficulty and rarity of it all, the diet was mostly non-animal. I think what she was saying about *The China Study* was interesting. I picked up the book a couple of weeks ago and started reading some of it. I'm thinking of doing a paper on it."

"But, Em, what about the plan the oncologist is mapping out for you? Don't you trust her? She comes so highly recommended."

"Yeah, Mom, I trust her. But you know how close I was to Aunt Lisa. All that chemo and radiation. I'm not *about* to go through that shit if I can help it!" she said, raising her voice and choking up, reflecting on her mother's sister who had since died. A few of the other patrons were watching.

"Shhhh!" said Sandra, taking Emmy's hand. "Please don't yell; I get the message."

"Sorry. I need a sense of control, Ma, something I can do to feel like I have some power in this. The stuff that Paisley was talking about is right up my alley."

Sandra sipped her coffee.

"I suppose it is, at that. You know, glamor girl, not *everything* has to be a fight. You don't have to knock out or choke out everything that comes your way."

"True, but wouldn't you prefer that I choke this cancer out before it chokes me out?" asked Emmy with arched eyebrows. "Without, I might add, poisoning myself to death in the process?"

Sandra put her coffee down and looked away from her daughter. She had promised herself she would be strong for her—no public tears. Yet here they came. She rummaged through her purse for tissue. Emmy signaled the waitress with authority.

"Yes, ma'am?"

"We need some more napkins now, please."

"Sure thing. Be right back," said the waitress, who had recognized Emmy when they sat down.

The waitress returned with napkins—and tissue from the back—for Emmy's mom. Emmy thanked her. The waitress, who was about twenty, hesitated. Emmy glanced up at her.

"Oh, I'm sorry, Ms. McNair—could I have your autograph?" Emmy smiled and nodded while the waitress turned over part of a menu on the back of her credit card presenter and handed it to Emmy. "I just wanna say, I think you're a *spectacular* fighter! The Ortiz fight was just, just, out of this world! Huge fan here, huge fan!" Emmy grinned and thanked her, signed her menu, and turned back to her mom, who had been trying to collect herself. The waitress headed back to the register to show the other employees. As Sandra pulled herself together, she watched all this with fascination.

"My daughter the luminary." She leaned her head back. "You think you're hot snot, don't you?"

Emmy batted her eyelashes. "Don't hate me because I'm beautiful," she teased. "Nah. It kinda comes with the territory. Eddie warned me there would be some of this. If I'm actually a role model for young women, then it makes me happy, I guess. Does that sound arrogant?"

"No, but just don't forget where you came from, okay?"

"You sound like Grams."

"Good! That's a good thing."

Emmy agreed.

Later in the Week
Emmy's Bungalow
Muskogee, Oklahoma

Emmy stood at the counter of her small kitchen and closed her eyes. She began her meditation, something she had been doing with frequency since her diagnosis. Breathing deeply, she focused her third eye on food and the transforming and healing power she was certain it had. She could smell the broccoli, cauliflower, and kale heating in the pan in front of her. In her typical summer tank top, she held her powerful arms over the food and imagined the journey her ancestors made nearly two hundred years ago. Letting the ancestors guide her time and attention, she hummed as she meditated. Two gallon jugs of distilled water sat on the counter. She imagined the water pouring through her, going to all the places it should go. She then pictured the food doing the same. After a few minutes, she opened her eyes and turned up the burner on the stir-fry.

She sipped her Pau d' Arco tea and recalled that some of her ancestors had used the herb as a healing tonic after it was brought from South America. She reflected on the Ortiz fight. Her jaw was still sore from the powerful elbow Ortiz had tagged her with. She worked it gently from side to side while she stirred the veggies. She thought her air conditioning was kind of half-assed, and she glanced at the ceiling vent, pretending it was cooler than it actually was. Just then, she heard a knock at the door. She looked up; it was Standingcloud. He waved and she motioned for him to come in.

"How ya doin', asshole?"

"Fine, bitch."

She grinned at him and shook her head.

"Smells good even," Eddie observed. The room smelled like soup due to Emmy having sauteed the veggies in broth rather than oil, one of Paisley's recommendations.

"Want some? There's plenty."

"Nah," he said, looking over her shoulder. "That shit's too healthy for me."

"What's up?"

"Em, I'm getting calls."

"Is that painful?"

"Hee-hee, ha-ha, funnn-ny. More interview requests. Podcasts, mostly. They're all important things to do, but I can keep them at bay for a while if you need time."

"Let me think about it, Eddie. It's not that I don't want to . . . just, just overwhelmed at times, ya know?"

"Precisely why I asked, dreamboat."

"You're always looking out for me, aren't you?"

"That's the name of the game, girl." He smiled and sat on one of Emmy's bar stools. She glanced at him. He was studying her, like he used to do when she was in early training.

"Uh-oh," she said. "I know that look. What else is going on?"

He rubbed his face as if he had a long beard—he didn't. In fact, he was always clean-shaven. Emmy had always considered that his "thinking face." She waited for his response, stirring her veggies again, which were now done. She banged the wooden spoon on the counter over the pan. She put it down and wiped her hands with a kitchen towel.

"I had a long conversation with Bill Stoddard," he said, rubbing his face again and looking down at the counter as if to concentrate. Stoddard was Emmy's main financial sponsor. Stoddard sometimes teamed with people like Elias Pumpkin to promote fighters. He was interested in female fighters, especially Emmy.

Emmy pulled the other stool over to her and sat, opening one of the gallon jugs of water. She spooned her food into a bowl. She looked down at it and closed her eyes. Eddie glanced at her and then closed his. This—this rare and spirit-filled tendency to give sincere thanks under adverse conditions—was one of the things he loved most about his fighter. He had known when he met her that he was onto something special.

Emmy opened her eyes. "Go," she said, taking a big bite and looking at her manager/trainer with respect and attention.

"Bill asked me, Emmy, what I truly thought of you and your abilities."

"What the hell kind of question is that?" she said, crunching her greens. "Does he think you would have backed a lame horse all this time?"

"Slow it down, dreamboat, chill," he said in his Native drawl, holding up his hands as if to calm her. She nodded, then showed him a piece of broccoli that had gotten lodged between her front teeth.

"Any-dang you zay, O' great one. I only do dis for thy love and avect-shee-on," she teased, flicking the broccoli stem and making it wiggle as she moved her eyebrows up and down.

"Will you please cut the crap and pay attention to me?" he said, irritated. She pulled the stem out with a napkin.

"Sorry, big boy," she said, "didn't mean to get your delicate panties in a twist."

He glared at her. "You done?"

"Okay, okay," she said lightheartedly. "I'm all ears."

"Basically, Bill wanted to know what I thought your true potential was," Eddie said, scanning her eyes for understanding. "You know—just how far can we take you?" he added.

Emmy took a swig of the water and wiped her mouth with a cloth napkin she pulled from a basket made by Cherokee National Treasure Lena Stick. She knew the root of Eddie's question was the almighty dollar. "And what, pray tell, did you say?"

Looking down, Eddie took a deep breath and exhaled. He looked into her eyes. "I told him I think you're the greatest fighter since Amanda Nunes."

Emmy had just put some food in her mouth. She put her head down, choking slightly, then put her right hand up, shaking her head. She chewed and swallowed, downed some more water, then spoke.

"Eddie, look—"

"I also told him you would say what I think you're about to say."

"Eddie, there's a lot of talent out there. Truth is, Ortiz just pissed me off in a way that I don't know can be duplicated. It just was what it was." She gulped another bite of veggies.

Eddie nodded knowingly, indicating he had been right about her response.

"I adore you for having brought me this far, and I'm glad we're a team, but I think you let your judgment get clouded when it comes to me. You're extremely biased," Emmy added.

"Well, yeah, I trained you, bitch, what'd you expect?"

"You know what I mean," she said with a look, swigging more from her water jug.

"Clouded judgment, huh?" he said. "Kinda like you beggin' me to fight Ortiz, kinda like kinda, huh?"

"Point taken," she said with a grin.

Standingcloud opened his heart. "Emily," he began.

"I wish you wouldn't call me that," she said, looking down at her thighs and rubbing her left one nervously, refusing to lock eyes with her trainer.

"Em, you're the best I've ever seen."

She looked up at him again.

"When I saw you cover that ring in two seconds and use that bitch as a stepladder and make some serious improvements to her ugly face, my heart just shot through the top of that arena. They're still out there lookin' for it, girl." She smiled and looked down again, rubbing her thighs more, unable to lock eyes with the man who had turned her into a human battering ram, an earthmoving machine, a Cherokee storm.

"You overestimate me, Standingcloud."

"*Bull*shit! I know how good you are, and *you* know how good you are. And I know you know I know. Just look at what you did to Wellingham. You hit that girl so hard I can *still* hear her teeth rattling and that was a year and a half ago. Remember? Ran smack into your right hook after eleven seconds in the first round. Damn eyes rolled back into her head, landed on that cute little tush of hers, and went out faster than an Oklahoma generator in the summertime.

"I wanted to say this to you now, before you start your treatments—or whatever you choose to do." Emmy closed her eyes, remembering the good times with Eddie, which were numerous. "You got the goods, girl—to go all the way. I told you that you were gonna shit thunder, and that's just what you did." Emmy stared at the edge of the counter. "You thunderclapped that woman while carrying a tumor, and made all of us so unbelievably stinking proud. She had every fighter in the league scared to death 'cept you. And I told Bill that, no matter what happens with your health, I'll always back my girl because

I found the best female MMA fighter of all time and I'm damn well gonna protect her."

Emmy shot from her stool into Eddie's arms and squeezed, eyes soaking wet. "Wado, Eddie." He patted her back. "I won't tap out on you, Eddie, just won't."

"I know that, dreamboat. But remember, there's a difference between tapping out and just being plain smart, which you are. Hell, I don't even know what a master's degree is. Jesus Christ." She laughed and hugged him harder, kissing his cheek and placing her head on his shoulder. He pulled her back so he could see her face. "You hearin' me? It ain't tapping out to protect your health—and your life never mind. That comes first, always. That's really all I was trying to convey when we argued in my office."

"'Convey?' Wow, Eddie, you gonna go for a master's, too?" she teased, wiping her eyes with the napkin. "Impressed here."

"Hey, I'll have you know I read fucking *MAD* magazine. I gots culture," he said with a wry smile.

They laughed and he pulled her back to him, patting her back again.

"You let me know how you're feelin' in the next week or so, okay? And listen: I'm gonna send my smoke and blessing to you every day. I'm gonna keep wishing for nothing but the best for you—that good things start happening for you that outweigh the bad. You're my girl, hear?"

He rose to leave. Emmy kissed his cheek again, took another drink from her water jug, and walked him the few feet to the door.

"Thanks for coming by and, well—you know," she said, crinkling her nose at him. He smiled on his way out.

"See you later, bitch," he said.

"Not if I see you first, asshole," she responded. She could hear him laughing as she closed the door.

19

Big Sis Grabs Some Soul

Present Day
Last Saturday of March
Vinita, Oklahoma
District Eleven, Cherokee Nation

"Hungry," said Molly, carefully stretching her left leg and resting her bare foot on the dash of Emmy's 1969 royal blue Mustang Mach 1, which she had named *Ned Christie*, after the falsely accused Cherokee outlaw. "Let's do the Archway!" Molly exclaimed, looking over at Emmy.

"Of course," said Emmy with a smile. "Thought you might want to. God, you *loved* that place as a kid. You should have seen yourself, your little nose plastered to the glass, watching all the cars zoom by underneath, your eyes as big as saucers. You were actually cute then."

"Hey!" Molly shouted, slugging her sister's shoulder, which felt like hitting a wood post.

"Ow, dang!" she said, shaking her hand to relieve the sting. Emmy laughed. Then Molly seemed pensive. "Hey," she said, "I'm sorry. I know that kind of food isn't part of your diet. We can wait and go to—"

"Nah, it's okay. I'll grab a veggie sandwich from Subway there. We can meet in the middle and find a table near the window. No problem. That's why I have all these bags of almonds," she said, holding one up. "Helps with the protein.

Plus, I'll need to gas up at the Kum & Go anyway. One thing I'm learning—the diet can't be perfect all the time, but I can do my best with what I've got."

"Cool!" said Molly, just loving the time with Emmy in any case. Emmy needed to replace one of the vintage taillight covers on *Ned Christie*, which she could only get at a customized shop in Vinita, and Molly had asked to come along in order to spend time with her. Plus, Molly *loved* Emmy's car and adored how Emmy raced down the highways, seemingly fearless of the cops and oblivious to traffic obstacles, which she had a tendency to just race on by or around. Emmy was her own person, and Molly loved that about her.

Soon enough, Emmy decelerated the 428 Cobra Jet engine, veering off the Will Rogers Turnpike onto the exit road. She zipped the Mustang around to the left and backed it into a space next to the highway, so she could keep an eye on *Ned Christie*. They exited the car and walked toward the Will Rogers Archway. Emmy, still adjusting to her new diet, farted as they walked.

"Dang, Em!" Molly shouted.

They hadn't gone ten yards when three men approached them from the side.

"Well, helllllooo, ladies," said a tall, lean man wearing a white cowboy hat. He was probably twenty-five or twenty-six, and he had just placed his hand on Emmy's shoulder when she turned to face him. Instinctively, Emmy trapped the man's hand to her chest with her left hand and popped him sharply in the solar plexus with a right inverted punch, dropping him to his knees. Plastering his hand to her chest while backing up, she put him in a bent-arm kagi, whereby all she had to do was bend forward at the waist to break his wrist.

"Ow, *fuck*!" yelled the man as he squirmed, then stopped because his right hand felt like it was in a vise.

"Don't ever do that," Emmy said calmly, confidently. The man moaned, raising his left hand in surrender. "Get behind me, Molly—*now*!" Emmy commanded, gesturing with her head. Molly stepped behind Emmy with a frightened expression, holding her arms close to her chest, unsure what these three large strangers had in mind. Emmy pushed her back with her body, dragging the cowboy forward as she did, the man screaming again.

"Hey, now," said the largest man, moving toward Emmy. "No need to get nasty."

Emmy dropped the cowboy's hand and adopted a reverse punch stance, drawing a Smith & Wesson .380 Bodyguard so fast Molly almost missed it. Emmy was wearing a blouse which tapered her waist perfectly, flowing over her belt. Unbeknownst to Molly, the belt supported an inside-the-waistband holster for the little semiautomatic pistol.

"Freeze it right there," Emmy barked, "or I'll turn all three of you assholes into zoo food." They froze.

The next sound was the "whoop-whoop!" of a siren as an unmarked police car pulled up next to the five of them. Emmy kept the men covered, who just stood there in shock. The officer exited his vehicle.

"Ma'am, I need you to holster that weapon." Emmy hesitated. "Now, please. Put it away." He was slowly walking toward them with his right hand on his own weapon, a SIG Sauer P226, motioning with his left hand for her to holster her gun. Emmy looked at the cowboy and his friends, then holstered. The cowboy was holding his right wrist and groaning, still on one knee.

"That good?" she asked.

"Yes, thank you," said the officer, who was wearing a polo shirt with the Oklahoma State Bureau of Investigation logo and "OSBI" beneath it. He was about five feet ten, had medium-length blond hair, and blue eyes.

Molly glued herself to her big sister, arms on Emmy's shoulders. "They came toward us," said Molly, her voice cracking. "He grabbed my sister."

"I know," the officer said. "I was right over there, trying to finish my lunch. Saw the whole thing." He pointed to an area of parking spaces near the Kum & Go, a line of tractor trailers behind filled with truckers at rest, some of whom were no doubt watching with interest.

Emmy glanced at the men, then at the officer. "Probably should have filed my front sight, huh?"

"What?" said the officer, looking confused.

"Would have shot that one first," Emmy said, pointing to the large guy to the cowboy's right, "then I would've shot him," pointing to the one on his left. "Then I would've shoved my gun up this one's ass, sideways," she added, pointing to the cowboy. A snicker escaped Molly and she covered her mouth to suppress it. The cowboy glanced up at her, annoyed. The other two laughed at their friend, which annoyed him even more.

"Okay, okay," said the officer with a gleam in his eye and holding up both hands. "I get it—very funny. Just do me a favor and stay there for a minute." He motioned to the men. "Guys, let me talk to you over here, and let me see some ID," he said, taking them aside and using his handheld radio to call in his location. The cowboy got to his feet and joined his friends, eyeing Emmy as if still trying to figure out what had just happened.

"Damn, Em; I didn't know you had a gun on you!" said Molly.

"That's the general idea," her sister retorted.

"Whada we do? Are we in trouble?"

"No. At least we better not be," Emmy replied. "Just chill for a sec."

As the officer questioned the men and checked their IDs, he seemed to be trying to calm the cowboy, who appeared frustrated and confused. After talking to the three men for a few more minutes, the officer led the men back to Emmy and Molly. The cowboy stepped forward, tipped his hat to them and said, "Sorry, ladies. This was a misunderstanding. We're from Texas. I was just gonna ask you if you were from around here."

"Uh-huh," Emmy said, keeping space between them and her sister. "No problem," she said, and nodded. The men turned to leave, the cowboy shaking his head and holding his wrist. They got into a Chevy truck with Texas tags and drove away.

The officer approached them with an odd look on his face. It was a smile, but with a question mark behind it somewhere. "So," he said, "you two okay?"

"We're fine," said Emmy. Molly decided to come out from behind Emmy's formidable hiding place.

"You're Emily McNair, aren't you—The Cherokee Storm?"

Emmy seemed surprised. She nodded.

"Yeah," he said in a way that seemed to hold her in awe. "Saw you beat Ortiz on pay TV. That was some kind of fight. You were . . . you were *amazing*! Just fantastic!" he said, his front teeth gleaming when he smiled. He was square-shouldered, and when he spoke, he gestured with his left hand. When he did this, the bicep on his left arm flexed. Molly grinned. Omigod, she said to herself, this guy is a *total teddy bear*!

"Wow," Emmy said softly, "thanks. Trust me, she had it comin'." She winked. Molly watched the officer stand there, mouth open.

"Listen," he finally said, shaking his head as if coming out of a momentary stupor, "even though this turned out not to be much of anything, you *did* pull a gun on someone in my presence. I at least have to check your pistol license . . . make sure it's valid, that kind of thing."

Emmy nodded and produced her ID and handgun license. He thanked her, and then studied them for a moment.

"Okay," he said. "Everything seems to be in order here." He hesitated, like he didn't want to give it back.

Molly noticed that the officer couldn't take his eyes off Emmy. She wore her hair in a thick ponytail and the officer seemed to be admiring it, along with her feather earrings. She didn't think he was being creepy; he was truly marveling at her, as if beholding a statue of Aphrodite or Helen of Troy. Emmy's tight jeans didn't seem to be hurting her situation, either.

"There a problem?" Emmy asked.

"Uh, no. I mean, not really. Uh . . . " He seemed indecisive and confused. Molly wondered if he was starstruck. She scanned his finger for a wedding band. Nothing. *Excellent.* Emmy leaned her head forward and smiled wistfully. The officer seemed hypnotized, but finally gave her back her documents. The three of them just stood there, as if someone had just told them all a joke and they were waiting for the punchline.

"Can we go in and eat now?" Emmy finally asked. "Kinda hungry here."

"Ah, sure. Yeah, um, absolutely," he stammered. He likes her, Molly said to herself. He *definitely* likes her. "Ah, listen!" he said, nearly shouting and stopping her gently with his hand. "Why don't, ah, here—take my card. Um, ah, you know, in case you need to contact me for anything."

Emmy stared at him.

"Why would I need to contact you?" she asked with a blank expression.

Molly slipped behind her sister again with a sort of fake cough/throat-clearing sound and whispered "Dude's prettier than a newborn baby's ass never mind; take the damn card already," in one breath. Emmy glanced to the side to acknowledge her pain-in-the-ass sister, then took the card from the cop.

"I'm Special Agent Soul," he said. "Mike." He grinned and his blue eyes sparkled. Molly noticed Emmy's eyes lit up in a millisecond of involuntary response. In that one instant, Molly thought, serious fireworks were exploding somewhere within the cosmos. Emmy smiled and examined Mike's card. "So," he added, "you got a card or anything?"

"Not really," Emmy said with a shrug.

Damn, Sis! She clearly needed help. "Actually," chimed Molly, "I'm Molly. My sister is pretty easy to find. She's also a grad student and likes to go to the lake on the weekends and *loves* the occasional Prairie Bomb and—"

Emmy cleared her throat to interrupt. Molly stopped, but was batting her eyelashes at Mike. "Why don't you grab your food? I'll be right there," said Emmy with her forever big sister look. Molly just stood there, beaming. "Like *now*?" Emmy added.

"Oh, yeah. Okay! Um, until we meet again, Agent Mike. Have a nice day!" she said, slowly backing away, then quickening her pace when her sister glared at her.

"Nice to meet you, Molly," said Agent Soul with a smile. Emmy shook her head, then looked at the cop and shrugged.

"Give me your hand, Special Agent Mike," said Emmy, gripping him with her penetrating eyes. He put out his hand. Emmy turned it over. "Got a pen?" she asked. He smiled and reached into his shirt pocket and handed her a pen. "Just in case you need to contact me for any reason," she said with a coy smile, jotting her number on the palm of his hand. He grinned back, his blue eyes sparkling as they stood there, lost in time.

Molly made her way to the door leading to the steps to the top of the Archway. She looked back to see Emmy smiling and writing something on Mike's hand. "Yyyess!" Molly yelled, fist-pumping as she made her way inside, people streaming past her on the way out.

Molly got her food from McDonald's and found a table smack in the middle of the Archway next to the window, where she waited while Emmy bought her sandwich from Subway. Molly daydreamed about being a little girl, just as Emmy had remembered, with her head glued to the window, watching the vehicles race through the short tunnel on their way toward Joplin or, in the other direction, toward Tulsa. She chomped on her fries as Emmy sat down across from her. Emmy smiled and looked out the window.

"So," she asked, "this good?" Molly grinned and nodded. She noticed that Emmy had placed Agent Soul's card on the table, instead of in her wallet or pocket. She felt guilty because there she was, in perfect health, eating a burger with two patties, smothered with cheese, onions, and bacon, with fries and a chocolate shake. She watched as Emmy methodically cut up her foot-long, spinach-loaded, plant-based whole wheat hoagie into quarters with her folding tactical knife. Then she wiped the blade with a napkin and put it away. No soda or tea; just water.

My sister the ninja, Molly mused: UFC contender, tactical knife–wielding, Smith & Wesson–carrying Cherokee badass. Magnet for hunky special agents. How can she sit there and pretend this didn't just now happen? Molly wondered. Like, she got out of a totally boss car, kicked one guy's ass, almost shot two others, then got the number of a hot guy with a steady job who thinks she's the bomb. That's some Katniss Everdeen shit.

They stared out at the parking lot, the Mustang sitting pretty in the distance.

"*Love* that car," Molly said.

"Yeah," Emmy responded, "me too." She watched Molly for a few moments. "You know," she added, "if anything happens to me, it's yours, right?" Molly jerked her eyes back to Emmy. She looked down, then began to cry. She pulled her chestnut hair away from her face and rested her head in her hands.

"Please don't say that, Emmy." She looked up, grabbed more napkins from the holder, and wiped her eyes. "I can't lose *you*; just fucking can't."

"Hey," Emmy responded, "I'm not giving up. But we have to be realistic. I might not survive this." Molly didn't want to hear it, but she knew deep inside that her sister was right. Emmy placed her hand on Molly's.

"Hey, I promise not to tap out, okay? Okay?" She smiled. "Subject change. Go."

"Okay," Molly answered, grabbing more napkins. "Well?" Molly inquired, wiping her eyes again and gesturing toward Agent Soul's card. She couldn't stand it any longer.

"Well what, Nine-Speed?"

"Oh, give me a freaking break, Em! You know what! Agent Mikey-Mike is what!"

Emmy smiled.

Molly mouthed a wide O-M-G. "That is one gorgeous guy! What'd he say, what'd he say?" She waved her arms like a three-year-old.

"None of your business, grandma!" Emmy chided.

"Really? Seriously? I can tell you like him. Like, he's got something, right? I mean besides being an adorable underwear model."

"Jesus, Molly!"

"No really. Some kinda magic going on there, Em. And he's obviously totally into you. I thought he was gonna ask for your autograph for a minute!"

"He got it—on his hand!" They both laughed and Molly high-fived her sister.

"I dunno," Emmy said. "We might go out; hard to say. I think he was just more interested in the persona of me being a pro fighter." She seemed sad when she said it. "That happens sometimes," she added, lost in thought.

Molly studied her. Suddenly, it dawned on her that something had happened to Emmy at some point. But what? Something told Molly that an event had transpired—an unpleasant one—somewhere along the line that she didn't know about. Maybe it was the reason she began studying the martial arts, then became a fighter. Or the reason for the gun. Emmy's vibrating phone interrupted her thoughts. Emmy checked it and Molly could see excitement behind her eyes. Emmy typed something.

"So sweet," Emmy said, gazing down at her phone.

"What, what?"

"Mike asked very politely and professionally if he could see me sometime. When I said yes, he asked, 'How about next Saturday?'" Emmy couldn't hide a grin and rolled her eyes.

"I KNEW it!" Molly screeched.

"Shush," said Emmy. "Eat your burger, grandma."

Molly grinned and took a huge bite out of the last half of her burger. They sat in silence and watched the cars race beneath them.

20

Mary Takes a Stand

Early November 1838
Lawrenceburg, Tennessee
Old Cherokee Nation

Mary looked around.

Two more Cherokees were dead. One, an elder named Walk Behind Owl, a highly traditional and rural Cherokee who spoke no English and barely managed Cherokee, collapsed on the trail. His dysentery was so severe he literally exploded from mouth and anus, in one final burst of vomiting and excretion, and just dropped dead on the spot. Captain Ambrose allowed time to clean him up and bury him, and for the Cherokee to pay their respects. It seemed as if Ambrose was becoming as tortured by the events as some of the Cherokees. Mary had noticed expressions of sadness on his face, and she had overheard a conversation between the captain and a lieutenant. Captain Ambrose had shared his sorrow and frustration about having to force the Indians to move.

The other Cherokee was a child named Matoo Underwood, a seven-year-old who gave in to what Doc Arbogast thought might be a strange, unknown virus. So much pain, so much grief, so much death, Mary thought. This cannot be the will of the God she had come to worship as a practicing Methodist.

Mary's section of the party had halted temporarily so that a McNair wagon axle could be checked because Nick noticed some instability. As Mary was trying to regain her wits, a wagon master became impatient at this particular stopping point and commanded his team of horses to drive on through. A little girl named Delilah Adair stood in the path of the wagon as the man tried to gain speed. Whether he saw her or not was unclear; he was looking over the heads of the horses and angrily using his whip to accelerate them up a slight embankment, where Delilah stood, sucking her thumb. Mary shot to her feet and ran past the girl to confront the wagon headed in her direction. She planted her feet and thrust out her right arm, palm facing out. Her look of determination said it all.

"Mary!" yelled Nicholas from his own wagon.

"WHOA!" yelled the wagon master as he brought the team to a screaming halt just feet from where Mary had taken her stand. The horses bucked and whinnied. As the dust cleared, the man yelled, "Lady, what in the hell do you think you're doin'? Get outta the way, bitch!"

Nick hopped from his wagon, where he had been writing a letter to Governor Cannon of Tennessee regarding Pretty Water's baby, and ran the fifteen or so yards to the other wagon. He leaped into the buckboard and seized the wagon master by the neck, taking him to the ground. Nick pounded the man about the head, the rage of the past couple of weeks unleashing itself. Several soldiers and Sergeant Thomas managed to separate the men and subdue Nick. Someone had grabbed Delilah and moved her from the path, and Mary tried to confront the wagon master herself, but was duly restrained by the soldiers.

Sergeant Thomas conferred with Captain Ambrose, who insisted that the wagon master and Nick be at opposite ends of the detachment moving forward. He ordered the wagon master be sent, with an escort of two soldiers, to the front of the line and told him to remain there for the duration.

"And if I *don't*?" the wagon master had said, glaring at Nick from a distance.

"Then I'll kill you where you stand," said Ambrose calmly, almost peaceably. He then turned and walked away, leaving

Sergeant Thomas to order the wagon master to leave at gunpoint. The wagon master muttered obscenities and then drove his supply wagon on ahead.

Later, in the quiet of rest and reflection at camp, Nick sat next to Mary while she bathed Martha from a pail of water. He reached over, gently took her chin in his hand, and said, "That was the bravest thing I've ever seen. Your father would be proud." She smiled at her husband and looked down shyly, then resumed bathing their daughter.

Some of the oxen and two horses became quite ill and had to be shot. Doc Arbogast said he couldn't determine what was happening, but he thought it best that they stay on the move as much as possible. His gut told him idleness would lead to more deaths of both human and beast. Augustine became sick and at one point Nick was sure he was going to have to put him out of his misery. He vomited several times, but then showed improvement. He was protective of the McNair household—including Enoch and his family—and soldiers had to ask permission to talk to Deborah or Martha for fear of being bitten. Some of the soldiers became more restless as the trip wore on. They would drink and play cards, upsetting the missionaries and coaxing some of the Cherokees weakest in mind and spirit to get drunk on the raw whiskey that was being passed around.

Two Cherokees, Thumper and Henry Edge, got into a fight after several soldiers egged them on. They wanted to see Thumper "Indian wrestle" Henry and they placed bets on who would win. Thumper had managed to get hold of a gun and he shot Henry in the arm because Henry was winning. Doc Arbogast and two assistants from the tribe had to treat Henry's arm. As they were treating him, Henry apparently broke free of his caretakers and went back in search of Thumper. He was so drunk that he ran headlong into a beech tree and knocked himself cold. When he came to, he realized that Doc Arbogast had treated him where he lay, and he just went back to sleep. Ida Bird, a self-proclaimed pickpocket, stole coins from his pants and absconded with his earring, deciding to wear it herself. She paraded around the camp, proudly showing the other Cherokees her new earring.

The general chaos was dizzying. Nick and Mary took more precautions to protect their family. Despite everyone's fatigue, rowdiness among the people providing transportation of supplies, the soldiers, and the Cherokees themselves, grew with each passing week. The McNairs worried about whether they would arrive in Indian Territory without having to shoot someone.

At daybreak on a Thursday, the party prepared for another day of travel. Mary rushed about, trying to ready Martha for the difficult day ahead. Strangely, Martha had not cried on the journey nearly as much as Nick and Mary thought she would. Mary had just placed a blanket on the wagon when Ida Bird came by, wearing Henry's earring and giggling as she showed Mary a pocket watch she had lifted from Sergeant Hollingsworth. She pointed to him, about thirty yards away, furiously searching his belongings for the timepiece. Mary could hear him swearing that he had just placed it in his breast pocket not twenty minutes ago.

"Not too smart white man," Ida said and cackled, placing her hand on Mary's arm. The women laughed and put their heads together.

"What's so funny over here?" asked Nick as he came around the side of the wagon, patting one of the horses on its side.

"Nothing," said Mary, looking at Ida with a knowing smile.

"Uh-huh," said Nick. He knew enough to know that he likely didn't want to know anyway.

Ida, one of the many Cherokee elders on this trip, winked at Mary and shuffled away, mumbling. Mary watched her walk past Moses McDaniel's wagon and bump into a young corporal. The corporal was impatient and nasty with her, saying, "Hey, watch where you're going, old lady!"

Ida nodded and said, "Oh-oh, 'scuse 'em!" and skillfully relieved the soldier of his sheathed dagger and a small shot bag.

Mary watched Ida hide them in her dress as she lumbered along, occasionally glancing back at the corporal with an expression of satisfaction.

21

A Celebration of the Soul

Present Day, Early April
Office of Marie Trevino
Fort Gibson, Oklahoma
District Four, Cherokee Nation

It was a beautiful afternoon as Emmy drove her Mustang into the parking lot. She was beaming and she knew it. How long would it take Marie to figure it out? Would she be happy for her, or just neutral? Would she jinx herself by telling Marie?

Emmy entered the building, a favorite of hers because it overlooked the Neosho River. She walked down the hall and opened the door next to a sign that read "Marie Trevino, LPC." She took a seat in the outer office and gathered her thoughts. She glanced at the shelf which housed her favorite teddy bear. He was beige with a little red bow tie. "Hi!" he seemed to be saying. "My name's Mike! That's *Mikey-Mike* to you, Goddess," he said with a wink and a smile. She giggled. The door to Marie's office opened.

"Well, you seem to be in a good mood, yes?" said Marie, smiling and holding her arms open. Emmy hugged her.

"I guess," she said, trying to downplay her excitement.

"Okey-dokey, then," said Marie, who knew her patient well. They entered Marie's office and took their usual seats.

"So," said Marie with an inquisitive expression, "what it be like, sista?" They laughed and Marie settled into her chair and leaned back in her usual relaxed but open and alert posture. "How are you, Emmy?"

Marie had a way of probing one's soul in the least intrusive way, and Emmy found herself regurgitating things she had no plans of getting into. It was supremely frustrating and liberating at the same time. Marie smiled again, waiting for the window to open and carry the wind of Emmy's thoughts and dreams to a place of birth and restoration. Her long, dark, straight hair and dark eyes revealed her Spanish and Italian ancestry. Today she wore a thin gray sweater. She moved her head slightly, awaiting Emmy's response.

"I'm fine, I guess," said Emmy with a slight shake of her head and confident smile.

"Okay. Good to hear."

Silence.

Emmy made a face by moving her eyes side to side, then pursed her lips in a "Well, what can I say?" movement. She spread her right arm out over the back of the sofa. She played with her left earring, a brown turtle, while the other dangled. More silence. Emmy blew out a long, collected breath, followed by another goofy expression. She looked as if she were ready to explode.

"You haven't had a bout since the Ortiz fight, right?" Marie asked.

"Right. What makes you ask that?"

"I mean, no other significant sub-card fights or such?"

"No. Why on earth are you asking me that?"

"Emily McNair, the only time you grin like that is after you've sufficiently pounded the living hell out of someone and earned a nice paycheck, or . . ."

Emmy moved her arm from the sofa and unconsciously hugged herself and rocked briefly to and fro. "Or . . . " Emmy whispered.

Marie's eyebrows arched and she shook her head questioningly.

Emmy inhaled deeply. "Or . . . I might have *met* someone, maybe?" She smiled as she slapped both hands to her face and turned red. "There, I said it!"

"Congratulations!" said Marie with genuine enthusiasm. Emmy threw her hands up in a "What can I say?" gesture. She sat back, taking in another deep breath. Suddenly, she grabbed a pillow from the sofa and flung it straight up. It landed on the tissue box on the coffee table in front of them.

"Okay okay okay. You ready for this? He is *so fucking cute!*" She squealed and roared with laughter, seizing the pillow again and collapsing back onto the sofa, which caused Marie to laugh.

"Congrats, Emmy, really. I am overjoyed for you. You deserve it," she said. During the rest of the hour, Emmy detailed how it all had come about. Marie took her usual notes, smiling and nodding, amused at certain places in the story. At one point, she put down her notebook and took a breath for herself, then once again wished Emmy the best in her new journey.

"Wado, Marie. You know," she said, hesitating and tearing up, looking away, "if it weren't for you . . . goddamn, Marie, if it weren't for you . . ." She stared out the window at the river before looking back at her therapist. Marie pointed to the tissues on the table. Emmy waved her off. "Thanks. I'm okay, really."

Marie let the flow of things take their course during the hour, listening to this new chapter of Emmy's story, saying that their time was almost up. She glanced briefly through her notes and then spoke.

"So, before we stop, let me make sure I'm tracking you accurately. You and Molly were returning from Vinita on a day trip to obtain parts for *Ned Christie*, and you decided to grab a bite at the Archway. By the way, I thought it was a nice moment when Molly expressed empathy and concern for you regarding your special diet." Emmy nodded, changed her mind about the tissues, and blew her nose. "You were suddenly caught off guard by three large, strange men in the parking lot, one of whom made the unfortunate mistake of putting a hand on you. Basically, due to your training, you motherfucked this poor Texas cowboy with some kind of judo thing—sending him to his knees—about which he's no doubt still having nightmares."

Emmy, knees curled up to her chest, was peeking over the top of her tissue and blinking as Marie read her notes aloud. "Then you scared the bejesus out of the other two with your gun. You then rousted the attention of what is apparently the sexiest . . . let's see, what is his title now—special agent—in the entire state bureau of investigation, who then evidently went cuckoo for Cocoa Puffs over you. He gave you his card—in a 'professional way' you said—which impressed you—and at one point you thought Molly was going to go into full-on hallucinations due to his sheer animal magnetism. In a moment of obvious pre-erotica, you wrote your number on his palm and then, in an apparent meltdown of man-boy impatience, he texted you thirty minutes later for a date. You accepted, have had several since, and I think it's fair to say that you kinda sorta like him. That about right?"

At first, Emmy was quiet, slowly pulling the tissue away from her face. Then she exploded with laughter, affirming that, yes, Marie had gotten it essentially right.

Marie smiled warmly. "Good for you, Emmy. *Good for you.*"

Emmy came away from the session feeling that it had been one of the most enjoyable hours in years. As she stopped by the river to go to water, honoring her Cherokee tradition, and felt the sun on her face, she smiled and gave thanks for her relationship with Marie and, of course, Mike.

22

A Kind and Generous Heart

Present Day
Community Baptist Church
Muskogee, Oklahoma

Devon emerged from the front doors of the church at dusk carrying a small spiral notebook. He was tired, resigned. He dragged himself down the steps, turning right toward the church office, and then stopped in his tracks. There, in the first parking space, leaning against her '69 Mach 1 with her arms crossed, was Emmy. Devon didn't know if he should muster the energy to run or just take whatever beating was coming.

"Evening, Devon."

"'Siyo, Emmy. Ah, how's it goin'?"

She nodded slowly. "How was your meeting?"

He shrugged.

"Not an answer."

"I don't know. Okay, I guess. They last about an hour." She said nothing, just flexed her arm muscles. She wore a red tank top which wasn't tucked in, along with her go-to denim jeans and Walmart shoes. Her hair was in a bun this evening, no earrings, nothing to get tangled or broken. She stared at him.

"Yeah," he added with hesitation, "we're ah, we're in there for an hour," nodding as if she needed reassurance on the matter. "Hey, hey, now," he said, smirking, "you're not gonna go all MMA on me and choke me down right here in front of the Lord and everybody, are you?" He pointed back toward the large structure with white columns.

Emmy narrowed her eyes and studied him harder.

"Just kiddin'," he said, putting a hand up again. "Juuust kiddin'."

"How was it?" she repeated.

"The hell you mean, 'how was it?'" he mimicked impatiently. She continued to glare at him. Something told him that wasn't the A answer. He began to fidget, scratching his arm with the spiral rings on his notebook. "I mean, what, whad'ya want me to say, Em? I don't know . . . we had a meeting, a guy meeting . . . you know." Running definitely was looking better by the second. He watched as she took a slow, deep breath, glanced up the street toward Harmony House, then brought her eyes back at him.

"One more fucking time, Dev. *How did it go in there*?"

"Oh! I mean, okay. You know." He looked down, as if ashamed. "They say we should make amends at this stage, you know." He stared at the sidewalk as if counting the microscopic bits of cement. She waited for him to look up at her again.

"Okay." She nodded with what seemed like some compassion. "And what do you think about that?"

"What do you mean?"

"I mean, Devon, do *you* think you should make amends?"

He nodded.

"Why?"

"'Cause, 'cause I offended Molly, I guess."

"You *guess*?"

"No, I mean yes, I did. And like, you know, I did send her flowers, so . . ."

"Yeah, but is it really about the flowers, Dev? I mean, honestly."

"Well yeah, kinda, it's just—"

"It was a rhetorical question, you asshat."

"Yeah, yeah, okay, okay," he said, holding out his right palm and looking away as if trying to keep her at a distance.

"I've been watching you, Devon, from afar, so to speak."

He shot a glance at her. This freaked him out. He felt a sudden infusion of courage, though. He pointed at her and boasted, "Hey, you know, I could, like, you know, like, file on you. Yeah—could file charges on you and shit—like for assault."

Arms still crossed, Emmy sighed and looked up the road again, then back at Devon. "Shit-ass, you file anything, it had better be those raunchy fingernails of yours, you hear me?"

"Yeah, yeah; I was just joshin' ya," he replied sheepishly. "Hey, Em, I've been coming regular. Only missed one meeting so far—" Emmy arched her eyebrows. "Nah, nah! Listen, couldn't be helped. Got called in to work that night. They were shorthanded, you know what I'm sayin'? Had to. But I'm coming here every week, I swear, it's been okay, been good." He opened his notebook and told her about the group's discussion on restoration, and the leader encouraging Devon to do his part in repairing injuries.

"That's good, Devon. I'm glad to hear it," Emmy said. She seemed sincere, he thought, less intimidating. "How do you think you can do that regarding Molly?"

"Not sure," he said, closing the notebook and looking down again. "I know she hates me now."

"Let me tell you something, Devon. The Great Spirit gave Molly a gift. You know what that gift is?"

Devon shook his head.

"A good heart. He gave her a good heart, Dev, a kind and generous heart. But it's also fragile. She wants to believe the best about everyone, and that can get her fragile heart broken. You broke my sister's heart, Dev. After all these years, you trashed her heart and then assumed it was all about you. Surprise, fuck face, it's *never* all about you. Responsibilities, Dev my man. We all have responsibilities toward one another.

Fulfill yours, Devon. If you're going to have anything further to do with the exquisite butterfly whose heart you crushed, get real about your responsibilities."

"Ah, how? I mean, how do I do that—especially if she won't talk to me?"

"Kindness, Devon. That's all it takes for now. Be *kind*. Do unto others as you would have them do unto you, don't 'do unto others *before* they do unto you.'" She crinkled her nose with a slight head shake. "Lousy policy, that second one."

"Okay. Got it. But if she won't—"

"If Molly never speaks to you again, take that as a message to go out of your way to be kind to the next girl. And deal with it. That's what real men do, Devon. Only Molly can decide where to go next, not you, got it?"

"Yeah."

"Kay-den. You have a good night, Devon," she said, turning back toward the *Ned Christie*.

"Ah, hey, a buddy brought me down here tonight. Ain't got no ride. Could I maybe hitch a ride with you?"

Turning back, Emmy shook her head and said, "No, knucklehead, you can't get in the car with me." He held up his arm again and nodded. "But," she continued, "I know a lot of people. Want me to call you a ride?"

"Oh, nah, I don't wanna put you out. I can just—"

"*Devon*," she interrupted, "would you like me to call someone for you?" She was staring him down again.

"Okay, sure, yes, ma'am. I mean 'Emmy!' Yes, that's fine, I mean, please."

She nodded and pulled out her phone. "How about Frankie Ragsdale? You know him, right?"

Devon nodded.

"All right," she said, hitting the call button. "Frankie, how ya doin', handsome? Emmy here."

"'Siyo, Storm!" he heard Frankie say in a loud voice.

"Listen," she said, "I need a favor."

When she was done with the call, she told him Frankie lived only five minutes away and would be there soon.

"That good?" she asked.

Devon nodded and she smiled at him for the first time.

"Kay-den. You have a nice evening and keep up the good work with the meetings. I'll check in on you again down the road."

Opening the driver's door, she turned, drilled him with her blazing brown eyes, and said with certain conviction, "Be at these meetings, Devon; be at these fucking meetings." He nodded and looked down again. With that, she got into her car and roared away.

Grateful that he was still alive, with all his body parts intact, Devon sighed, returned to the church steps, and sat down to wait for Frankie to pick him up.

McNair House
Muskogee, Oklahoma
District Four, Cherokee Nation

Molly lay on her bed with her legs angled at forty-five degrees, feet on the wall, chewing the ends of her hair. She replayed the movie night with Devon in her mind. She had been eager about their date. At any other time, she would have been turned on by Devon's heavy kisses, minus the groping and arm squeezes. What the hell, exactly, was his problem? Her mind went back to the time she had chased him around the large sycamore in front of the Lutheran church where they went to kindergarten. He pulled her hair; she beat him up. Simple, right? So what happened to all the simple? She wished she could have beaten him up at the theater. But then, not really. She just wanted the old Devon back. The boy who pulled her braids and teased her. What happened to that cute little Cherokee boy with the olive skin and happy smile?

She realized she was gnawing on her poor split ends again and stopped, putting her hands behind her head, elbows out. Was it her? Was she the one who changed? Or maybe she needed to adapt? Things are different these days. And guys in college probably have higher expectations. Yeah, that's it, she thought. She needed to be more flexible and meet college guy expectations. Molly sighed.

I don't *think* so.

Why not?

You did good. You stayed sacred. Not all women have a choice in the moment. You did.

What if he never speaks to me again?

-Silence-

Well? Answer me that!

-Silence-

I'm really sad about Emmy. And I'm really happy for Becks and Tara. It's weird, isn't it? All that time and I didn't put two and two together. Well, I guess they didn't, either. It must be hard for them. Like, I know what I want—being straight—yet I can't seem to find it, and here they are—obviously madly in love. What am I doing wrong? Nothing to say about that one, huh?

-Silence-

I guess I don't blame you. The good girl—the one no guys wanna be near anymore, the puritan—

Pity party for one, please; table in the back.

Oh, *very* funny! Ha-ha, such crap. You think you're so damn hilarious, don't you?

Nope. Just dead.

I'm sorry you are. Really. *So* sorry it happened.

Molly, everyone dies. I survived the Trail of Tears, remember? Died later. Young, but later. It was my time.

Oh, God, here I go with the tears again—eerr! "I wish it hadn't been your time. I really need you here," Molly said aloud.

I am here, Pretty Feet.

"Yeah, I guess."

Count on it.

"So look, if Mom came in right now, would she be able to—"

Nah. She would just think you're crazy as hell, talking to yourself.

"Oh, that's just great. Well, I guess I'm back to silent mode with you, then."

Whatever.

You know, we're Christians.

Of course. So am I. I was raised Methodist.

So, like, shouldn't I be talking to Jesus or something? You know, instead of you?

Want me to go grab him for you?

Cool! Yes, could you? Wow!

Molly raised up on her elbows with excitement.

Not really. Just kidding. My guess would be that he's kinda busy.

Then *why* the hell did you do that?

It was fun. You should have seen your face! Oh, God, granddaughter, you are just adorable!

That is *so* infuriating! Is this what you do? Float around, mucking with people?

Just you for now.

But Jesus exists, right? I mean, he's there, isn't he?

What do *you* think?

Well, yeah. Like, duh, right?

Well, there ya go, then.

Should I be going to church more often? Would that help?

I don't know, should you? And would it?

Maybe. I still get angry 'cause we lost Dad. Now Emmy with cancer. It just seems so unfair.

I agree.

So how do you handle stuff like that?

I pray. And I believe, Pretty Feet. I believe in you. And I believe in Emmy. She's a warrior, that one. Could Amtrak that girl and she'd just get up from the track like one of those little flat cartoon characters and go wax that car of hers. The *Ned Christie*—that's pretty funny, by the way.

Is she gonna live, Mary?

-Silence-

No! Please, God, don't check out on me now. I *have* to know!

Be sweet.

Please!

Oh, you need to check that PowWowUs thingy, or whatever it is.

Why? Who? What?

Donadago-huh-ee.

"God, that's exasperating!"

"What is, kiddo?" Molly's mom asked, popping her head around the corner.

"Nothing. Um, just, I was just thinking about a homework assignment, that's all," Molly said with a faint smile.

"Not one you're ignoring, I trust?"

"No, 'course not. Just . . . stuff."

"Hmm. Well, there's a lot of that in the world, isn't there, Lollipop?" She flicked Molly with a hand towel she was holding.

"Hey! Dang, Mom—that hurt," Molly whined, rubbing her elbow.

Sandra mimicked playing the violin, saluting Molly's drama.

"Why is it everyone's doing that to me?" Molly demanded, clearly pissed.

"What? You mean, like this?" her mom said, flicking her again.

"Mom!"

Sandra laughed and said dinner was ready and not to linger or it would get cold.

"All right already; be there in a sec. Gotta send an email."

"Make it quick, Peewee," Sandra hollered behind her as she made her way down the hall.

"*Okay.*" Molly rolled her eyes, shook her head, sighed dramatically, and picked up her phone. She clicked the PowWowUs app and checked in. There was a friend request: Clayton Blackfox. "Ohh . . . well, okay, then," Molly whispered to herself. She clicked the accept button and there was a message.

> Osiyo, Molly! We are having a "Recommend and Recruit" day at the college. I immediately thought of you. You had mentioned something once about maybe majoring in elementary education. Thought any more about that? If you're interested, you can come up and I can show you around, talk to you about scholarship opportunities, introduce you to the dean, that sort of thing. Maybe afterward we could go have lunch? Let me know. Clay

Clay Blackfox's mom was a friend of Molly's mom, and Clay had been two grades ahead of Molly in school. She had always liked Clay. She remembered him as friendly and treating people nice. She felt her palms sweat at the thought of going to the college, meeting a dean, and having lunch with Clay. She responded with a "Yes!" asked what time would be most convenient for Clay, and pressed "Enter."

"Molly! Let's eat, my little drama queen!" her mom called. Molly smiled and signed out.

23

The Sacred and the Profane

Suffering may be a rod to chastise; it may be a scepter to empower. Make it a scepter.

—Henry Ward Beecher

Present Day
Mid April
Marina Del Rey Resort
Grand Lake O' the Cherokees
District Ten, Cherokee Nation

Mike leaned back in the rocking chair on the porch of the cabin. He smiled at Emmy.

"Thanks for taking some time with me," he said. She nodded and smiled, slowly rocking in her own chair as they surveyed their surroundings. It appeared to Mike that it felt good for Emmy to unwind. She admired the cabins lining the lake, their large, red, A-frame roofs and red front doors reminding her of a row of small churches, each awaiting their respective congregations. Mike loved Emmy's braid and couldn't decide if he liked it or her thick ponytail best. Her tree stump earrings swayed in the afternoon breeze as she rocked. He couldn't believe how beautiful her thighs were, feminine yet extraordinarily powerful. They seemed to be browning in front of his eyes under the Oklahoma sunshine. She wore a multicolored beaded turtle necklace that her grandmother had made. She seemed relaxed and comfortable in her denim cutoff shorts and red tank top, which highlighted her supple and muscular arms. Her hands lightly gripped the rocking chair armrests and he studied the callouses on her knuckles. Even those were beautiful.

"Why are we really here, Michael?" asked Emmy.

"Maybe to have a nice time?"

"Uh-huh. But I mean, like, *why* did you bring me here? You really pushed for it. What gives?"

He was silent for a moment. He hesitated, as if trying to choose his words.

"I just thought that, well, you know—we've talked a lot but we haven't really *talked*, you know?"

"You going girlfriend on me, Agent Mike?" she quipped with a grin. He laughed.

"Nah, I just . . . look, I don't know; I thought you might like it here, that's all."

"I do like it here."

"Great!"

"Now answer the damn question."

Mike sighed. "I think I've been pretty clear that I think you're great, haven't I? I mean, amazing, really."

She smiled. "Yes, you have."

"Sometimes I think you forget what I do for a living. I read people, Emmy. It's my job. I know when someone's lying or not telling me everything. You're hiding something."

"Since when do I have to tell you everything? What are you—my priest?" Mike leaned back in his rocker and rubbed his head in frustration. "What?" she challenged. "What? What?" He shook his head and sighed.

"I can't fight you, Emmy. Not you, fentanyl, heroin, homicide, rape, arson, terrorism, and everything else I have to deal with. It's just too much." She looked scared for the first time since he had known her.

"Wha—what are you saying? Did you bring me all the way out here just to break it off? If so, that's a *shitty* thing to do, Mike. I swear to God, I'm not about to—"

"Hey, hey, take it easy," he said, leaning forward and taking her hands in his. "Of course not, babe. No way." He rubbed her rough hands and then let them go and eased back into the rocker. "But this is what I'm talking about." He looked into her eyes. "Don't you ever get tired of living so defensively? I mean, isn't it exhausting?" His frankness caught her off guard.

She looked out toward the other cabins. "Don't know what you mean," she said, knowing full well it was bullshit.

"Emily, you're a highly intelligent woman working on a master's degree. The hell you *don't*. You read people, too. Every time you step in that cage, you become an expert by reading your opponent. Well, Goddess, that's me. I don't have a lot of skills, but this is one of them, and I'm just asking you to be straight with me. I know it's not just the cancer. It's something else. If it's me, I need to know."

She shook her head and rested it on the back of the rocker, staring off into space. Marie and her questions: Do you love him? Fuck! She looked at him. First, she wondered, why does he have to be so cute? Second, why so smart? Third, what was I thinking—dating a handsome and smart guy who interrogates people for a living? Really, why not just shove my cancerous tit into a food processor?

"It's not you, promise," she managed with a smile. "I just have some shit I need to sort through; doesn't have anything to do with you."

"Oh, really? We've all got shit, Goddess. Me especially. But I've been as up front with you as I know how to be. I mean, aside from little things like breaking my arm in the seventh grade or my first kiss in the eighth, I think I've been pretty honest. And I admire you for telling me about the cancer, but I would expect that, of course, because as things progress, well, you can't really hide something like that. And for you to say that this doesn't have anything to do with me, well, that's actually pretty damn insulting at this stage. The way you say it, it sounds like there might be another guy involved, and I'm a one-woman man. Hey, you're a beautiful, semi-famous woman, so I can see why you'd have men after you. If there's someone else, just tell me now so we can decide what to do. You're the most amazing woman I've ever known and I recognize something special when I see it. If you're wanting to break it off with me, then just get it the hell over with. Like, flush me now and be done with it. I don't know what you think our relationship is based on, but I happen to think it's pretty damn special and I don't appreciate being shut out like—"

"I was gang-raped when I was eighteen."

Mike stopped, sat upright, crossed his hands in a nonthreatening way, and gave her his absolute, full attention. Somehow, he had known it had to be something like this. "I'm sorry," he said quietly.

She glimpsed at him, looked out at the grounds, then shot him another quick glance. "College. My first year. A party. Some asshole's apartment. There were five of them."

Mike could feel every muscle in his body tighten. His arms flexed involuntarily, and he suddenly had the impulse to quick-draw his weapon, which, of course, he wasn't wearing. He was on vacation. Or was he?

"Yeah," she said. "Five white assholes got me drunk then took turns on me. Mostly from behind. One of them used his beer bottle."

Strangely, Mike noticed, it became hard to breathe, even in the crisp open air. He knew he couldn't be neutral about this. He wanted to kill all of them. Slowly. In the four years since he had become an investigator, he had learned the importance of objectivity, of letting the facts guide the conclusion. This was different. But he managed to stay focused on this vulnerable, injured warrior that now sat before him.

She rested her head back on the chair again, then tilted slightly toward him and spoke with one eye open, squinting in the early afternoon sun that was reaching across the landscape.

"And no one could hear me, of course, because they had my head buried in a pillow and I could barely breathe. I thought I was going to suffocate and die, but I wasn't that lucky."

She then turned and looked straight ahead, back to property-gazing. Mike moved his chair closer to hers, so they were side by side, facing the same direction. He put his hand over hers, slowly rocking his chair. She didn't take his, but just kept talking. She was hauntingly calm considering the subject matter.

"One of them said that fucking me was better than the time he fucked his sister when she was thirteen." Mike sensed his breathing becoming more rapid, his muscles tightening again. Remember your training, remember your training, he repeated to himself. "The big one—he yanked that guy off me when he was done and said, 'Yeah, well, when I'm done with this bitch, she won't *remember* when she was thirteen.'" Mike swallowed, concentrated on his own breathing, and recalled being with victims—usually in the hospital ER, and always with a female officer. This one was his to handle alone.

"He was the worst. It felt like he was on top of me for hours. He literally pulled shreds of my hair out getting off on me. The bastard made sure he used his full weight with every thrust. At one point, he said, 'Oh, man, never done an Indian before!' I remember leaving my body—like, I went places. Went to be with my ancestors. In retrospect, they kept me sane. They saved me. One of them was named Mary. Anyway, the others—they kept saying, 'Roll her over, roll her over!' He squeezed my shoulders so hard they were bruised for weeks, just mashing my face into the pillow to get his rocks off. He told them, 'Nah, not yet. I'm saving the good stuff for later. You know she's gotta be good.' At some point, I blacked out, but I don't know for how long. When I came to, I realized they had rolled me over and there was semen all over me. I assumed they had all taken their turn. I was so thankful it was over." Mike never moved his hand. He just kept it gently over Emmy's. For a moment, he felt her hand lightly squeeze his.

"But I was wrong. The big one—he wasn't done. He slapped me several times, called me the filthiest of names, then entered me from the front. It's weird because he seemed like such a little child; just no development there. No empathy, no nothing. He raped me for forty-five minutes, like a machine—a broken, distorted machine stuck in some loop. He would do his business, keep me pinned, then start again. He kept telling the others, 'Go away, this radish is mine' and 'Shut up and let me fuck this prairie nigger.' His grunts, his filthy smell, all like it was yesterday.

"There was a scrawny guy with them. He didn't seem to want to do anything but the others kept egging him on. The big guy bullied him into climbing on me. When the little guy objected, the big one slapped him, too, and yelled, 'Don't be a pussy! Get down there and get you some of that red ink!' They all hollered, 'Shag that bitch, junior!' and then forced him onto me. Just a big spectacle for everybody. Sometime before they all passed out from the booze, the big guy made me give him oral sex. Said that if I bit him he would kill me right there. Being terrified and wasted, I did as I was told. He made me do it until I vomited, then he shoved me back on the bed and just lay on top of me, smothering me while he eventually passed out. He was well over two hundred pounds.

"I remember the exact time because of a stupid little alarm clock radio beside the bed. I just lay there and watched as the green numbers changed over and over. The shit you remember, huh? I guess you've heard this kind of thing dozens of times by now, right?" She managed a weak smile. She seemed done. For the first time since he had known her, she seemed vulnerable, delicate. She was truly remarkable, he thought. He hadn't noticed a perceptible change in her heart rate or breathing patterns. She had clearly processed all this with someone. He knew it was beyond time to come clean with his feelings.

"Can you please look at me?"

She stared at a large oak tree in the center of the property.

"Emily, look at me."

She relented and slowly turned her head in his direction, squinting again in the warm sun.

"I love you."

She remembered her toughest fight in the cage. She would rather get back in there right now than have this wonderful guy say shit like that. Why must he be so sweet? She couldn't speak.

"I love you," he repeated. "You know something? Even if you don't love me, I can handle that. I don't know if I realized it immediately—the day you put that cowboy on his knees with the wrist lock—or if it's been a more gradual thing, but, damn, girl, I just think you're the best. I wish I could go back in time and change everything—be there for you when you needed it. Would've killed every one of those bastards for you. They ever catch 'em?"

She shook her head. "Of course not. I was scared, didn't report it. And they were white and I was Indian. It was what it was. And it was so long ago . . ." They were silent for a minute or two, the energy dictating the time.

He knew there was no point in reminding her that this was still within the state's statute of limitations time frame. She had arrived at a certain place with it; the pain of rehashing it in the legal process would be too great, that much he knew from his work. Breaking some tension, Mike smiled, remembering. "Man . . . the way you ripped that Bodyguard from your holster . . . you're even faster than me, and I'm fast!" He laughed. "I remember tossing my food aside—thanks a lot by the way—and thinking wow, now that's the kind of gal I'd like to meet!"

She smiled and wrapped her hand around his now. "I love you, too, Mike; I do. I'm just scared." He jerked his head in surprise and caressed her thumb with his.

"You? Scared? Hmm. Of what?"

She sighed. "Oh, I don't know, let's see: Maybe that you might not want anything to do with me after what I just told you. Maybe the fact that you're solid and we Native chicks have a hard time with that. Like, finding it, for one. Maybe that I've never been able to hold a relationship for longer than a few months. That could be due to the rape, or it could just be the way I am. Dunno. Or, maybe, the unpleasant reality that the woman you recently met has breast cancer—do you want me to go on?"

"Stop it," he said. "Just fucking stop it right there." He got up. "Stand up," he said, motioning for her to stand, which she did. He took her seat in the rocker, which was one of the "grandfather" size rockers, big enough to hold the weight of two people. It was warm from her body heat. "Come here," he said, holding out his arms.

"Well, okay then," she said with a faint smile, and sat in his lap. He pulled her to him, kissing her muscular deltoid.

"Listen to what I'm saying to you. I'm in for the full ride, you got it? You, your cancer, your history, the whole deal," he added, his face to her shoulder. "If you think you're the only one here with a U-Haul full of shit to tote, you're wrong, okay?" She pulled her head back and playfully examined him.

"Yeah," she said with a slow, mocking nod, "now that I think on it, you're actually a genuine mess, aren't you?" He laughed and kissed her arm again. "No, seriously!" she chided, playfully shaking his shoulders. "You work all the damn time, I have to constantly remind you what day it is, and I gotta work on your wardrobe. I mean, you're just too damn pretty all the time. Gotta get you some Native threads, Mikey-Mike. Put you in some denim and a pocket T-shirt more often. Jesus Christ!" They laughed together for the first time on the trip. He took her face in his hands and gently kissed her.

"The whole package, got it?"

"Be careful what you wish for, Michael, seriously. It's more complicated than that. And *I'm* more complicated than that. I have to stay dedicated to my studies. I mean, who knows? I may even go for a Ph.D. I have to focus on the UFC and—" He kissed her again. He didn't want to get too romantic considering the sacred and profound story he just heard, so he finished with a soft peck on her nose. He loved her nose.

"I hear you," he whispered. "Let's just be us for now, how's that?" She nodded with relief.

"Yeah," she said, "I can hang with that." She grinned and hugged him.

Mike stood over the stove in the cabin and stirred a large pan of sizzling veggies. He had promised her an amazing plant-based dinner. They had gone for a run together, and now Emmy had just finished up her shower. It was all Mike could do to keep up with a professional athlete, one where serious roadwork was second nature. At one point, he was certain he was going to collapse. Her ragging him during the run with things like "What're you—trying out for Miss Oklahoma?" and "Mush, little bitch!" forced him to keep going. It was, in short, humiliating.

"Looks great!" she said, kissing his cheek. She went over to set the table. For the next couple of hours, they had a number of conversations, learning more about each other than they had previously. Mike decided to push the envelope a bit by asking about how she had processed her assault so well.

"Yeah, I got counseling for it early on, actually," she began, sitting on the carpeted floor in the cabin's living room with her left knee up, left arm resting on top. "Not all women do, and for many, not right away, and that's okay. It only works when you're ready. As you can imagine, the whole thing really had an impact on my studies. I left college for nine months—couldn't function. They had an okay counselor who referred me out, and that's how I met Marie. She's awesome. We've come a long way together. And it was during the first counseling period—with the college counselor—that I started studying martial arts.

"At first, I was tentative. But then I dove headlong into it. It was a constructive outlet for my rage. I began driving the distance to Tulsa four times a week, sometimes during the day, others in the evening. My sensei was Dan Stevens. It started out as karate, jujitsu, and kick-boxing classes. Dan was great, though, about the importance of tradition in the arts. So much martial arts today, as you probably know, is just strip mall–led bullshit, people getting their black belts in a year or two, that sort of thing. Dan would never allow that. In fact, I was in my third year of very regular attendance and testing and had just earned my second kyu brown belt when a guy walked in one Saturday morning. He and Dan were old friends and they were going to lunch after class. Dan told me his name was Eddie Standingcloud, a former UFC fighter.

"Well, Eddie took a liking to me and thought I had talent. He had watched me in the dojo that morning and really liked me, saw something in me. And that's how I came to fight professionally. Dan really wanted me to be one of his black belts because I'm a good teacher, but he said he understood and that if I wanted to fight, I needed to do it while I was young.

"Eddie was so great, Mike. He finally had me focus on three things: boxing, Japanese (not Brazilian) jujitsu, and Shorinji Kempo. He got me a special coach for that, an intelligence agency man with a tenth-degree black belt who created something called Unconventional Personal Combat for intelligence types. He put those things together for me—along with the stuff I learned from Dan—and it was the toughest, most rewarding fourteen months I've ever spent. A lot of that amounted to full-time work. I was exhausted." She laughed. "He did the whole Burgess Meredith-in-*Rocky*-thing: said that when he was done with me, I was gonna be able to 'chew lightning and shit thunder.'" Mike laughed loudly at that, his blue eyes sparkling from the recliner next to her as he rubbed her neck. "But yeah, glad I started young like I did. Don't know how long I could keep this up even without the cancer."

He patted her hand. "Yeah, that's for sure," he said. "I've seen enough from self-defense and weaponry at the academy to know that there's a world of training you have to go through, and retirement can come early."

"Yeah, you're not ready for a real fight until you've been training for a while. Especially if you're not doing it truly full time. More men and women are fighting into their thirties and forties, but that's rare. It takes its toll. It takes a lot of roadwork, the typical routine of sparring, weights, and so on. It's not for the faint of heart!" She smiled as she popped an after-dinner blueberry in her mouth. Mike had surprised her with a vegan blueberry cobbler, and she had a small bowl beside her.

"And your grad work—why did you choose a master's in public health?"

"Well, you know, it's important for Cherokees to give back to the community. I suck at art; it's just not a talent of mine. I never learned to weave baskets, which is a big thing in our culture. I don't know much of the language. So I wanted to have an impact on the tribe in *some* way, and public health seemed like a good idea after majoring in something as bland as English!" She laughed. "And of course, there's the fighting. It's good for the Native communities to have fighters. And I've had some generous financial backers—people like Elias Pumpkin and Bill Stoddard. They've been very kind. Pumpkin's always right there, pulling for me!"

"Well, as far as you not being good at art, I don't know about that," said Mike. "The way you climbed all over Ortiz in that fight, the way you splattered her on that mat—that was some serious artwork!" Emmy snorted and laughed. He loved her snorts.

"I will have a capstone project next semester or the one after that, depending on my schedule. It will last most of a semester with a final report or paper, sort of like a thesis project."

"What are you doing it on?"

"I had some ideas before the diagnosis, and now, after meeting Paisley—"

"That's Dr. Walkingstick?"

Emmy nodded.

"Now I'm not so sure. I might make it about nutrition. You know—and I'm not judging—that our people are in an epidemic of obesity." Mike nodded. "I mean, I think it's great that people want to embrace tradition around food and whatnot, but the truth is most Natives are in the dark about how to achieve good health. It's the elephant on every reservation no one wants to talk about. And, like everything else—as you were saying earlier today—not talking about it isn't going to take us anywhere."

Mike winked.

"Look," she said, "I admit fry bread is tasty, but for most people—especially heart patients—I wouldn't call it the choice of common sense. I think fry bread and Indian tacos are psychological tools, an addiction, really. They are important symbols of our tradition, but there are healthier choices that also represent our tradition—beans are one example, for Christ's sake. But nobody wants to talk about that. In fact, if you bring this up in some circles, get ready to have your throat cut!"

"I'm proud of you for what you're doing. People will see these things down the road. You're a trailblazer, a warrior. You rock."

She smiled in a coy way. "Are you flirting with me?"

"*Hell* yes!" They laughed together.

"So, you've been with Eddie ever since?"

"Yep," she said, reflecting. "He's been like another father to me, or an older brother, I guess. I told you our dad died when we were younger, yeah?"

Mike nodded.

"Heart attack if I didn't say that already. Mom raised us, for the most part. Grams helped out, though, especially with Molly."

"And Molly worries you, I'm guessing?"

"Well, I wouldn't say 'worry' so much. Just want her to be safe and be all she can be. She's stubborn as hell."

"Can't imagine where she gets it from," said Mike playfully.

"Hey, now! Well, I have to remember that she's becoming a young woman, with all that entails. It's hard because I still see her as a little girl sometimes, and I know I shouldn't. There's seven years between us."

"So you're protective. That's okay. That's good, really." He smiled as he watched her relax. It was nice seeing her animated—watching her eyes light up here and there as she talked about the people in her life.

"Well, golly gee, blame the big sis," she said in a sarcastic tone that turned deadly serious. "Let's just say I'd fucking kill anybody that is out to hurt her. I mean, you can take a sworn statement right here and now, Michael. You might as well just cuff me now and haul my ass in, because there's no limit to what I'd do to someone who hurt Molly the way I was hurt. I promise you, they're as good as fucking dead."

"I think you made that clear at the Archway," he said, grinning.

"Seriously, Mike. This whole 'Let's treat Native women like dog shit and throw them aside because we can'—this crap has to stop! I mean it. I know you know that we're the largest demographic for assault and missing persons. I try to do my part in keeping that at the forefront so these asshole politicians don't forget it."

"I think that's great. I support you in that; I hope you know that by now," he said. Then he smiled again. "It was just fun—and a little ironic—watching you spin some of your magic on a six-foot cowboy at the Will Rogers Turnpike."

"Yeah, well . . ." She snorted again as she spooned the last of her cobbler into her mouth. "That poor guy," she said, turning her head to the side, suppressing a laugh. "I scared the shit out of him, didn't I?" She giggled, dropping her spoon in the bowl and putting her hands to her face, which began to turn red. They both laughed. He loved the little girl in her.

"I think he's going to think twice about just casually putting his hand on a strange woman after that," said Mike. "By the way, you owe me for that one. Technically, he could have charged you with assault. I talked him down for you."

"Well," she said, rising and wiping her hands and face with her napkin, "very Special Agent Michael Soul, what can I do to make it up to you?" She winked as she circled around and approached him, then stood between his knees and looked down at him, her earlier damp hair now frizzed from the shower. She crinkled her nose at him, then eased into his lap and straddled him, her hands behind his neck. She was wearing a light sundress and her neck and chest smelled like baby lotion. He pulled her close and hugged her, rubbing her back.

"You know," he began, "I want to make love to you, but after hearing your story, I don't know how you want me to be with you. I just want to respect your boundaries. And I am happy to be here with you this weekend and relax. We can just chill; we can swim, hike, play board games, whatever."

She pulled away from him, appreciation in her eyes. "Well," she said, running her fingers playfully up his abdomen and chest, "why don't you just hold me tonight? That would mean a lot."

"You got it," he whispered, putting his forehead to hers.

They went to bed that evening with him doing just that—holding her and nothing more. Sometime around 2:30 a.m., Mike awoke from a relaxing sleep to something vibrating, then realized it was the bed. He grunted and looked around. It was Emmy. She was shaking and crying, seeming childlike in a tight, tiny embryo position.

"Hey," he said, moving closer to her and pulling her tightly to him. "It's okay. Shhhhh. It's okay; you're safe." Her fighter's body heaved in great movements, the sobbing intensifying, as she tried to hide her face in her hands.

"Oh, God—the things they did to me." She cried harder. "Shit, Mike, what they *said* to me . . . the names, Michael—the goddamned names they called me. What they *took* from me. What they took from *my people* . . . Ohhh, God!" she bawled. He held her so tight he began to sweat almost immediately. But he stayed close as she poured out the kind of sorrow he had never known.

"I love you, Emily. I'm here. Shhhhhh . . ."

Mike was relieved when the air conditioning kicked into its high gear cycle. He pulled the sheet around them and patted her side and kissed her forehead and wiped her tears. He knew there was nothing he could say. He could only be.

24

Answer the Phone

Present Day
McNair House
Muskogee, Oklahoma
District Four, Cherokee Nation

Molly's ringtone demanded her attention. "Hello?"

"Osiyo, Molly. This is Tommy Drum, from the Remember the Removal office. How are you doing today?"

"Oh, fine, I guess."

"Yeah? Listen, I want you to know I heard something from Sara Amos and, ah, I don't want to pry, Molly, but she said your sister is sick, and, ah, just checking in to see how you're doing, especially with your knee and all."

"Well, I'm sad, you know . . ."

"I'm sure you must be, Molly. What's going on?"

"Emmy has breast cancer."

"I see," he replied, though Molly sensed that he had already known and just didn't want to presume.

"Well, we want—that is, the staff here—we want you to know that we are sending smoke and prayers, Molly, and we are here if you need us for anything."

"Thanks," she said, a lump in her throat.

"We're all proud of your sister, by the way. She's a fantastic fighter, I'm sure in more ways than one. I know you must be proud, too."

Molly realized she was unable to talk; nothing would come when she tried to speak.

"Molly? You there?"

Molly wept. The significance of her sister's situation and her own injury was becoming more real with each passing day, each conversation. Now she found herself in breakdown mode.

"It's okay, Molly. I will sit here, at my kitchen table, and stay on the phone with you for as long as you need, okay? Do you hear what I'm saying to you, Molly?"

Molly nodded, then realized that he couldn't see her. Finally, she spoke.

"Wado, Tommy. Oh, Jesus, I'm afraid I'm gonna lose my sister, Tommy. I don't want her to die!"

"I know. It's okay, Molly." He sat, as he promised, and listened as Molly spoke about how she has always looked up to Emmy and tried to be like her. He let her talk for a good ten or fifteen minutes, then tried to reassure her with the knowledge that medicine has come a long way and that Emmy had access to great doctors.

"My training is starting to slack off, Tommy. I just don't have any energy on some days, plus, this knee starts to get better—at least it feels like it—then it starts hurting again. That IHS doctor said it was an unusually bad jolt to the knee and I really don't know why, 'cause I was just peddling is all. Anyway, I'm tryin' to walk most days."

"That seems reasonable, Molly, given all that you are dealing with. Molly, time being what it is, summer closing in on us and whatnot, I think it would be best for you to set aside the race this year. I want you to know I held out as long as I could, but I have to make a tough decision. I know that's a hard pill to swallow, but that's what seems to make the most sense right now. I will personally see to it that we hold you a place for next year if you still want to ride then. Everyone will understand, Molly, so don't you worry about that."

She winced at the thought of putting off the ride a year. She had already put in so much time and training. She felt herself getting in better and better shape. But she knew Tommy was right.

"Okay," she said. "I wouldn't want to do anything to slow down the progress of the other riders. This is killing me, though, Tommy. It hurts more than my damn knee."

"I have no doubt about that, Molly. You know, it's hard to envision at your age, but as you get older, time really flies, and next year's ride will be here before you know it. The waiting will seem agonizing at times but, if I know you like I think I do, you'll be going on to college later this year and your plate will be full with some pretty important things. If I have anything to say about it, the ride will always be there. Meantime, you just hang in there; don't be hard on yourself about any of this. What will be will be, okay?"

She hated that expression. "Okay, Tommy, thanks for calling. I'll talk to you later."

"*Dona dago huh ee*," he said. "Call me if you need anything."

"Okay, bye." She just sat there, numb. She felt like a tree stump in the woods, rotting away for decades until someone comes along to carve her up into dust. She had never felt so alone and afraid: afraid for Emmy and for her own future.

Molly had moved from the kitchen table to her bedroom, contemplating her life, the conversation with Tommy, Emmy's cancer, and everything else. What if there's no college, after all?

Life really is just one big piece of flaming dog shit, left at someone's doorstep only to be hosed down and smashed flat. Fuck everything and everybody.

What if you walked in my tracks and not someone else's?

"Oh, shit. Please, don't start with me," she said to herself, wiping her nose with her forearm. She stood and snatched a tissue from the container on her dresser, then sat in her chair again, which faced the small desk where she did her homework each night. The desk was a family heirloom, passed down from her father's mother's side. It was a mahogany antique, with a nice flat surface with rounded corners. She wiped her nose, then placed her head in her hands and just squeezed.

We're a tribe, but never forget that you don't have to be part of a group to express the best of yourself.

Molly wasn't sure what to make of this. It was the clearest message she had yet received. It hung there, in the void of space and time. What was that supposed to mean—the best part of myself? She waited for another message. Nothing. Seriously? She tried to be as quiet and introspective as she could be. It was so quiet that she could hear a yellow jacket or bee just outside her window—and the air conditioning was running. Please, she silently begged, say something else. Anything.

-Silence-

See! See? It's all just bullshit, isn't it? You, this goddamn ride, cancer, this fucking hick city, Devon. You're all just a bunch of damn liars and hypocrites! And *screw* your bullshit self-pity jokes and play-on-words Indian crap!

I believe in you, Pretty Feet. Why else would I be here?

To fuck me over.

Never.

Look, you've got the wrong person. I'm not—I'm not *equipped* or whatever for this!

Then how would you explain this conversation?

I *wouldn't* explain it! It's not a conversation, lady! You're not even here, goddammit! Look, I just wanna be left alone. I can't handle all this. I just can't. No damn wonder Becks gets high all the time. I get it now. That's what I'm gonna do. I need to find Becks and hit her up for some of that shit. I'd rather have crazy conversations with some mechanical Cherokee medicine man with sexy eyes than put up with this shit any longer. To *hell* with everything!

Your phone is ringing.

Are you *listening* to me?! Why can't I get a break here? Rebecca and Tara have each other, all my other girlfriends have guys or girls or whatever, and I just push guys away. I pushed the ride away. I push my whole life away. It's a freakin' mess is what it is, and you don't really actually give a shit, do you? I mean, like, really. Emmy's practically famous now and lands this really hot guy 'cause she's like, well, *such* a babe, but me? Noooooooooooooo!

Answer the phone.

I'm so tired. This fucking book report. Gotta get going with that. And gotta get some new clothes, some shoes never mind . . .

Molly realized her phone had been vibrating on the desk beneath her. It was face down. Truth be told, she didn't even want to look at it. But something made her flip it over. It read "Maybe Clayton Blackfox" just before going to voicemail.

"Oh, *shit*! Oh, holy crap," she whispered. She quickly put the phone down as if it had burned her, seizing the end of her hair and biting on it. She eyed it, as if it might sprout wings and take off down the hall. The last time she saw Clay, he was taller. He had nice, dark skin with the kind eyes she remembered as a kid. He had, like, a really great chiseled jawline, and—

The phone buzzed briefly, indicating a voicemail. Molly slowly looked to her right and then down, then up, then to her left, downward then upward again. Nothing. No voice. Just the quiet of her room. She clicked to confirm the voicemail was from Clay. She wondered why he had called. Before they had only been communicating via social app. Tall, with a chiseled jawline. She sat there with her mouth open.

25

The Only Good Indian

Waynesboro, Tennessee
Along the Green River
Bell Detachment Camp
Old Cherokee Nation

The John Bell detachment was not Captain Ambrose's first experience with Cherokee removal, and he had learned some hard lessons during the previous trips. He was prone on this trip to allow frequent stops and breaks, though he still had his orders and a schedule to keep. He knew he couldn't allow the Cherokees to linger for long, sick or not, dying or not. Despite what Nick McNair might have thought, he was doing his best to be humane while at the same time expedient, and he was going to demonstrate that. Unfortunately, insensitivity to the Cherokees abounded. Wagon drivers would inform the wagon master about a sick or dying Cherokee, and the response was usually "Keep moving!" and "Drive on!" From Nick's point of view, this negligence and abuse was the typical southern American attitude. From Captain Ambrose's perspective, it was just the opposite. The more religious among them had their observations as well.

Entry of missionary Simon Rhodes:

The poor but resolute Indians have managed to drag themselves from encampment to encampment. There have been fights and sickness and death and despair. The Lord is most assuredly our rock and our salvation. What little clothes they came with, most of them only that which they had on their backs, have been destroyed by the elements or simple usage and many of those not destroyed have been left by the wayside on dusty trails or in creeks or rivers because daily use has proven exhaustible.

Many of the Cherokees do not trust white doctors and some have suffered mightily and others have died due to this distrust. Food has been quite scarce. Rations for the Indians have been mostly kept to coffee, green corn that they roast, and foraging nuts. We started out with ample supplies of bacon but much of that seems to have gone by the wayside and I do not think the Cherokees are to blame. Once in a great while the soldiers will kill a buffalo and share some of the meat with the Indians. But much of the time the poor savages are destined for lesser things such as the slippery elm bark they often find to sustain themselves. They seem expert at locating these trees and will use their knives to strip the bark from the tree and the chief hunter passes the strips around until the others are fed before he partakes himself. They are a Noble breed.

It is my estimation that more will die before we complete this journey. I have endeavored to preach the gospel nightly and a small group from the party will attend, usually more Cherokees, interestingly enough, than the whites who are often busying themselves with card games and whiskey. The devil is a roaming fortress who finds habitation in this detachment with abandon and soon I'm afraid the great battle for their souls will play out on these ungodly trails and river-creeks.

Captain Ambrose and Lieutenant Whitworth, after going up and down the line of wagons, riders, and walkers, called a meeting using runners to alert those invited. It was evident that Ambrose wanted the wealthiest Cherokees to attend. It had something to do with money. It always did. Toward evening a runner stopped by the McNair's meager campsite and told Nick about the captain's meeting, which would be held in the small clearing northwest of their campsite. Nick ensured his family was secure and made his way there.

When Nick arrived, he found Captain Ambrose, Lieutenant Whitworth, and Sergeant Hollingsworth—his least favorite sergeant—standing amid a small but growing group of men. Other Cherokees present were Moses McDaniel, John Bell, Catcher, John Sanders, Drowning Bear, and Archy Preacher—all well-to-do-enough Cherokees who had hired out their wagons and some supplies for the journey. Nick, John Sanders, and the Drowning Bear had been neighbors, and they stood together. Putting his hand on Sanders's shoulder, Nick asked what they were discussing.

"Our funds," said John. "They are asking for some of it back, Nick. They're dipping into what they already gave us. Can you believe this?"

"The hell you say!" said Nick. Sanders nodded.

A handful of other wagon owners arrived, Ellis Hogner and Absolom Taylor among them. Nick nodded to the newcomers as Captain Ambrose brought things to order.

"Listen, people, we're running low on funds and need to borrow some to get us through. And you folks are gonna cooperate, you understand?"

The men just stood there, some mumbling among a few of them. Nick gritted his teeth. Now, he thought, now I've seen every goddamn thing.

After what amounted to a lecture from Ambrose, the Cherokees were ordered back to their respective camps. Drowning Bear didn't speak English well and was silent on the walk back. John Sanders was furious.

"Look," he said, stopping Nick with his hand and turning back to look at Ambrose, still in discussion with his men, "why don't we just get the word out among our people . . . and we just rush them once and for all and kill them? There's more of us than them!"

Nick shook his head. "Even if we could do that, John, we'd never get away with it. The main reason I supported the treaty was because we must minimize the loss of life of our people. We do something like that and I guarantee you the government will send so many troops they will just kill us all. That's what Major Ridge and Mary's brothers were trying to avoid in the first place. If we resist through great numbers—especially using violent means—they'll just massacre us. No one will be left. You want *all* of our people to be wiped from the face of the earth? Jackson was a crazy son of a bitch, but this Van Buren is worse. The motherfucker's disposition to extreme violence and anarchy oughta be obvious to anybody now."

John Sanders looked at his friend and nodded slowly. He visibly shook. Nick put his arm around his friend's shoulder and escorted him back. He turned to Drowning Bear, who was still silent but had picked up most of what Nick said.

"What do you think, Yona?"

Drowning Bear stopped, looked back at the soldiers in the distance, and said, "We been best to fight. Best to fight white army men."

"No," Nick said, shaking his head.

"Yes."

"No, sir. No!" Nick was adamant, but so was Drowning Bear.

"You," said Drowning Bear while pounding his open palm on Nick's chest, "you—respect. No hard feeling. But me—no coward. I cut throat now," he said, moving back toward the soldiers.

'No!" exclaimed Nick. "No, no cut throat, for God's sake, not here, not now," he insisted, dragging his friend back. Sanders got on the other side of Drowning Bear and they escorted him back before there was even more death to contend with.

Later in the evening, Wattie Muskrat, another Cherokee woman going into labor, was disrupting the detachment at the far end of the line. She had been falling behind for weeks and now was so close to birthing that she convulsed in pain spasms and screamed. Her blood was leaving a trail for animals, some predatory. The soldiers had run out of patience. A private approached Sergeant Hollingsworth.

"Whad'ya wanna do about her?" he inquired. Two other soldiers had gathered. Sergeant Hollingsworth seemed to consider the situation.

"She's holdin' us up," he finally said. "Can't have that. Kill the bitch," he commanded coldly.

"*Sergeant*?" said the private, his eyes widening.

"You heard me."

"Yessir, but, ah, I dunno, Sarge, I think—"

"It ain't your damn job to think, private; it's mine. Now do as I say."

Another private spoke up. "Sergeant, that's against regulations. We can't—"

Hollingsworth slapped his face. "I'm goddamned running out of patience with this shit, boys, and you can bet I ain't shutting down this here part of the detachment and facing a discipline 'cause of this Indian whore. Hell, I bet she can't even tell you whose kid that is. Get rid of her!" The men just looked at one another. Finally, after a period of silence, Hollingsworth threw his hands up. "All right, boys, all right. Forget I said anything. I'll figure somethin' out. Get back to your stations. Disperse!" The men nodded and, relieved, returned to their assigned areas of the detachment.

The Green River and the area tributaries had been filled with unseasonable rushes of sometimes blinding showers that would last for days. Sergeant Hollingsworth lit a cigar as another rainstorm moved in over the detachment. He sat back against a rock and considered his options. He had joined up under Andrew Jackson and had seen little action. Coming from a broken home with an abusive father and an alcoholic mother, he longed for the open prairie and a chance to get his hands dirty for God and country. He flicked the remainder of his cigar into the woods, and it was instantly extinguished by the increasing and cold raindrops. He muttered a few obscenities before gaining an hour or so of shut-eye.

Wattie Muskrat went down the bank to the cold river to wash. Her pains were almost beyond comprehension at this point. She found herself drifting in and out of consciousness a number of times. With no husband or family to help her, she was one of the unfortunate ones who were on their own. At the rear of the detachment, stragglers faced the ever-present possibility of being left behind to fend for themselves.

She made her way back up the bank, pulling her rain-soaked and deteriorating dress up so she could waddle up the hill. Dodging the protruding rocks, she looked up just in time to see Sergeant Hollingsworth stick his bayonet into her heart. She gasped a long, wheezing breath, her eyes wide and mouth open. It felt so odd that she didn't think for a second that it was supposed to hurt. As she exhaled and breathed in again in a long, sucking motion laced with some of the blood that had filled her lungs, he yanked the bayonet out and jammed it straight through her right eye. He released the weapon and turned Wattie to face the river, then kicked her back down the hill, her body flipping in different directions as she bounced off the rocks on the way down. She hit the water with a dull thud, followed by a barely audible splashing sound muffled by the pouring rain.

Sergeant Hollingsworth sauntered down to the water to rinse his bayonet. He grunted as he watched Muskrat and her unborn baby float downstream. *One less filthy straggler.* He returned to his rock to get another hour or two of sleep before the morning preparations for the day's journey. He knew that no one would ever know. Any questions from the rear, and he just needed a good story. She probably just fell off a cliff. How the hell else would you explain it, sirs?

Just another savage, just another Indian, and, as was so often said, "The only good Indian was a dead Indian."

26

The Delight Behind the Demons

Office of Marie Trevino
Fort Gibson, Oklahoma
District Four, Cherokee Nation

Emmy had installed a state-of-the-art sound system in *Ned Christie*. As she turned down the road leading to Marie's building, she drove slowly, listening to her chill-out playlist. Everything seemed slow today. One of her favorite seventies jazz tunes, "Land of Make Believe" by Chuck Mangione, was playing, and it never failed to soothe and invigorate her at the same time. She pulled into a parking space close to Marie's first-floor office, shifted to neutral, and just listened. Once described by Marie as "a bit of an old soul," she closed her eyes to the instrumental and let it invade her being. She practiced her breathing as she allowed everything pleasant of late to overcome the less pleasant. She opened her eyes, turned off the ignition, and went in to face her demons.

Emmy stared at her therapist. Something about Emmy's energy cued Marie to be more alert than usual, discerning. She sat upright, not quite her usual relaxed-but-alert posture, her notebook closed but ready. She set her own breathing cadence, smiled warmly, and looked her patient in the eye.

"Well," said Emmy, "I told him."

"Told him what?"

Emmy gave her a look. "Really? I mean, seriously?"

"You mean about the rape?"

"Yes."

"Okay. And how did he take that?"

"Ah, good. Great, actually."

Marie nodded, making a note.

Silence.

After at least a minute, Emmy rubbed her temples, kicked off her slides, and curled her knees to her chest, her preferred posture in psychotherapy. She rubbed her thighs through her jeans. "I felt small, Marie, just *small*. Hate feeling like that." She shook her head. "Shit . . ."

"What do you mean 'small,' Emmy?"

"I dunno. Just . . . damn. Small. I had a meltdown after bed. We had *such* a great conversation during and after dinner. I felt like I could tell Michael anything. He's a great listener." Marie smiled and nodded.

Silence.

"We had a great time and I just went and fucked it up by having a meltdown in the middle of the night. I did my 'cradle' thing—just fucking fell apart."

"How so?"

"Goddammit, you know how . . . me and my chickenshit PTSD in the middle of the fucking night is how! What the hell do you think?" She put her hands to her face. "Ah, I'm sorry, Marie. Don't mean to take it out on you." She started to cry and Marie nodded toward the tissue box.

"That's why I charge the insurance companies the big bucks. Pretty sure I can take it, Emmy," she said with a smile. Emmy laughed and wiped her eyes with a tissue.

Silence.

"I'm such a fucking coward, Marie. He held me there—so sweetly—while I shriveled up like a pathetic prune. Just when I think I'm getting past this thing, *fuck it!*" She slugged the back of the sofa with a stout backfist, dust escaping the fabric in a small cloud. Leaning forward, hands to her head, she massaged her temples again. She looked at Marie. "Sorry, really."

"Flea market shit," said Marie with a shake of her head. "We'll take it out of your next session," she added with a wink.

"Wouldn't blame you," said Emmy, hugging her knees again.

"You said Michael was understanding, comforting, even— if I'm hearing you right?"

Emmy nodded.

"Do you sense that he's burdened by your experience? That is, does it seem as if this discovery is too much for him to handle? Let's not forget what the man does for a living."

"No, it's just that . . . I just can't get past this notion of coming so far—with you, the UFC, grad school." Marie nodded and furiously scribbled in her notes. "I just keep reverting back to this little girl, this cradle coward that won't go the hell away."

Emmy spent the better part of the hour processing her fear and frustration. In time, she took a deep breath and noticed how exhausted she felt. Strange that she could be a pro athlete and yet exhausted by an hour of talking. Her self-blame was debilitating. Marie put her pen on the coffee table and turned her notes face down. She leaned forward slightly with a lighthearted expression.

"Emmy, I'm going to make a rare—oh, I don't know—once every year or so therapist confession, with an observation." Emmy gave Marie her full attention. "I never told you, but I watched your fight with LaToya Ortiz on pay-TV. Frankly, aside from the Olympics, I've never seen a woman do anything like what I saw you do in that cage. It was awe-inspiring. Breathtaking, actually. Almost like something from outer space. Violent, to be sure, but I think I understand your mission in all that. You lived through hell on earth as a young co-ed and have managed to turn that nightmare into the noble objective of serving your people in the field of public health and representing them as a fighting warrior. And I'm reflecting on how you responded to those men at the Archway, how you protected Molly—evidently without a second thought."

Emmy nodded, considering Marie's observation.

"You've evolved into a protective force, a way of being, it appears."

"What do you mean?"

Marie pondered. "Well, for one, you're a professional fighter. Not just for yourself, but for your tribe; that seems obvious. You represent a feminine force of nature. Two, suppose, God forbid—and I *do* mean God forbid—suppose one of these mass shooters we're so plagued with entered this building right now. Or maybe some sexual deviant from off the street looking to do his thing. Not that I would require or expect it, but I would imagine you would protect me. It's just who you are—who you've become." She shook her head slightly. "'Cradle coward'? *Seriously*?" She then gave her patient an "I doubt it" look and turned her notes right side up again. Emmy thought she spotted a tear in the corner of Marie's eye. "And it's okay— more than okay—for that little girl in you to come out in the middle of the night. She's gonna have to go *somewhere*. She's looking for a place of safety. Maybe she found it in Michael. And maybe that's a place he needs right now to show his love for you. Just a thought on that regarding Mike, not a conclusion. More of a question."

Emmy smiled and nodded, then looked down, rubbing her thighs again.

"I just don't like that part of myself, ya know?"

Silence.

"I want to be rid of it, but I know better. I have enough education and enough distance from it to know better. And Michael . . . he's just, he's . . . he's a little *too* good, you know what I mean? I mean, he just *had* to come along at this time in my life. Damn."

"How so?"

Emmy sighed. "You know . . . he's, he's what I always wanted in a guy and . . . oh, dammit." The tears welled up again. "He's just, just, *inconveniently spectacular*." She threw her hands up and sighed again and looked at Marie. Marie looked

Emmy in the eye, unblinking. Emmy quipped, "Um, can I phone a friend? Maybe do a 50:50 or ask the audience?"

"Nope."

Emmy laughed and pulled more tissues as Marie returned to her notes. Emmy stretched out her legs, then crossed her left over her right. "Did I ever tell you . . . did I ever say that Eddie took a shine to me because, as he put it, I hit like a man?"

Marie nodded without looking up from her notes.

"He said, 'Never seen anything like you, dreamboat! 'Cept you remind me of Gina Carano—hit like a dude while breaking their hearts with your smoldering beauty.'" Marie smiled at that. "He even said, 'Hell, *I'm* scared of you, and I don't scare, bitch!'" They both laughed.

Silence.

Thinking it through, Emmy said, "I guess I just don't want to screw things up this time. I don't want to frighten this guy away."

"Frighten him away?"

"Well, not literally, of course. I mean, he's a pretty tough guy—being a cop and all that. Just . . . the breakdowns, the night sweats, the anxiety. That's a lot to put on any guy, especially one as busy as Michael, and especially because of what he does for a living. But I like what you said about that possibly being a way for him to share his love for me."

Marie nodded and scribbled.

"He's got a great ass by the way, did I ever tell you that?"

Marie smiled and shook her head. "No, but *so* good to know, girlfriend," she said, playfully tapping her temple with her finger.

"Yeah," said Emmy, lost in thought. "Just . . ." holding up her palms, as if taking a photo, "just . . . yum, pow—right there, makes me just wanna slap it like he's a miniature Chippendale on a Shetland pony. *Smack!*"

"Well, all righty then!"

Emmy laughed, bringing her arms up and hugging herself, feeling the powerful air conditioner send cold air through Marie's ceiling vent. She gazed out the window at the river.

"Emmy," Marie began, "pretty soon our time will be up. I want to encourage you to think about how being vulnerable with Mike is or is not hamstringing you. Are you giving this guy the credit he deserves—that is, in the area of understanding and response? Do you fully trust Mike, and do you believe he fully trusts you in the day-to-day of things? That sort of thing. Also, in looking at your family diagram, I'm curious about the triangle between you, Mike, and your dad. Remember when we talked about this before? Though your father's dead, we can presume an emotional connection between him and you, and think about how that might play into the emotional process between you and Michael. And let's not forget the ancients— those grandmothers and aunts—and the role they have played in your formation, especially during your recovery."

Emmy wore her intense look as she stared out the window at the calm of the winding river. It was the look of uncompromising integrity, the look of determination and ferocity that made Emmy "The Cherokee Storm," the look that struck fear into opponents who realized after being in the cage with her less than sixty seconds that they had made an irreversible mistake. It wasn't a perpetual look, yet somehow one affected by the space-time continuum, ever present in another reality, always ready to come back to this one, the same look that said, *No one will ever touch me like that again and live to tell about it.*

"We can take it up from there next time, yes?"

Emmy came back to earth, nodded, and put both feet on the floor. She smiled, raised her right palm, and said, "Wado, sista!" Marie slapped her palm in response.

7:00 pm
Emmy's Bungalow
Muskogee, Oklahoma

Emmy and Mike were stretched out on the carpet after dinner. Mike had the next two days off, and Emmy relished the precious time together. She had bought him a Cherokee Nation T-shirt—a sky blue one, to match his eyes—and he wore it along with a pair of khaki shorts. They were stretching, part of her regular routine, and Mike was finding it helpful, since he was in a car or at a desk doing paperwork much of his day. He kept getting whiffs of her Black Rose perfume, making it hard for him to concentrate on what he was doing. They were side by side, facing the front door. He glanced her way. She wore her full ponytail especially for him. Tonight she had it up high and had made it as thick as she could. She was in one of her tank tops—an orange one—she refused to wear pink—and a gray pair of sweatpants. She smiled at him and winked.

"Do the guys come on to you a lot? You know—at the gym or school or what-have-you?"

"Nah," she said with a dismissive shake of her head.

"No? Really?"

"You kiddin'? Most of them are scared to death of me! 'Sides, they don't like a woman who can fight. It's intimidating. They don't want to believe that I can beat their ass, even though most of the time they know it's true."

"Seriously?"

She grinned. "Actually, they *all* want me, Mikey-Mike. They write me love notes, send me flowers, buy me drinks, whisper in my ear—all when you're out of town, of course." She laughed.

"Hey!" he yelled, quickly rolling on top of her. "I'll hunt them all down, Goddess. Make them all wish their fathers had never met their mothers." He made a face at her. She trapped his legs with hers and instantly flipped him over, pinning him.

"So glad to hear that," she said with a twinkle in her eye. "That was the right answer!" She touched her fingers to her lips and kissed them, then placed them on his. "It's okay," she said, "you can still be my bitch." She snorted and laughed. "Oh, hey," she said, "don't forget to do a brief downward dog. It will help stretch that lumbar region. Too much time in the squad car, bro."

He nodded and stretched upward, taking a minute to flex everything and relax, then lowered himself. This time, they stretched out, facing each other, resting on their elbows. Emmy reached for his hand, wrapping hers around it gently. She caressed it, turning it back and forth, as if examining it for study. She looked at him and moved her eyebrows up and down. He held her hand firmly, then kissed it. She smiled, tightening her grip.

"Wanna go for it?" she asked, clearly challenging him to arm wrestle. Her smile widened.

"You've got to be kidding me," he said with a funny look.

"I'll crush you," she said, "like a grape in a wine press. *Bitch*."

"Ha-ha. Pretty funny, but I think I'll pass," he said as he shook his head.

Emmy clucked like a chicken.

"You think that's gonna make me wrestle you?"

"Bak-bak-bak, baaaaaaaaaaaaak!"

He glared at her. "Doesn't seem right, Em. It's not because you're a woman, it's just, just ... I don't know—weird, ya know?"

"You've tussled with women before, right? Cuffed 'em?"

"Yeah, but that's, I don't know—different somehow. I don't wanna wrestle *you*. You're my lady."

"Berrk," she quickly squawked.

"SERIOUSLY?" Now he was irritated.

She held on with her right hand and made a flapping motion under her arm with her left, grinning uncontrollably. She found this hilarious.

"All right, dammit! Now you've done it!" he said, pulling back the upper part of the sleeve on his Cherokee Nation shirt and flexing. She loved the freckles on his shoulder. "You're gonna wish you never started this." He shook his head in exasperation.

"*Berrk!*" she gobbled once again, firing him up even more and flicking his right nostril with her left index finger. She squeezed his hand harder and he steadied himself. Her tank top showed off her incredible arm and shoulder muscles.

"You're gonna regret this, Em, I swear to God," he said, flinching and rubbing his nose. "You can only push me so far. You think you got my number, but you don't. I can put up with a lot of bull, but I'm telling you—"

"We gonna do this," she interrupted, "or are you gonna charge me money for that speech?"

"Oh, you are *so* gonna regret this!" he roared.

"Oh, I'm so *skured*," she teased with a giggle, which pissed him off even more.

They readied themselves, each trying to stare the other down. As they did, she blew on the inside of his left wrist.

"Hey, cut the shit, will you?" he whined.

"What? You had some lint there." She half-snorted and tried her best not to chortle. They locked eyes.

"Ready?" she said, tightening her grip to the point that Mike was beginning to question the very essence of his manhood. They stared as the tension rose. Emmy's eyes twinkled, her seductive upper lip protruding.

"GO!" she said, and off they went. Hmm, she thought, he's stronger than I would have guessed. She flexed her bicep and focused her energy into her wrist with her mind. She smiled as his neck muscles bulged. He pressed on the floor with his left hand for support.

"Huh-uh, nope!" she admonished.

He stopped, struggled for a moment, then gave it his all.

Not a wimp, that's for sure, she thought, secretly proud of him. This must be hard, she guessed. Would be for any self-respecting guy. She started it, though. She aimed to finish. But she felt him taking the lead.

"Mike," she said in a barely perceptible whisper as her arm began to give. He didn't look up.

"Michael," she said, a little louder.

"Nope, ain't doin' it," he said, straining, his face turning red now as he forced her arm. "Ain't lookin'."

"Michael, please," she said in a pitiful voice.

He glanced up, perhaps wondering if he had hurt her. As he did, she gave him the most voluptuous, sultry, and deliberate air-kiss she could muster, closing her eyes in the sexiest manner possible. She then leaned closer and blew directly on his lips.

"Oh, *shiiiittt!*" was all he could say as she slammed his arm to the carpet. He rolled onto his back, desperately trying to catch a breath.

"Whoo-hoo!" she roared, then laughed with her trademark snort, rolling over on him. She giggled and kissed his chest. "Ooooh, Mikey," she teased, squeezing his chin, "you are so *charming* when you hyperventilate!"

"Oh, my God, you cheater! You little cheating, be-atch! Disqualification, disqualification!" he managed to shout.

"All's fair in the cage, bitch!" she teased. She gently cradled his hand again, then kissed it.

"You win, I guess," he said, gazing up at her, his blue eyes sparkling.

She leaned down and kissed him softly.

"Michael?"

"Yeah?"

"Make love to me."

He lifted his head, looking at her quizzically.

"You sure?"

She nodded.

"Look," he said, "your situation is different, Em. I want it to be just right. I want you to be positive."

She drilled him with her mocha-chocolate-mocha browns. "I am," she said.

"Yeah?" he asked, taking her ponytail in his hands and rubbing it, running his hand through it.

"Yes. Make love to me, Michael. *Please.*"

He nodded and then kissed her forehead. She smiled and rested her head on his chest. When they awoke the next morning, Emmy knew she found someone she could love for the long-term.

27

You're Going to Have to Do More

November 1838
Bell Detachment
Indian Creek Region, Tennessee
Old Cherokee Nation

Enoch was busy repairing broken spokes on the McNair wagon, while Annabelle occupied herself cleaning the McNair family's clothes. She made multiple trips to the creek and a nearby cottonmouth barely missed her when she didn't see it resting on the bank near the water and got too close. Sergeant Hollingsworth rode up to the McNair's portion of the camp and slowed his horse when he saw Enoch steadfastly at work.

"You!" he shouted. "Yeah, you, boy. Drop what you're doing there and get over here and take a look at my horse's shoe." Enoch looked up, then glanced at Nick, who was stretching out some leather that had gotten soaked from the rains. The weather was turning cold and with that came some sunshine. "I say *now*, jigaboo! Getcha skinny ass over here and check these shoes for loosenin'." Nick nodded to Enoch.

"Best do as he says, Enoch. You can finish that wheel later. It's okay—go on now," Nick said with a nod.

"Yezz-sir," said Enoch, shuffling over to Sergeant Hollingsworth as he dismounted.

"Check that rear left shoe, boy," said the soldier, spitting on the ground. Enoch just looked at him and squatted next to the horse to examine the hooves.

Sergeant Hollingsworth removed his hat and hit it against his leg to knock the road dust off. He glanced back up at Nick, who flattened the leather as best he could, shaping it with his palm in the sun. He had a bad feeling about Hollingsworth and mostly tried to ignore him on the sojourn.

Hollingsworth belched and rubbed his nose with the back of his hand. He glanced toward the creek and sneered. "That's a fine lookin' Indian woman you gotcha yerself, there, Mr. Mac-Nair. Yessirree, fine looking woman indeed," Hollingsworth repeated, watching Mary help Annabelle with the clothes. "My guess is she was worth the trouble you had to go to!" He leered at Mary, following the outline of her body as she worked.

Without saying a word, Nick walked to the rear of the wagon, reached under a covering, and pulled his Springfield Model 1835 rifle from underneath. He swung it out, marched over to Hollingsworth, and took aim, cocking the weapon. Each Cherokee family in this particular detachment was permitted one firearm and this was his.

"Listen to me, you foul-minded, dirt-scraping, ass-sniffing *mule fucker*!" He got close enough to Hollingsworth to kill him with the rifle, but not close enough for the soldier to grab it. Several other soldiers jumped up and rushed over, covering Nick with their own rifles, and ordered him to drop it. Lieutenant Whitworth rode up just in time to see it all unfolding.

"McNair! What the hell are you doing? Drop it, now!"

"Lieutenant," said Nick, aiming directly for the sergeant's startled face, "we got ourselves a *dicey* situation here! You tell this backwoods ape to shut his fucking face when it comes to my wife, or I'll blow his balls all the way back to Fort Cass, you understand me?"

"Drop it, McNair—right now!" Whitworth commanded, bringing his own weapon to the ready.

"Understand something, *all* you motherfuckers!" Nick roared, steadfast in his posture, eyes wide and looking around him. Nearby campers were staring at him—including Mary, who put a hand to her mouth and headed in his direction. Her husband had reached his limits, and his crazed eyes and manner were unnerving. "We are NOT under your goddamned command! You are *escorting* this party, assholes! You're supposed to be protecting us! We're not your soldiers, and I'm telling you I don't like this son of a bitch!" He looked back at Lieutenant Whitworth, then turned violently toward Hollingsworth with his rifle. "Go on, dammit, tell him I don't like him! Do it now, Lieutenant!"

"McNair don't like you, Sergeant!" the lieutenant yelled, trying to avoid a mutiny. "Back off of him now!" Hollingsworth slowly eased back a couple of steps.

"Tell him I'm gonna kill his ass if he acts untoward in this camp again—tell him that, goddammit!"

"You heard the man, Sergeant! All right, all right, McNair, calm down, just *calm down*," the lieutenant said, lowering his weapon and signaling the others to do the same. "Let's just take it easy here, all right?"

"Here's what you do, Lieutenant: You tell that fucking Ambrose that this guy disrespects my wife again, you're gonna have a damn funeral on your hands. You hear me, mister? You tell him that!" He took two steps toward Hollingsworth, aiming the rifle at his private parts. "You get the hell out of my camp and get out of my face, donkey-humper, or President Van Buren's gonna be sending your mama a sympathy note for Christmas with your blood on it, you pasty-faced potato-masher! Get outta my space, bastard!" Nick raised the rifle again to the soldier's head, taking careful aim at his nose. Hollingsworth held up his hands, as if to ward off an oncoming shot with his arms.

"Sergeant!" commanded Lieutenant Whitworth, "report to Captain Ambrose—on the double. Move out!"

"Yes, sir!" said Hollingsworth, clearly surprised and shaken. He took his horse back from Enoch, who had managed to make one repair with a hammer, and rode away.

As things cooled down, Nick put his rifle back, aware that his wife had caught most of the last part of the exchange. He looked at her and she looked down, and he wondered how hurt she might have been because of all of this. Lieutenant Whitworth dismounted, apologized to Nick and Mary for his man's behavior, and said he would speak to Captain Ambrose about it.

"That man should *not* be wearing the uniform of the United States, Lieutenant. I don't trust that bastard; he's been up to no good since we set out. I know your men think you can get by with a lot out here, but not all of us are ignorant, confused, 'tree trash' as some of your people like to say. I'm puttin' you on notice, sir, and the whole damn army as far as I'm concerned. Certain indignities will *not* be tolerated," Nick said, his arm now around his wife's waist. She had marched up to be with her husband, and grabbed the back of his pants to keep him from walking anywhere.

As Nick's speech had grown to its crescendo, numerous mixed-blood Cherokees—most of them well-educated with money—began to appear from around wagons, trees, and mule teams. Moses McDaniel, John Baldridge, Bill and Harry Crittenton, George Falling—who had appeared with his own rifle—Ed Shipley, David Welch, and a few others slowly approached and stood behind Nick in an act of solidarity.

Lieutenant Whitworth tried to reassure the Cherokees, but they were doubtful, based on events to date. When the conversation ended, Nick turned to see his neighbors smile and nod their approval, John Baldridge and George Falling patting Nick on the shoulder before walking away. Later, in a moment of quiet reflection as they were getting the wagon in order for the next leg of the journey, Mary took her husband's right hand and rubbed it, admiring it—and him.

She pulled his hand to her face, kissed his knuckles, and said, "James, second chapter: 'For as the body apart from the spirit is dead, so also faith apart from works is dead." Her Sunday school teacher experience had not deserted her. He smiled and looked down. When he looked up again, she was slowly walking away, her hair pulled up in a large, tied cloth, looking at him over her shoulder and holding her belly.

We might all die from this, he thought, but I'm glad I took that stand. "God," he said quietly to himself when his wife was gone, "you're going to have to do more. You're just going to have to do more for us. Meet us in the middle . . . meet us in the middle, and we'll meet you. You listening, old man? Are you even *there*?"

28

A Sister's Love

Present Day
McNair House
Muskogee, Oklahoma
District Four, Cherokee Nation

Molly got on the stationary bike. She seemed to do okay for a while until . . .

"Ow, dang!"

"How's it coming, Peewee?" Sandra studied her daughter from the dining room doorway.

"Still hurts, Mom," said Molly as she slowly tried to pedal. "There's—I dunno—something about this motion—I can walk better than I can ride. Dammit!"

"Look," said Sandra, walking into the living room and glancing out at the cloudy sky, "I'm having some ice cream. Want any? I bought you some chocolate chip." Molly nodded and eased off the bike. Sandra went to the kitchen and opened the freezer while Molly got into the recliner and stretched her leg out to rest it. Sandra brought Molly a bowl with an extra helping, along with an ice wrap from the freezer for her knee. Sandra took a seat on the sofa and put her legs up. They stared for a moment at the gray skies, thunder rumbling in the distance.

"This is such crap, Mom. I can't believe this is happening. I mean, the one thing I've really been looking forward to. I've cried so much about Emmy that I can't even cry about this; I'm just pissed off."

Sandra eyed Molly.

"I know. And, frankly, you have a right to be. I'm proud of you. Your grades have been excellent, your teachers speak highly of you, you have a lot of friends. You can be mad—that's okay; but you also have a lot to be thankful for."

Molly rolled her eyes.

Sandra would not be moved. "You *do*."

Molly shrugged.

"Yeah, I guess," she said with a dramatic sigh.

Sandra took another spoonful of ice cream and tried to get Molly's mind off of Molly. "Speaking of friends," she began, "is there something you'd like to tell me about Tara and Rebecca?"

Molly shot her a quick glance. "No" was the immediate response. "I mean, why would you ask me that?"

"Well, I just happened to see them—they didn't see me— over at Eagle Feather last night. I was on my way home and stopped at Wanda's for some makeup. They were sitting in Tara's family SUV being, well, how shall I put this—intimate?" Her mom continued to looked at her.

Molly spooned more ice cream into her mouth, getting some of it on her face. She wiped it with a napkin Sandra had given her and stared at her mom. Sandra seemed surprised. "You didn't know? Hmm . . . "

"Yeah," Molly admitted, "I knew. They told me a couple of weeks ago." She licked her spoon, then looked at her mother with an almost secret, girls-club-only smile.

"Did you see this coming?"

"No, I mean, not really; but yeah, in a way. Know what I mean? It was like, like, things all of a sudden made sense. Were *you* surprised?" Her mom leaned back on the sofa, her attractive face in reflective mode.

"I might have suspected it with Tara, I suppose. Well, I will say I *was* shocked to see my daughter's two best friends making out in Tara's mother's car . . . so yeah kinda sorta." They both laughed. Molly dropped her spoon in the bowl in her lap, then put her hands to her face and giggled, making sure her ice wrap didn't fall from her knee.

"Omigod . . . that is so funny. I mean, it's weird, ya know? Like, if they were strangers I wouldn't think anything of it, but, they're my best friends forever—known Becks since grade school. Just weird, but good, ya know? I mean, I'm happy for them. They're in love, Mom, they said so." Sandra shook her head in wonderment.

"Well, that's what it's all about—what matters most," she said with authority, spooning some more chocolate chip.

"That's what I said!" exclaimed Molly.

"Do their parents know?"

"Oh, shit, Mom, no!"

Sandra raised her hand with a "stop that" motion.

"Will you please?" she begged. "You're getting as bad as your sister."

"Sorry. I just mean . . . Oh, Mom, no! Please don't say anything. You know Mr. Taylor—if he finds out, he'll probably disown her."

Sandra reflected on that one, nodding.

"You're probably right about that. Don't worry, I'm not saying a word," Sandra assured her. "But," she added, "I would also say, 'Good luck hiding this one!'" She saluted Molly with her ice-cream spoon. Molly looked relieved, but thoughtful. They were quiet as they finished off their chocolate chip. The house darkened and the Oklahoma landscape grew sinister from the approaching storm. "Damn," said Sandra offhandedly. "Hope we don't lose power."

"'*Damn*,' Mom? Really? Well! You're almost as bad as your daughter!" Molly chided jokingly.

Sandra put her hand over her mouth with a look of surprise.

"Oh, dear . . . you caught me. My mistake."

They laughed. Things got quiet again, then Molly spoke.

"Tommy Drum texted to check on me after our call. He says he still supports me, and he asked about Emmy again." Sandra nodded in appreciation. She looked carefully at Molly.

"Molly, listen to me. You listening?"

Molly nodded.

"Something happens as you get older. Grams and others weren't kidding about the years going by faster."

"That's what Tommy said!"

"Well, he's right. When you get to be my age, they really start zooming by. I know that, to you, a year seems like forever. I remember; I do. I haven't forgotten what that feels like. But during the next few years—whether it's college or something else—you'll find your time being occupied in different, more urgent ways."

"More urgent? Oh, geez, I can't wait," Molly said sarcastically. Her mother laughed.

"I think it's very kind of Tommy and the staff to hold the slot open for you next year if you still want it. Most of the riders are older anyway, right? I know how much your genealogy has meant to you this past year, and you've done a wonderful job with it. You know, you've taught *me* some things! With today's technology, you have so much more to go on. Sure, we Cherokee have our oral tradition—which is so important—but the details that you have been piecing together are really impressive. I'm sorry I haven't been available enough to you lately to tell you that. You've become quite the researcher, and I'm proud of you."

"Thanks, Mom. It has been a lot of work. It's been fun doing both as parallel activities."

"Do you think you will be okay *not* doing the ride this year?"

"Well, I guess so. I can't really focus like I want to because I'm thinking about Emmy, and now this darn knee being worse than we thought—it's a lot. Maybe I should be glad that Tommy wrote me off this year." She wiped her hands again.

"Hey!" exclaimed Sandra. "He *did not* write you off. He cares about you and wants what's best. And he has to think about the rest of the team—you know that."

"I know, Mom; you're right. Sorry. I keep thinking that— getting this feeling that—like, Emmy is going to need me this year—soon, maybe, I don't know. Anyway, I can't concentrate a lot of the time because of her diagnosis." She smiled weakly at her mother. "I think so, Mom; I think I can live with putting it off a year."

"Of course you can. You're my other warrior." Molly smiled at being compared to Emmy. "And I'm also proud of you for thinking of your sister first. Maybe more than anything else you do, I'm *so* proud of you for that." Molly smiled and shrugged, then looked back up at her mom, wanting to change the subject.

"So how do you feel about Emmy and Mike, anyway?"

Her mom looked thoughtful.

"I *like* Mike," she responded. "He's a good one. He's not tribal, and I always figured Em would go for a Native, but she loves him, and that's the big thing. He's a sweet man. And I heard through the grapevine that he's won a couple of medals during his time with the OSBI."

Molly's eyes lit up. "That is *so* cool. He's dreamy. And he's got *such* a cute butt! Omigod!"

"Molly McNair! You better not let your sister hear you talk that way. She'll stuff you in the closet and hang you upside down like a bat!" She laughed and Molly giggled like a child. "Remember when you were little?" she said, licking her spoon dry. "That time when you were eight and she was fifteen. You were driving her crazy so she turned you over her knee and beat your ass, then opened the side window and hung you out by your ankles—she was offering you up for sale to the highest bidder. You were screaming your poor little lungs out, thinking you were going to get shipped off to some foreign country! Mark Doughtery and Joey Littlejohn happened to walk by and said, 'Yeah, we'll take her!' Joey said, 'We can sell her at the airport!' Oh, you cried and cried! I had to take you in my arms and hold you for twenty minutes to convince you that you weren't being sold off. I really let Em have it for that one!"

"Omigod, right? She was *such* a bitch to me then!" They laughed again, then grew quiet once more. "Mom, did something happen to Emmy?"

"What do you mean?"

"I don't know. Just something about her when we were at the Archway . . . I mean, I dunno—like something from her past?" Her mom seemed to turn ashen, distant.

"I . . . really don't know, Peewee. Not that I can think of." She looked away, toward the window, as large raindrops splattered against the pane. Molly had the feeling that she was the only one who hadn't gotten the memo about something important.

Molly wondered if her mom knew about the gun. She couldn't help herself—she had to ask. "Did you know Emmy packs heat?"

Sandra rolled her eyes.

"Yes, I know," she said with a sigh. But then she seemed thoughtful about it and said, "I talked to Standingcloud about it one day—the day she told him about her cancer, actually. He said it was probably a good idea and for me not to worry. As if, right? He said that because she's becoming more well-known, there's an increased chance of weirdos coming out of the woodwork—just the thing I needed to hear, right?" she said with a nervous laugh. "He told me he taught her to shoot at the rock pile. Says she's a crack shot, which somehow doesn't surprise me. He looks out for her, and I'm so thankful for that."

"You should have seen her at the Archway, Mom. She pulled that gun so fast I thought those three big dudes were gonna crap their pants!" She laughed.

Sandra put her hands to her ears, pretending not to hear this, shaking her head and saying, "No, no!" in a silly tone. "Ignoring you, ignoring you!"

Molly laughed, then her mood changed as she thought about it more. "She was protecting me, Mom, she was . . ." Molly became emotional, her voice cracking. "She, oh, God, Mom," she cried, putting her hands to her head as Sandra sat forward and held her arms out for Molly, who joined her on the sofa. "She shoved me behind her . . . she was gonna *deal* with those guys, Mom!" she moaned in a sniveling voice, collapsing into her mom's arms. Sandra pulled Molly to her and Molly put her head in her mother's lap and sobbed as her mom stroked her hair like she did when she was little. She handed Molly a clean napkin to wipe her eyes. "I DON'T WANNA LOSE MY SISTER, Mom!" she screamed, unleashing the past couple of months' built-up grief. "Oh, Em! Please *don't die!*" she wailed, closing her eyes and burying her head in Sandra's lap.

Sandra held her daughter and proclaimed, "We won't, Molly. We *will not* lose her, hear me?" She snuggled Molly's head to her chest and rubbed her shoulders. Well, Sandra thought, I certainly got her mind off her knee . . . God, please, come to us . . . be with us.

She held Molly until her tears abated. After a couple of minutes of sitting quietly, she cleared her throat and said, "One other thing. Contessa Blackfox called." Molly's eyes widened as she looked straight ahead, still resting in her mother's lap. *Clay. College, maybe. Meeting with a dean . . .*

"Oh?" said Molly, feigning sheer ignorance. "What about?"

"Well, she said Clay talked to you about going over to the college, taking a tour, that sort of thing. You gonna do that?" she asked, leaning her head toward Molly's face.

"Ah, yeah, I think so. No big deal. Just a tour." *Yeah right!*

"Uh-huh," her mom responded in a "I knew you before you knew you" sort of way. "Well, I'm looking forward to hearing how that goes," she said. She kissed Molly's forehead. "We'll figure a way, sweetie; we'll figure a way for you to go to college, don't you worry."

In less than ten minutes, the sun came out.

29

Leaving the Old Country Behind

November 11-12, 1838
Bell Detachment
Savannah, Tennessee
Tennessee-Cherokee Nation Boundary
Leaving the Old Cherokee Nation

C aptain Ambrose stared across the Tennessee River to the other side. Lieutenant Whitworth stood next to him.

"Sir, this marks the end of the Cherokee Nation territory. We cross this river, these people become strangers in a strange land." Ambrose closed his eyes. When he opened them, a ferry was making its way back across the river. Ambrose looked up to his left, to the great house perched on the hill. The Robinson home; the largest in Savannah. Its owner was a dealmaker of sorts in the area. His son guided the ferry across the water and brought it to a stop not far from the group of lead horses that headed the Bell Detachment. He nodded to the captain.

"Alex F. Robinson," he shouted as he and his assistant anchored the craft. "What's all this?" he inquired, looking at the long, sad line of people. The Cherokees were shivering in the chilly air, their faces telling a tale of woe, loss, and death. Captain Ambrose stepped forward.

"Captain Thomas Ambrose, United States Army, Fourth Artillery Division. I have to get these people across, Mr. Robinson, posthaste. Six hundred sixty souls, more or less."

Robinson stared at the increasingly long line of wagons, horses, oxen, Indians, and soldiers and just shook his head.

"You can't be serious, Captain. *All* of these people?"

"I'm deadly serious, sir. Or better yet, President Van Buren is. His orders, his army. We're taking this route as a protective measure. This here's what's known as the 'Treaty Party' of Cherokee. We're on escort duty to prevent infighting between them and the Chief Ross detachment, up to the north."

"I see," said Mr. Robinson. "And just who proposes to pay me for this monumental effort?"

"The United States government, sir, I assure you. I have the money on hold, ready to make good on such a transaction."

David Welch had made his way to the front of the line during the day's travel. He grunted and turned away after listening to Ambrose. The sun shone brilliantly, its rays bouncing across the surface of the water, which moved steadily with a northwest current.

"I see," said Robinson again. "Well, now, I'll, ah, take half up front, the other half when the job is done. Good enough? By the looks of it, we're lookin' at a couple days' work, for sure."

"Done. Just get us across this damn river, Mr. Robinson. Just get us across," said Captain Ambrose.

As the ferry got underway, the McNair group made its way to the front of the line. The Robinsons's grand mansion stood on the hill to the left, overlooking the Tennessee River. Welch took time away from his family to spend part of the day with Nick and Mary. He hunched his shoulders from the chilly air and gladly took a cup of coffee from Enoch, who made some from the rations provided. He stood next to Nick in a conspiratorial way, as if hoping others wouldn't hear their conversation.

"According to Lieutenant Whitworth, this is the boundary, Nick," he said, pointing to the ground. "This here spot—it's the last we're going to see of our homeland."

"Let me tell you something, Dave," Nick responded, venom in his voice, "I'll be *back*, you can count on that. I know how we got out here, and I know how to get the hell back."

"It's hopeless, my friend," said David, his hand on Nick's shoulder. "They'll just figure out a way to arrest us, send us right back out here again. We're vermin to them, boy, trash, shit in the outhouse bowl. Hell, we're no better in their eyes than a rattlesnake makin' his way across the ground to eat a buncha baby birds. We're flotsam to them." Nick grimaced. He, too, was white. And yet he was also brown. Life just wasn't that simple. It was, he thought, horribly complex and bent toward the elite. He was, at least in part, a member of that elite, and hated himself in the moment for it. He sighed, looking at the cold ground, cursing the realities of human existence. Just then, Mary appeared. Welch tipped his hat to her.

"Morning, Mary," he said with a nod.

"David," she acknowledged. "I know that look," she said to her husband, "what is the matter?" Nick glanced at Dave, who just looked away. Nick turned back to his wife.

"We, ah, we've reached the edge, Mary, the boundary. This is it for us. From here on out—at least until the Indian Territory—it's all state-owned. We're leaving our homeland." He looked down.

"Oh, my word," she said, putting her hands to her face. The weight of Nick's words were considerable, burdensome, as pregnant as she. Mary sobbed. She took her husband's hands in hers and, as he joined in, they both prayed:

> Our Father, who art in heaven, hallowed be Thy name. Thy kingdom come, Thy will be done; on earth as it is in heaven. Give us this day our daily bread, and forgive us our trespasses, as we forgive those who trespass against us. And lead us not into temptation, for Thine is the kingdom, the power and the glory, forever and ever, amen.

Dave Welch appeared to be trying to overhear what Lieutenant Whitworth and Captain Ambrose were discussing— along with Sergeant Thomas—in a small huddle closer to the water. Whitworth was examining a map again and pointing in the distance.

The sound of horse hooves approaching interrupted husband and wife. It was Sergeant Hollingsworth. He glanced Nick's way as he approached, looking as if he might say something.

"Get the hell away from me," said Nick. Hollingsworth put up his hand as if to indicate a "no problem here" message. A different detachment in different circumstances might have prevented Nick from speaking his mind and feelings so freely. The reality of his social and political standing within the tribe, and the Treaty Party members' general cooperation with removal made such things feasible. Dave Welch turned, giving the soldier a nasty look.

Captain Ambrose heard Nick's comment and, looking over his shoulder, called out to Hollingsworth. "Deploy those two wagons near the water's edge, Sergeant."

"Yes, sir," came the response, and Hollingsworth rode back without looking in the McNairs' direction.

"And they call *us* savages," Mary said with a chill. Nick observed his wife. He knew Mary was pondering her family back home in Georgia: her two younger sisters, her many brothers. Two of her brothers had signed and helped develop the Treaty of New Echota, making the whole family appear to some as traitors to their people. Nick knew that she admired Chief Ross, believing him to be a good leader. She had expressed mixed feelings about the treaty, but she understood why her brothers, Major Ridge, and others had signed the Cherokee lands over to the government. Total tribal extermination was a real possibility, and it seemed to make more sense to preserve and maintain their nation and people in another location than to have no tribe at all. Nick appreciated that Mary was able to see both sides, and she admired Ross and the rest of her people for wanting to hold their ground.

The McNairs waited to be ferried across. The sun shone even brighter as Robinson's ferry floated across the causeway. The sun's rays were dynamic and incandescent and rode the ripples in the watercourse. At one point a child fell overboard. He was being carried away by the current until Amos Deer Skin dove in after him and pulled him back to the ferry, which had to stop in the center of the channel to pick them up. The boy didn't seem at all disturbed, despite the frigid waters and many upset adults.

When it was their turn, Nick guided the horses and wagon onto the craft. There was just enough room for his family and slaves. Alex Robinson eased the vessel along the current to minimize sway and drift. Mary wrapped herself in her blanket, huddling close with Martha and protecting her unborn baby. She looked up, trying to glean as much sun as she could in the cold, breezy air. Nick remained on the buckboard and observed the moving waters that surrounded the boat. A largemouth bass leapt from the water in a short, fast arc. Sure looks tasty, he thought, trying not to think about food. He was happy to see Joshua Sanders awaiting him at the other side with what appeared to be a more hopeful expression than the one he had worn during the creek incident. They waved to each other. Nick noticed that other Cherokees moved up the trail on the other side in order to make room for new arrivals.

Mr. Robinson's ferry was cable-driven. Sometimes called a "flying bridge," it was propelled by ropes or chains—in this case—new, powerful chains that were state-of-the-art. He attached the chains to both shores and, with the use of an elaborate pulley system which he operated on the craft, he would guide the ferry over the water by pulling the lead chain. It was noisy, but more efficient and reliable than the older ferry systems. As he worked with the slack on the leading end, the opposite end would ratchet up with a loud, "creeeek, rad-tad-tad-tad-tad-tad" sound until the ferry was about a third of the way across. It would slow to a near stop, then Robinson would get it cranking again and off they would go the rest of the way. If the river ran rapid or the winds were high, the boat would veer off course for a ways, but thanks to this newer system of pulley and chain, the ferry would right itself in the end.

Mr. Robinson guided the giant wooden platform to the edge of the shore, the chain grinding through the pulley system and the party making moderate contact with the shore, a loud "thump!" signaling their crossing's completion. Mr. Robinson unlatched the large wooden gate at the craft's bow, permitting the horses to pull the wagons off the landing. Nick nodded to Robinson, who quickly secured the gate and started heading back to the other side, knowing that his work would be steady all day and into the evening, his father and brother taking turns to relieve him. Nick drove the wagon team up a moderate hill and pulled over to the right, letting several other wagons go by that had been resting and reorganizing supplies after coming across. He hopped off the buckboard and waited as Augustine shook, then hopped off the back end onto the ground, then shook again. Nick petted him and patted his belly. Augustine always waited for Mary to help Martha down from the wagon, then stayed close by, ever the protector.

Joshua approached Nick and shook his hand. "Good to see you make it over, cousin-nephew," he said.

"Wado," Nick responded. "How's your spirit, Joshua?"

"Better," said Joshua, "thanks to you," and nodded. He moved on ahead to catch up with his family.

Nick gathered his family and they walked halfway back down the hill and stood off to the side. Nick, Mary, Enoch, and Annabelle left their children briefly to play on their own. Deborah looked after Martha by carrying her around and pointing at things for her to look at. The adults stood on the upper bank of the Tennessee River and gazed across the water at their former home—the old Cherokee Nation. They could only stand in silence. Enoch looked at Nick for guidance.

"So what do we do *now*, Mr. Nick?"

Mary glanced at her husband, Annabelle looked at him quizzically, and Enoch searched his face for answers. It was some time before Nick spoke.

"We go forward, is what we do. We've been driven through most of Tennessee like the buffalo that we're not. Our only hope at this point is to show them that we know how to live well. We show them that we're the resilient people that our parents were." Enoch and his wife nodded. "Enoch," he said, "time for you to take the reins again. I'm going to walk a spell with my wife," he said, looking at her proudly.

"Why, yes, sir, Mr. Nick, I'll do just that," Enoch said with a smile.

The members of the Bell route had access to riding more often than did Cherokees on other routes, particularly the John Ross detachments, and Nick offered the other half of the buckboard to rotating members of the detachment whenever possible.

He found himself enthralled with many of the stories from friends and neighbors who shared part of the ride with him. At one point, he told Mary that it was quite the learning experience for him. He heard many hard-luck stories, naturally, but also some uplifting ones. For example, Bull Frog told him about finally being able to acquire new materials for his small farm, and what an exciting project it had become up until the army came and told him it was time. Bull Frog managed to sell his property on the side—one of very few people able to do so. He pocketed the proceeds and was able to bring them along to help his family in the new Indian Territory.

In another case, Mary Hubbard, whose four children were with her—including her oldest, Robert, an adult—told Nick a different tale. Mary heard the soldiers were on their way for the roundup. From Cherokee runners who sprinted from home to home in some areas giving warning, she discovered the soldiers were dispossessing the Cherokees of their hard-earned cabins, houses, and other property, even burning many of them. She was having none of it, she said. Mary grabbed what she knew she and her children needed to survive, then burned down her own cabin before they got there. When a corporal realized it was she who had done it, he told her with an arrogant smile that it was just as well—he would have burned it if she hadn't.

"I gave him one of these," she proudly proclaimed to Nick, holding up her middle finger, then crossing her arms with smugness. Nick laughed as Mary, a fluent English speaker educated at the Salem Academy, said she told the corporal his mother was anally infested and that, unbeknownst to his mother, she had had carnal knowledge of his inadequate father in a black cherry tree. The corporal became furious and slapped her. But she said it was "worth every ounce" just to see the veins in his neck bulge.

Nick had laughed—as much as a laugh can be a laugh during such times—and leaned over and kissed the widow's cheek.

She patted his knee and told him they were all going to make it—that they would survive this ordeal. She had a unique way of inspiring confidence, and he appreciated that, given the many despairing days of this journey.

Enoch brought the team to readiness, though Nick told him before heading out that he and his wife would walk for a while. When she got tired, he would put her back on the wagon. As usual, Deborah held Martha as the wagon pulled away. They waved—Mary assuring her daughter that she was right behind her. Augustine just looked on mournfully as the wagon began making its way to the next destination, the head tilt so indicative of his breed—a look that said, "We're family—a pack; don't leave us for long." But he also had the noble look of a dog that says, "I got this covered."

A wealthy plantation owner, James Graham, had a substantial amount of corn and fodder. His dual-chimney brick home stood to the south of the Savannah River departure point. When Captain Ambrose heard about Mr. Graham's large volume of supplies, he sent a corporal and private, in lieu of an advance purchasing agent, to make a purchase for the Bell Detachment. A deal was struck—some of it made with Cherokee money again—and Mr. Graham had his workers haul the supplies to the Robinson ferry landing, where he was reimbursed for the goods and the passage across the river.

Various wagon teams began passing Nick and Mary as they marched on. Sergeant Thomas's horse trotted by, and the sergeant made a point of speaking to the McNairs. "Things good here, sir?" he asked, tipping his hat and slowing his horse. Nick nodded and the sergeant said, "Good enough, then," and picked up speed. Nick guessed that Captain Ambrose or Lieutenant Whitworth had made a point of ordering the sergeant to check on them after the incident with Sergeant Hollingsworth, who was now somewhere closer to the front of the line.

Old Stage Road
Trail leading to
Adamsville & the Purdy Crossroads
State of Tennessee

The detachment camped at a clearing in the woods not far from the river. The next day, Nick and Mary walked a popular stage road, with new versions of the common stagecoach traveling the area more than ever. Nick held his wife's hand as they shuffled along on a trail that became narrower as they went along. The trees and brushwood closed in as the detachment advanced. They arrived at the edge of Adamsville in the late afternoon, long after Nick put Mary back on the wagon. Captain Ambrose originally planned to have the detachment camp near the town's main road. As they passed through, however, a large contingent of townspeople gathered, and many were rowdy, having consumed large quantities of whiskey beforehand. Several drunk people tried to block the main passageway through town, and more than once Captain Ambrose readied his men for a potential conflict.

A peace officer sauntered up at one point, trying to quell the unrest. Captain Ambrose told him in no uncertain terms that if he had to fire on his townspeople, that's what he would do. This seemed to frighten the officer, who turned out to be a recently installed county sheriff. It was hard to tell if the people were protesting the Cherokee removal or expressing hate for the Indians, and things soon got out of hand. One citizen threw a bottle at a passing wagon and before anyone knew what was happening, some of the townspeople were throwing rocks. One hit Lieutenant Whitworth in the side of the head, causing him to bleed. When a large man with a huge belly cursed and picked up a boulder the size of a grapefruit and employed a running start to heave it, Ambrose shot him through the shoulder.

"Hey!" the big man screamed, "you done shot me here!" weaving to keep from falling.

"That's right, you dumb bastard!" Ambrose spewed. "Constable!" Ambrose shouted in the sheriff's direction. "You best get ahold of your people!" The sheriff looked frantic, running around trying to gain control. The big man fell to the ground, then managed to get up again. Ambrose caught him out of the corner of his eye. "You stay right there and don't move, fatty!" he roared. "Private Lewis," he called to an approaching private.

"Yes, sir?"

"See that big lump of shit? If he makes another move on this detachment, kill 'im!"

"Yes, sir!" Private Lewis answered, drawing his breech lock pistol and steering his horse within several feet of the man. Moses McDaniel stopped his wagon next to Private Lewis and pulled out his Springfield rifle, training it on the big man.

"Don't you even *breathe* wrong, boy," he said, backing up the private.

The large man wobbled again, rotated his trunk like he was unscrewing himself, then, eyes rolling back in his head, garbled, "Oh, my God, he done sh . . . done sh . . . done shot meeee!" He then fell backward and passed out.

The townspeople began slowly filtering away after seeing that the army meant business. Only a few tossed rocks or other items at the rest of the detachment before it made its way through. The soldiers sped things along as best they could to avoid injuries or death, so the Cherokees were in and out of the town faster than Ambrose would have guessed. Later he conferred with Lieutenant Whitworth about where might be best to camp for the evening. They decided they could make it to the Purdy Crossroads before midnight.

As another long day came to an end, the Bell detail began populating the area surrounding Purdy Crossroads. Doc Arbogast applied a mustard seed poultice to Lieutenant Whitworth's temple.

"Rocks," said the doctor as he treated the lieutenant's wound, "are some kinda special dirty. Can cause a messy spot, smudgy—can predispose you to the redness and swelling. Very strange. We need to keep such a mishap at bay, Lieutenant. So you best keep this applied to your noggin. Then have someone clean and change the wet cloth," he insisted. The lieutenant nodded and leaned back against a tree to rest.

Captain Ambrose sat against his own tree, sipping coffee, and made journal entries for General Scott or C. A. Harris, the Commissioner of Indian Affairs. The interesting thing about his journal entries was what *wasn't* mentioned. As Rev. Daniel S. Butrick would write in his own journal on Cherokee removal, newspapers and other sources of public information represented the Cherokee relocation as a peaceful, if not pleasant, endeavor. No one—including Ambrose—wrote about the rapes, murders, assaults, and other brutalities in their official reports. In Ambrose's mind—and certainly General Scott's—duties within the realm of forced relocation were being done in an orderly, proficient, military manner. And though Ambrose was slowly becoming sensitized to the brutal nature of forced migration, part of his brain refused to recognize the truths that made this a moral dilemma for any human being.

He glanced back at his entry from November 3 to the commissioner:

We have pursued the direct road thro' Fayetville and Pulaski leading to Memphis part of which we found very rough, but our rate of traveling has averaged between 10 and 12 miles a day. Nothing of much importance has taken place since I last wrote. Some of the Indians have lost a number of oxen from eating poisonous weeds, but the progress of the party was not interrupted on that account. The people are generally healthy, and everything relative to our movements is at present going on well.

He seemed pleased with the form and structure of the notation, never acknowledging the more severe aspects of the journey for which he had volunteered.

30

Sister Time

Present Day
Local College Campus
Muskogee, Oklahoma

Thanks for driving me over here, Em," said Molly, applying lip gloss while looking into her compact mirror, which she subsequently dropped into her shoulder bag.

"No problem," said Emmy as she wheeled *Ned Christie* down the main drive of the campus. Molly noticed a group of students walking by, one of them pointing to the car. She thought she heard a guy say, "Hey, that was The Cherokee Storm!" Molly smiled and shook her head.

"You can just drop me at the front steps; that'll be cool." Emmy drove on by, pulled to a stop, then began backing into a nearby parking space. "Did you hear me?"

"I heard you," said Emmy, continuing to back into the space.

Molly threw her hands up, shaking her head. "Nobody *listens* to me."

"Cool your panties, Nine-Speed. Just wanna say hello to Clay. You know, ask after his mom, that sorta thing."

Molly rolled her eyes, checking herself in the mirror again. "Omigod, this is *so* embarrassing," she said.

"Oh, m'god; this *so* EM-BARR-a-sing," Emmy mimicked. "Get the hell outta my car, princess."

They got out and Molly looked around, a sense of wonder surging up within her. She grinned, which made Emmy smile. As they approached the front steps, they heard a voice calling out.

"Molly!" It was Clay. Molly's palms moistened with sweat. "Osiyo, Molly. Good to see you again!" said Clay.

"'Siyo, Clay," said Molly bashfully. "How are you?"

He reached out his hand to shake hers.

"Osda, just fine. Hi, Emmy, long time no see," he said with a smile.

Emmy extended her hand, wrapping his in an aikido handshake, her forefinger beneath his outer wrist bone. She removed her shades and Molly noticed a glimmer in her eyes, similar to the day she met Mike. Oh, God, please, thought Molly, as she watched Emmy hold onto Clay's hand and turn it slightly as they shook. She's *not* doing this—can't be. She's *not* charming him, is she? Holy cow! Please, Em, you've got your own guy. Don't take this one, *please.* Emmy let go of Clay's hand and smiled. Clay nodded, but Molly caught him rubbing his hand afterward with a slight grimace.

"It is so sweet of you to show Molly around, Clay! Awesome. Wado!" she said in an odd but convincing and authoritative voice. "I'm *sure* you'll take very good care of her."

"Oh, it's my pleasure, Emmy. And hey—didn't see the fight live but saw the highlights on YouTube. You were amazing!"

Oh, boy, Molly thought. *Here we go.*

"Thanks, Clay. It was an important matchup. Glad so many people were able to watch," she said with what Molly was certain was a flirtatious grin.

Yeah, yeah, yeah, fucking yeah. The Amazing Emily: my sister, the tightrope walker, the flame-eater, the goddamn American Gladiator. Really, Em? Just really?

"Um, Clay, could you excuse us for just a minute? I'll be *right* there," said Molly.

"Sure! I've gotta return a phone call anyway. Take your time and let me know when you're ready. I'll take you to meet the dean, then we can go from there." Molly nodded and smiled.

She and Emmy walked away, out of earshot.

"What the hell, Em?"

"What?" said Emmy, surprised.

"Like, enough already, okay? I can't believe you're standing there, flirting. For God's sake, Em!"

"*Flirting*? Are you serious?"

"The hand grip, the following me up here just to show off, that whole . . . seductive smile thing you do. Damn, Em . . ."

"I wasn't flirting, Molly. I was simply sending Clay a message: be *good* to you. That's all."

"Omigod. Who's the grandma, now, sis, huh? Unbelievable." Molly put her hands to her face, feeling the squeeze from the strap of her bag on her shoulder. She readjusted it and looked pleadingly at her sister. "I'll be fine, *Mighty Thor*, okay? I don't need a bodyguard. Omigod, this is humiliating."

"Okay, sorry." Emmy studied her little sister. "You know, you're right. I'm sorry. Really. Just wasn't thinking. You guys have a nice time. I'm gonna go grab a bite to eat myself, then head over to Dunham's Sports and get some equipment. If it runs long I've got other things I can do, too. Just text me when you're ready, okay? And hey—sorry." She gave Molly a quick hug.

Molly pulled away slightly and said, "Okay, okay, forgiven. I got this, grandma," she said, making a little shooing motion with her hands.

Emmy couldn't help but needle her a bit more.

"Yeah? Ya sure, ya think, yeah?" she said with a grin, using her best puppy-dog voice as she playfully pinched Molly's chin.

"Yeah-yeah-yeah," said Molly impatiently, jerking her head back. "Go on, Gal Gadot; I'm good here." She waved her off.

Emmy laughed and headed back to the car.

During the next hour and a half, Clay took Molly to meet the dean of students, showed her around campus, discussed scholarship possibilities, and bought her lunch at the college dining hall, which, to Molly's pleasant surprise, was tasty. *Rizz my guy up, will you?* she thought, replaying Emmy massaging Clay's hand. *Just for that, I'm having the fucking mac and cheese.*

They brought each other up to date, and she told him about Emmy's diagnosis, which seemed to upset him. They talked about the ride, too, covering many important topics in a short period of time. He never touched her hand or anything, but she was profoundly moved by how he gave his attention fully to her. It was a nice change. Clay struck her as someone with a mission, a vision, serious about who he was and where he was going. She admired that.

"So good to see you again, Molly," said Clay as they wrapped up their lunch visit. "I remember when we were kids, and your mom sometimes came to our house for that sewing club—remember? Yeah, and then it would be held at your house, or Mrs. Bumgarner's house, or wherever. I remember that sometimes my mom would bring me over to your house to pick up sewing material and there you'd be, all tomboy, just waiting for me so we could play one-on-one kickball in the front yard. Remember that?"

Molly nodded. "Yeah, and then we'd get tired and watch TV until your mom was ready." Clay nodded.

"Okay, confession?"

Molly shrugged and nodded.

"I had a crush on you—big time!"

Did he just say what I thought he said? Molly recalled the "conversation" she was having just before Clay called. *Your phone is ringing. Answer your phone.* Holy moly, she thought.

He smiled again and took a swig of his iced tea, finishing it. Only a small lump of ice remained.

"Um, ah, oh wow . . ."

Clay held up his hands. "Sorry," he said, "I didn't mean to embarrass you. Just a nice memory."

"Oh, no, I'm not embarrassed at all, Clay." He cocked his head, as if wondering if she might say more.

"Anyway," he said, smiling again and rising from his chair, "I'll get rid of these trays."

"Clay," said Molly, looking up at him, "thank you—wado. Actually, that was very flattering. I'm honored." She gave him an alert, non-flirty smile. "And thank you for all you did for me today. The dean seems nice."

"Yeah," said Clay, holding off on the trays. "He's a pretty good guy. He really likes meeting new students. And he's impressed with you. He told me that before he even met you, you know, from your application and references." Molly stood and held out her hand.

"Here," she said, "I'll help you trash these." They emptied their trays and walked to the front of the building, where Molly sent Emmy a text saying she was ready. Emmy responded:

Be there in 10.

They chatted for a while longer while Molly waited.

"Listen," said Clay, "I get that you've made no decisions and need to explore your other options. But I just want to plug the school again. We have a great faculty. The atmosphere here is chill. We don't have an environment where our professors feel threatened or have to walk on eggshells because of some inane politically correct rebel force. And, being a Christian-based institution, we do our best to adhere to those principles. On the other hand, we're small; a lot of people want to be where the action is—big schools. Or where they can just party every weekend and do their time for the four years. Depends on what you're looking for, I guess."

"I never asked you—what's your major?"

"Ah," he smiled, "pre-law. Well, English and pre-law. Actually, English is a great major for a lot of things—law included, even without the pre-law courses."

"Huh," said Molly. "You know, Mom's a paralegal."

"Oh, yeah, that's right!" he said. "I should come by sometime, pick her brain. I'd love to see her again!"

Oh hell yeah, oh definitely; Omigod, yeah, like, come by any time and I'll show you around my house and anything else you wanna see, just sayin' . . . "Yeah, oh, yes—definitely! I know we'd, I mean, she—you know, would like that. Can't wait to tell her I saw you today!" Did I just sound like a little girl? she wondered.

"Oh, hey—I see Emmy's car out there," said Clay. "What a rockin' ride!"

"Yeah, she loves that car. Its name is *Ned Christie*."

"No kidding!" he exclaimed with a laugh. "I mean, that's really wild—I'm a descendant of Ned's."

"No way!"

"Yeah, seriously."

"Are you an outlaw, too?" she asked with a coy smile, risking being corny.

"No, not yet!" he laughed again. "But hey, *you* be the outlaw and I'll keep you out of jail after law school!" They both laughed and he bumped shoulders with her as they made their way out the door to the steps.

Yeah, he did. He just shoulder-bumped me and I liked it. I liked it so much I wish to hell he would do it again because it was totally hot and now my palms aren't the only things sweating . . .

"Well, Clay," said Molly, turning around. "Thanks so much for everything today." They looked at each other for a little longer than what might be considered casual interest between friends who haven't seen each other in years. Molly reached up and hugged Clay, who hugged her back and said how happy he was that she was considering the college.

They said their goodbyes with the promise to keep in touch, and Molly headed down the stairs toward *Ned Christie*. She walked to the car and got in. She glanced over at her sister, who had been watching.

"Hmm, nice hug, Nine-Speed," Emmy teased.

"Yeah, yeah," Molly responded, tossing her bag into the back seat, partially loaded with bags from Dunham's.

"Things go okay? I mean, did you like what you saw of the place?" Molly nodded, her mind elsewhere. "Nice dean?" Molly stared back at the campus. "Smaller classes, I hear, which is good, right?" Nothing. Emmy sighed. "So, did the two of you shit in the main hallway after double martinis, or what?"

Molly shook her head.

"What? No, what? Oh, sorry! No, it was great. He was great. Nice place . . ." She felt like she might be smiling slightly, but in reality, she was beaming and just somehow anesthetized to it. Emmy grinned and touched Molly's jaw muscle with her index finger.

"What's this? Dimple action?"

"What dimple?" said Molly, trying to swipe Emmy's hand away.

"*This* dimple, girlfriend! This wittle demple right here!" she laughed and jabbed at the crater in Molly's jaw. Molly giggled and swatted Emmy's hand.

"Stop it!" she shouted with the same beaming expression.

"Oh, you *like* him! Oh, my God, girl. You got dimple fever for this guy! Look at this—boing, boing," she said, poking again at her sister's face and laughing.

"I don't *have* dimples, thank you very much!" Molly protested, crossing her arms.

"Oh, bullshit in the grass, girl! I 'knew you before you knew you' and all that shit. Ha!"

"Omigod, Em, stop with that already, pa-leeze!"

Emmy made a show of opening her door. "I can't stand it; gonna go back and tell *Clay*-ton that my sister regrets to inform him that she has chosen not to attend this particular college because the doors are too small. Her dimples won't fit through the front entrance. Oh, Clay-baby!" she halfway shouted as she was climbing from the car.

"NO! EMMY! What the fuck? You can't! Don't! Please get your ass back in this car, Em."

Emmy was laughing so hard she could hardly talk as she shut the door. She poked her sister in the ribs, under her arms, tickling her until Molly couldn't take it anymore and began cackling. They wrestled briefly, Emmy threatening again to shout Clay's name at the top of her lungs. Molly tried to break free of her sister's hold—an impossibility, of course. Finally, Emmy let her go and kissed her sister's cheek, giving her a little shove upright into the passenger seat.

"You know," she snickered, "you are positively adorable when you 'go dimple'. And that smile—it looks like you're going to implode—just like when you were little." She laughed again. Molly gave her the finger and asked her—no, begged her—to please just drive out of there, which only made Emmy laugh louder.

Finally, Emmy cranked the car and put it in gear. She looked over at Molly and chuckled, patting her sister behind the head and rubbing her neck. They headed back to Emmy's place because Sandra was working late and Emmy offered to cook her a good meal later. They chatted about the cancer, Molly's knee, college, what grad school was like, and so on.

Though Molly hated burdening her sister with all that she was facing, she defaulted to being the little sister. She told Emmy about her fears and frustrations regarding the ride, having to put it off a year, wanting to retrace the Trail of Tears and being depressed over that, and so on. Her big sis listened patiently. She loved her for that. Molly thought about the day, about what hanging around with someone like Clay was like, and about Emmy and Mike.

"Emmy, I'm sorry about what I said earlier." Emmy looked at her. "You know—about flirting with Clay and all that. I don't know what's wrong with me. It's like, you being sick is totally freaking me out, and I can't think straight. And I feel guilty because you're the one having to go through it. It's just nuts. And the other stuff . . . my knee, the ride, stuff like that."

"It's okay, kiddo. I think my being sick is making all of us a little crazy: me, you, Mom, Eddie."

"What about Mike?"

Emmy looked thoughtful about that. "Actually, no. He's been my rock. Solid all the way."

"You love Mike, don't you?"

Emmy smiled. "Yeah, I suppose I do."

"He's so adorable!" said Molly, patting her chest.

"Hey, now, no moving in on my guy. Don't make me do to you what I did to Ortiz," she said with a smile. Molly laughed.

"Is he ever intimidated by you?" asked Molly.

"Michael?" said Emmy, looking over at her while passing a slowpoke on the highway. Molly nodded.

"Nah," she said. "I mean, not really, I guess. He's a pretty tough guy, you know. Actually, just the other day he told me about being at one of the oil fields the day before. You know, they investigate crimes in the fields as part of their duties," she said, watching traffic but talking to Molly through her shades. Molly nodded. "Some roughneck they suspected of a felony got nasty as they were questioning him and threatened Michael."

"Oh!" said Molly with concern. "What happened?"

"Apparently he took a swing at Mike and he and Leon—his partner for that tour—got him cuffed, but not before Mike broke his nose." She laughed. "He said the judge wasn't gonna be crazy about that one, but would understand because the other guy swung first. So, he's a pretty tough cat, my man," she said proudly. She checked her side mirror as two bikers on Harley Davidsons wearing club colors passed on her side, one of them eyeing Emmy.

"Bet you could take those two guys!" said Molly, admiring her big sis as they roared by.

Emmy glanced at her through her dark shades. "Sure wouldn't wanna have to find out, would you?"

"Nope," said Molly in agreement. She reflected for a moment. "You packing that gun?" she asked.

Emmy glanced at her again, then looked back at the road.

"I'll take that as a yes."

Emmy said nothing.

"So," she said, changing the subject before she pissed off her sister, "Mike's a pretty tough dude all right, but I bet he couldn't take you, could he?" She grinned.

Emmy flipped her shades up on top of her head and looked over at Molly. "Are you kidding me?" she said with stark seriousness. "He's a guy, isn't he? I mean, come on."

Molly stared at her sister, guessing she was wrong.

"I can't believe you'd even ask me that!" exclaimed Emmy.

She seemed offended, and Molly worried that she hurt her feelings.

Then Emmy flashed her million-dollar smile. "Sista, I'd beat his ass up one side of that cage and then down the other," she said, waving her finger and rolling her shoulders. She flipped her shades back down, right hand slapping the steering wheel. Molly exploded with laughter. Emmy put her forefinger to her lips. "Shhhh. Don't tell him that, though. You gotta keep these men happy, see? Make 'em feel good about themselves." She smiled, reaching over and tickling Molly's ribs again with her free hand. Molly giggled again at her sister's humor as Emmy turned up the volume on the radio.

31

Golden Eagle

Present Day
Office of Linda Prescott, MD
Tulsa, Oklahoma

"**D**oes this hurt?"

"Not really," answered Emmy as Dr. Prescott, her oncologist, examined her breast.

"Not really or no? Or yes?"

"It's a damn tit squeeze, Doc, so it's not exactly pleasant," she said, looking up at the doctor from the exam table.

Dr. Prescott continued with her exam. "What about here?" she asked, manipulating another area of the breast.

Emmy shook her head.

"Here?"

"Nah, I'm good."

"And . . . what about . . . here?" she inquired as she dug deeper. Emmy winced. Dr. Prescott looked at her inquisitively.

"What did you say?" said Emmy, feigning deafness.

"Does it hurt there?"

"Where?"

"Where I was pushing?"

"When you say 'hurt,' define that."

"Was she this much trouble as a child?" the doctor asked Sandra, who was sitting and skimming a *Woman's Day* magazine.

"More."

"Pain is the opposite of comfortable in my book," said Dr. Prescott, looking down at Emmy over her green-framed glasses, which matched her eyes. Dr. Prescott was thirty-three, with shoulder-length blonde hair and a curious expression—a researcher's face, Emmy liked to call it.

"Define comfortable," she responded. "I mean, depending on your metrics, it could mean a number of things, right? As could pain." Sitting up and gesturing with her hands, Emmy continued. "For example, if you're the type that gets off on having your boobs crushed between two of those Acme anvils that Wile E. Coyote likes to throw around, then pain and comfort become a bit harder to define, I would think. Then again, if we take the time to examine other definitions of pain versus comfort—"

"*Emmy*," said Dr. Prescott, shaking her head.

Sandra lowered the magazine and looked at Emmy.

"Please don't do this," she said, giving her daughter the eye.

"Do what? I'm answering the good doctor's questions, am I not?" said Emmy, pretending to be clueless. Dr. Prescott pushed her glasses up to her face and gazed at Emmy, studying her, while her mother glared at her. Dr. Prescott motioned for her to put her shirt back on.

"Okay, get this," said Emmy with a girlish smile as she reached for her shirt, the front of which was inscribed with "I hit bitches—*real* hard." She pulled the shirt over her head and slipped it back on. "A woman walks into her oncologist's office holding a shopping bag with a ginormous pair of purple tits in it. She places the bag on the exam table and says, 'See! I told you I could find them at half price!' Then the oncologist says—"

"Emmy, *damn* it. I asked you not to do this!" Sandra exclaimed. Dr. Prescott suppressed a laugh before ever hearing the punchline, looking down and clearing her throat.

"Oh, come on, you two—lighten up, will ya? You can see where I get the profanity from, Dr. Prescott," said Emily with a droll expression. "Crying shame, isn't it? It's sadly ingrained; some studies even indicate a genetic tendency, for heaven's sake . . ."

Sandra threw the copy of *Woman's Day* back on the small table where she found it and leaned forward. "You want profanity? Okay, I'll *give* it to you," she emphasized. "Dr. Prescott," she said with a warm smile, but without breaking eye contact with Emmy, "would you fucking excuse us please? I wish to speak with my eldest but least mature *dipshit* of an offspring. The one apparently matriculating from a master's in public health to a master's in public bitch."

"Certainly," said Dr. Prescott, looking down and trying to maintain decorum. "I'll put my notes into the hallway computer. Take your time." She turned to Emmy before leaving and said, "Emmy, we all know you're a fighter. But I know fear when I see it. You're still very early stage. Celebrate that, okay?" She winked and walked out.

The room was quiet.

Finally, Sandra shook her head. "Look, I don't know—maybe it was a mistake coming with you today. Nice to see that you find this all so amusing. I was just trying to be a support."

"I know that, Ma," Emmy whispered. She looked down, kneading her thighs.

"I'm still your mother and you're still my daughter. I only want what's best for you. Please have some respect for me by taking this seriously."

Emmy made a heaving motion and a sound similar to a chipmunk calling out for its mother. Sandra looked at her, cocking her head. Emmy's shoulders shook as she put one hand to her face. "Oh, *shit*, Ma," she cried. "I beat the living hell out of the scariest woman in the league, but this tumor has me petrified!" She wept as she held her breast, which was tender from the probing and prodding, her calloused hand covering it as if to protect it. Sandra stood and walked to her, arms out.

"Oh, baby, it's gonna be okay," she said, taking Emmy in her arms and holding her, wondering if in fact it really *would* be okay. "You just let it out—it's okay," she said, as Emmy cried on her shoulder. Of the many things bound to visit Native women, Sandra thought, haven't we had enough? I mean, really? She rocked her oldest in her arms for another minute while Emmy collected herself.

When they were ready, they told the nurse and she alerted Dr. Prescott, who suggested an MRI to see where they stand. She emphasized that it would be used as a measure for the next MRI or CT as a comparison regarding any potentially serious changes. Emmy and Sandra went to lunch afterward, as usual.

They went back to the plant-based restaurant Paisley had recommended. The same waitress from before appeared at the table, beaming.

"Hello, Ms. McNair and Ms. McNair!" she said. "Welcome back!"

"Thanks," said Emmy. "What is your name again?"

"Lily," she said, admiring Emmy's hair, down and in a bit of a frizz.

"Osiyo, Lily. This is my mom, Sandra." Her mom smiled at Lily.

"Nice to meet you, Sandra. Hey, Storm, I put your signed menu up on the wall in my apartment. Had it framed. That was so awesome of you; thank you again!" She grinned at Emmy, moving her torso and hips side to side, holding her left upper arm behind her back with her right hand. There was a twinkle in her eye as she asked if they wanted water. They said yes, and Lily said she would be right back, but then turned and added, "Oh, and *hot* water for you, right, Storm?" Emmy nodded. She had been ordering hot water regularly so she could put her Pau D 'Arco tea in it.

"Well," said Sandra with a smile, "*that* girl definitely has the hots for you."

"Yeah," said Emmy, "her and Tina Gallager." She laughed and shook her head.

"Really? Tina?" her mom asked, leaning in close to Emmy with a surprised look. "No!"

"Oh, God, Mom. She'd jump me tonight if I let her," she said with another laugh.

"That is *so* funny!"

"She's a *great* fighter, Mom. A really good friend, too. I trust Tina. She has the *cutest* little boy—Edgar. He always grins at me when she brings him in. He says, 'Hey, you! Lady over there!' and points, then puts his hands up like he wants to box. Oh, Lord, he is adorable." She seemed relaxed now. Lily was back with water and the menus, took their drink orders, and said she would return. She headed to another table where a man had just sat down.

"Well, that is hilarious about you and Tina. Sounds like Mike might have his hands full. I mean, there might be 'trouble in paradise!'" Sandra said with a grin.

"Oh, stop, Ma!"

Lily returned to take their order and the menus. Sandra requested the cauliflower wings and a large salad, while Emmy chose the black bean burger with a small side salad with maple mustard dressing. Lily grinned at Emmy again and then turned around and ran right into another waitress walking by. She smiled self-consciously and headed for the back. Sandra laughed when she was gone and told Emmy she might have to scale down and go grunge in public if she wanted to avoid the attention and public crushes.

"The price you pay for being a babe, I suppose," said Sandra. "I'm sure I wouldn't know."

"Oh, please, Ma. You're still a fox."

Her mom blushed.

"No, seriously." She leaned in toward her mom, lowering her voice. "I meant to tell you this about two or three weeks ago—remember Willie Ray Starr?"

Her mom nodded.

"Saw him at the Tractor Supply store one day and he asked about you."

"Oh, God, girl. Seriously? He's such a goofball," said Sandra, closing her eyes and moving her arm if trying to brush away the thought of Willie Ray Starr.

"He said, 'Tell that sweet thing I'm gonna get up the nerve to call her one of these days!'"

"Oh, Jesus Christ. Let's hope he has a complete failure in courage—for my sake." They laughed.

"Seriously, Ma, ever think about dating? Or do you date? Just curious."

"Oh, praise the ancestors," Sandra said, looking up. "My coffee is here."

Emmy just smiled and shook her head while Lily placed their tea and coffee before them. They chatted for a bit waiting on the food. They talked about Dr. Prescott, Paisley, Mike's latest assignment, and Molly's knee. Lily brought the cauliflower wings and Emmy's salad. She blushed when Emmy smiled at her.

Emmy said a quick blessing and they dug in.

"Em," her mom began, "Molly asked me if something had happened to you." Emmy looked up at her as she chewed, then looked down again. "I think she knows something might have. Have you ever thought about telling her?"

Emmy shrugged, digging her fork into her salad. "Once or twice."

"Maybe it would help her to know."

"How, Ma? Just how the hell would that help?"

Sandra put her hand in Emmy's. "Not here to confront," she said, pulling Emmy's hand up and kissing it. "Just thinking about us as a family. Nothing more."

Emmy thought about it.

"I don't think it would help anything. I have a great therapist in Marie, and that's where I think it should stay."

"Does Mike know?"

Emmy looked at her mom, her lovely eyes pleading.

"Okay," Sandra said, holding up her hand, "sorry. None of my business."

"Yeah," Emmy sighed, "he knows. He was *wonderful*, Mom. Really. The best." Her mom smiled at her, seeing that Emmy was unquestionably in love. "You know, the kind of work he does—wasn't like it was a shock or anything."

Sandra stared out one of the cafe windows.

"Yeah," she responded thoughtfully, "and that's another kind of crime, isn't it?" She shook her head again for her daughter and the millions of others. She studied Emmy for a moment, an awed, yet almost terrified look on her face. "You would have killed those men at the Archway, wouldn't you?"

"Yes," said Emmy without hesitation, sucking down a shredded carrot slice. "Right between the eyes, Ma. All of them. You can *make book* on it." She looked down again and casually took another bite, as if she were merely discussing the weather or ordering a beer.

Sandra scratched again, but then stopped. "I love you. You know that, right?"

Emmy nodded. "Of course. Things are good, Ma, really," she reassured her. "I'm doing fine on that score, don't worry." Sandra nodded. Emmy patted her mother's hand and resumed eating.

Changing the subject, Sandra put her hand on the table with emphasis. "Thinking about what you said about Tina—and

this waitress, never mind—you know how I hate to gossip, but—
"

"Oh, Ma, *really*? You are *such* a gossip!" It was, actually, one of the things Emmy disliked about her mom.

"Am not."

"Are too."

"Am not."

Emmy just rolled her eyes. She wasn't taking the bait. She took a long sip of her water then dug into the black bean burger that had just arrived.

Sandra was about to bust, and Emmy took great pleasure in pretending that her mom hadn't said anything at all, playing with her food and trying not to laugh in Sandra's face.

"All right, dammit!" Sandra whispered, "I'm going to tell you anyway!"

Emmy burst out laughing.

"I *knew* it! You just can't help yourself, can you?" She wiped her mouth with her napkin.

Sandra ignored her oldest child's attempt to school her. She told Emmy about seeing Rebecca and Tara, and her chat with Molly on that subject. Emmy just continued to chomp on her burger.

"Well?" said Sandra, "are you surprised at all, especially since we've known those girls since they were little? Just seemed like it came out of the blue."

Emmy shrugged again. "I don't know. People today, Ma. I don't know . . . things are just different than they used to be. More kids feel safer than ever to come out as one persuasion or the other. In so many places now, if you're young and straight, you're often in the minority. So, I don't know how much of it is genuine and how much is experimentation. Tara is gay, no doubt. I could tell by the way she used to stare at Molly and the Chief when they would all hang out at our house. Rebecca? I think she may be more in the questioning phase, but I don't know. Only she should determine that. Not some damn doctor or teacher or professor telling her she's one thing or another. That's for the person to decide, goddamn it, and I hate that shit."

"Wow," Sandra exclaimed, "you've certainly given this some thought."

"I think we all are called to," said Emmy. "We should have clarity in our own heads about things or it's going to be hard to make sense of anything in the future. That's how fast things are moving, Ma. I know that, when my time as an MMA fighter comes to an end and I go into public health, I will have to have clear positions in my mind on some of these things."

Sandra admired her daughter.

"You know, maybe I did a pretty good job with you after all," she said as she sipped her coffee. "Very proud of you."

Emmy looked down at the table. "I'm just a bunny rabbit, Mom. A rabbit running from the coyote at dusk in the heat of the Oklahoma desert," she humbly intoned, closing her eyes and shaking her head, ashamed of her behavior in Dr. Prescott's office. She massaged her thighs.

Her mother leaned in close and whispered, *"Bullshit.* You're a golden eagle, soaring in on the southern winds over the Arkansas River on a cool April morning in the sunshine," she said poetically. "Ever present, ever watching. I knew you before you knew you and shit." She grinned and winked, briefly holding Emmy's hand again.

"Wado, Mom," Emmy whispered back, looking at her plate and taking a deep breath and stroking her legs once more.

"Ga-gay-you-ee, my girl," Sandra responded, letting her know she was loved. She raised her coffee cup to Emmy's cup of Pau d'Arco tea, and they toasted.

32

Those Chair-a-Keys!

November 16, 1838
Bell Detachment
Bolivar Region
State of Tennessee

Once again, the community charged Captain Ambrose tolls that, to no one's surprise, came from funds allotted for the Indians. As the Bell Detachment approached Bolivar, they encountered a bridge that spanned the Hatchie River. A man by the name of Harry Oliver enforced toll regulations, and he shook his head as he saw the military and civilian caravans coming together in the distance. It was the longest train of people and animals he had ever seen. He mounted his horse and rode out to meet them head-on.

"Whoa! Harry L. Oliver, for the townspeople of Bolivar. Who goes there in the present year of our Lord?"

"Captain Ambrose, United States Army, Fourth Artillery Division. I am in command of this detachment of the Cherokee people, and we are coming through, sir!"

"The hell you say."

"The hell I do, sir, indeed. Prepare the way for a vast number of wagons and human and animal real estate. I am authorized by the government and your president, sir, to make payment for passage across this river."

"I would vouchsafe to say that you are indeed, Captain. I will provide that passage and do so for a pretty but reasonable penny. Do you plan to do this in the present moment, or will there be a delay for this accommodation?"

"Starting now, sir. Posthaste. We mustn't tarry. Much experience in these matters tells me that the most consistent movement is the wisest manner of strategy. I will follow you to the crossing, sir, if that suits you. At that point, I will dismount and we can do our business and start moving these poor savages to the other side. Satisfactory?"

"That will do, Captain. Follow me, sir." Ambrose signaled to Lieutenant Whitworth, and he, guided by Mr. Oliver, led the people to the river. Crossing the Hatchie was uneventful and faster than many of their crossings. It wasn't until they came across some of the adjacent swamps that things became more challenging. The swampland presented a crooked and dangerous path for the wagons and animals.

Most of the Cherokees found themselves wading up to their chests and, in some cases, heads. Children and babies had to be carried overhead to prevent loss or drowning. One child didn't make it, and it took twenty minutes to locate his body. One horse broke his leg and had to be shot. At least three wagons broke axles, and front wheels came off several others. Due to chaos in the swamps, Captain Ambrose decided to halt the party until runners could determine that all groups in the detachment were ready to move forward, making a command decision to camp just outside of Bolivar, with the hope of making up that time the following morning.

The next day, as people and animals began to dry out, the wagons, horses, donkeys, and walkers seemed to be going in slow motion. Back on foot together, Mary and Nick moved along, the wider dirt road through Bolivar cold and uninviting. The detachment was deliberate, experienced now, as the people and wagons quietly made their way in a long, steady, and solemn succession of weary people and animals. The McNairs approached the central section of what was basically the town's main street. They passed what was called The Little Court House on the left and a Cherokee elder, Pigeon, who had his own horse, rode by with his wife. He pointed to the courthouse.

"Nick-o-las," he said, "Mr. Davy Crockett—he speak for us—there, at courthouse—much grateful. He take stand for our people." Nick and Mary nodded.

"Yes, he did, Pigeon," Nick affirmed. "We too are grateful," he added with a nod.

"Too bad his words not enough," Pigeon moaned before moving on.

Mary squeezed her husband's hand and sighed, looking down as they walked and hearing occasional shouts from the soldiers of "Keep it movin', people," "Gotta make up time!" and "No slowin' down here—keep walking!" The shouts were not hateful, but firm reminders of the inevitability of their destination. A few minutes later, a large house on a hill across the street came into view. It was apparently in the process of conversion from log cabin to stately manner. Three of four completed columns stood in front on either side of a grand front door. They noticed a woman with light-colored hair standing on a balcony above the front door. She stood, hands on the wrought iron railing, observing the party and holding a monocle over one eye.

She turned toward the interior of the building and called out, "Levi, Lee-vie! Look out here-ah."

A man walked to the balcony and stood with her.

"Thatsa them, hon," she said, "that would be them-ah; those *Chair*-a-keys!" To Mary, it seemed as if she and her family were on display at an auction or the like. "Oh, *my*," she chortled, "look-ah that one they-ah! Why, why, she's *lovely*, Lee-vie; just love-lee. See her there-ah? The preg-a-nant one. Why, she's just *gore-a-gous*, she is! The poor-ah thang. Why, bless her-ah heart!"

Mary looked up and locked eyes with the woman; she was not far from her but may as well have been a thousand miles away based on their respective ideas of reality. Mary, her full, dark hair down to her waist, her raven-like eyes, haunting in their beauty, her unborn child hanging lower by the week, kept her shoulders high and held her man's hand in a show of dignity and faithfulness. Enoch, at the reins of the McNair wagon again, tipped his hat to the couple on the balcony. He smiled, but had other ideas in mind.

"And top of the day to you, my flamboyant, bombastic, cosmopolitan *crackers*," he muttered under his breath in his best Shakespearean inflection. He smiled again, tipping his hat once more, and started cackling to himself as the carriage rolled past the mansion. Augustine yawned. Deborah, who had a powerful work ethic for such a young teen, noticed a girl, a few years younger than she and wearing a new dress straight from the Boston colonies, staring at her from beside a rose bush at the corner of the mansion's property. She gazed at Deborah, as if she had never even seen a Negro girl, and Deborah watched as the corners of the girl's mouth turned upward into a faint smile. Deborah smiled back and waved, causing the girl to turn and run to the steps leading to the grand front door. The Bell Detachment continued on.

November 18, 1838
Bell Detachment
Somerville, Tennessee

The Cherokees continued to show fatigue, and chose to camp for two nights instead of one. On the second night of encampment in Somerville, a middle-aged man named, ironically enough, Path Walker, bid goodnight to his fellow Indians and walked to an isolated spot near the camp. He seized his rifle, sat beneath a large oak tree, put his toe on the trigger, pointed the weapon at his head, and blew his brains out. Someone had heard him say that he would "go no further to that country of Arkansas." Nick and Mary grieved yet another death among their people. The numbers were growing, making it harder for Mary to hide her grief. She broke down twice in four hours after Path Walker killed himself, thinking that being driven to self-slaughter was the most grievous of the horrible penalties inflicted by the government.

She kept a regular eye on Pretty Water in the Morning throughout the journey and at one point realized that Pretty Water had taken on caring for Old Nancy. Old Nancy was infirm and Pretty Water seemed to have transferred her maternal instincts into helping Old Nancy with her basic needs, much as she would have done with her baby. She took it on as her responsibility to feed her, bathe her, dress her, and so on. It was one of the most astonishing things Mary and Nick had ever witnessed. Diana McLendon said it was "a shining example of the triumph of the human spirit." Mary sensed that she could back away from caring for Pretty Water as much as she had before. But her grief for the repeated losses was rising, and she felt a disconnection from her spirit at times, which worried Nick in the quiet hours of the night.

Oddly enough, none of the soldiers caught on that Ida Bird had picked their pockets. In fact, the man from whom Ida had stolen the dagger and shot bag assumed he lost them somewhere along the trail. Mary was bathing Martha in a large tub when she spotted Ida swiping Sergeant Thomas's personal tobacco canister. Although she was thankful that Sergeant Thomas had been kind to her family and the other Cherokees, she secretly thought it marvelous that Ida was still up to her tricks, and that she had survived the journey to date. She could hear Brother Simon Rhodes preaching the Gospel from a nearby tent, and her tears flowed as she quoted Scripture along with him. Many of the Cherokees who were not Christian were getting caught up in card games devised by the soldiers and civilian teamsters, and she knew they were being taken advantage of. She confided her worries to Nick, who said they had to be strong and look out for their own family first, come hell or more high water.

At one point while doing daily chores, Mary twisted her left knee in an awkward motion. She began to limp and the pain became severe. The extra weight of the baby made the load on her knee that much more strenuous. She hobbled about for a while, then rested. As she tried to calm herself before the day's travel, Nick brought her his pipe. He stuffed fresh tobacco leaves into the chamber and gathered some embers from the previous evening's fire. After some effort he managed to light the leaves, took a few puffs to test it, then handed the pipe to Mary.

As she lay sprawled against a tree, belly protruding, she inhaled deeply. The smoke rose through the air, some of it blowing back on her and her free-flowing hair before making its way in Nick's direction. Husband and wife sat quietly for a few minutes, contemplating their situation. As Mary's pain subsided, Nick moved down and addressed her feet.

Nick pulled a few leaves from his tobacco pouch and ground them even more. He spit on them then applied the mushy compound to Mary's blisters, soothing the pain from the abrasions and swelling. She looked at him lovingly, then resumed smoking from the pipe.

"You need more time on the wagon," he said with irritation in his voice.

"No."

"Yes."

"No. Many others must walk—so should I."

"Many others are not with child, woman."

"Some are," she argued, exhaling her last round of nicotine into the air. Nick sighed and dabbed more of the poultice on the largest blister on her right foot. He removed his pocket watch and wound it, placing it on the ground beside him.

"All right," he said, looking at Mary with conviction. "You get thirty minutes at most on the ground, then it's back in the wagon. You can walk at two-hour intervals. That clear?"

Mary looked at him with an expression that surely said, "And just who in the hell do you think you're talking to?"

He looked away, toward the ground, then back at his beloved. "Please?"

She smiled, then winked. "Agreed," she said, wincing as she moved to a more upright position before standing.

Nick helped her to her feet and looked down at her belly. "And you," he said to the child within, "mind your manners."

She smiled at him, blinking her eyes and trying not to look as tired as she clearly was. "Be right back," he said, and walked over to the wagon, where Mary noticed a piece of wood with slices of bark and wood shavings on it. Nick had discovered a willow tree and cut off some of the watery bark to relieve her pain. He brought some to Mary and she gratefully sucked on some of the shavings, as best she could. Before he took the remaining bark back to the wagon for safekeeping, Mary stopped him by touching his arm, then thanked him with a kiss.

33

The Viking & the Vicar

It's a nickname, and I *earned* it.

—The late Wilma Mankiller, when once asked
by a taxi driver about her surname

Present Day
Sacred Grounds Coffee Shop
Muskogee, Oklahoma

A gorgeous afternoon found Molly, Tara, and Rebecca stopping at Lotus Gold so that Becks could grab some hemp. Molly just shook her head and laughed as Rebecca traipsed into the marijuana dispensary with a smile on her face.

"You know, I've never been into it much," said Molly as they watched her go inside. "You?"

Tara smiled and shrugged. "Not so much, but I have a little every now and then. Gives me a headache if I take a certain amount. And I can't smoke it; can't stand to. Sublingual only for this girl. Becks walked into her doc's office and said, 'I'm fucking depressed.' Presto! Marijuana card!"

"I'm starting to get it, though," said Molly with frustration. "Life . . . geez Louise."

"Tell me about it," said Tara. "Enough stress to go around for all of us ten times over. You know, Native rights being overlooked, coming out of the pandemic, school, university or no university, Cherokee and colonial ideals forever clashing, family stuff for different people all the time, hell." Molly nodded.

They chatted for a few minutes before eventually turning to their phones. Molly checked PowWowUs and Tara read her texts. About that time Rebecca came out, grinning. She started dancing on the sidewalk, doing her best Beyoncé-style J-Setting moves. Tara and Molly laughed. Molly glanced over at Tara and she could see her face glowing, eyes twinkling as she watched Becks showing off, which made Molly smile.

Rebecca got in and they drove across to Sacred Grounds. Tara—an excellent driver—swung the SUV skillfully into the parking space directly in front of the cafe. "Ohhh," said Molly, rubbing her temples, "*so* looking forward to a latte right now, Jesus." They got out and headed for the door, Tara and Rebecca holding hands. Tara rested her head on Rebecca's shoulder as they got in a short line behind a group of out-of-place white kids with freshly scrubbed faces and conservative clothing.

"Gotta go water the bushes," said Molly, indicating the restroom. Rebecca nodded and Tara asked her what she wanted, saying that she would place the order and that it was on her today.

Molly returned from the restroom just in time to witness a startling scene. Rebecca had her arm around Tara's waist, and Tara looked frightened.

A teen about Molly's age, blonde, sporting ironed white pants and a green polka dot print blouse, wearing a large, gaudy gold cross around her neck, was chastising Tara and Rebecca as they waited in line. "You're both foredoomed until you repent!" she preached, her hands on her hips. The girl was smug, cocksure. Her version of the Bible was clearly the correct one; any other interpretation was null and void. "You are harlots at the brink of the embers of hell!"

Molly glanced at her friends. She could tell they were surprised, in shock, and deeply hurt.

Though Tara was not generally as emotional as Becks, Molly could see what looked like a tear in Tara's right eye, and she seemed to have slipped behind Rebecca for protection. Rebecca, often the first of the three to pounce on injustice when she saw it, seemed immobilized. The girl stepped closer to the couple and thrust her finger in their faces, insisting that the friends Molly had known since childhood were horrible, unrepentant subhumans destined for something even worse than hell.

"You will both spend eternity in the fires of Gehenna, a trash heap where the lost and most disrespecting to Jesus go to rot! Trash will remain trash until it burns into righteousness!" she boomed, gesticulating as if she were standing behind a pulpit holding a rattlesnake. In her imagination, at least, she had the entire congregation in the cafe hanging on her every word.

Rebecca, who looked the most Native of the three of them, wore a Cherokee National Holiday shirt. The blonde pointed to it and proclaimed, "You! You worshipers of the sun and false gods, your pathway is one of misdeeds and sloth! And women who lay together will suffer the punishment of God's almighty sword! You are an abomination to the Lord our God!"

Her companions nodded and muttered agreement with an "amen!" thrown in here and there. The few other patrons in the building seemed stupefied, and Molly noticed that the employees behind the counter were stunned and hesitant. One timid customer who had just gotten her beverage left as quickly as possible, passing a woman on her way in as the door closed behind her. The woman coming in arrived just in time to hear the girl's last comments about Tara and Rebecca.

Molly couldn't explain why she did it; she just did it. She walked over to the gospel hawker and slapped her face. It sounded like a firecracker. The girl's eyes widened into a startled, perplexed look, as if she had been shocked by an electrical device. The girl stared at Molly. Molly was so hurt and taken by surprise, she couldn't find the words she wanted.

"OWWWW!" screamed the blonde zealot. Her friends were frozen, unable to respond. They gaped at their leader, stunned that such a thing could ever happen to one of God's chosen. The girl rubbed her face and started crying. "That hurrrt!" she whined. Rebecca and Tara looked at each other with wide eyes, surprised at their friend. Molly had worn her grandmother's spider earrings that day. Her chestnut hair swayed with the blow as her hand rebounded from the white girl's face.

"Hey!" yelled the assistant manager, "we have a no-tolerance policy here. All of you are going to have to go—now."

Molly finally found her words. "You know," she said to the blonde, trying to hold her fury, "it's so-called 'Christians' like you who make Christians like me almost ashamed of the cross! And by the way," she roared, pointing to the garish gold cross, "you disgrace us by wearing that around your neck, you . . . you . . . miserable *bitch!*"

Tara put her hand to her mouth and shot a glance at Rebecca, who wore a slight smile.

Molly, an enormous lump in her throat, arms outstretched in frustration, moved toward the counter to explain herself to the staff. Before she could take another step, she felt a strong arm around her belly from behind. She turned to see a young woman about Emmy's age—though she could pass for someone much younger; she had a kind face, one of confidence but not arrogance. Her brownish hair had a painted red streak running down the left side, stylishly falling over her eye in an attractive way. A black leather Harley-Davidson strap adorned her left wrist. With one hand on Molly's waist, she patted her cheek with the other.

"I've got it from here, Probie," said the stranger with a calm, reassuring smile. She studied Molly briefly and winked. Molly looked over at her friends, who seemed just as alarmed by this newcomer. The woman had a worn, almost ragged clergy collar, unclasped and hanging rather carelessly from her neck, as if she had had a long, rough day and was glad to be done with the day and the collar as well.

"I said all of you kids have to go now. Sorry, store policy," the young assistant manager repeated.

The woman slowly guided Molly over to her friends, who looked worried. She then went to the counter and introduced herself to the assistant manager. "Hi, I'm Reverend Claire Sanders, pastor of Come to the Circle. I think we can resolve this, don't you?" The cafe employee shrugged.

"I'm supposed to call the police," he said, looking unsure of himself.

"Don't," said Claire with authority, handing him a business card. He didn't.

She looked at the girl and her friends. She spoke with precision, but did not yell. Her volume was enough for everyone in the cafe to hear. "On behalf of my friends here, I apologize that this came to a slap. But can you understand why? No, you probably can't. Let me say this: You need to know that you *all* are violating the law by disturbing the peace and intimidating these women. You are also in violation of the 1964 Civil Rights Act, a federal offense. Federal time, that's, uh, that's ugly." She shook her head. "Not only that, you are further in violation of Title 21-850 of the Oklahoma general statutes, a hate crime. You just committed a misdemeanor in my presence and can go to jail for it."

The blonde girl seemed confounded as she rubbed her face, her companions looking petrified. "If you approach these two women again for the same thing, that is a felony punishable by up to ten years in prison. Now, why don't all of you take your drinks and leave before this goes any further and the cops get called, hmm? Just as a reminder, you may be in your beloved state of Oklahoma, but you are also on tribal land—Indian Territory—so minding your manners is advised. Oh, and by the way, since you profess scriptural authority, take some time to read Matthew 7:12 in several different translations. And, though it might be a challenge, try and be nice for a change, okay? You might be surprised how far that can take you."

The startled fanatics exchanged glances and almost ran out of the building, the blonde girl still holding her cheek and whining. Molly shook from the cortisol rush. Pastor Claire looked at the assistant manager.

"Will that do?" The assistant smiled and nodded. Two white women with window seats and an elderly black man holding a cane applauded both Molly and Claire.

"Yes, ma'am. What can I get ya?" the assistant manager inquired.

"Iced green tea, unsweetened."

"On the house," he said.

"Not necessary," she replied.

"Oh, no, Reverend, my pleasure, believe me. You might have just saved us a lot of trouble and commotion, not to mention an evening news story."

"Whatever," said Claire with a smile. She turned back to Molly and her friends. "You guys okay?" Tara and Rebecca nodded. Molly looked at the stranger.

"Wado. I mean, thank you. Really. You were awesome!" she said.

"Howa," she replied, telling Molly she was welcome.

"You're Cherokee!" exclaimed Molly.

"Yes," said Claire, "by ancestry. I'm not a tribal citizen. I'm a Sanders descendant. My ancestors traveled the Trail of Tears on the Bell route."

Molly's eyes widened and she glanced at her friends.

"Mine too!" she said. "Yeah—same route even!"

"Oh, well, there ya go, sista!" Claire said as she leaned in and hugged Molly. Molly hung onto Claire for a moment, unsure of just why. She pulled back and looked down.

"Nice job, young warrior," said Claire quietly. "A bit violent, but message delivered, I would think."

"Oh, I'm no warrior," said Molly self-consciously, looking down again.

"If you say so," answered Claire, strangely in the same way Mary would. She gave Molly one of her cards. "Feel free to call me anytime," she said, looking at Molly in what seemed like a clairvoyant way. "We'll have lunch, chat up the ancestors," she said with another grin.

Not knowing what to say or how to feel, Molly said, "I'm sorry I slapped her in front of you."

"What's your name, cousin?"

"Molly."

"Well, Molly, I'm sure white Jesus will get over it, ya think? His propensity for overturning tables and whatnot." They laughed.

Molly had the strangest feeling their meeting was no accident. She scanned the room for Mary. Did she set this up? Was she watching all this? She remembered her "chat" with Mary: *Do I need to go to church more often?* I don't know, do you? Molly suddenly got the chills. She stared at Pastor Claire's card. It felt as if it almost had a life of its own, a vibration even.

"Okay," said Molly shyly, "I'd love to have lunch sometime." Pastor Claire got her green tea and reminded the girls about Come to the Circle, then departed. Molly held her card, looking at it and wondering what had come over her. Tara handed Molly her latte and asked the manager if they had to leave. He said technically, yes, but if they sat outside he could officially say they left the building. He smiled at them. While they were getting their napkins and cup covers, one of the women by the window walked over.

"I have no idea who you are, but I want to say how proud I am of you." She hugged Molly, who seemed astounded, and waited while her friend cleared their little table. "I'm a Christian, too. I'm Roman Catholic, and just wanted to say that was a very noble thing to do." Molly just smiled and looked down. The woman leaned in and whispered, "Truth be known, I wanted to slap that little witch myself!" Rebecca heard her and giggled. The woman wished them a nice rest of the evening and she and her friend left. Molly noticed them holding hands on the way to their car.

As the girls headed for the door, Rebecca grabbed Molly and blew a snort-burpie on her neck like they would do to each other when they were little. She hung on as they moved along, leaning into Molly. Imitating Cameron in *Ferris Bueller's Day Off*, she said, "Molly McNair, you're my *hero*!"

Molly snickered and pushed her away, saying, "Stop it, Becks!"

In a moment of seriousness, Tara blocked Molly's path and took her latte back, placing it on the table next to them. She teared up as she looked Molly in the eye and hugged her. "You're a serious badass viking, you know that?" she said into her ear and kissed her friend's cheek.

"Am not."

"Are too."

"Not really."

"Yeah-huh!" Tara said, getting in the last word.

"Hey," said Rebecca as they made their way out to the patio, "we should stick her ass in the cage with Emmy. Bet she could give her a run for her money!" Tara nodded.

"Yeah *right*," said Molly with a laugh. "Two hits: Emmy hitting me, me hitting the mat. Period." They laughed.

Come to the Circle Space
Unitarian Universalist Church
Office of Rev. Claire Sanders
Muskogee, Oklahoma

Molly entered the front door of the Unitarian Universalist church and took a left—down the stairs, to a corner office with Claire's name on the door. She sat behind a small desk and smiled when Molly appeared.

"How's my young warrior?" she asked, getting up and approaching her for a hug.

"Fine," said Molly with a slight wince, her knee aggravating her. She had texted Claire to take her up on her invitation for lunch.

"Ouch," said Claire, noticing Molly's knee brace. "Doesn't much look like it. Is that recent? Didn't notice it the other day."

"Sort of," said Molly. "I had on jeans the other day, though, so you wouldn't have seen it."

"Oh, yeah. Right," said Claire, remembering. She motioned for Molly to sit in the chair across from the desk. Claire pulled her rolling chair around the desk so that they could be face-to-face.

"Are you Unitarian?" Molly asked with a look of confusion and some apprehension. Claire laughed.

"No, but I could be," she said. "I like the Unitarians. They tend to treat one another better than we Trinitarians do! When I first came to town about eight months ago, I approached several churches about sharing space, and the Unitarians were the first to say yes, so I grabbed it. Not a lot of room here," she said, looking around her little office, "but it's cozy and welcoming." Molly smiled. "I'm actually dually aligned with two different denominations. I'm Baptist-based." Molly nodded. "I graduated seminary last year and wanted to try and plant a welcoming church here in Indian Country. I have some financial help from the denominations, so that's good." She studied Molly as she looked around Claire's office, pretending to be interested in the artwork, the church-related symbols, and so on. "All right, cousin, what's *wrong*?" She smiled compassionately.

For reasons Molly couldn't explain, she had a sudden attack of diarrhea of the mouth. She poured out everything she had been holding in since Emmy's diagnosis. She didn't get too emotional, welling up only once. She talked about being raised Episcopalian, growing up with Devon, what Devon did at the theater, her friends becoming lovers, the Remember the

Removal Ride going down in flames, her knee, meeting Clay, being fearful about Emmy, and so on. When she was done, thirty minutes had gone by. She suddenly leaned forward and put her head in her hands, sighing. Then she looked up at Claire.

"Damn," she said. "I just totally screwed up lunch, didn't I?" Then she felt bad for swearing in front of a pastor.

Claire smiled. "Nope, sure didn't. This is an office day for me, no pastoral care or the like. We're doing just fine." Molly smiled weakly. "So," Claire boomed, slapping her knees and standing, "what say we get outta here and go grab some chow?"

Molly couldn't help it. She giggled. Then giggled some more. Then, as Claire was grabbing her shoulder bag, she giggled once more. What the hell? Was it stress relief or what? she wondered. Finally, as Claire shut the door, she stopped snickering and rubbed her head, wondering if she had made a mistake coming here.

No, you didn't.

Molly looked around. She glanced down the hall, then back the other way.

"Something wrong?" asked Claire with a puzzled look.

"Ah, no. Just thought I heard something is all."

Once on the road, Claire asked where Molly wanted to go. Molly told her about Emmy's new diet and that out of respect for her, she was trying to eat better, which made Claire smile. Claire took her to Harmony House, where Claire asked for a table on the patio since it was a milder than usual day.

"So," she asked as the waiter brought their menus, "Emmy eats plant-based for her health, huh?"

"Yeah," said Molly. "This doctor has told her about studies that show eating that way can prevent and even reverse some breast cancer."

"That's really terrific, Molly. I've read something about that, too. Hard to break the habit of so many of the things we eat, though, isn't it?"

"Tell me about it!" said Molly with a laugh. "I'm addicted to chips, I swear. Emmy tells me to just sub stovetop popcorn for them instead," she said with a shrug. Claire nodded and smiled. "It's important for her, though, not just 'cause the cancer, but because she's a professional athlete. They have to be real careful anyway about what they eat." The waiter returned, bringing them both iced tea and water, and they ordered.

Claire raised her glass of tea to Molly and said, "Here's to your courage, Molly."

Molly smiled and returned the toast. "And to yours. You were really *awesome* with those girls," she said, shaking her head. "I don't understand some people," said Molly. "Never could get behind those fundamentalist types that insist their way is the only way, like, like, God speaks only to them."

Claire nodded. "Some of that goes back in the generations, and a lot of it is someone with a dynamic personality taking advantage of young people—infecting their minds with extremist thinking. It's okay for people to have different beliefs. It's okay to take the Bible literally if that is your thing. But it's never your job to impose your ideals on others. That's where things get ugly." Molly nodded in agreement.

"How old are you?" asked Molly.

"Twenty-six last week!"

"Oh! Happy birthday last week," said Molly, raising her glass again for another toast. "Yeah—you're a couple of years older than Emmy. You could pass for nineteen though, seriously!" They laughed.

"I believe in welcoming people to the table, as long as they are not causing harm to others in the process. I have an open-door policy, but I did have one church member whose boyfriend was abusing her, so I sent him on his way. Told him I would have the cops lock him up if he didn't stop. I'm more moderate-to-liberal in my theology, I suppose, but I do have some conservative social leanings. For example, my father is a retired police captain—a good man. I really hated it when my more 'liberal' clergy friends started calling cops cancer and murderers of unarmed black men and the like. I could tell how much it hurt him, and that hurt me."

Molly nodded. "Yeah, our family has friends in law enforcement, and Emmy's boyfriend is a cop—a special agent for the OSBI. So, yeah, it hits home, especially when you know cops personally who are good people." Claire nodded as she stirred her iced tea with a spoon.

"So how do you feel about your sister being a fighter?"

"Well, you know—it's weird; she's my sister, right? But sometimes it seems as if she's this other being, like a stranger. Not in a bad way. But because she's becoming kinda famous, it's just—I dunno—odd. Never expected that."

"She probably didn't either," said Claire.

"Did you see the Ortiz fight?" asked Molly.

"Nah, but I saw highlights on the news or somewhere. Sounded like a big victory for Indian Country."

"It was. She wiped the ring with her!" Molly exclaimed proudly. Then she looked down. "It's just that Ortiz—she's a pretty dirty fighter and mean as hell. She insulted our family in the ring—told Emmy we were all trailer trash and whatnot. So Emmy beat her ass real good." Claire smiled.

"Well," she replied, "I don't follow mixed martial arts much but I do respect those gals—they have a lot of heart. I *can* tell you this: My cousin Steve is a big fan and does a little bit on the amateur side himself. He told me that your sister is probably the greatest female UFC fighter of all time."

It was stunning to Molly to actually hear the words. "Wow," she said, shaking her head in wonderment. "But that's what I mean, see? It's like it isn't real—like people are talking about someone else and not my big sis."

"That makes sense. You know her as your sister, Emmy."

"Exactly!" said Molly. She took another swig of iced tea and the waiter arrived with their food.

As they enjoyed lunch, Molly talked more about the ride, her knee, and Mary. Claire listened intently and with great interest. When Molly paused at one point, Claire looked at her and posed an interesting question.

"Molly, have you ever thought about retracing Mary's journey on the Bell route? I mean, it doesn't have to be an either/or. You could always do the ride in a year or two, or whenever, since Tommy is willing to hold it for you."

Molly just looked at her. What if you walked in my tracks and not someone else's? Holy shit, she thought. She put her fork in her dessert—peach cobbler—and took a bite. "Gosh," she said, considering this, "I don't know."

"You could make it a summer project, whether or not you go to college this year. You could figure out a way to film it, like a mini-documentary. If you did that, you could no doubt use it for college credit in one course or another. Plus, you've got something you can keep forever—something to pass down the generations."

"Wow. I'll have to give that some thought, I guess."

"So," said Claire, "tell me about your ancestors. Who is your family? How far back can you go?"

This lit Molly up. "Well," she said with some excitement, "back in Tennessee, David McNair married Delilah Vann. They had like six kids, and one of them was a guy named Nicholas McNair. He married Mary Rogers, and they were on the Trail of Tears Bell route. They had a bunch of children, too, and one of them was also named Nicholas. A bunch of sons come down the line, and that's where I get my surname, through my dad, of course. He died of a heart attack when I was eleven."

"Oh, I'm sorry."

"Ah, that's okay. It's been almost seven years now," said Molly with a shrug.

"Well, wow, that's quite a history. Good on you, Probie!" Molly laughed. "So, it sounds like we had ancestors who took a terrible and heartbreaking trip together, doesn't it?" Molly nodded solemnly. "My ancestors in the Bell Detachment were

Robert Sanders and his wife, who was named Mary, too. Lot of Marys back then. One thing led to another over the generations and my Dawes ancestor got stricken from the roll due to death. I have a great-grandmother and some others on different rolls like the Miller Roll, but no more citizen qualifiers."

"That sucks," said Molly.

"Yeah, but it doesn't really matter to me. Cherokees around here treat me pretty well—like part of the family." She smiled.

Molly drank some of her water, leaned back in her seat, and played with the ends of her hair. "Guess I'll come up with a plan about the Trail of Tears that works for me . . ."

"No hurry; just an idea." She watched as Molly sat forward and began playing with her cobbler, her chin resting in one hand as if lost in thought. "What else is going on in that head of yours?"

"You know," she said, "I slapped that chick because I thought she was being cruel. She was being horrible to my friends." Claire nodded. "Do you think I overreacted?"

"Do *you* think you overreacted?"

"I don't know. Maybe. I didn't like the way it felt."

"That's a good sign."

"I mean, I don't know how Emmy does it—waling on people like that."

"Emmy's a professional. It's her job. And the people she wales on are volunteers, in case you hadn't noticed," she said with a smile.

"And Mike—Emmy's boyfriend. He got into a fight at work and busted some oil worker's nose."

"And that's *his* job, assuming he was justified."

"The other guy swung first."

"And there ya go."

Molly shrugged.

"You feel bad because you used violence to stop an abusive situation. Do you think all encounters of abuse can be handled nonviolently?"

"I don't know. Probably not."

"Most likely not. Could this one have been? Probably. But your love for your friends sent you to a place of compassion for them and, I'm guessing, a desire for justice. We're only human, Molly." Claire made a tiny sign of the cross, blessing Molly. "The Creator says you get a pass on that one, okay?"

Molly grinned. "Okay. Thanks."

"One thing you can do with folks like that," said Claire, "assuming you have the time and the patience, is ask them questions. For example, in the case of that hyper-aggressive blonde, you could ask her precisely where in the Bible she's getting the narrative to formulate her opinion. Then have her *produce* a Bible, saying, 'Well, show me where it says that.' Then have the person calmly explain to you their rationale. Usually, they can't. That is, when forced to unpack what the words actually mean, they will often become frustrated because their mission is to 'correct' you, not to ultimately help you. *That* is their idea of Matthew 28—the Great Commission. Instead of 'making disciples' as Jesus suggested, for them it's about redressing or 'straightening you out,' unfortunately. Not a helpful way to interpret the text."

"Huh, that's interesting," said Molly, trying to take everything in.

"I will admit, it usually takes some experience and practice. Even then, these types will almost invariably choose to see you in a negative light. For them, like I said, it's about being 'correct' in their theology more than any idea of being compassionate. Often, you're just better off saying, 'You have your beliefs, and I have mine. Let's just leave it at that.'"

"But what if they won't *let* you leave it at that—then what? Like the way they trapped my friends and humiliated them in public?"

"Well then," Claire shrugged with a silly expression. "Jesus ... money changers ... Molly ... right hook."

Molly put her hands to her face and giggled. Claire winked at her and picked up the check and examined it. "I can pay for mine," said Molly.

"Nah; it's on me. The church committee folk will probably think I'm not doing my job if I don't do enough of these," she said with a smile. "Got to keep everyone happy, I'm learning." She put her credit card on the table.

"Why'd you become a minister? Was it like a divine revelation or something?"

"You could say that." She swallowed some iced tea from her second refill. "I was assaulted by a guy I was dating my last year in college. He was an abuser."

"I'm sorry," said Molly, thinking about their conversation—and Devon.

"Oh, it's okay," said Claire, compassion behind her green eyes. "He was a real piece of work, that one. He's actually living proof that nonviolence does *not* work in some situations. Things had gotten really bad and it culminated in my trying to leave him one night, so he nearly beat me to death. Put me in the hospital. The medics had taken me and I went out on them in the ambulance just as they were pulling into the ER. I had a near-death experience, and that was partially why I sought ordination. It's actually a much longer story; I'll tell you about it sometime." She smiled again. "Matter of fact, I am planning to speak on it in the near future. I'll let you know in case you want to come hear it."

"Ooh, I'd really like that, Claire. You know, you're not like most ministers I know."

"That's what they tell me," she replied, her eyebrows bobbing up and down. Molly snickered.

"You're the only one I know that wears a Harley-Davidson bracelet, that's for sure!"

"That's another one I'll tell you about sometime. C'mon," she said, pushing her chair back and standing, "I should be getting back and you no doubt have things to do."

"Thanks for meeting with me, Claire. And for letting me talk. It really helped."

"Good!" replied Claire. "Then I'm doing something right this week! That happens about once a month, so I'm one for one this month!"

"So," Molly asked as they were walking to Claire's car, "whatever happened to that guy you were dating—the one who hurt you?" She was thinking about Devon.

"He's doing twenty years in the can," she said without emotion.

"Oh! Well . . . that's good," said Molly, thinking about how many Native women are assaulted, murdered, and missing.

"Molly, how are you doing with this Devon thing?" She put her arm around Molly's shoulder.

"I don't know, Claire, honest to God I don't. Do you think he's a horrible person for what he did? I mean, I don't, really, but I guess because I've known him most of my life. He was always so sweet when we were kids. It's not like he's some major criminal or anything. And even though he got too rough, he didn't actually succeed in what he was trying to do. Becks and Tara were furious, though. Becks wanted to hook his balls up to an electric cattle prod." Claire laughed at that. They arrived at the car.

"What do you want to do in this situation?" she asked Molly, leaning against the passenger door with her arms crossed, her funky, red-streaked hair giving her a rather hip yet wise look.

"I don't know. I don't want Devon to get in trouble. I'm almost certain he's never done this to any other girl. He's always had a big thing for me. I mean, I don't want to sound stuck-up, but I think he's always been in love with me. I think it's those damn steroids or something, Claire. He's bigger—much stronger—than he's ever been. He has a short fuse now but he was never like that when he wrestled the first two years of high school. I just noticed subtle changes in him over time. And hey—I still wanted to date the guy." She crossed her arms and became emotional. "Okay, look. I'll admit it, Claire: I really wanted him, like, we had been flirting most of the past year," she said, wiping her nose. "I mean, I really wanted to screw the guy, okay? There—I said it." She rubbed her head, her grandmother's earrings bouncing in response. "But not like *that*, you know?" She teared up and Claire gave her a slight hug.

"Molly," she said, pulling away and leaning back again on her Toyota, "you're a young woman now. Nothing at all wrong with any of that. Hormones are hormones. You know our call, right? Stay sacred. And men had damn well better respect it. It's beyond time for us to take a stronger stand. And it sure sounds like you did just that at the theater. Devon's Coke-stained shorts were testimony to that! So good for you."

Molly regained her composure and laughed, wiping her eyes. "Oh, shit," she said without thinking. She looked at Claire and apologized for her language again. Claire smiled, then got serious. She held up her hand as if to get Molly's attention.

"Listen, Molly. I think I've heard you. And I understand your lifelong emotional attachment to this young man. But guess what? That doesn't mean much in the greater scheme of things. Technically, what Devon did was attempted rape, with aggravated circumstances because he bruised you. That's a felony. That's just plain wrong. If you are looking for a moral answer—that's it. Devon should be punished for that. But I'm not a judge, and I'm not you. Because you are still a minor—when do you turn eighteen?"

"August."

"Because you are technically still a minor, I should report this."

Molly looked panicked.

"Just chill," Claire said. "Do you love this guy?"

"Well, as a friend—yeah, 'course I do. But not 'in love' I guess you would say. I was hoping to get there some day, though."

"You don't want to see him go to jail, then?"

"No, please don't, Claire. You know, it's weird; I haven't really seen him anywhere since it happened. Like, he just disappeared."

"Well, that sounds like a good thing, at least for now. You said back at my office that you didn't want to tell your mom. How come?"

"I dunno. I guess—now that I'm talking to you—I didn't want him to get in trouble, you know—go to jail or anything."

Claire sighed and looked down, then looked up again. "I'm in kind of a tough spot here, Molly. Devon is eighteen and legally responsible for his own actions. I'm not doing you or any other potential victim a favor by pretending this didn't happen. You're a minor. It would still be a crime even if you were eighteen, but, because you're a minor, *I* could get in trouble—be arrested even—if it's not reported."

"Oh, my God!" Molly cried and put her hands to her face.

"Calm down. I'll make a deal with you. You and I talk to your Mom, let her know what Devon did. Whatever your mom wants to do, that's what should be done, agreed?"

"No, fuck no. I don't agree," Molly said, crossing her arms and shaking her head like a little girl standing in front of the tub refusing to be bathed.

"Molly."

"I came to you for help, goddamn it!" Now she was truly crying. She raised her arms, then put her hands behind her head, squeezing her temples with her upper arms. "Just to fucking talk, never mind . . . oh, God."

"I understand. I care about you, Molly. Do you *honestly* think it's in Devon's best interest to get away with this, as if nothing at all happened? What if, Molly, what *if* he pulls this crap with another woman and then rapes her. You good with that?" Claire looked at her questioningly. Molly thought about this. She let out a breath and sighed.

"No, not really, I guess."

Claire reached over and hugged Molly one more time. "Listen, I know it seems like the world is coming to an end, but it isn't." She patted Molly's back and let go. "Here's what you do. You tell your mom we met—and tell her *how* we met, girlfriend, because you were amazing! Tell her I want to meet her and just invite me for coffee or tea or whatever it is and then just leave it to me. I promise I won't compromise you, Molly. I won't hang you out to dry. If your mom is as reasonable as you are—and I figure she has to be—between the three of us we can come up with the best answer. It just has to come out in the open, sweetie. It's the only way you're gonna have any peace with this, okay? Sorry, Probie, but part of being a warrior woman is dealing with situations like this, and you really are a true warrior." She cocked her head and waited for Molly's response.

Molly just nodded. She seemed exhausted.

"Kay-den," said Claire. "Let's head back. Things will work out—promise." But Molly wasn't so sure.

"I feel like such a heel," said Molly as they drove back toward the church, her head on the headrest.

"That's the genuine righteousness in you. Honestly, if you weren't conflicted, I'd be worried about you. Besides, you just never know who or what might be working in your favor without you even knowing it," said Claire with a smile, nodding at Molly reassuringly. "And please don't underestimate your mom. You just might be surprised."

34

Facing the Music

Beauty, terrible beauty! Deathless goddess—so she strikes our eyes!
—Homer, *The Iliad*, Book 3, in reference to Helen of Troy

Present Day
Saturday
Central Business Area
Muskogee, Oklahoma

The *Ned Christie* zoomed down Ockmulgee Ave. Mike was driving, and he looked over at his lady and smiled. "Thanks for going Italian today. I know it's not strictly on your diet." Emmy glanced at him.

"Anything for my sexy bitch," she said and grinned.

"Just hope we don't cut you out with a mere salad," he said.

"Don't worry. I called them ahead of time. They'll make a special plate for *me*," she said, batting her eyelashes. "Pays to have muscles," she said in a coy way, posing with her bicep and reducing the word "muscles" to nearly a whisper.

"Oh, jeez," he responded, rolling his eyes. "You really are full of it, you know that?"

Emmy laughed. "Yes, I know. And you *love* that about me, don't you?"

He grinned. "Honestly? Yeah!"

Emmy had just turned up the radio when she spotted something in the lot across the road from Community Baptist.

"WHOA!" she shouted. "Turn this thing around!"

"What? What the hell, Em?" Mike said as he hit the brakes, scaring himself.

"*Son of a bitch!*" Emmy said, gritting her teeth. "Just do as I say, Mike. Go back!" she exclaimed, turning the volume back down.

"Go back where? What the hell is the matter with you?"

"Back to the vacant building. I'll explain later. C'mon, or we'll lose him." Mike did a U-turn, almost running into a postal truck. He stopped to back up, the postal carrier now frozen in the middle of the road, looking at him and holding up his arms.

"Sorry!" said Mike, holding his badge out the window, "sorry!" The carrier just waved him on and Mike sped away, back toward the vacant building lot.

They approached the building and Emmy said, "Turn here!" As Mike turned left into the parking lot, they saw Devon handing a man a roll of bills. Devon glanced up and recognized the car.

He shouted "Oh, shit!" and shot down the sidewalk.

"Step on it!" screamed Emmy. "Catch that Stretch Armstrong little prick!" she bellowed, ignoring the other guy, who disappeared in the opposite direction.

"Emmy, just what the hell are we doing? Who is that? Wait—that's not that Devon kid, is it?" He stopped to check for cars before pulling out again.

"Yeah," said Emmy, concentrating on the road as if she were driving. "Remember what I told you about Molly? Well . . . he's like, like a little project of mine is all," she said, glancing over at Mike.

"Oh, shit," said Mike, shaking his head because he was learning more about his lady with each passing week. "You beat this guy's ass, didn't you? Didn't you?" he shouted. Emmy didn't answer, but had the expression of slight excitement and mischievousness one would see on a thirteen-year-old who took the car out for a neighborhood drive without permission.

"Well, not really. We just had a . . . a little *chat*, you might say," she said with one of her you-really-don't-want-to-know looks.

"Aw, shit!" said Mike. "You shouldn't be telling me this stuff, Goddess, seriously!"

"Well, you asked," she retorted.

Devon sprinted around and behind two buildings, then jetted down Broadway toward Ninth, trying to make the block. Mike had to U-turn and roared back to the vacant lot, turning left at the corner, thinking he would have to catch up to Devon out on Broadway. Emmy told Mike to stop the car as Devon raced up the road in the opposite direction. Emmy flung open the passenger door, and Mike yelled, "Goddess, you can't keep getting involved with this stuff!" Ignoring him, she slammed the door and took off after Devon. "Ahh, shit creek!" yelled Mike, stopped by a red light. Traffic was increasing. He hoped to catch up to them before either Emmy killed Devon or vice versa. The kid could have a weapon, Mike thought.

Out on the pavement, Devon saw Emmy chasing him. She was wearing Standingcloud's favorite blouse again, her cutoffs, and her fifteen-dollar Walmart shoes. Like a champion thoroughbred at Steeplechase, she gained momentum. Devon panicked as she closed the gap. He wondered if she was annoyed because he had been buying drugs less than one hundred yards from the church where he was supposed to be making amends. Whatever the case, she floored it.

Hell, he thought, I might not be able to take her, but I can sure as hell *outrun* the bitch. He stepped it up, kicking gravel dust behind him and putting his head down, pumping his shoulders as he boogied up Broadway. He was sure he had smoked her now. But he could—to his consternation—hear feet scooting closer, as if barely touching the ground, the sound of a young gazelle wearing warehouse specials.

Motherfucker! Here we go again with the Deer Woman bullshit, he fumed. Maybe that story really was true, he thought. How can she be that *fast*?

"Why you fucking chasing me?" he yelled, glancing back, eyes wild and sweat drenching his forehead.

"Why you fucking running?"

"Goddamn antelope shit!" he screeched, facing forward again and nearly falling. "Aghhh!"

Panting, he made a left at the corner at the Soul Food Kitchen and glanced back again. She was practically on top of him, her giant ponytail swinging from the motion. He knew it was hopeless; the woman was an animal. Mike had zipped around after spotting them on Ninth, backed up, and headed their way.

She caught up to him at a large oak tree beside the sidewalk, seized him, and flung him to the ground. As Devon stood and struggled to catch his breath, he thought seriously about fighting his way out of this one. He instinctively squatted into a wrestler's ready stance. Emmy held up her hand, palm facing Devon. She wasn't even breathing hard, for God's sake.

"Don't try it, Devon," she commanded. "You don't stand a chance. I promise you, this time I really *will* fuck you up. So just don't. I'll jack your ass so hard, you'll have to cut your hair to take a shit."

Mike drove around and stopped the Mustang in the lot of the television appliance shop next door. To everyone's surprise, Devon ran to the tree and seized the lowest branch and started climbing. "Damn Deer Woman—gonna murder me. Help!" he screamed in a high pitch as he shimmied, his hair disheveled. He seemed out of control, crazed. Mike approached, checking the position of his off-duty weapon as Devon frantically scaled the tree like a baboon, bark and a few leaves falling in his wake.

"Where the hell do you think you're going?" said Emmy, hands on her hips.

Spotting Mike, Devon yelled, "Keep that fucking deer spirit away from me, man!"

"What?" said Mike, looking up.

"Goddamn succubus, man. They'll find me fucking dead in a week! Check her feet for hooves, man! *Fucking check 'em out!*" Mike looked at Emmy's feet, perplexed.

"What the hell's he talking about?" said Mike.

"Come down, Devon, right now," Emmy ordered.

"Hell no, ain't doin' it!" Devon protested, his face panic-stricken.

"Did you blow a damn gasket?"

"Go away—fucking Cherokee Medusa crap!"

"You think I can't climb a tree? Get down here, chooch, or I'll fucking jungle cat your ass!"

"Hey," said Mike, "ease up, okay?" Emmy shook her head and sighed.

To Emmy's surprise, Devon was trembling, not so much in a fearful way, but more in the way of the shakes. He hugged the tree, then started crying, which also surprised her.

"Please, Emmy," he said, weakly holding on with one arm, his eyes bloodshot and looking as if he hadn't slept in a week. "Please don't kill me," he begged.

Emmy calmed, putting her arms at her side, then held up her hands in a nonthreatening way. "I won't, Dev. It's okay. Come on down, over here," Emmy directed, pointing to the grass. Devon hesitated, clearly making a last-ditch estimation about either running or fighting his way out of this. "*Devon,*" said Emmy reproachfully. "Don't even *think* about it."

Realizing he had nowhere to run, he slid down to the lower branch and dropped to the ground. Emmy gently took his arm. Someone had set a smoking bench outside the rear door of the appliance shop, and she walked him to it.

Mike walked up and sat on one side of Devon while Emmy sat on the other. The couple rested while Devon caught his breath. Mike pulled out his phone and opened his notes section.

"I'm sorry, Emmy," said Devon, sitting up and shaking his head. "I'm sorry about Molly, sorry about lying to you, sorry about a lot of goddamn shit. I can't stop, Em, can't stop using," he cried, his hands shaking as he put his head down again. Emmy reached over and patted his back.

"It's okay, Devon," she said. "It's gonna be okay." She gave him a minute to collect himself, then turned to him.

"Look at me, Dev," she said. He couldn't. He just buried his head in his hands again. Emmy sighed. "Devon, look at me," she repeated. Finally, he looked up in frustration, then turned to her. "Dev, the next few minutes of your life are pivotal. Your future lies in your hands, right here—right now." Puzzled, he looked at her and cocked his head. Suddenly, in his strung-out state, he realized there was some guy there, just sitting with his pasty white self, not saying a damn word.

"Who the fuck is this?" Devon asked with junkie irritation.

"Show him, Mike," she said. Devon glanced down as Mike reached into his rear pocket. Mike produced his badge and ID. Devon looked up, grabbing either side of his head with his hands as if to rip his own hair out.

"Fuck!" he yelled, then the crying started again. He just shook his head and squeezed, trying to find a hiding place somewhere within himself. Emmy rubbed Devon's back gently.

"This is my friend, Mike. He's gonna search you for that shit, Dev. I know it's on you or I would have seen you toss it. We saw you, Dev, saw you buy that stuff. That gives Mike— what's that called?"

"Reasonable suspicion," said Mike.

"Yeah—reasonable suspicion—to search you for a weapon. And you're gonna comply, Devon, or you and me—we start this shit all over again from the top. And I don't think you want that." He nodded in agreement. She leaned toward Mike and whispered, "Go easy, okay? Simple shit, maybe?" with a pretty-please look. Mike nodded.

"Look, Devon," said Mike, "why don't you just give me the drugs, okay? Just hand it over and let's see if we can't keep this to a minimum, maybe even keep you out of court, okay?"

"You can do that?"

"I can't promise you anything. But you need to give me the name of that asshole who's pushing this stuff, or you're gonna be in a world of hurt, buddy." Devon looked at Emmy and she nodded, patting his back again.

Devon thought about it. "Nah," he said. "No way. I ain't gonna be no goddamn snitch." He tried standing, but they both put a hand on his shoulder and sat him back down. "Aw, shit, man!" he protested.

"Right here, right now, Devon," Emmy repeated, keeping her hand on his shoulder. "The rest of your life, Dev. Think about it, kiddo." He burst out crying again, leaning over and putting his head on Emmy's shoulder. She patted his back again a couple of times, then pushed him upright. "Be a man, Devon. Don't go to jail for this jerk; don't do it, nephew."

"Emmy says you have a chance, Devon, a future," said Mike. "A lot of young people I see on the job are hopeless—no chance at all. Don't do time for this fool." Devon sat and stared, looking like he just watched ten million dollars slip overboard in the middle of the Pacific Ocean. He turned to Mike and his lip quivered.

"I can't snitch, man, you know that, right? I'm a dead man if I do that."

"You've been watching too many movies, Devon," said Mike with assurance. "It's not like that. This guy—if we do this right—he won't even know. Hand it over, Devon. Give it to me," said Mike with an outstretched hand. Devon sighed heavily. His mind was working overtime, trying to think of a way out of this.

"Officers, help me!" shouted Devon, looking up toward the road. As Mike and Emmy glanced up, Devon tried bolting. Emmy seized him by a rear belt loop and Devon found himself running in place, like a cartoon character in a blur of legs. She yanked him back violently onto the bench and against the wall, standing and wrapping her right hand around his throat.

"I'm running out of patience with you, bitch!" she roared.

"Emmy," said Mike, grabbing her arm. "Come on, now." She shook her head furiously, but let Devon go. Mike decided to speed things up. "Okay, Devon, on your feet. I'll just call a squad car from the PD to pick you up."

"No!" said Devon, panic-stricken. "I can't!" Emmy seized his right elbow and hoisted him off the bench.

"Bullshit!" she shouted. "*Eee-NEY-na*, shit stick!"

"NO, no! Okay, okay already, goddamn." Devon sat down as fast as he had shot upward, as if gluing himself to the bench. "All right, already, I'll fucking tell, okay? Just don't lock me up, man," he pleaded, looking at Mike for help now.

"Hand them over, Devon—NOW!" Mike yelled, playing the bad cop this time. Devon fished a large plastic bag of pills out from under his shirt and underwear and handed it to Mike.

"Ooohh, gross," said Emmy. "I'm definitely glad he's givin' 'em to you!" Devon looked humiliated. She leaned toward Devon and quietly demanded, "Okay, Hercules: what's his name?" Devon couldn't take the heat anymore and Emmy was just too damn scary. He told them everything—the guy's name, his address, who *his* boss was, where to find him, everything. When he was done, he leaned back against the wall, defeated. Mike signaled Emmy for a private chat. They got up and walked toward the car, but stayed close enough to keep an eye on Devon.

"What do you want to do with him?" said Mike.

"Do you have to lock him up now?"

"Nah, no point in busting him for simple possession under these circumstances. If you really want to keep sticking your neck out for this kid, let me see what I can do with an assistant district attorney I know, and maybe Judge Boyer. He's probably our best shot. The kid has no prescription, so technically it's a misdemeanor, but honestly, Em, it's a waste of everyone's time. You know we're cross-deputized with the Cherokee Marshals, right?"

She nodded.

"I've got a Marshal friend, Callie."

Emmy grinned. "Yeah, I know Callie! She's a sweetie."

"Let me talk to her and maybe we can get the kid into a program and some community service—make him work this shit off. It might work. Plus, I'll admit, if he has someone like you on his back, he might be more motivated to complete his work. One thing's for sure, you've got him scared to death. Hell, you're scaring me, and I don't scare!" She snorted and laughed, remembering Standingcloud. "What?" he asked, puzzled.

She waved it off and said, "Never mind; tell you later. Thanks, Mike."

"Don't thank me. These things don't often end well. His chances are fifty-fifty at best. And I'll only do this on one condition: if I think you need to back away and let this kid sink, you'll do as I say, okay?" She nodded. "I mean it, Emmy. Promise?"

"Kay-den," she said, giving his hand a squeeze.

"Hey," he said, holding onto her hand, a curious look on his face. "Why *are* you doing this, Emmy? I mean, the guy almost raped your kid sister. Why?"

She looked over at Devon, shaking her head. "I don't know, Michael, to be honest. I mean, that night at Eagle Feather, I came really damn close to breaking his neck—seriously—right there in that damn dark parking lot. No one would have been the wiser. Could have snapped it like a toothpick. Just another dead Native guy. No cameras around, no witnesses, really. I just don't know."

"Maybe it's because you see yourself in him," Mike offered.

"The fuck does that mean?" she said, eyes wide and more than just a little pissed.

"Because maybe, when all is said and done, he's just another indigenous victim of the system, like you were."

"Oh, bitch, please," she protested. He smiled, touched her nose, then gave her a soft kiss.

"Or maybe," he said as he pulled away, "it's because you're the greatest of the warriors, the ones who are inevitably the most merciful."

She smiled and looked down. "Are you flirting again?" she said shyly.

He nodded and grinned.

"Let's take him home, and then go eat—that still good?"

He nodded again.

At that point, a patrol car pulled up in the medical building parking lot across the street. Someone had no doubt seen the commotion and dialed 911. Mike met the officer in the road, producing his ID and explaining. The officer asked if he needed backup and Mike said, no, he had it covered. The officer left.

They escorted Devon back to the car after Mike searched him for weapons and more drugs. He was clean, and, just as Mike said, scared to death. Mike didn't cuff him—they just put him in the passenger's seat while Emmy drove, and he and Devon had a long chat on the way home. Emmy demanded that either Devon go and get detoxed or the cops were going to come pick him up and she would be done with him. He agreed.

The next day, Sunday, Mike used his connections to get Devon into a local halfway house to dry out, driving him there himself, making sure he understood that having Emmy in his life was better than a probation officer any day, even though she might be scarier.

35

Mr. Henry & the George Guess

November 20, 1838
Bell Detachment
Raleigh Area
State of Tennessee

J ust outside of Memphis, Tennessee, the detachment marched into the Raleigh community. As the head of the Bell group, John Bell was becoming more proactive with Captain Ambrose and Lieutenant Whitworth. Nick couldn't understand why Bell had been absent for much of the trip. George Welch speculated that he was carrying messages back and forth, but to whom? And why?

As they approached a small wooden building marked "Mr. Henry's Feed & Supplies," with smoke rising from the chimney, meeting the cold air in billowing clouds, Bell halted his horse and dismounted. Their advance purchasing agent, Thomas Likens, had tried to buy goods from this particular location and had reported much trouble with no success.

"Gonna need these supplies, Lieutenant," he said to Whitworth as he walked to the front door and banged on it.

"Who the hell goes there?" boomed a voice from inside.

"John Bell, sir. My party needs supplies," he responded.

"Don't know any John Bell. Go away!" Bell shrugged and threw his arms up as if flabbergasted.

"Sir, Mr. Likens—advance agent for our party—informed me that you would not sell. May I ask why, sir?"

"No you may not, imbecile! Off with thee!"

Lieutenant Whitworth dismounted and approached the door. He knocked.

"I said go away, you eternal miscreant!" came the voice once more, which sounded nasal, a cross between a steamboat horn and an ailing sheep.

"Sir, this is the U.S. Army. We need supplies and are prepared to make a sizable purchase. Please let us in so that we might make a transaction," said Whitworth.

"I'm tryin' to take a shit in here, you silly sidewinder! Leave me be!"

"Captain," Lieutenant Whitworth called out as he saw Ambrose riding up. "This man won't open the door. He's being disagreeable, to say the least, sir. He was the one who rejected Mr. Likens. What should I do?" Ambrose told him to knock again.

"Away with thee!" came the mysterious foghorn voice again. "What about this do you not understand, you malicious, pesky varmint?"

"Captain Ambrose, United States Army, Fourth Artillery!" yelled the captain. "Open that door, sir!"

"Listen, you little fly titty, I'm tryin' here to relieve my bowels in the most peaceable of ways and you, sir, are interfering with one of the great movements of our time! Get lost, you godforsaken trail rabbit!"

"Sir! I and the president of the United States will give you five minutes to complete your business, lest you lose control and fall into that bowl and be lost forever. Then, sir, you best get yourself together and come outside or I shall be forced to enter that dwelling and move your bowels for you, you civilian cow-humper!" The newly arriving soldiers laughed as Ambrose grumbled.

When the five minutes was up, Captain Ambrose called out, again stating he was with the army and they needed supplies.

Nothing.

"What now, sir?" said Lieutenant Whitworth.

"MISTER! Open this door and accommodate us! We are in need, sir!" yelled Ambrose. "Maybe he really did fall in," he added, looking around at his men, to their amusement.

"Sir, can you imagine what the place must smell like if he's using the outhouse bowl inside?" said Sergeant Thomas.

Ambrose was about to dismount with his musket when they heard the bowl moving around and the strident voice returned, as if the oddity inside had required time to think of his next response.

"Can't *be no army* in these parts this time of year! So, ha! The prank is on *you*, you reject from *Macbeth*! Go away, sir, whoever you may be, and leave me absent your practical jokes! I will not bandy with thee much longer! I have completed my duties most basic to defecation and I hereby charge you with your leave, sir!"

"We cannot take leave, sir. We are escorting the Indians to the Indian Territory and must burden you regardless for a supply run. Do please open up and sell us what we need, sir, and we will indeed be on our way. We will pay top dollar."

They waited for a response.

They heard a loud fart.

Sergeant Thomas made a face. "Oh, that's disgusting, sir. We don't have to go in there, do we?"

"Did you *hear* me in there? I demand satisfaction, sir, this minute!" yelled Captain Ambrose.

"Have *coitus* with yourself, sir!" came the response in a formal, almost dignified manner, as if profound thought and consideration had been put into it.

"No, sir! No!" bellowed Ambrose, now red-faced and overdrawn, pointing his finger at the door. "*You* engage in carnality with *your*self instead, sir, posthaste!" he roared, clearly having lost his patience and decorum.

"Not at all, sir! I say *fuck* yourself, sir, *twice*! With hearty abandon, at that!" the foghorn shouted yet again. The Cherokees pulling up with the white civilian wagon masters were all looking at one another, trying to figure out this strange predicament.

"You, sir, are as big an anal orifice as I have yet encountered!" screamed Ambrose, spitting on the ground near the door. Lieutenant Whitworth stood there, scratching his head, concerned about his captain. The young soldiers gathered round were fascinated, waiting to hear the next exchange with anticipation.

"That is an *inaccurate* statement, my horrible fellow! Now, for your information and pleasure I have indeed just used my *anal* orifice with the sharpest of precision, but no, sir, that I *will not* indulge! But if it so dresses your palate, you may happily gnaw on my twittel, you ghastly birthing accident, you!"

Ambrose would not be moved. "Thus far I find you to be an apostate of hell, sir!"

"Whether you do or not is not a matter of my concern in this neck of the woods. And despite anything my Hebrew brethren might postulate, the Lord does *not* tarry in these here parts, so on with you now before He strikes you with his mighty sword! That is to say, surely you will reverse your tracks and go *back* to the viper hole from whence you came, sir!"

"I WILL NOT, sir! Come out of that dwelling this minute or face the consequences!"

"*Gnaw on my twittel*, I say!"

"I will not! Produce yourself, you ambiguous toad!"

A Cherokee named Muskrat stood off to the side listening to the encounter, picking his nose and shaking his head.

"Not *gonna*! Your hairy-chested mother, sir," the mysterious voice continued, "trusses herself in the most masculine of vestments while smoking one of them Her-*nan*-doe de *So*-to *cee*-gars on the back of a rented mule down by the river at Christmastime!"

"Goddammit!" Ambrose dismounted with his musket. He charged the door with a hard right kick. "You best open this door, you little backwoods beaver-biting imbecile! What the hell is wrong with you, anyway?"

As if the entire exchange had never occurred, they heard a soft clicking noise which sounded like someone lifting a door-length wooden locking latch. The door cracked ever so slightly—about three or four inches—and a small bespectacled man that resembled a prairie dog with dark circles under his eyes poked his head out and softly crooned, "Yeessssss?"

"YES?" Ambrose roared, bewildered and dumbfounded. "All right, look," he said with a heavy sigh. "See my uniform? See these captain's bars? I'm an officer for the United States government, for God's sake."

"Why yes I see that very thing," said the odd character in one breath, with a nod of the head.

"I am bound to ask it: are you deficient of mind, sir? We need supplies for the road ahead. Would it, sir, really and truly, be of such a burden to make this transaction?" Ambrose queried with his last ounce of patience.

The little raccoon-like man farted again and said, "Well, why didn't you just show me those bars in the first place, son? Get on in here and state your business." He opened the door for Ambrose. "I haven't got all day, ya know."

The captain just shook his head, turning to Whitworth and mumbling, "*Damn.*"

November 22, 1838
Mississippi River
Tennessee-Arkansas Border
Bell Detachment Crossing

"Oh, my God," said Mary, putting her hand to her mouth as the McNair wagon stopped near the banks of the mighty Mississippi River. She had never seen such a large body of water. In her relatively short life to date, she had never journeyed to the Atlantic Ocean, not even when she lived in Georgia with her family as a girl. They sat and stared into the distance. Beyond the bank was a vast amount of water, with land in the background they were told was Arkansas.

Captain Ambrose had made advance arrangements: soldiers were quickly moving up and down the wagon lines, telling the Cherokees to unload their pottery, if any, along with all excess baggage, and put it on the ground beside them. A soldier would come by and load it on a separate wagon, which would then be rolled to the front of the line, where Mary and Nick could see a large, dirty, wooden flatboat drifting to shore. Captain Ambrose would soon pack the boat with as many extraneous items as he could manage, to be sailed down the Mississippi, then up the Arkansas River to the Indian Territory. In theory, this would make the detachment lighter and more expedient.

Caty Walking Stick, for whom Mary knew the trip had been excruciating, sauntered to a nearby hill overlooking the Mississippi, looked heavenward, and dropped dead on the spot.

"Oh, dear God, no!" exclaimed Mary, who spotted Caty from the buckboard. Nick stopped her when she tried to get up.

"Listen to me—if she's past caring, it won't matter. I need you *here*, woman, with our baby. You, me, our family first. That's just the way it's gotta be, understand?" Nick was resolute, with no room for argument. He gripped her arm firmly. He was concerned she was going to lose this child due to sheer worry.

Moses McDaniel saw it happen and sprang from his wagon toward Caty. He pounded the ground with his hand and when two soldiers walked up to see what was going on, he began beating one of them with his fists, then seized the man by his throat and tried to strangle him. A corporal struck Moses in the back of the head with the butt of his rifle, knocking him to the ground, bleeding.

Doc Arbogast ran to tend to Moses. As he used an old rag he carried to slow the bleeding, he looked up at the corporal. "You—you savage bastard!" he shouted. "Haven't these people suffered enough?" The corporal gave him a hateful look and pointed his rifle at Doc Arbogast's forehead.

"You just tend to that bush monkey, Doc, and leave the rest to us, understand?"

"CORPORAL!" yelled Sergeant Thomas, who had just arrived on the scene. "Put that rifle away this minute!"

"Whatever you say, Sarge. I was jest tryin' to *ejecate* the good doctor here on proper procedure regarding contact with these swamp rats," he answered with a sneer as he lowered his weapon. Nick looked over at Mary, who, exhausted and conflicted, lowered her head. She looked down at her belly, gently rubbing it, no doubt wishing she were back on their faraway farm, walking in the sunshine. He took her hand in his. For the first time in a long while, he wanted to sit and cry.

Sergeant Thomas walked over to the corporal and, with a right hand lead, knocked him flat. The astonished soldier looked up at his sergeant in fear. Thomas reached down and grabbed him by the shirt and yanked him to his feet. Another soldier moved forward, apparently to restrain Thomas.

"DON'T!" Thomas thundered, staring the other soldier down. The young man backed away. "Listen to me, all of ya!" he yelled, addressing the young soldiers in the group, all of whom were newly minted privates, except the corporal. "I've already had to tell one of you little fuckers on this trip to mind his manners. Do I gotta tell the lot of ya, or you think you got the message?" All of them—including the corporal with the now-bloody lip—nodded. "What say?" Thomas shouted, looking the corporal in the eyes but addressing the group.

"Yes, Sergeant!" they all said. Thomas nodded, then pushed the corporal away and told everyone to stand easy for now until they received orders otherwise. As he walked back in the direction of the McNair wagon, he glanced at Nick, who gave him a slight nod, and the sergeant returned the nod.

Sergeant Thomas made his way back to his horse and happened to notice Lieutenant Whitworth standing off to the side, evidently having witnessed the ugliness.

"Well done, Sergeant," said Whitworth quietly. Sergeant Thomas instantly stood at attention with a salute. Whitworth returned the salute and said, "A lieutenant's bar would look good on those shoulders, Sergeant."

"If you say so, sir." Whitworth realized Sergeant Thomas was crying. Thomas looked his superior in the eye.

"I'm tired, sir. Just so *damn* tired, if you'll forgive me, sir. This ain't what I signed on for."

"Understood," replied the lieutenant. "See to yourself, Sergeant. Do it now. Take fifteen. I've got it from here for the moment."

"Thank you, sir," said Thomas gratefully, saluting once more. He wandered into some trees on an opposite hill to be alone with his thoughts.

Captain Ambrose could see his own breath in the air as he stood on the Tennessee side of the Mississippi and, hand over his eyes to block the sun, squinted as he watched one boat depart and another approach. The flatboat, manned by a civilian ferry captain familiar with the Indian Territory, sailed away with some of the McNair's belongings, along with those of everyone else. It was to float down the Mississippi River to the fork where the two great rivers met, then up the Arkansas River toward Little Rock. Although a significant amount of rope had been used in an attempt to secure the cargo, Nick was willing to bet that at least some of the cargo would never make it to its destination.

Ambrose and John Bell stood at the head of their party and watched as the steamboat *George Guess* huffed into the river's harbor. The great ship floated into sight, looking like a typical neighborhood community on the small waves. As the steam craft made its way closer to shore, a loud "clank!" was heard, then several "chuga-chuga" sounds, followed by a "thud!" Steam shot upward through the smokestack funnel, followed by an enormous cloud of black, billowing smoke. It was a frightening sight. The front portion of the Bell Detachment felt a large, underground rumble, and those on foot fled backward. Soldiers on horseback were slightly panicked because the horses were startled and some galloped about. The ship was close enough to shore that, with monumental effort, it was able to be maneuvered the short distance needed, close enough to be anchored for repair.

To Ambrose's extreme frustration, the mighty *George Guess* was grounded.

According to the ship's captain, the pilot had been unaware of a hidden sandbar that extended farther from shore than anyone had anticipated. The boat's rudders dug in and everything went wrong from there, including the pilot losing his ability to steer. It took most of that day to make repairs on the *George Guess*. The small crew worked tirelessly to restore a damaged boiler and part of the propeller. When they were done, a late afternoon venture to load a significant number of passengers began, and, with Captain Ambrose determined not to let the ceasing of daylight hours prevent the passage of migrants to Arkansas, he convinced the ship's captain to make nighttime travel a reality.

The voyage across the Mississippi River wasn't so much difficult as it was time-consuming. Nick estimated that his family made it across to Arkansas at about three in the morning. Upon disembarking on the other side, folks were running into one another, horses seemed confused, Augustine barked a lot, and Ida Bird was bitten by a timber rattlesnake when she stepped on a large rock in the dark. The snake had been resting on the rock and was startled by Ida's presence. Doc Arbogast's assistant tended to her immediately, but afterward Ida treated herself by using herbs from the homeland that she carried in her medicine bag. She set fire to some of them using the flint she had stolen from Sergeant Hollingsworth, burned them to a sacred ash, then applied the ash to the bite. She then asked Jeter Silk to suck the poison out. Jeter became quite ill from that, but Ida seemed to do just fine.

Sometime around 9:00 a.m. on November 24, Captain Ambrose, after a few hours of sleep, smiled at Lieutenant Whitworth and said, "Well, Lieutenant, we made it to Arkansas! Should we have the fortune to cross this state safely, our work here is done."

"Yes, sir!" smiled Whitworth, with a salute.

Augustine trotted alongside the McNair wagon in step with the horses, occasionally dipping down a hill to get a drink from one of the many small creeks that flowed throughout the region. He would fall behind, then scamper along until he was back with his pack. At one point he encountered a bobcat near a water source and the two engaged in quite the wrestling match. Augustine returned to Nick and Mary, tail between his legs, with a look that had him questioning the self-righteousness of the bobcat that dared to defend his drinking hole. Mary treated his face scratches with valerian root and squeezed his face in her hands, kissing him on the forehead and telling him in Cherokee to stay close to the wagons. He seemed to understand.

The area around Marion, Arkansas, and beyond was sparse and dryer than what the party had seen in Tennessee. The next couple of days made for monotonous, boring ground coverage for which no one was the wiser or happier. They were approaching the St. Francis River, where Captain Ambrose and John Bell decided they would camp before the next leg of the journey.

36

The Common Good (Gadugi)

Present Day
Saturday Afternoon
McNair House
Muskogee, Oklahoma
District Four, Cherokee Nation

Things were warming up and the humidity was high. Claire wiped her brow as she knocked on the front door. Molly let her in. Sandra was in the kitchen, putting together a snack tray. Molly hugged Claire and whispered, "I'm nervous—just sayin'."

"Try not to be, Molly. All will be well," Claire responded. "Oooh, that air feels good," she said, grateful for the air conditioning. Molly showed her into the living room. "You have a lovely home," said Claire, admiring the various pieces of artwork around the room, most done by Cherokee artists.

"Thanks," said Molly. She looked so upset that Claire thought she might throw up.

"God is with you, Probie, always. Take it slow, take it light." They sat on the sofa together. Sandra came in with the tray.

"Osiyo, Claire. I'm Sandra," she said, extending her hand. "So nice to meet you! Molly has told me a lot about you."

"Nice to meet you, too, Sandra. Did she tell you how awesome I think she is?" she asked with her confident smile.

"Ah, no, she skipped that one," said Sandra with a laugh. Molly smiled self-consciously, still wanting to run like hell. Mary, where are you when I need you? Sandra put the tray on the coffee table. "What can I get you to drink?"

"Well," said Claire thoughtfully, "I would prefer something cold given the sudden heat wave. I realize you may have prepared coffee, and if you did, I'll have some—along with a glass of ice water, if that's okay."

"I know—this early heat, right? I think I'll join you in that," said Sandra as she returned to the kitchen.

"Be there in a minute, Mom," said Molly, trying to act normally. She leaned forward, head in hands, quietly repeating, "Shit, shit, shit, shit, shit, *shit*." Claire rubbed her back and told her again that things would be fine. Molly went in to help her mom with the drinks.

The three of them had talked about Claire's new church, what it's like to be a minister, denominational differences, Molly's knee, school, and the like when it appeared to Molly that her mom could tell something wasn't right. Molly kept looking at Claire as if she had a secret, and Sandra knew her daughter. Finally, after a break in the conversation, Sandra put her coffee cup on the coaster on the table.

"Okay, would someone like to tell me what's really going on here?"

Claire smiled. "Sure, I think that might be my department," she said, looking at Molly.

"Oh, my God," said Sandra, a hand to her chest. "You're pregnant, aren't you?"

"What? No, Mom. Jesus Christ!"

That made Claire laugh. "No, Sandra, that's not why I'm here—and no, Molly is *not* pregnant. Are you?" she said, giving Molly a playful elbow.

"Uh, like, *no*," said Molly with irritation.

"Okay, good. Well, then, I'm here because—"

Just then the back door opened and Mike and Emmy walked in.

"'Siyo, Ma, Molly. Didn't realize you had company. Um, we can, uh, we can come back later, if you need us to."

"Well," said Sandra uncomfortably, "I guess if it's not urgent, maybe that would be good."

Emmy nodded and was about to turn when Claire spoke up.

"Mrs. McNair, I think it would be good if they stayed, if it's okay with Molly." Molly's eyes got big, but she didn't object; she was so numb now she wasn't sure what was a good idea and what was not. "Okay, Molly?" Molly nodded.

"Okaaay," said Emmy. "And you are?"

Claire stood. "Reverand Claire Sanders, pastor of Come to the Circle, near downtown."

Emmy smiled. "Yeah, I've seen the little sign at the UU church, right?"

"That's the one!" said Claire with her usual enthusiasm.

"Emmy," she said, pointing to herself, "and this is my boyfriend, Michael."

They all shook hands and sat.

"Emily," said Sandra, "will you grab something to drink for you and Mike, please?"

"Sure, Ma," she said, recognizing that something was definitely in the air. Mike leaned over and kissed Sandra hello on the cheek. She patted his hand.

Mike smiled at Molly. "How ya doin', Blue Jay?" Molly felt as if she might pee her pants.

Within a minute or two, all five of them were sitting in the living room as if it were a funeral wake. A heaviness permeated the room. Sandra sighed, then looked at Claire. "Well, okay then. I think you were about to tell me something about Molly?"

Claire nodded. She looked at Molly, still seated next to her. Molly had pulled her knees to her chest and began rocking herself, eyes focused on her glass of iced tea on the table. Her third refill since Claire had arrived. She really needed to pee. Claire patted Molly's hand, and Sandra and Emmy glanced at each other.

"First, I want to say it's been a real pleasure getting to know Molly. Sandra, did Molly tell you the circumstances under which we met?"

"A little. She told me about that ugly incident at Sacred Grounds." Emmy arched her eyebrows, and Mike narrowed his eyes a little. "Tell you both later," Sandra said to them. "She did good, our girl."

Emmy nodded. "Well okay then!" she said. They turned their attention back to Claire.

"As Molly and I have gotten to know each other better, she told me something in confidence. But due to current law, I'm obligated to tell you what it was." Sandra looked afraid, Emmy alarmed, and Mike intrigued. "Molly told me that she went out on a date with Devon Farmer and that he attacked her."

Sandra looked as if she hadn't heard Claire correctly. Molly slowly closed her eyes, hoping Mary was around somewhere. *Please don't leave me.*

"I'm sorry, what?" said Sandra, stunned.

Emmy puffed out her cheeks, her eyes got big, and she blew the air out with an "Oh, shit!" expression.

"Basically, Mrs. McNair, Devon almost raped Molly in a movie theater."

"WHAT THE FUCK!" screamed Sandra. Molly squeezed her eyes shut even tighter. Claire took her hand again. Sandra looked over at Emmy and could tell immediately that Emmy knew something. "What, Emily, what, what—what do you know about this?"

Mike shifted in his chair and cleared his throat.

Emmy looked at Mike, who looked back at her, who looked at Molly and then to Claire, then shrugged.

Before Emmy could respond, Claire added, "Also, it's really odd in that Molly has told me that she hasn't seen Devon anywhere since. Like, he just disappeared."

"Oh, boy," said Mike under his breath without thinking.

Sandra looked at Mike. "Mike? What the hell is going on here? Tell me now, dammit, and I want to know why the mother is the last to know about something like this. Spill it, Michael, and don't you dare lie to me!" Mike held up his hands, as if trying to calm the situation. Sandra shifted her frustration from Mike to Emmy. "Emmy? Please, for God's sake, will someone tell me what's really going on here?" Claire looked on with curiosity. Molly had lowered her legs to the floor and was staring at both Emmy and Mike.

"Em?" she inquired weakly.

"All right, okay, okay," said Emmy, holding up her own hands. "I knew, Mom," she said, looking over at her mother and feeling like she had betrayed her for life. Sandra just stared at Emmy, a look of disappointment shrouding her face. Molly looked at her sister with surprise and trepidation. "The Chief came by my place one night and told me, Molly," she said with an apologetic look. Claire looked confused and nudged Molly.

"Rebecca," she confirmed for Clair. Claire nodded. Sandra was dumbfounded, still trying to absorb the shock of what she had been told.

"That's how I got that bruise on my arm, Mom," said Molly, reminding her of the welt that Sandra had asked about the day after it happened. Molly had lied and said it was from wrestling with Becks like they did when they were little. Sandra held up her hands this time, as if to try to help herself sort out the confusing information.

"Okay, wait, wait. Emmy, if you knew, then what—what happened? I mean . . . and just *where* the hell *is* Devon, by the way? I'd like to hang his ass from an oak tree in any case, but where is he in all this and why—why didn't you *tell* me, girl?" she asked, looking at Molly. "I mean, why?" She looked bewildered and hurt. Molly felt terrible.

"I'm sorry, Mom; I just didn't know what to do. Honestly, I just wanted to forget about it. He didn't actually rape me. He got overly aggressive in the movie and when I told him I wanted him to stop, it was like—like he was deaf. It just wasn't like him, Mom. It's like he's not the same guy I grew up with."

"But he didn't . . ."

"No, ma'am," said Claire, answering for Molly. "He tried, but our young warrior here dumped Devon's soda in his lap after twisting his, his, well . . . you know."

Emmy burst out laughing.

"Atta girl!" she said. "Becks didn't tell me about that one. That's pretty damn funny!"

"Emily!" yelled Sandra. "Honestly, girl! And when are *you* gonna tell me the rest of what *you* know about this?"

"I gotta pee," said Molly, as if she were eight.

"Hold it," snapped Sandra, as if Molly were seven.

"Well," Emmy began, glancing at Mike, who looked away, "I, um, well—after Rebecca told me that night, I eventually stopped by Devon's job and well, you know—just, um, kinda had a little . . . *chat* with him, is all."

"Oh, my God!" said Sandra, leaning forward and putting her head in her hands and shaking her head. Molly bolted upright.

Molly's jaw dropped what seemed like a foot. "*Oh. My. God. That's* why I haven't seen him around! You *killed* Devon, didn't you? Oh, Jesus H. Christ, Emmy! You fucking shot him with that gun of yours, didn't you! Didn't you? Oh, God," she moaned, putting her hands to her face.

Mike raised his hands again. "No, Blue Jay, she didn't kill *any*body, okay? Can we get that straight here, please? Especially since we have a member of the clergy here. We promise, Molly. She didn't kill Devon, so relax, okay?"

"Sure thought about it, though," Emmy mumbled under her breath, her arms crossed. Claire's eyes shot back and forth between family members, clearly taking in this interesting transaction.

"What?" barked Sandra, looking over at Emmy.

"Nothing," said Emmy.

Mike looked around at everybody. "Let's just take it easy, okay? Devon's at a halfway house, Molly. This is what we came over to tell you. Emmy's been trying to . . . well, trying to help Devon, so to speak. She's basically been acting as his probation officer, as it turns out."

He looked to Emmy to explain the rest. She sighed, then told them about insisting that Devon go to meetings, checking up on him, and then about the recent drug buy. Molly just sat in astonishment. Sandra looked as if she were processing every scrap of information since the meeting began. Molly shot to her feet.

"I've got to *fucking* piss, dammit!" she bellowed, hands on her head.

Her mom looked up at her. "Okay, okay. Go on. We'll be right here then," she said, still trying to make sense of it all. Molly turned to leave, then turned back to face her sister.

"You lied to me," she said, her voice drowning in disappointment.

"No, Molly, I didn't, I swear—"

"*Yes,*" Molly insisted, "you absolutely did!"

"I was just trying to protect you, Molly!" Emmy argued, standing.

"Bullshit!" Molly screamed. "You fucking lied to me by doing all this shit behind my back! And I hate your ass for it!" She stormed down the hallway to the bathroom and slammed the door. Emmy started after her, but Mike stopped her and shook his head.

Claire smiled. She tried to take up some of the conversation from there, knowing the shock to everyone's system. She asked questions and shared her observations, doing her best to take a pastoral perspective. Sandra said Claire might as well stay for dinner, insisting that Mike and Emmy stay, too, and not leave the house without some peace and resolution to this mess. Mike suggested that this was just too much on Sandra or anyone to cook, and that they order some decent takeout and he would pick it up and bring it back. Everyone agreed on Thai and decided to get a big grab-fest from an online menu.

"I bet you didn't expect to be here all day," Sandra said to Claire ten minutes later, as they stood side by side and handwashed the few dirty dishes and glasses from the snack tray together.

"Actually, I'd planned on it as a contingency. This is a big deal, wouldn't you say?" she asked, looking Sandra in the eye with compassion. Sandra nodded sadly and Claire dried her hands and patted Sandra's back. When Mike and Emmy came into the kitchen, Claire shared her own assault story with the family—the one she had told Molly about. Soon, they could hear Molly in her room, crying. Mike started in that direction when Emmy stopped him.

"Ordinarily," she said, "I would let you because I know she thinks you hung the moon. But this is my mess. I'll clean it up." She kissed his cheek, took a deep breath, and then headed that way. She turned back to them and said with a sad expression, "Actually, I'd rather fight Ortiz again than have this conversation."

Emmy knocked on Molly's door and stuck her head in.

"Go away," said Molly, lying on her bed.

"Can't do that, Nine-Speed. Love you too much."

"Fuck that shit. You *lied* to me."

"No, I didn't. I just didn't tell you things I didn't think you needed to know. There's a difference."

"Not really."

"Okay, Molly. If it satisfies you for me to say it, then I lied to you. So there. Are you going to hate me from now on because of it? I'm only human, Peewee, and a pretty messed-up one at that." Molly lay on her side, face halfway on her pillow, holding the plush Snoopy she'd had from childhood.

Emmy came and stood by the bed. She kneed the bed.

"Go on," she said, arms behind her back. "I'll give you a free shot. Hit me."

"Go the fuck away, please."

"No. C'mon, lay one on me. Freebie. Indian taco shit-stain to the face. Go ahead."

"No."

"Yes," she challenged, kicking the bed and hoping to rile her sister.

"No, dammit."

"Stand up, bitch."

"NO! I don't want to hit you, Em. I'm just . . . just disappointed. In you. In Devon. In God. Fucking karma shit." She hugged her Snoopy harder. Emmy sighed, then gently moved Molly's legs out of the way and sat on the bed beside her. "Dog-tired, Em. Just leave me be," she moaned sadly, mashing her face between the mattress, the pillow, and Snoopy.

Emmy sat and nodded, leaning forward with her elbows on her knees. "Oh, crap, that reminds me," she said, shaking her head as if she had forgotten something. Molly ignored her. "Did you hear about Charlie Bunch's dog? You know—he's got that gorgeous giant poodle, Zeppelin." Molly stirred slightly. "It's rough, man, rough. Hated to hear it," Emmy shook her head again, flexing her biceps involuntarily like a boxer. Ever the animal lover, especially dogs, Molly turned, peering over her Snoopy.

"What? Somethin' happen to Zeppelin?"

"Well," Emmy said solemnly, "Charlie took him to the groomer—you know that prissy little guy over on Hoskins Ave.? Doobie Parker, I think?"

"Dewey Parker," Molly replied, sitting up slightly.

"Yeah yeah, Dewey. Anyway, Charlie takes Zeppelin in for his monthly digs, right? Puts him up on one of those froufrou tables, ya know? So Dewey's doing his thing, examining him before the groom, you know."

Molly shook her head slightly, then lay face down again, not giving her sister any benefit.

"Well," Emmy continued, "Dewey's looking him over real good and Charlie—well, Charlie's just standing there—off to the side, helping Dewey steady Zeppelin."

"There a point to this goddamn story?" Molly mumbled through her Snoopy.

"Well, the damnedest thing happened," Emmy continued. Molly just lay there, refusing to budge, her face against Snoopy's right ear, her breath blowing the ear out so it stood on end. "Dewey—in his prissy way—says, 'Hey, I don't want to overstep, but I'm noticing some really horrible, just terrible, disgusting breath here. Has that been a problem?' So, it's like pregnant silence for a few seconds, and Dewey's thinking he's embarrassed Charlie and lost this valuable customer, right? Suddenly, Zeppelin's ears shoot straight up and he turns to Dewey and whispers, 'No, actually. It only bothers me after the fucker licks himself!'"

Emmy snorted at her own joke, leaning in toward Molly and giggling. Molly's upper body shook with laughter, increasing more with each evident thought about what Emmy just said.

Emmy plopped down next to her sister and tickled her the way she had in the car at the college. Molly laughed hysterically.

"Who's your favorite sister?" Emmy snickered as she prodded Molly.

"Stop it!" Molly yelled as Emmy blew a loud raspberry onto her neck. "CUT IT OUT, EM!" she roared as she tried to roll away, cackling.

"Well," said Sandra with relief from the living room, where the others had returned, "I do believe they've made up, don't you?" Claire and Mike laughed, nodding.

A few minutes later, Mike appeared at Molly's door and said he was going to pick up their dinner, asking if anybody else wanted to come. Emmy, who was standing and stretching, shook her head. She gave him a look and told him to tell Sandra and Claire that she needed about fifteen minutes alone with Molly. He nodded, pulled the door to, and left to deliver the message and get the food. Emmy smiled at Molly, who was sitting up now, leaning against the headboard with her Snoopy tucked under one arm.

"Room for me?" Molly nodded and slid over, giving Emmy just enough room on the double bed for both of them. Emmy leaned back, putting one of Molly's pillows behind her head. She put her arm around her little sister and they stared at the opposite wall, occasionally glancing out the window. "Again, I'm sorry. I'll do my best never to keep anything from you again. I dunno—it's a big sister thing, I suppose."

Molly just nodded, exhausted.

"On that subject," said Emmy, brushing Molly's hair away from her face, "I'm going to tell you something that happened to me in college . . ."

Sometime later—after a few minutes of listening to Molly wail for her sister—Sandra knocked on the door and checked in. Emmy, holding Molly close—Molly's face buried in Emmy's tear-stained chest, arms wrapped tightly around her sister and trembling—nodded and told her they would be out in just a little while. Snoopy sat upright against the headboard behind them, facing them as if listening intently to the most sacred narrative imaginable. Sandra nodded and quietly closed the door.

The food was spread out on the dining room table. Sandra sat at one end, Mike at the other, with Claire on one side, and Emmy and Molly on the other. Emmy's arm was around Molly's shoulders, lightly rubbing her neck and back. Sandra asked Claire to say the blessing, and she offered up a meaningful message, keeping it brief. She spoke about the beauty and power of Native women and Mike, especially, seemed touched. Everyone had their eye on Molly, who, after the earlier discussion and then hearing Emmy's story, looked utterly depleted. As they ate, the conversation necessarily turned to the subject of Devon and Molly, and what more, if anything, should be done.

"Michael," said Sandra, "what do you think?" Claire nodded, as if wondering the same thing.

"Well, first, and with respect to Blue Jay here—Devon technically didn't rape Molly. There has to be penetration for that, right? So, that's off the table. Second, it's aggravated assault—of a minor. Trying to prove attempt or malice aforethought is incredibly difficult in a situation like this, especially for a guy with no prior record and a drug problem. Because it's Native on Native, I would turn this over to Callie, and she could charge him with the assault. Third, Molly has conflicted feelings about what to do here, so . . . ?" His hands were folded as he spoke, and he unfolded them and opened them in the form of a question. Clearing his throat, he said, "I want to emphasize to Molly that, from a criminal justice point of view especially—but from *any* point of view—that rape and sexual assault are crimes of violence, not 'sex crimes.'" He glanced at Emmy, who had been watching him intently. Leaning forward, with her elbow on the table, chin in hand, she slowly closed her eyes and opened them, then smiled at him adoringly, mouthing "thank you." He looked back at Molly. "Do you understand the difference, Blue Jay?"

"I guess so," she said, haggard and frail from a day of great emotional output. "I mean, I think," she added, rubbing her head, both of her own elbows now on the table. She sighed.

"No, kiddo. Sorry, that doesn't cut it," he said, which made Emmy and Sandra sit up and take notice.

Claire smiled knowingly.

Molly just looked at him, trying to comprehend.

"The fact that Devon didn't take no for an answer—that he disregarded your wishes and your verbal statement—that is unacceptable, you understand?"

She nodded.

"It doesn't matter how long your families have known each other or that you two were childhood friends. Devon used force. He ignored your knee injury on top of everything else, and he bruised you as a result. Do you understand that's never okay— under *any* circumstances?"

She nodded again.

"We—all of us here—are invested in you, Blue Jay. We need to hear you say that you understand what I'm saying to you."

"I understand."

"What, Molly," asked Sandra. "what do you understand?"

"I understand what Devon did was wrong. Period." Emmy and Claire nodded, and Mike nodded with a look of satisfaction.

"Well, I'm just haggard from this thinking process. I'm so blown away—we've known this family since he and Molly were in kindergarten," Sandra said, addressing Claire. "But like Mike is saying, it shouldn't be a moral dilemma, though, should it?"

"Yes and no. It's not that simple," said Claire.

"Exactly," said Emmy with a nod. Sandra also nodded slowly, then shook her head, perplexed by it all and yet furious at Devon. She looked over at Molly, who wasn't eating. "Eat something, Molly, please." Molly rolled her eyes and stuck her chopsticks into a piece of chicken and put it in her mouth. Sandra looked around the table, almost as if asking permission of the group for this next question.

"Molly, what would you have me do in this situation? I want to hear from you."

Molly put her chopsticks down and sighed, crossing her arms. "I don't know," she said softly. "In a way, like I've said, I just wanna forget this. Can't anybody see that I'm just trying to move on with my life?" She glanced at Claire, who looked down. Sandra came to Claire's defense.

"Claire did what she thought was right, Molly; what she *had* to do, actually. And I'm grateful, by the way," she added, smiling at Claire.

"Well, I *don't* want that to happen to another girl, that's for sure," said Molly. "I just—I don't know." She rubbed her arm where he had bruised her. "And he *did* hurt me, I just don't understand why." Emmy glanced at Mike.

"Should've killed that bastard at Eagle Feather," she sparked.

Mike shook his head.

Molly huffed and sat back, crossing her arms.

Emmy immediately patted Molly's leg, saying, "Okay. Sorry."

"Look," said Mike, holding up his hands again. "Here's what I think. Not much will likely come of this in the legal sense. So much of this rests on Devon, and his mindset from now on." Molly listened to Mike with interest. She valued his opinion as much as the others. "I can tell you one thing," he said with a grin. "That guy is scared to *death* of Emmy." Molly managed a smile, then lightly rested her head on Emmy's shoulder. Emmy put a hand to her kid sister's face and patted it.

"I mean, here I am—out there with my badge and my Glock 9mm—trying to play the bad cop, and all Emmy has to do is flex her biceps and this guy nearly craps his pants!"

Everyone—even Molly—laughed.

"Say, what was that business about calling you a deer woman? What'd he mean by that?"

"*Yes!*" said Claire with a snicker, giving Emmy two thumbs up. The women laughed.

"Never mind," said Emmy. "Tell you later."

Mike continued. "So, I guess what I'm saying is maybe we let this play out, see if Devon can dry out and go back to meetings, maybe unsupervised probation. If he can't, then we let the system have him. What do you think?"

"Yes, yes," said Molly with her last ounce of energy, raising her head and nodding soberly. "I'm for that."

"Agreed," piped Claire.

Sandra looked at Emmy, then at Claire, who nodded. Then she sighed and said, "All right, then. I guess that make sense."

Molly managed another smile and said, "Thanks, Mom."

"Sure I can't kill him?" Emmy offered to no one in particular, arms outstretched with a crack of her knuckles. "It'd be quick and painless."

"Yes!" shouted Claire and Mike at the same time. "We're sure," they said simultaneously.

Emmy rolled her eyes and sighed. "Fine . . ." She smiled at Molly and patted her face again.

Molly, looking spent, leaned into her sister's shoulder and said, "I just wanna sleep."

37

Bankrupt 'Em Boyer

Present Day
State District Court of Judge Boyer
Muskogee, Oklahoma

J udge Boyer brooked no nonsense.

The defendant standing before him had refused counsel, going on the assumption it wasn't needed. He wore a dirty white tank top unsuitable for day-to-day life, much less court. Judge Boyer confirmed that he had a good job as a plumber. He seemed cocky and unbothered by the judge's presence or the fact that he was standing opposite Alan Trapp, one of the most aggressive and successful assistant district attorneys in the DA's office.

Judge Boyer looked at him, wondering why this seemed so insignificant to him. A serial repeater, the defendant stared back at Boyer and asked, "This gonna take long, Judge? I gotta get back to my job."

"Run that by me again, son?"

"Gotta job waitin' on me over in Broken Arrow. Serious bucks, Judge."

Judge Boyer looked at ADA Trapp. "I see. Well, pardon me all to hell, Mr. Todd," he said, addressing the defendant, who was scratching his underarm. "Charges, Mr. Trapp?"

"Assault on a female, Your Honor. Also resisting, public drunkenness, assault on a law enforcement officer, and defacing public property."

"What's that last one?" Judge Boyer asked.

"Urinating on a patrol car, Judge."

A probation officer who looked just like Pippi Longstocking, doing court intake and sitting over in the seats to the side—giggled and played with one of her red braids.

"Sheeeet, das a lie," said the defendant.

Judge Boyer shook his head and asked the ADA for the recommended sentencing. "It's his seventh arrest for assault on a female in eighteen months, Your Honor," said Trapp. "State recommends six months straight time with three years unsupervised probation with counseling. His wife did not want to come in, Judge, but she was pretty marked up from their last encounter. She mainly wants him out of the house for a while."

"I'm sure she does," said the judge, rubbing his chin and lightly tapping his forehead with his fist while thinking, a clear sign that Judge Boyer was considering dropping the hammer as he scanned the case notes.

"I got somethin' to say to that, Judge," said Mr. Todd.

Judge Boyer sat back. "Oh, well, please, Mr. Todd—I mean for heaven's sake, I'm waiting on pins and needles, sir." Pippi Longstocking laughed out loud at that one.

"She's always nagging me, Judge. Can't do anything right by the woman. I mean, like, she's always in my shit about other women and says I drink too much, but I pay the bills, ya know what I mean, sir?"

"Umm, I do indeed, sir, I do indeed."

"Not only that, Judge, but—"

"Stop, Mr. Todd," said Boyer, holding up his hand. "You're givin' me a headache." Pippi snickered again. "Mr. Todd, I'm sittin' up here, holding copies of X-rays from your wife's last visit to the ER. I'm also looking at the severe bruising on her face from photos taken the same day. Your personal problems just don't seem to interest me, sir. Does the state have anything further it wishes to add, Mr. Trapp?"

"No, sir," said the ADA with a satisfied expression. The probation officer just shook her head, knowing what was coming.

"Madam clerk," said Judge Boyer loudly into the microphone, "so noted: The defendant is hereby sentenced to not less than twelve months in the county jail, followed by supervised probation of no more or no less than three years."

The defendant's jaw dropped.

"Furthermore, the conditions of probation are to wit," Boyer added as the probation officer furiously took notes. When Judge Boyer was finished with the conditions of probation, which included frequent visits from a probation officer, extreme drug and alcohol testing, and mandated counseling for the entire period of probation, Mr. Todd wished he'd never set foot in the courtroom of "Bankrupt 'Em Boyer." "Mr. Sheriff," Boyer said to a deputy the size of a professional wrestler, "Take him away, son. And Miss Arrington," the judge said to the probation officer, "see to it that Mr. Todd understands I mean business, will you?"

"Yes, sir," she responded, returning to her notes.

Stunned, the defendant left the courtroom in handcuffs.

"Next case!" yelled the judge with a rap of the gavel.

Devon's court-appointed attorney, Lydia Thornwell, leaned over to Devon and whispered, "We're next. Mind your manners." He nodded. Emmy, Mike, and Marshal Callie, who had just joined them in the courtroom, sat behind Devon and his lawyer.

"State versus Devon Farmer, Your Honor," said the ADA. "Judge, I'll call your attention to the earlier plea conference in chambers." The judge nodded and skimmed his paperwork. That morning, Lydia Thornwell, ADA Trapp, Callie, and Mike had met with Judge Boyer, going over the entire story with him. Devon was allowed to sit in for parts; for others, he was excused. Mike had explained Emmy's role in the situation, but the judge had not met her. Judge Boyer looked over the paperwork again, glanced up at the party behind the defense counsel, and nodded.

"Both parties approach the bench, please," he said, motioning them to come forward. "You, too, Ms. McNair." He smiled. "It's an honor to have you in my court, Storm," the judge added with a twinkle in his eye. People in the courtroom sat up and took notice when they realized who the judge was talking to.

"Oh, pa-leeze!" Callie whispered as they approached, playfully elbowing Emmy in the ribs. "He thinks you're the absolute *shit*." Mike grinned at that.

The judge pushed the court microphone down and to the side, then flicked it off to have a private conversation. "Mr. Trapp, you good with what we discussed this morning?"

ADA Trapp nodded.

"Ms. Thornwell?"

"Yes, Judge. Mr. Farmer is ready to comply." She had told Devon to wait at the counsel table.

"Well, well, well," Judge Boyer said with a grin. "The Cherokee Storm—right here in my court. That was quite the fight, Storm. That Ortiz woman is *still* pulling your boot out of her ass, I'm guessing? One hell of a fight! Saw it at O'Dean's over on Third Street. That bar went total apeshit when you dropped that girl. One of the hardcores almost went into anaphylactic shock when you choked her out!"

Emmy just smiled and looked down. "Thanks, Judge." He smiled and nodded.

"Agent Soul here tells me you've made quite the impression on this young man. Anything you want to say at this time?"

Emmy put her involvement with Devon in a nutshell for him, the content of which was exactly what Mike had told the judge earlier, minus, of course, Emmy's little "chat" with Devon early on. Judge Boyer listened intently, nodding now and again.

"All right, then," Judge Boyer said with a sigh, "if everybody's still good with this, I'll pronounce sentence." Those who had been present nodded. "Marshal, this gonna work on your end?"

Callie nodded. "I'll go with Emmy's request on this one, Judge," she said with a smile. "The Cherokee Nation court will be set to deal with Devon regarding the assault charge."

"How's that looking, ya think?" the judge asked.

"Well, Emmy's sister is willing to drop the charges if Devon complies with all of the conditions you impose in state court, sir."

"Hmm, I see," said Judge Boyer, mulling that over. "Ms. McNair? That satisfactory?"

Emmy nodded. "Yes, Judge," she said, verbalizing her agreement.

Boyer grinned at Emmy again. "You keep makin' us proud, Storm, hear me?"

Emmy smiled and nodded.

"All right, then," he said, motioning for everyone to return. Boyer thought twice and said, "Callie, Ms. McNair," gesturing for them to come back. "Listen to me," he whispered, double-checking that the mic was off. "Look, I try to keep things lighthearted in here, believe it or not. But I'm warning you *both* not to let this young man drag you down with him—if that's the way he wants to go. *Do not* let him mess up your career, Storm, you understand me?" Emmy nodded. "This shit doesn't always turn out so well; I'd give him a fifty-fifty shot at best."

"Funny," said Emmy, "that's what Mike said."

"Ohh, 'Mike' is it?" said the judge with a knowing smile. Emmy grinned and shrugged. "Okay," he said, "step back." As they were returning, Judge Boyer smiled and said, "Thanks for showing up today, Ms. McNair."

Emmy turned and smiled, thanking the judge for the hearing, as Callie guided her back to the counsel table.

Lydia stood with Devon as Judge Boyer pronounced sentence. With respect to the possession charge, Devon got off easy with a fine and some community service, with a period of unsupervised probation. Judge Boyer told Devon that if he complied with everything and finished college, he could return to court to have his record expunged.

"I happen to know the Cherokee Nation deputy chief," said Judge Boyer. "I imagine he might have some interesting community service projects he could line up for you, Mr. Farmer." Devon just stood there and stared, as if hypnotized. Lydia glanced at her client and turned to the judge.

"Um, that would be great, Your Honor. Thank you!" she said.

When the judge went over the details and hours of community service—which were demanding and extensive, Devon let out a loud sigh, shook his head, and mumbled, "Oh, man."

Judge Boyer looked up. "What was that?"

"Told you to button it!" Lydia whispered to Devon, who just nodded and looked at the floor.

"Did someone just sigh in my damn courtroom?" boomed the judge, dropping his arm down on the bench. "Mr. Farmer," he roared, "do you have a problem with the way I hand down sentencing in my beloved court?"

Silence. Lydia nudged Devon, who was staring at the judge again as if trying to figure out a calculus problem.

"Well?" Boyer demanded.

Callie, standing on the other side of Devon from Lydia, and Emmy, standing behind, simultaneously slapped Devon upside the back of the head. Probation officer Arrington giggled again.

"Uh, uh, no. I mean, yes, Your Honor. I mean, I'm good with it, sir."

"Yeah," said Judge Boyer, smiling at the women, "I thought you might be." Turning solemn, Judge Boyer added,

"You've got *serious* people in your corner, Mr. Farmer. Do yourself a favor and be thankful. Don't foul this up, son!"

Lydia nudged Devon once more.

"Yes, sir. I mean, I won't, sir."

"Next case!" thundered Boyer with a slam of his gavel.

38

Sleek and Proud

She was a phantom of delight
When she first gleamed upon my sight;
A lovely apparition, sent
To be a moment's ornament;
Her eyes as stars of twilight fair;
Like twilight's, too, her dusky hair . . . .
—William Wordsworth

Present Day
Third Week of May
McNair House
Muskogee, Oklahoma
District Four, Cherokee Nation

S andra watched Molly watching Clay as he talked about his
pre-law classes. She noticed that Molly laughed at nearly
everything Clay said, even when it wasn't funny. Then she
noticed the dimples. Oh, no, Sandra thought, *not* the dimples.

"Would you get Clay some more tea, Molly?"

Molly just sat there like an imbecile, smiling at Clay.

"Molly!"

"Oh, yeah, sure, Mom," she answered, going back to the
fridge for some iced tea.

"So, Clay," said Sandra, "any thought so early on what type of law you might like to go into someday?"

"Well, yeah, I'm thinking about—"

"He's really into the idea of tort law, Mom. His dad being in construction all these years—he's had a lot of help from lawyers regarding personal injury and such," chimed in Molly, walking back and handing Clay his iced tea refill.

"I see," said Sandra, nodding at Clay, wondering when the next interruption was coming. "So the idea of trial law appeals to you to some degree, then?"

"I think so," Clay answered. "I'm not opposed to—"

"He's not opposed to other areas, either," blurted Molly. "He was telling me that constitutional law is interesting to him, too. He likes the idea of learning the Bill of Rights and protecting them and being of service to his country and to our people in the Cherokee Nation and he likes the idea of fighting systemic racism, especially against the tribes, and he wants to maybe apply to the Oklahoma City University School of Law and probably Ole Miss and maybe even Stanford—"

"Molly," Sandra interjected.

"—plus he's trying to decide if he wants to do more with his English major, like maybe do journalism as a job for a year and—"

"Molly!"

This jolted Molly back to earth. "*What?*" asked Molly.

Sandra noticed that Clay was grinning at Molly and admiring her hair, which was up in a beautiful bun that accented her grandmother's spider earrings. Sandra also noticed that Molly had sprayed perfume before Clay came over.

"You're making the iced tea nervous, Peewee. Truly, girlfriend, *slow down.*"

That made Clay laugh.

Molly turned red and put her hands to her face. "Oh, I'm sorry, Mom." She looked at Clay self-consciously and said, "I had three glasses of tea before you got here. Guess I'm a little jacked. Sorry about that."

"Open your mouth, Clay," said Sandra with a funny look. He glanced at Molly, then turned back to her mom, opening his mouth slightly. "Oh, my gosh, Molly, he still has his tongue. I'll just bet he can speak for himself." She winked at Molly.

Clay laughed loudly at that.

"It's okay, Mrs. McNair. I like listening to Molly." Molly beamed and rubbed her left forearm. "Everything Molly said is basically true. I guess my eyes are bigger than my stomach. Seems like a great thing about the law, though, is that you have a lot of options as to which area to go into."

"True," said Sandra. "And you have plenty of time to decide. How are you liking the school in general? It seems to have made a nice impression on Molly during her visit."

"Well, I can tell you this: the dean sure liked her. He was very impressed with Molly and her teacher references." He smiled at Molly when he said it, and Sandra glanced at Molly, who was completely in outer space, somewhere between the Big Dipper and the North Star. She did, however, manage to bat her eyelashes at Clay in response. "It's a great school, Mrs. McNair. The overwhelming majority of the students there are serious about their studies and aren't just using it as a place to hide out for four years." Molly let out a belly laugh, as if that was the funniest thing she'd ever heard.

Molly touched Clay's arm gingerly and said, "That's *too* funny!" and beamed at Clay.

Oh, for God's sake, Sandra thought.

"No, seriously," Clay added, "a lot of people are just going through the motions these days at college, with no idea at all about what they want to do or who they want to be. I try to stay focused, ya know?"

Sandra nodded her approval and Molly gazed at Clay as if he were an astronaut who just saved earth from a cosmic catastrophe.

"I'm hoping to do an internship my last semester senior year at a law firm. That might help give me a better idea about things."

"It definitely couldn't hurt," said Sandra. "I know an attorney here and there after all these years. I might be able to recommend someone when the time comes."

"That would be awesome, Mrs. McNair! I can't wait for it all to come together like that. Being a sophomore this year was interesting, but I'm looking forward to being a junior. And I'm hoping to see Molly there as a freshman!" He grinned at her.

Molly was resting her chin in her hand, elbow on the table. "Umm . . ." she said in a dreamy, faraway kind of voice. Sandra just shook her head. "That would be *so* rad," said Molly, gazing at Clay as if her mom were not in the room.

"Hey, we just need to make it all happen, girl!" he said, throwing up his hands with another smile.

He seems safe and he respects your mom. Laugh again like he's the funniest guy on earth, but try not to drool on the floor like a Saint Bernard.

Molly let out another prolonged, girlish giggle, touching the front of her neck and rubbing her left arm again. Clay smiled and looked down. Sandra had the sudden urge to puke. Jesus, Molly, she thought.

"Okay," she said. "Well, Clay, I'm so glad you came by for a visit. I'm going to go clean up the kitchen, but you two kids feel free to keep chatting. Clay, give your mom my best."

"Thanks, Mrs. McNair, and wado for the dinner—it was terrific! I really appreciate you talking to me and giving me some ideas."

"You're welcome, Clay." She disappeared into the kitchen and Molly and Clay went to the living room.

"How's Emmy doing?" he asked as they sat down on the sofa.

"She's doing pretty good. Not letting this cancer get the best of her, that's for sure. Did I tell you that she has a special diet—the plant-based thing—and she sees a naturopath who does native herbs and different stuff like that?" He shook his head. "Yeah, she's really diligent about her health. Our Aunt Lisa went through chemo and radiation and she didn't make it, and Emmy wants to try a different way. She's been doing a lot of studying and research and believes that cancer can be treated in different ways—that it doesn't have to be 'burning and poisoning' as she likes to call it."

"Yeah, I have a cousin named Wancha and he went through the same kind of thing. The treatment almost killed him, but he made it."

"That's good," said Molly. They sat in silence for a few moments. Finally, Molly spoke.

"Hey, I *really* appreciated the tour at the college. That was nice of you."

"No problem. Glad to do it. So, have you thought more about it? Remember, there's scholarship money available, too."

"That sounds strange. I mean, for some reason, I never thought about having to apply for one."

"Oh, hey," he said, holding up a hand. "It can be rough these days getting through college without one—even when you're working. I waited tables for a while, worked some construction at my dad's firm, did some sales work—that kind of thing. Still really hard to cover expenses even when you're making some good money. You get along okay with your mom?"

"Yeah, sure. Why do you ask?"

"Well, staying on campus can be cool, Molly, but you'd save a lot each year if she let you stay here for the four years. That can be hard, though. I did it with my folks for the whole year last year, then decided to move in with a buddy of mine in a duplex over by the school. Works out okay—we're not there half the time anyway! I mean, obviously, it's our time to spread our wings and become more independent as people. It all depends on the individual situation, though."

"Yeah, I don't know. Haven't really thought that far ahead yet. So much going on, you know?"

"Yeah, of course. Oh, hey, God . . . sorry. I totally forgot to ask about your knee. How is it?"

"Sore. This tendonitis is taking longer than we wanted it to. After deciding to put the ride off a year, well, it doesn't really matter as much now."

They had both inched closer on the sofa during the conversation, and she was now looking up at him, her tawny, glistening hair in perfect form atop her head. They gazed at each other until Molly leaned in slightly, Clay meeting her halfway for the kiss.

They held it just long enough for Molly's heart to skip a beat, then pulled away.

"Thank you," she said softly, looking down.

"What do you mean?" he asked.

"Ah, I'll tell you about it another time. I just really appreciate you being a gentleman."

"Wow," he said. "Then I guess I'm happy to be one!" They laughed. He took her hand and held it for a moment, as she patted his and smiled up at him again.

"Thanks for coming over," she whispered. "And for helping me with college choices and all. I have to think about it, but I really did like what I saw."

"Good," he said, taking his cue to get up. They stood and hugged. Like before, they both looked at each other just a little longer than one would expect from just friends. He reached over, placing his hand on her face, and briefly kissed her again. "You look amazing, by the way," he said with a smile. She walked him to the door. "Tell your mom I said thanks again and hopefully I can chat with her more later."

"Okay," she said. "Goodnight, Clay."

"Night, Molly," he replied with a grin. She shut the door and leaned against it.

Well done, Pretty Feet. Easy does it.

"Yeah . . ." said Molly with a dreamy sigh. She heard her mom coming back from the kitchen and opening the swinging door, which she had closed to give them some privacy.

"Have a nice visit?" she asked.

"Yeah, yeah—I think so," said Molly thoughtfully.

"Good." She walked over and pulled some remaining items from the dining room table, bending over to reach the far side. "That is a *good-looking* man, Molly Martha McNair. Go easy, okay?" She straightened before returning to the kitchen, eyeing her daughter and capturing Molly's attention.

"Okay. I love you, Mom."

"Love you, too, kiddo."

McNair House
Backyard Corner

"Now," said Clay, holding Molly's head steady in his hands. "Put it up to your mouth and blow."

Molly inhaled and blew gently.

"No, blow on it, Molly. Blow harder."

"Like this?" she asked, looking up at him and blowing with a slight puff.

"Yeah, but put your mouth to it like this," he said, bending toward her so she could see him and puckering his lips. "Then steady your breathing—and *blow*." He rested his hand on the back of her head.

"Okay," she said with a sigh, "if you say so." She did as he said, glancing down the shaft and giving a soft "pfftt!" Molly looked up to see if the result had satisfied Clay.

"Bullseye!" he shouted with a smile. "Nicely done, Molly, really!"

"All right!" screamed Molly, giving Clay a high five and kissing the shaft of her new blowgun, a gift from Clay. He handed her another blow dart and she sent it on toward the target. Not a bullseye, but close. She beamed. He placed his left arm on her shoulder, handing her another dart.

"Now," he said, patting her shoulder, "steady . . . blow!" The next one went straight to the bullseye again. "Outstanding! You're a natural, Molly," he said with a grin.

"Wado," she said. "This is a really special gift, Clay, thank you." She examined the smooth river cane and held the weapon in her arms like a baby. "I always wanted one of these but just never bothered to learn."

"Glad you like it," he said with another smile. "It reminded me of you when I saw it—sleek and proud."

He digs you. He's loving those dimples. And those eyebrows, but for the right reasons. Now laugh at what he said, but don't be a nincompoop.

Molly laughed and touched Clay's shoulder with the end of the blowgun. "Thank you. That's sweet."

Yeah, and he's got that hunky thing going on, too. You're one of the lucky ones, Pretty Feet.

Molly smiled again. She leaned over on her tiptoes, kissing him lightly on the cheek. "Wado, Clay, for taking the time with me. This is really awesome."

"Well, I was thinking that, with all you've been through lately, you deserve some fun—a change of pace." He nodded and smiled, putting his hands in his pockets. Molly just stared at him, back between the Big Dipper and the North Star.

Hello . . . afterlife to Molly . . . I said you're lucky, not available for the taking. Make him earn your respect.

"Well," said Molly in a thoughtful way, "I think maybe you're right." She nodded her head. "Clay, why did you reach out to me? I mean, in the first place—about college? Why? There are a lot of other girls wanting to go to college—girls a lot prettier than me, by the way."

"Is that what you think, Molly? That I contacted you for a date? That it's about you being pretty—well, beautiful, if you ask me, but that's beside the point. Seriously?"

She shrugged.

"Isn't it? I mean, that's what most guys are ultimately interested in, right?"

"Jeez, Molly," said Clay, shaking his head and walking over to the chairs that were usually in the yard. He sat down, shook his head again, and looked up at her. "I'm sorry you see it that way, Molly. That's not the case, so you know."

Molly would not be moved. She crossed her arms and cocked her head at him, as if still waiting to hear the real answer.

"All right," he said. "You want to know the real reason?"

"That'd be nice." An enormous, almost insurmountable feeling of disappointment came over Molly. Why? Why do they all lie like this? What is it about me? Did Devon set this up? Is he *paying* Clay to mess with me?

"It's going to sound silly," he said, shaking his head. He looked straight ahead, toward the back fence. "I kept getting like, I don't know, kinda weird messages—to call you, you know, to reach out and say hello. Almost as if someone were tapping on my shoulder. Like I said back at the school, I used to have a crush on you, so I don't know if that had anything to do with it or not." He glanced at her sheepishly and shrugged.

He's opening up to you.

Molly uncrossed her arms and walked over and sat in the other chair, giving him her attention.

"It's not like I was hearing voices or anything—I'm not going crazy, so don't worry. Just, instinct, maybe. Something telling me to say hello and see how you were doing. I mean, yeah, I think you're attractive and like being with you, no question. I'm a guy, right?" Molly nodded and looked down, as if considering what he was saying. "It's just that, well, it seems like most of the people we grew up with and many of the ones I meet now are coming out as trans, gay, bi, questioning, perpetually confused, Bigfoot, alien, hell . . . I don't know . . ."

Molly laughed loudly.

"Yeah, seems that way," she said, nodding in agreement.

He reached over and held her hand briefly. "I guess you stood out in my mind. I knew you were straight and had a good head on your shoulders. But honestly, Molly, I was really thinking about how great it would be if you went to the college I was going to, that's all. We weren't from the same neighborhood, but we knew each other when we were kids and I always thought you were nice, decent. Also, I had hoped that, you know—maybe I could help someone. Sounds corny, I know, but that was the main reason. And I know my family really respects yours."

Tell him.

She nodded. "I'm sorry, Clay. I didn't mean to offend. It's just that . . . well, remember when I told you I would tell you something another time?" He nodded. "I went out with a guy— a guy I've known most of my life, actually." She hesitated, surprised to see her own hands trembling. And Clay noticed it, she could tell. "Well, he attacked me. He went after me, you know? I mean, in a damn movie theater, of all places—basically tried to rape me."

"What?" He looked shocked.

"Yeah. His name isn't important. I was caught off guard. I mean, I've known him forever and he was never like this until he got involved with steroids. He has a drug problem."

"Ah, I see," said Clay, nodding. "We've got some of that going on now and then at school. One of our basketball players got caught up in that. He got kicked off the team, then he just quit and disappeared. It's sad, really. I know a lot of the pro athletes dope, but the smart ones—if you want to call it that— they do it under a doctor's supervision with a prescription. At least that part of it is legal. That kinda thing's just not for me, though."

"I'm glad to hear that," said Molly. "Trust me, I couldn't be with you if . . . I mean, I wouldn't want to hang out with you if you did." She rubbed the blowgun again, admiring it.

"Yeah, in aikido, they taught us that a drugfree life would take us farther, and I still believe that. You know, it's a mind-body-spirit thing."

"You do martial arts!" Molly's eyes widened and she opened her mouth in excitement.

Saint Bernard . . . just sayin'.

Molly closed her gaping jaw and smiled. "I didn't know. That's so cool. I mean, with Emmy and all, it's been a big subject around the house for years, of course." She leaned toward him as if she had a secret. "Mom hates it all! It's funny!" She laughed.

"Really? She shouldn't. Aikido isn't about violence; just the opposite. But . . . I can see where she doesn't like to think about Emmy doing it, being her daughter and everything. Plus, what Emmy does . . . man, that's a *whole* different ballgame. Those women are seriously tough. Wouldn't want to have to tangle with one."

"You mean you wouldn't want to get in the ring with Emmy to test your stuff?" Molly asked with a gleam in her eye, trying to throw some smack.

"Oh, hell no!" he said. "She'd break me in half, Molly!" Molly giggled. "Plus, I'm a lover, not a fighter," he said with a wink. She smiled at him bashfully. "So," he said, getting back to her original subject, "did you report the guy that tried to do this to you?"

Molly nodded. "That's a long story. Turns out Emmy dealt with him at first. Because he's an old family friend, we gave him a second chance, but he has court conditions to abide by. Remember me telling you Mike—Emmy's boyfriend—is a cop?" He nodded. "Well, thanks to the two of them, it got reported the right way. I was confused and scared—you know, didn't know what to do—and Mike helped set me straight about that. But I'm where I need to be with it now." She smiled again.

"That's good. So Emmy 'dealt' with him, huh? Man, I'd hate to have her after me! She's scary, and I don't consider myself someone who scares easily!" Molly laughed.

"*Everybody* says that about her! She's just like—you know—my big sis. Funny, still trying to get used to her being a celebrity. Crazy." She shook her head.

"You know," he said, pointing to the river cane, "the blowgun is a lot like aikido. It's about finding your center, in some ways. Learning a new way to focus. Want to do some more?"

"Yes!" she said, grinning.

Sandra had been watching part of their exchange from the kitchen window. "Go easy, Peewee, go easy. *Please*." She looked upward, then back down, nodding, as if she had her own chat buddy up there. She finished wiping down the counter.

39

Cherokee Princess

"Where are all the Indians?"

"They're probably at K Mart."

—Brief exchange between frustrated tourists confused by stereotypes and Wilma Mankiller during her tenure as principal chief of the Cherokee Nation

Present Day
Meg & Mike's
Muskogee, Oklahoma

Claire, Molly, Tara, and Rebecca sat chatting at the snack table near the door. The girls came to admire Claire, and they respected her willingness to accept people as she found them, Christian or not, churchgoers or not, whatever one was or believed. Molly was pensive, telling them about Clay and what might or might not be a relationship.

"My brother was friends with Clay," said Rebecca. "Seems like I remember something about him," she said, winking at Claire and Tara. "Tall, right? Molly?" Molly sat and gazed at the stand across from them that had American and Cherokee Nation flags for sale. Claire laughed.

"Yeah," said Claire, "think it just *might* be a relationship!"

Tara nudged Molly. "'Siyo! Earth to Molly."

Molly, resting her chin in her hand as she was prone to do when thinking about Clay, mumbled, "Yeah, tall . . ."

"Oh, hell—looka those dimples!" Tara teased.

"Seriously!" said Becks, pushing on them the way Emmy had. Molly blushed and they all laughed. Tara sighed and said, "Oh, I wish I had your eyebrows, Molly; they're dreamy."

"Yeah," said Rebecca, "I've always liked them, too."

Tara smiled. "How's the knee, Molly?"

"I still get a lock-like kinda thing, you know what I mean? Like, the pain is mostly gone, but, man, that IHS doc wasn't kidding. It's been nearly three months and I can still tell something isn't right. I don't really limp now, but it still catches at times. I tried riding a couple of weeks ago and that was a no-go. So I guess Tommy used good judgment in having me wait."

Claire nodded. "I think so, Probie. You don't want to be messed up for a year or more because you didn't use your common sense." Rebecca and Tara nodded in agreement.

Two women walked in who could only have been tourists. One of them, a tall strawberry blond with thinning hair, just had the look of someone who could annoy others within thirty seconds. She wandered about, fingering the merchandise. Claire and the girls watched as she made numerous comments to her friend about items she came across. Looking through some art-inspired letterhead and envelopes, she mispronounced Nez Perce and Osage, calling the latter "O-sag-ee." She looked around, as if performing an in-store inspection for some kind of corporate headquarters, and the girls caught her eye.

The woman, weaving in and out of the aisles, approached the table.

"Christ, what does this Karen want?" Rebecca mumbled under her breath.

Claire playfully kicked her chair and said, "Settle down, Chief."

Rebecca turned and looked as the woman tip-toed up.

"Excuse me," she said in a falsely tentative, almost kindergarten teacher sort of way. She spoke to Rebecca, who wore a beaded necklace and a Cherokee Nation ball cap, her black hair in a ponytail jutting out from over the back strap. She touched Rebecca on the shoulder.

"Yes?" said Rebecca politely.

"You're, um, you're . . . *for real*, right?"

"Excuse me?"

"What I mean is, well, you're like, a *real* Indian, am I correct?"

"Uh, yeah," said Rebecca with a "what the hell?" expression. She sat erect and, robotically, said, "That I am. How!"

Tara snickered.

Claire gave Becks a look that said, *Really?*

Rebecca held up her right hand. "I am real Injun!" she said lightheartedly, the woman laughing in response without really knowing why. Molly looked uncomfortable and crossed her arms. Holding out her hands to introduce the group, Rebecca said in a warm and sincere way, "So are my friends here, just so you know."

The woman, not getting it, pressed on. "Well, I mean, I was looking for an *actual* Indian—like you. I mean, no disrespect intended," she said, looking at the others and wistfully motioning with her hand in their direction. "Just that my friend and I were hoping to have our picture taken with an honest-to-goodness Native American—preferably a Cherokee. I'm part Cherokee, by the way. My great-great grandmother was a Cherokee princess from Kentucky. She was born on the river in a tepee!"

Molly spoke up. "Um, actually, ma'am, that's really not how we determine who's Indian and who isn't. I mean—you know—the physical feature thing. Kind of like, like I don't ask my black friends if they're real Africans, ya know?"

The woman eyed Molly.

"Well, that's hardly the same thing, now is it?" she finally said, taking a professor's tone with Molly, frustration in her voice.

Molly shrugged with an annoyed expression.

"Okay," said the woman with a smirk, "how *would* you determine who is an Indian?"

"Well—"

"Of course DNA is the big thing these days," the woman interrupted. "I had mine tested a couple of years back and I'm just fascinated by the results. I think more Native Americans should be doing it."

"That doesn't really—"

"Did you get yours tested?"

"Nope," said Molly, growing impatient, "didn't have to. Actually, ma'am, tribal citizenship—our people—is what really determines that I'm Cherokee. Also, you have some people who can't qualify for enrollment, but they have documentation of their ancestors and are part of our tribal community—like our friend Claire," she added, pointing to Claire.

"It's about kinship and loyalty, ma'am," said Tara, trying to support Molly's kindness.

"I know, right?" said the woman. "My daddy's daddy was so proud of his Cherokee kin. He was a Hyatt." To Claire, Molly looked steamrolled and just smiled weakly. "You all know any Hyatts? He played the flute and hunted deer with a bow and ar*row*," she said in her southeastern accent, sealing her fate.

"Well!" said Rebecca in mocked fascination, standing and pushing her smartphone over to Molly. "By all means, then, we should get a picture!" Tara lowered her head and rubbed her temples.

"Chief . . ." said Claire, shaking her head.

"It's all good, pastor! Hey, she's a Cherokee medicine woman!" said Rebecca, pointing to Claire for the benefit of the tourist.

"Is she now? That's just *mah-valess*!" the woman crowed. Molly, apparently to keep from laughing out loud, looked toward the door. Rebecca put her arm around the woman's shoulder briskly and pulled her close, saying, "Friend Molly—

take em photo now of me with white woman!" with a sarcastic smile, placing two fingers behind the woman's head as Molly snapped the photo.

"Oh, my goodness," said the woman's friend, hands to her mouth and watching from the edge of the candy isle. The first woman realized what was happening and pulled away from Rebecca.

"Well!" said the woman, "you didn't have to be rude!" She turned and strode away. She and her friend walked toward the back, the woman gesticulating to her friend about Rebecca.

Meg caught the last part of it all when she returned to the counter and mumbled, "Oh shit." She looked over at the girls.

"Don't fuck with my customers, Chief!" she whispered, cupping her hand around her mouth so the women wouldn't hear it. Rebecca made a pig face at her.

"Check my boogers, Megster!" Rebecca whispered with her snout face. "Lookin' all sexy, I am!"

The women continued browsing. At one point, with a look of some frustration, the woman turned back to Meg from the candy aisle and, in the same condescending tone she had used with the girls, inquired, "Pardon me! I know you're a small outfit and probably don't have what I need, but do you have any books on the Trail of Tears? I'm just *dying* to teach it in my Sunday school class! They really need to be educated on this, being Christians and all. It is *such* a discouraging aspect of our history though, isn't it? Oh, those poor people!"

Molly rolled her eyes.

"It certainly is," said Meg. "Yes, you'll find a few in the book section—over there where it says 'Books.'" Molly and Rebecca snickered and the woman did a double take at Meg.

"Careful in that candy aisle," Tara hollered. "That's where the Little People hang out." The woman and her friend looked around.

"Little People?" she asked.

"Yeah," answered Tara. "They've been acting up again—throwing hatchets over there. One woman died recently from catastrophic loss of blood. It was on CNN." The woman looked around again.

"Hatchets?"

Rebecca nodded seriously. "Oh, yes—yes, ma'am. Trickster shit—so much of it these days, especially since COVID." The woman looked at Rebecca and narrowed her eyes.

"Another woman," Tara continued, "if she hadn't ducked, she would have been splattered on the spot. Strangely, it caused her to run to the home of her lover, who seduced her during a sultry, sweaty weekend." Rebecca jerked her head at Tara with a wide-eyed expression of mock surprise.

"You girls are *terrible*," said Claire in a low voice, shaking her head. Molly was now in a continuous state of the giggles.

The woman thought for a second and scoffed. "Honestly," she said, "Little People indeed!"

"No, seriously," said Tara, her hand slapping the table, "you *are* part Cherokee, right? Surely you know about the Little People. They help little children, but hate older people like you." Meg stood at the register, cleaning her teeth with a toothpick and shaking her head. Molly convulsed.

"Oh!" said the woman, "*those* little people. Of course." She turned back to her friend, who had waved her over to the book section.

"Ova heara, Ginger," said the friend.

"*Ginger*?" said Claire quietly. "Seriously?" The girls snickered again. The women soon realized they were being hazed and Ginger, the part-time Cherokee, tossed her book back on the shelf and made a show of dusting off her hands.

"I'm not buying anything *here*, that's for sure. Let's go."

"Wait, Ginger! I want thi-us!" her friend crooned, pointing to a small pewter animal.

"Whatever!" said Ginger, shaking her head in frustration. Her friend then spotted something else near the back of the store. Ginger turned to the girls and decided to have the last say.

She came back out to the floor and, hands on hips and purse wrapped around her shoulder, said, "You know, as someone who is part Cherokee, I don't appreciate your behavior one iota. One would think you people would appreciate our tax dah-las. I don't like to talk about it generally, but I have Cherokee royalty in my background, and I just don't—"

"Okay, okay, just hold it right there . . . please." Claire, who had been sitting with her elbows on the little table, thumbs under her chin, had finally had enough. She put her hands up, her Harley Davidson leather strap catching the woman's eye. "First, just so you know, one is either Cherokee or one isn't. There are no parts in the equation."

Molly breathed a sigh of relief. She seemed grateful for Claire's intervention.

The woman stopped and seemed to listen, perhaps because Claire was older than the others.

"Second, you approached us a few minutes ago in a very disrespectful way. I'd be happy to talk to you about it sometime if you're interested—explain what might be more appropriate. You were correct about one thing: You are a *tourist*. Third, it's not our fault that you don't know what you don't know. Please don't blame us for that."

The woman sighed and crossed her arms.

"The girls were just having a little fun; I apologize if we hurt your feelings. But it might interest you to know that not only do we not have 'royalty' as such, there was never any such thing as a Cherokee princess. Just trying to be informative."

"Well, my daddy's people knew more about Indians than most. He was a quarter-blood. And he had the high, rich cheekbones, you know. If he were here, I'm sure he could tell you all a thing or two, being from the old country and all." She stood defiantly in front of the Elder Downing Zoltar, who seemed to be gazing at the back of her head with an amused expression.

Claire threw her hands up. "I stand corrected. I'm sure you're right."

Rebecca couldn't help herself, and she wasn't even high. She scurried past Ginger—who scowled at her—to the children's section and grabbed a feathered headset, then walked over to the apparel aisle and waited. Ginger rejoined her friend, who was still shopping. Meg went back to what she was doing at the counter and the others waited to see what Rebecca was going to do. Ginger's friend finally grabbed what she wanted, and the women headed for the counter. As Ginger's friend bought a tiny totem that was made in China, Rebecca snatched a Pendleton blanket and made for the door. Rebecca dramatically swung the blanket around her, removed her ball cap, placed the feathers on her head, and stood perfectly still next to the exit.

Ginger approached the door with her friend, asking, with great exasperation, "So what are *you* supposed to be, Miss Smarty Pants?"

Rebecca held up her right hand and, staring straight ahead, solemnly intoned, "Iron Eyes Cody say, 'People start pollution, people can *stop* it!'" imitating the Italian actor who portrayed an Indian in a TV commercial during the 1970s that she had seen on YouTube. The actual Cherokee women in the room could no longer control themselves and exploded with laughter. Molly put both hands over her mouth and laughed so hard she farted, which made Tara laugh even harder.

Ginger, probably in her forties, just shook her head at Rebecca and said, "Honestly, young lady! I just wanted a picture."

"Only you can prevent wildfires," the Chief continued, still staring ahead, this time quoting Smokey Bear. "Only *you*!" She dramatically thrust her index finger at the women.

Claire did her best to contain herself and Molly and Tara cackled incessantly.

The part-time Cherokee fumed, yelling, "OH! I just don't *understand* some people!" As they exited, Meg's flute music whistled crisply and Rebecca resumed her posture.

Meg burst out laughing, joining the others. Finally, she snapped her fingers at Rebecca, saying, "Give me that damn thing back!" and reaching for it with a smile.

Becks refused to hand Meg the merchandise, shaking her head and grunting "Uug!" Customers pulling up to the front door and getting out of their vehicles could hear the hysterics of a group of Cherokee women laughing so hard they shed tears. Soon enough, a rather small man in Bermuda shorts and what appeared to be his wife came in. The man glanced at Rebecca as they entered, the flute music doing its thing.

"How!" Rebecca nodded with utter seriousness, holding up her hand again. The couple seemed amused.

Soon after, Ricky Stovall, one of Rebecca's friends from school and a tribal citizen, walked in from the heat and glanced at her.

"*What* is going on there, girlfriend?" he asked with a perplexed expression in his typical high-pitched voice, his short, frizzy ponytail bouncing about.

Rebecca, keeping in character, gave a slow head nod, held up her right hand, and said, "Peace treaty copies on back shelf for negative forty-nine cents, little brown man, as they are and forever will be, fucking worthless. How!" Ricky let out a prolonged giggle as he waved to Meg and went to the refrigeration section for a Pepsi. The women once again cackled at their friend, snapping a few pics and applauding.

Ricky put his Pepsi on the counter for Meg to hold and quickly joined Rebecca at the entrance. He snatched the feathers from Rebecca's head, stood next to her, and crossed his arms and stuck out his chest like a cigar store Indian.

"Chief," he said in a formal way, staring ahead like Rebecca, "how many white folks does it take to change a light bulb?"

"Jiminy Cricket, Tonto, I don't know! How many white folk *does* it take to change a light bulb?"

"None. They hire us dumb injuns to do it for pennies on the dollar 'cause they're too fucking lazy to drive to the Tractor Supply!"

The women howled. The Bermuda shorts man and his wife were snickering as they shopped.

Maintaining her rigid decorum, eyes on the back wall, Becks asked, "Hey, Tonto! Why do some Native women have sex with other Native women?"

Holding up his right hand to match Rebecca's, he responded, "I'm chomping at the bit here, Chief. Please, tell me, why *do* some Native women have sex with other Native women?"

"Because it only takes one cooch to accomplish in one night what two dicks can't do in an entire lifetime!"

When Meg laughed at that one she sounded like a baby elephant at play.

"Oh, my, Chief! That sounds *racy* and controversial!" said Ricky in mock upset.

"That's not what your mother said last night, Tonto!"

Ricky erupted with another prolonged giggle and the women screamed with laughter.

Next, two white women in bathing suits strolled in, one of them an almost exact replica of Elle Fanning. She glanced at Rebecca, who, nodding ever so slightly, announced, "Zay-hey, young warrior: what beautiful legs you have! Please deposit seventy-five cents!"

The Elle look-alike seemed startled but kept walking, whispering to her friend, "Did you hear what that Indian said to me? I think she propositioned me!" They browsed the hatchet-populated candy aisle.

The girls guffawed once again at their friends. Molly realized she had peed herself and Tara laughed so hard she actually gave herself a headache. Claire admitted, "Jesus, I'd pay good money for this. This is gonna be good for at least one sermon." Then she pulled her chair back and said, "Becks, *stop* that and get back over here!" Molly and Tara had shot enough video and taken enough pics to satisfy their lust for humor.

Rebecca unwrapped the Pendleton, having become overheated. She bowed gracefully, nodding to her audience as they cheered, saying, "Oh, thank you, thank you, no, really, thank *you*." She acknowledged an imaginary crowd to her left. "Wado!" she said with great appreciation, blowing kisses to the crowd, then ending her dramatic piece with a curtsy. Ricky bowed, the feathers falling off as he did. He gave them back to Rebecca.

"Chief," said Meg, recovering from her own giggles, "either buy that shit or put it back on the shelf, hear me?"

Rebecca returned the items to their proper place. She walked back by the counter and made another face at Meg.

"Behave yourself, you little scamp!" Meg responded playfully, swatting at Rebecca with a broom she kept behind the counter. Ricky paid for his drink, bade his friends farewell, and bowed once more at the door as they cheered and applauded him.

40

Mary (may-lee)

No one has greater love than this, to lay down one's life for one's friends.
—John 15:13, NRSV

November 27-28, 1838
Bell Detachment
Black Fish Lake
St. Francis River Area
State of Arkansas

Wagons, people, and animals populated the area at Black Fish Lake. Despite a few escape attempts early in the journey, the Bell Detachment being what it was—a group of Cherokees mostly in favor of the Treaty of New Echota—army personnel were now more at ease with the reality of the Indians cooperating. At least, cooperating to the extent that they had resigned themselves to the idea that forced removal was happening and would forever be a part of their history.

Mary Cordery Rogers McNair sat with her back to the right front McNair wagon wheel, Martha snuggled up against her, and snacked on an ear of corn.

"You know I love you more than anything, right?" asked Nick, sitting next to her. Mary, looking straight ahead at the lake in a state of exhaustion, nodded. "Good, because you should know that you're dribbling corn." She swatted lightly at her chin, knocking some of the blue and white kernels from her face. "As a Christian gentleman, it behooves me to inform you that it is most unseemly on such an astoundingly beautiful face," he chided with a soft smile.

"As your corn-encrusted and unbecoming wife," she stated with formality, "I should direct you into the woods back there and play about yourself with great ambition, you silly bastard, because you shall receive no attention from this place." She maintained an expressionless face. Martha chomped on her ear of corn, oblivious to her parents' conversation. Nick laughed and munched on his own corn, finishing the last quarter in record time. He examined his wife. She looked as if she were aging more than she should with each week of the journey. Despite this reality, she was more stunning than ever. Black hair wrapped as usual in a head scarf, she employed an attractive way of wrapping the scarf just under what amounted to a waterfall of hair behind it, the sides hanging behind her ears like long, colorful earrings.

"Umm, tasty. Nothing in this world like a good ear of white eagle corn," said Nick, tossing the cob aside and wiping his hands on his filthy trousers. He seized Mary's hand and squeezed. She squeezed back. He let go and brushed aside some of his daughter's hair as she inhaled her corn, ending with a hiccup. The hiccups continued in earnest as they all got to their feet to begin another day.

Captain Ambrose paid for passage across Black Fish Lake. By now the detachment had gotten into the rhythm of water crossings, though they were still laborious and time-consuming. Nick and Mary learned that a Private Boyd had bravely come forward with suspicions about Sergeant Hollingsworth and the disappearance of a Cherokee woman near the back of the line. Lieutenant Whitworth brought the matter to Captain Ambrose after a Cherokee named Grits complained that Wattie Muskrat was nowhere to be found. Private Boyd had secretly confided to Sergeant Thomas, who informed Lieutenant Whitworth, who in turn reported to his captain.

When Ambrose and Whitworth questioned Sergeant Hollingsworth, he merely replied, "Beats me, sirs. She probably fell off a cliff or somethin' back during that god-awful rainstorm." When confronted about Private Boyd's suspicions, Hollingsworth laughed and said, "Captain, you can't possibly believe somethin' like that! Hell, maybe the private has forgotten that I woke him up from sleepin' at his post and he admitted to having nightmares. Hell, sir, he even wrapped his hand around my throat upon wakin' him up, threatening to kill me, sir. If you ask me, Captain, I think the good private wasn't prepared for the rigors of this here journey and is becoming unhinged, sir. But I'll pray for him, sir, I truly will."

Though Ambrose and Whitworth had their suspicions about Hollingsworth—especially after consulting with Sergeant Thomas, Hollingsworth's peer—they could come to no definite conclusions about what happened. And because Private Boyd was the only private to voice his concerns, it was his word against that of Hollingsworth, who outranked him. After careful consideration, but pressed by the urgency of completing his mission, Captain Ambrose wrote the incident of Wattie Muskrat off as a "probable death under mysterious circumstances—most likely accidental."

Between the crossing of Black Fish Lake and the approach of the St. Francis River, four Cherokee traditionalists—Old Stomper, Sap Sucker, Thumper, and Drowning Bear—contributed to the healing process of the journey in their own way. As the detachment made its way toward the river, the four men took it upon themselves to circle the entire detachment—carrying reeds with eagle feathers attached to the ends—seven times. As they did so, they would occasionally recite brief prayers in Cherokee for the safety and health of their people.

Soon enough, the Bell Detachment arrived at the St. Francis River. After Captain Ambrose paid for the ferrying of the masses, he set his focus on Strong's Place.

November 29-30, 1838
Bell Detachment
Strong's Place
St. Francis County, Arkansas

The weather turned colder, dimmer. Things were messy in the swampy area on the west side of the St. Francis River. Some of the small lakes in the region grew colder as well, the nighttime temperatures making the water feel freezing to the skin. Ambrose halted the party near William A. Strong's plantation. It was a grand home on massive acreage, and the Strong's Place community—which consisted of steamboat access, a post office for common mail delivery, stores, and a nice tavern—was a welcome sight after much travel in lone, open country. The people in Strong's Place welcomed the Cherokees. In fact, the local citizens seemed to tolerate the army presence, but they were fascinated by the Indians, even handing out small tokens of kindness here and there. One girl about Deborah's age gave Martha a piece of cloth material to play with.

Express purchasing agent Alfred Edington, who was assisting advance agent Likens, introduced Captain Ambrose to Mr. Strong. The two met outside the local tavern. It proved to be a happier and more rewarding meeting than some of the others.

"William A. Strong, sir, very pleased to meet you. How can I help the government and the Indian people of this party?" he said, standing alert and smiling.

"Thank you, indeed, Mr. Strong. Captain Ambrose, Fourth Artillery. I would be obliged if you could show me what you have available to help us stretch our wares until the upcoming disbandment. I would most surely appreciate it." The two men hit it off well and it seemed that the Cherokees might be in for a more orderly and restful couple of days than might have been imagined.

The McNair's Cherokee neighbors from Bradley County, the Fields, could not locate their twelve-year-old daughter, Tulip. A small party of Cherokees and three soldiers formed a search party in what amounted to a vast, widespread area. Mary, Nick, Enoch, and Annabelle had initially searched a portion together, but as the search broadened, the women became separated. In time, Annabelle and Mary decided to split up. The days were becoming shorter, and twilight threatened to give way to darkness sooner than later.

A peculiar-looking barn, small but substantial, stood against the skyline in an open cotton field. Mary approached it on the chance the girl had gotten lost and stumbled upon it. She could hear voices as she got closer. Carefully tiptoeing up to the door, she opened it until it stuck against the backdrop of hay, which was spread throughout the structure. She walked down a few stalls and there, sitting in a mound of hay, was young Tulip Fields. She stood when she saw Mary. Standing across from her was a man who appeared to be in his mid- to late twenties. He had been talking to Tulip when Mary arrived. He was a large, powerfully built man, well over six feet tall. Mary could see that Tulip's field dress was torn at the shoulder. She was covering her chest with her arms in a defensive posture. She looked up at the man, then glanced at Mary, her face full of fear.

The man had an eerie calmness about him. He nodded to Mary. "Evening, Missus." Mary nodded slightly, looking at Tulip and trying to lock eyes with her. The man stepped forward and firmly planted his hand on Tulip's shoulder. "Si'down, now. Go on," he said, pushing her down. Tulip fell back into her original position in the hay. The man turned toward Mary and smiled. "Now, ah, Missus, you should go. Go on, now."

"I've come for the child," said Mary, reminding the man of the fact that she was one.

"I un'rstand," he said, his voice quiet, almost hushed.

"You her mother?"

Mary shook her head.

"I see. Well, you can't have her just now. She's gonna help me with somethin'." He nodded toward the door. "Hurry on now, Missus."

"No."

"Ah, yes; I'm very much afraid so, ma'am. Go on now."

"Please don't do this."

"Got to, I'm afraid," he said, rubbing his genitals through his pants.

"Please," said Mary, taking a step toward him, "don't. She looks grown because she's well-developed, but please believe me, she's just a child. You mustn't."

"Gots to, Missus. Ya see, my own missus left me a while back. I'm feelin' awfully carnal, ma'am. Got this need and have to fulfill it. I promise I won't be rough. I promise now, but you gots to head on, now. Go back to your people." He turned toward Tulip, who was slowly backing up in the hay. "Hold on there, girl. You just wait right there," he said, unlatching his belt.

"Wait!" said Mary loudly, but avoiding a scream for fear of what he might do to the girl. "Please, in Jesus's holy name, please don't do this." He turned back to face Mary.

"The Lord, huh? Just where's he been lately, Missus? Tell me that. Where was he when I needed him?"

"I'm sorry for your troubles," she said. "I'm so sorry your wife took her leave. But surely, sir, that is no reason to violate this child." She looked at Tulip, who was eyeing the door, obviously thinking about bolting for it. Mary shook her head slightly, catching Tulip's eye and trying to calm her.

"She did, Missus, she took her leave. And I'm hurtin' here, you understand me? Now, I'm sorry it has to be this way—I was telling the young lady that. I gots to do what I gots to do, ma'am. Unless . . ." His voice trailed off as he examined Mary carefully.

He moved his eyes up and down, scrutinizing Mary from head to toe. "Unless . . ."

Mary exhaled. "Un*less*," she said quietly, definitively. She closed her eyes briefly, recalling all the good, then looked at the girl. "Tulip, come," she said, calling the child. She held out her hand, not breaking eye contact with the man, who glanced back and forth between her and Tulip. The girl hesitated, still protecting herself with her arms. "Tulip! Come," Mary repeated. Tulip shook her head slightly, but slowly rose. "*Come here!*" Tulip ran to Mary and took her hand. Mary nodded to the stranger, then stooped down and spoke to Tulip, telling her to go, run—toward the camp as fast as she could.

Tulip was picking up on what was happening, and she shook her head violently and began to scream "NO!" Mary put her hand over the girl's mouth and calmly but firmly ordered her in Cherokee to return to her parents. She told her to keep silent about the barn. Under no circumstances must she mention it. When Tulip disagreed once more, Mary slapped her face with just enough force to scare her into doing what Mary said. Mary pushed her away—toward the door.

"Go," she said. Tulip slowly backed away, tears streaming down her face. "Go!" yelled Mary. "*Go!*" she yelled. Tulip fled.

Mary turned to face the man, who was slowly circling her, looking down at her.

"That was brave of you, Missus," he said, grabbing her by the shoulders and smelling her.

"Please," she said, "spare my life so that I might have this baby."

"Of course I will, Missus. Of course I will," he muttered, backing her into the stall. She felt him kiss her neck as he effortlessly forced her down into the hay. He grunted violently, but did not strike her as he removed his trousers and shoved her back further into the hay, his right hand covering her face as if she meant less than trash. He yanked her scarf from her head. He was young and strong and she knew she had no chance; she was too far away from help for anyone to hear her screams. Trembling, she gently rubbed his ears with her thumbs, praying he would not leave bruises or marks on her, make this quick, and be on his way. He grunted again and pulled back her saddle dress to steal what wasn't his, the greatest of all thefts. Seeing Tulip in her mind's eye and stalwart about her decision to substitute for the girl, Mary turned her head to the side, closed her eyes, and endured his violation.

"Ayyyah!" she yelled. She covered her face with her hands as he trapped her on the ground, the mounds of hay providing no comfort.

Your reward in heaven will be great, she heard her Lord say to her in a strange but certain voice as the man forced himself upon her. During the next few moments, she found herself visited by her grandmother, a Wild Potato clan matriarch named Susannah. Strangely, Mary was not in the barn, but elsewhere, in a place where the spirits come to make their presence known. It was a place of respite deep in the crevices of her mind and spirit, outside the usual bands of time and space. There, she later realized, she was in a cocoon of protection, far removed from her present circumstances. She was soon returned, however, to the place where all things were temporary.

BONG!

The man suddenly collapsed onto her body. Standing above him was Annabelle, a shovel in her hand. For good measure, she pounded him again twice, once on the shoulder and then nearly caving in his head with the last blow.

Mary pushed the man—who began bleeding profusely—off of her and quickly sat up and covered herself with her dress. Annabelle dropped the shovel. She fell to her knees and yelled, "Mizz. Mary, Mizz. Mary! Oh, dear Lord, Mizz. Mary!" She was crying, full of concern for Mary. The two women stayed there briefly, both on their knees, hugging and trembling.

In the minutes that followed, Mary explained what happened as they made their way back into the cotton field.

Mary stopped Annabelle and made her swear that she would never mention it. Annabelle objected, but Mary insisted. She hugged Annabelle again and thanked her for coming to her rescue, making it clear that under no circumstances should Nick ever know. Annabelle tried valiantly to argue with her enslaver, but Mary made her swear to it.

"It's *too late*, Annabelle," she said. "He was inside me. He had his way. I must go to water."

"Oh, dear Lord!" Annabelle said once again, hands to her face. "We *must* tell Mr. Nick!"

"No, Annabelle! Keep quiet and take me to the lake to wash. You must do as I say—now!"

The women were at the lake in short order, Annabelle helping Mary into the frigid water, both women shivering in the early evening air. Mary prayed the Lord's Prayer, followed by requests for the forgiveness of sins, then a prayer for her unborn child. Annabelle helped Mary wash and, in the shallows of the cold water, managed an "Amen!" here and there, her teeth chattering from the cold. The necessity of brevity forced the women from the water, and they made haste to return to the encampment when they saw a soldier from the search party approaching.

"You need to be in camp!" the private barked. "The child has been located."

When they returned to the camp, Mary joined her husband and child in their small, makeshift enclosure in some shrubbery near their wagon. Nick looked at her.

"Where have you been?"

"Searching for the child," said Mary, avoiding eye contact with her husband.

"I was worried."

"All is well. Annabelle and I were separated briefly, and the coming darkness made things more complicated," she replied, still moving about and avoiding her husband's eyes. He moved to her and held her by the forearms.

"Are you sure everything is all right?"

Mary looked at her husband, focusing briefly on the bridge of his nose only. "Yes," she said, "of course it is." She inquired about Martha and began laying blankets down the way they did every night of the journey. "We should get our sleep," she said while working. "We will have another early rise upon the morning light."

"You're right about that," said Nick, yawning and stretching. With that, the couple settled in, Mary pulling Martha between them and closing her eyes, helplessly relying on her child to protect her from the coming nightmares.

The next morning, Nick found interaction with Annabelle odd in that she refused to look at him and seemed to go out of her way to avoid him. He noticed that Mary had been restless during the night, but nothing else out of the ordinary. He discovered her to be impatient, frustrated with things throughout the following day as the detachment moved on toward Little Rock.

Annabelle busied herself with her own routine of keeping the children together, preparing salt pork and the always scarce vegetables, and helping her masters with daily chores along the trail. Nick noticed that Augustine spent an unusual amount of time around Mary, as if guarding her from something. Despite this odd behavior, Nick knew that—to his mind anyway— women were women and *never* easy to comprehend. It was incumbent upon him to move his family along, to take them forward into this unknown territory, and nothing could get in the way of that.

41

Emily (a-may-lee)

A Thunderer in Slides

And though she be but little, she is fierce.
—Shakespeare, A Midsummer Night's Dream

Present Day
McNair House
Muskogee, Oklahoma
District Four, Cherokee Nation

"Oooohh," said Molly, snatching the new yellow top that Emmy had just bought and holding it up to herself. "This would look *so* good on me," she said to her sister with pleading eyes. Molly, Emmy, and Sandra were in the kitchen. Emmy and Mike had swung by on their way to dinner, Emmy having just returned from a brief shopping spree. Mike and Clay were in the living room, talking.

"Yeah, I can let you borrow it sometime. I'm slapping this baby on tonight because we're heading over to Tammy's Tavern. Never know when a sportswriter might pop up," she added, rolling her eyes.

"Oh, *please please please*, Em! Clay's taking me out to eat, too. I wanna wear this for him!" she said in a hushed voice.

"No, dingbat, I'm wearing it. Get your own top," said Emmy.

"All right, you two," said Sandra, hoping to avoid a "moment."

"Oh, come on, Em. Look at it—you *know* I would look hot in it!"

"For one thing," said Emmy, "it would hang on you too much. You're too small, squirt. For another, anyone who's convinced she's hot is not. Now gimme!" She tried to snatch it back.

"No."

"Yes."

Molly stuck out her tongue and hid behind her mom.

"Come on, Molly," complained Emmy. "We want to get going." She tried grabbing it again. Molly grinned and used Sandra as a shield. "You want me to grab you and put you over my knee like I used to?" Emmy scolded. "Now cut the crap and give it to me." Sandra rolled her eyes, somehow knowing where this was going. Molly ran to the other side of the kitchen island, just out of Emmy's reach, waving the shirt.

"You try that," she said, raising her voice, "and I'll put one of my blow darts in that big ol' muscle-bound butt of yours!"

Oh, dear, thought Sandra. That wasn't good.

"You pull that blowgun on me and I'll stick it so far up *your* skinny little ass, your eyes will be using it for windshield wipers in the rain, Snow White!"

"What's going on in there?" Mike hollered.

"*Somebody's* about to get their ass beat is what!" Emmy yelled. They could hear the guys laughing. Emmy, obviously fast on her feet, sprinted around the other side of the island.

"MOM!" shrieked Molly and made for the laundry room behind the kitchen. Molly slammed the door after darting inside and sprinted to the half-bath on the other side, closing that door and locking it just as Emmy arrived. Emmy banged on the door.

"Come on, Peewee, *please*? I was wanting to look good for Mike," she said in a soft, resigned voice. She sighed as Sandra peeked around the door through the laundry room.

"Just let her wear it, for heaven's sake," their mom said. Emmy threw her hands up.

"Fine." Just then, Molly opened the door and handed Emmy the top, looking down in shame.

"Sorry," she said. "I wasn't thinking." She fought back a tear.

Emmy smiled at Molly. "Hey, Nine-Speed, it's okay," she said, taking Molly in her arms and rubbing her back. "Please don't treat me with kid gloves just because I have cancer, okay? I'm gonna be fine, I swear." Molly put her head on Emmy's shoulder and wiped away the tear. "It'll take more than a chickenshit tumor to put this dog down, got it?" She pulled her sister back so Molly could see her smile and shoved the top back at her. "You wear it tonight and have a nice time, okay? I can wear it anytime."

"No," said Molly, shaking her head. "You wear it. I'll wear it another time—here, take it."

Sandra smiled and went into the living room, saying, "Indian bitches, boys—welcome to the McNair reality." The guys laughed.

After a few rounds of "you wear it," and "no, *you* wear it," Sandra could hear Emmy playfully spanking Molly on the rump.

As they came back around the corner, Sandra was standing at the island, separating some keys in her hands. She turned to them, and, standing as properly as she could manage, offered her best *Downton Abbey* accent: "So, I shall inform you both that I just told your men that *I* am woman enough for *both* of them. We shall—the three of us, that is—proceed to Tammy's Tavern without you. Should you feel called to stop this childishness and ever decide to *get* ready, you may join us for evening repast. Have Carson drive you in the Camry and meet us there. Ciao." She threw Molly the keys to her black 2019 Camry.

"What?" said Molly, her jaw dropping as she stood there like a buffalo.

Emmy laughed. "All right, squirt," she said to Molly as Sandra disappeared into the living room, "go put this on. It's okay, really. You wanna look good for that stud out there. I'll just wear what I've got on. I suppose I can make it work if somebody shoves a camera in my face. I'm just always having to look out for that sort of thing now, ya know?"

They heard an engine roar, then tires squealing. Molly ran to the living room window. "They're taking *Ned!*" she said, glancing back at Emmy, eyes as big as saucers.

"What the *fuck?*" said Emmy in astonishment. The sisters just stood and stared at each other. "She wasn't kidding."

"Holy shit," said Molly, looking down at the Camry keys. "Em?" she said, as Emmy walked to the window, mouth open, and stared.

"She stole my damn car!"

"And she stole our men!" said Molly in similar astonishment. "Well, let's go!" she said, motioning to Emmy with her arm.

But Emmy just stood at the window and mumbled over and over, "They fucking stole *Ned Christie.*" Then she turned to her kid sister and said, "Molly, do you know what just happened?"

"What?"

"Sista, we just got *motherjumped*—literally!"

Molly and Emmy arrived at Tammy's about fifteen minutes later because the Camry needed gas. When they walked in several regulars greeted "The Storm," and Tammy told them their party was in the back. Sure enough, in a back booth were Sandra, Mike, and Clay, all grinning. They had already ordered drinks and it looked as if their mom was on her second beer. Molly sat next to Clay and Emmy slid in next to Mike, who had his arm around her mom's shoulders.

"Moving in on your mom—hope you don't mind," he teased.

"Oh bitch, please," said Emmy, shaking her head. "Shove over," she growled, pushing him so she could have some room. She ordered a Prairie Bomb and Molly ordered a Roy Rogers. Tonya, Tammy's daughter, was their waiter, and she took orders when everyone was ready.

Mike looked at Emmy. "Hey, can you manage here tonight—with your food choices?" Emmy was trimming down on the plant-based lifestyle and her muscles were becoming more defined, less bulky.

"Yeah," Emmy said, nuzzling his cheek with her nose. "Fortunately for you, I can, bitch." Clay laughed. Molly loved his laugh. Clay was having iced tea. Everyone was bound to order something fried since it was, after all, Tammy's. Emmy gave her order to Tonya last and said, "Your mom knows what I like now. See if she can make some up for me, will you?" Tonya nodded and headed back, soon to return with their drinks. After she put them all down, a man about thirty or so returning from the men's room swatted Tonya on the butt.

"Lookin' good, girl!" he said with a grin. He was over six feet tall, probably weighed close to two hundred pounds, was broad-chested, and was clearly inebriated. He wore old jeans, work boots, and a T-shirt that had a construction logo on it. Tonya scowled at him as she headed for another table. The man laughed and winked at Molly, pausing to look her over as he stumbled back toward his friends.

Mike glanced at Emmy, who had just cracked her knuckles. "Easy, Laila," he said, referring to the boxer, Laila Ali. "Take it easy," he said again, smiling and bringing her calloused knuckles to his lips and kissing them. Emmy just sighed and shook her head. To Molly, Sandra looked as if she was starting to feel the buzz of her beer and had just ordered a margarita as well. When their food came, everyone had something different. Sandra had the catfish, but, to honor Emmy, everything else was meat and dairy free. Clay had a burger and fries, Molly had a shrimp salad with sweet potato fries, Mike had fried shrimp and a salad, and Tonya brought Emmy two huge baked potatoes smothered with black beans and vegan butter, and a spinach salad with almond slices.

Emmy drank water with her beer. She smiled at Molly wearing her yellow top. Mike didn't seem to mind, as he was admiring his lady in her usual sleeveless top—this one black to match her hair, down tonight—and it also went well with her white denim shorts.

During the meal, everyone got equal time as they chatted about all kinds of things—Molly's knee, Emmy's tumor, Clay's classes and Molly's visit with him, and Sandra's work—which intrigued Clay. The majority of patrons were watching major league baseball on the giant TV screens as the place grew louder in congruence with the amount of alcohol consumed. About three-quarters of the way through the meal, Emmy had to go to the ladies' room. Tonya was working hard, making her way back and forth between tables with only one other waiter on duty.

Apparently the big guy's bladder wasn't doing much of a job holding his beer because he had just returned from what seemed like his fifth visit to the can. Still stumbling somewhat, he managed to seize Tonya's arm as she was leaving the table next to them. "Hey, baby," he said, "you are looking so fine in those shorts. Lemme buy you a beer later." He pulled her close to him and grinned.

"Thanks," said Tonya politely, "but no thanks." As she tried to turn away, he jerked her back.

"Now that's not being very nice, is it?" he said, clearly using force to hold her in place. People took notice and grew quiet.

"Let *go* of me," she said with authority. Clay put his drink down and scooted closer to the edge of the booth.

"Clay!" said Molly, worried. By now the big guy's friends, two wiry little guys who looked as if they hadn't showered in a week, sauntered up, either to try to control their friend or back him up—it was hard to tell.

Mike motioned to Clay saying, "It's all right, Clay. I got this." He stood and approached the big man.

"What the hell do *you* want?" the man growled, still hanging on to Tonya.

Mike showed the man his badge and ID. "Why don't you go back and enjoy your meal, okay?"

"Why don't *you* mind your own damn business, asshole?" the man said, letting Tonya go and trying to dominate by closing in on Mike and using his size to intimidate. Molly felt nervous.

Emmy came out of the restroom and was stopped by a little Muscogee/Creek girl who wanted her autograph. The girl was about six or seven and Emmy flashed her infectious smile and said, "You betcha, sweetie!" She squatted down beside the girl as her father snapped a few photos. Molly could see that Emmy was perfectly in tune with what was going on with the bully and Mike, keeping her eye on the situation as she took time to chat briefly with the little girl. Part of the tavern was still into the ballgame, another part focused on the trouble brewing out on the floor, others were grinning at Emmy and the girl.

Mike stepped back with his right foot, his right hand automatically on his off-duty weapon beneath his shirt, in a posture to keep the man away from his sidearm. Emmy gave the little girl a hug and a kiss on the cheek, then ushered her toward her parents, saying, "Okay, sweetie, gotta go now. You go on—go back over there with your mom and dad, okay?" The girl nodded and scampered back to her parents as Emmy stood and evaluated what was happening.

"That damn badge don't scare me," said the big guy.

"Billy-Mac," said his friend, trying to talk him down. He was in his late twenties, greasy-looking, with a long, skinny mustache that formed into a partial chin beard.

"It's not meant to scare you," said Mike calmly. "It *is* meant to tell you that you can't be assaulting the waitstaff and that, one way or the other, I'm gonna make sure you don't. Now, seriously, you don't wanna go to jail tonight and I don't want to be stuck doing a bunch of paperwork. Let's just everybody chill out, okay? C'mon—we got small children in here tonight, ya know?" Molly knew that Mike was doing his best to be reasonable.

"I ain't required to report to you, oshifer!" the man mocked, looming again. He looked down at Mike and snarled, flexing.

"Yeah, well, I'm just a phone call away from having a bunch of my buddies from the PD come in here and break all ya bones. You want that?" he asked, hand still on his weapon.

"Billy-Mac," said the chin beard again, this time grabbing his friend's arm. "Come on now," he said, trying to get his friend to back away.

Billy-Mac took one step closer to Mike, saying, "That right? Well, by the time your buddies get here, I'ma break all *your* bones!" Molly could feel her underarms sweating.

Clay sat at the ready as Molly voiced her concern again, putting her hand on his shoulder. She abhorred the thought of him with a busted nose. "I won't do anything unless he tries to hurt someone," Clay reassured.

Emmy, already on her way over, rapidly pulled up her hair, this time into a tight swirl behind her head with her headband so there would be less to grab. She walked up and kicked off her slides, sending them across the floor, peanut shells flying about, one woman at a nearby table saying "Uh-oh!" and holding her partner's hand.

"Need a hand, officer?" said Emmy, calling attention to herself in the middle of the floor. The tavern hushed, and

Tammy came out from the kitchen holding her hand to her mouth in concern. Emmy violently thrust her right knee up, followed by her left, then threw a flurry of warm-up punches in the air, exhaling loudly and rolling her shoulders, bouncing on her toes.

"Oh brother," Mike mumbled to himself as he looked toward the ceiling. Billy-Mac and his buddy looked at Emmy.

"*Shit*," whispered Billy-Mac's skinny friend as Emmy cracked her knuckles. "Billy-*Mac*," he said again, "come on, let's let these good people go back to their dinner. Come on now . . ."

"I ain't scared of this greaser!" he roared.

"I *know* that, Billy-boy. Thing is, look at that statey. Look how he's wearin' that shirt. Now you know he's got one of them big SIG nines under that shirt."

"SO!" said Billy-Mac, letting the booze get the better of what little judgment he had left.

"And so, it ain't just that, boy. That standin' over there is that MACNair woman."

"So!"

"So? Goddamn, boy, that there is *The Cherokee Storm*, Billy-Mac. Damn Cherokee Storm and a state cop with a 9mm. C'mon, now, son, let's cut this one loose . . . live to fight another day, Billy-boy."

"Ain't afraid a no girl!" boomed Billy-Mac, looking hard at Emmy.

"I ain't with you on this one, Billy-Mac."

"Whatchoo mean you ain't with me? We can take this punk greaser!"

"BILLY-MAC!" his friend yelled, shaking him to get his attention. "I ain't *with* ya on this, I say. I'm not *about* to spend the rest of my night on my hands and knees, spittin' my teeth out like Chiclets and pukin' up beer on a filthy floor covered in peanut shells 'cause of some MMA dragon with thighs as big as my waist—no sir! Look at da arms on her! Her *up*-onents say she hits like George Foreman. I done seen what she did to that Ortiz woman in the cage—beat her so bad theys proly *still* tryin' to fix her ugly face. This woman—she'll hitchya so hard you'll be doin' construction with raccoon eyes and your jaw wired shut for months, son! You want those boys at the site seeing you like that? Be wearin' that big ol' nose on the back of your head, Billy-Mac. You on ya own here, boy!" he said, looking up at his friend. He turned to the McNair table and said with a brief salute, "Sorry for the in-*cone*-vee-nee-ence, folks. Y'all have a nice night." He shook his head and he and the other wiry guy headed for the door.

Mike took a step back, evidently to maintain some distance. Billy-Mac turned to Emmy and sneered, but seemed less cocky now.

"Ain't afraid of no girl," he repeated, attempting to salvage his masculinity.

Looking tired of the whole thing by now, Emmy rotated her head rapidly, cracking her neck, then stretched her arms and popped her knuckles again, crunching some peanut shells under her bare feet and kicking them away like an angry bull. She presented her arms, waving her fingers toward herself and super-flexing her quads, taking two steps toward him, then angling herself in a fighter's stance.

"*Sko-den!*" she bellowed. The tavern was pin-drop quiet. Billy-Mac looked around, glancing at Mike, hand on his weapon, then back at Emmy, who drilled him with her fiery eyes.

"Okay, *okay*," he said, holding up his hands and slowly backing away. "Sorry." He glanced back at Tonya, who had gone to stand with her mother. "*Sorry*. Okay already?" He stumbled toward the door.

"I'm trespassing you for now, sir!" said Tammy, coming out from behind the bar. "You're welcome back sober, but you can't get wasted in here again like that. And keep your damn hands off my daughter!" He made his way out the door and a great sigh of relief filled the tavern. Tammy tried to bring things back to life, saying, "Okay, y'all—show's over. Sorry about all that." She walked over to Emmy and hugged her shoulder. "Thanks, girlfriend. Goddamn, you're scary!" She laughed, swatting her playfully with a towel.

Finally, Mike and Emmy got to sit back down and finish their meal, which Tammy reheated for them. Returning with their plates, she smiled at Emmy. "Thanks again, Em."

"What am I, chopped liver?" said Mike, holding up his hands and looking around the table with a silly smile. Tammy grinned, reached over, and pinched his cheek, saying, "Oh, yes, and *you* too, pretty boy!" Molly and Clay laughed as Tammy went back to the kitchen.

"Here," said Mike to Emmy, having retrieved her slides for her. "I think you left these out on the dance floor, Cinderella." She puckered her lips at him and winked.

"Wado, Prince Charming," she teased, batting her eyelashes and slipping the slides back on.

Sandra had had a lot to drink and appeared glad the whole thing was over. The gang continued chatting while Mike and Emmy finished their dinner. Molly had observed that when the check came, Tammy had deleted Mike and Emmy's charges.

"Lemme pray for that," said Sandra, slurring her words and reaching for the bill. Mike pulled it away from her, shaking his head. Molly's eyes widened. She looked at Emmy.

"She drunk?" she mouthed. Emmy rolled her eyes and nodded.

Some people crowded around the table two booths down raised their glasses and a beer pitcher and simultaneously whooped, "Storm, Storm, *Storm!*" and then cheered, others adding their applause for Mike and Emmy. Emmy just grinned and waved them off, shaking her head in embarrassment. Tonya returned with another Prairie Bomb for Emmy and a gin and tonic for Mike, courtesy of some sports fans at table one by the front door. Mike and Emmy raised their glasses in appreciation.

"Well, that's just hunky doorknob," said Sandra, plastered now.

"Ma, really?" said Emmy, putting down her mug. She shot a glance at Molly, wondering what was going on. Molly shrugged.

"No no no no no no no," said Sandra, holding her glass and pointing at Emmy. "Thumb people might thay that I'm drunk, but I'm really under the affluence of incohol!" she crooned, then giggled like a schoolgirl.

"Omigod," said Molly, "how embarrassing!" She had her head in her hands, elbows on the table, wishing this wasn't happening. Mike and Clay grinned at each other and looked away.

"Mom," said Emmy, "what's going on? Tell me about it," she said, putting her hand on her mother's arm. "Something's wrong. What is it?"

Sandra shook her head. "I could tell ya, but I'd have to kill ya, bitch!" she said, leaning in and breathing on Emmy, then giggling.

Molly turned to Clay. "She *never* does this, I swear!" she whispered. Clay smiled and rubbed Molly's back.

"It's okay," he said softly, enjoying the show.

"Now, everyone," said Sandra, sitting upright and holding her glass in the toast position, "My daughter—the Roman glad-u-*ator*—has a troomer in her boob, and she—"

"Ma, *stop it. Now.*" This quieted their mom for the moment. Emmy and Molly looked at each other, Molly wishing her mother was somewhere else. Or that she was. Sandra became weepy. "Oh, shit, Ma, please, not here, not now," Emmy insisted.

Mike touched Emmy's arm. "Hey, it's okay, babe," he whispered. "Sandra," he said, "let me drive you home, okay?" Emmy nodded. Sandra seized Mike by the lapels and shook him.

"Michael, you take care of her, understand? Anything happens up on me, you take crare of my bay-bee!" she mewed.

"Jesus," said Molly, hiding her head in her hands again.

"Ma," said Emmy with her typical conviction, "*get up* from this booth and let us take you home, or I'm going to pressure-point you, put you out, then carry you out of here over my shoulder like a damn dead animal." Mike nudged Emmy, shaking his head.

"Well, then, my little dickachee, you must do as you see fit, seeing as you're so fit!" Sandra quipped, putting up her fists and hitting herself in the head.

"Oh goddamn," Molly said, putting her head down once more and praying no one could hear this.

"Gonna trank her out, Mike, I swear to God," Emmy snapped impatiently.

"Nah, wait!" he said, holding up his hand. "C'mon, Sandra," Mike repeated, "let us take you home. C'mon, let's go," he said, rising and taking her by the arm.

"Well, okey dokey, then, special agent man!" she said with a snicker.

Emmy looked at Molly, rolling her eyes again and shaking her head. "Thank Christ," she said under her breath.

"You're welcome!" boasted Sandra with an even louder giggle.

"Oh. My. God," said Molly, flabbergasted by her mom's behavior. They all got up to escort her out. "Thank you, Mike," she said, shaking her head and waving to Tonya.

"It's okay, Blue Jay," he said, coming around to her since Emmy had Sandra by the arm. Putting an arm around Molly's shoulder, he said, "Go easy on her, okay? She's dealing with a lot. Emmy's cancer, your knee and missing the ride, trying to figure out how to get you to college—that's a lot. Plus, she almost had to watch her daughter duke it out tonight with a guy the size of an NFL tight end. Cut her some slack."

"What*ever*," Molly retorted, pulling her hair back and looking up at Clay, wishing she were absolutely dead right now. Clay leaned in and kissed Molly's cheek as they all walked to the cars, telling her things were good.

42

Matriarchs and the Trail of Tears

Present Day
McNair House
Muskogee, Oklahoma
District Four, Cherokee Nation

Sandra rested on the sofa, propped up halfway by several large pillows. She gripped a glass of tomato juice in her left hand and was holding an ice pack on her head with her right. She glanced at her daughters.

Emmy sat in the recliner with her feet up. Molly postured on an old antique chair that had been in the family for a century. Molly's hair was in a tight braid, Emmy's in her typical ponytail. They stared at their mother.

"You both hate me, don't you?"

"No," said Emmy.

"Maybe," chimed Molly.

"I'm sorry, Peewee, really. I know I must have left quite the impression on Clay. You deserve better." Emmy looked over at Molly, who crossed her arms.

"Well," said Molly, rolling her eyes, "I kinda let you down, too, what with not telling you about Devon and all. It's just, I dunno—Mike's been around longer than Clay has. He's comfortable with you, respects you. Clay just met you again, sorta . . ."

"I know, I know," said Sandra, pressing the ice to her forehead harder. "Bet he never expected that one when he was a kid, huh?" said Sandra with a weak smile. Molly just shrugged.

"Ma, what's going on?"

"Please don't interrogate me right now, Em."

"Okay, sorry." She watched her mom pop a second Tylenol. "So, what's going on?"

Molly looked down and snickered, then back up at their mom for an answer.

Sandra looked at her girls as they gazed at her. "I don't know, baby—really, I just don't know. Mothers should be able to handle anything, especially these days. I guess I'm just not as strong as I thought I was. I'm sorry—to both of you. Without your dad, I don't know—I've tried to do my best."

"Ma, Dad died of a heart attack. Maybe it could have been prevented, but it sure as hell wasn't anybody's fault—least of all yours. We love you, Ma."

Molly nodded in agreement.

"You don't think I failed you?"

"Hell no. I mean, look at how perfect Molly and I turned out!"

Sandra laughed, then grimaced, pressing the ice in again. "I want to make sure you girls know I'm frustrated at all that's happened lately. Molly and her knee, this disappointing Devon situation." She took another swig of tomato juice. Looking at Emmy, she said, "Everything that you've been through—the evil, now this cancer. I wish I could take that from you, baby girl—I would take that diagnosis for you if I could."

"I know that, Ma."

"So would I," said Molly with utter seriousness.

"I know that, too, Nine-Speed. Did it ever occur to either one of you that maybe the universe has imposed this on me because it thinks I'm the strongest—the one who should have it in place of others?"

Molly seemed to consider this. It had not, in fact, occurred to her. But what kind of bullshit was that, anyway? Sandra smiled, staring at the ceiling. "My young matriarch," she said. "The Cherokee Storm. Well, what can I possibly say to that one?" Glancing at Emmy, she said, "I was so worried about you last night."

"Why? What do you mean? I was having a nice time—you know, the five of us just chilling out. I thought it was a nice evening overall. And it was fine, Ma, Tammy knows what to feed me. Little perturbed that you would swipe *Ned Christie*, but I'll get over it." She winked.

"No—I mean that godawful man—the one that grabbed Tonya and leered at Molly. He was *big*, Emmy. Just didn't want to see my firstborn get hurt. You've been hurt enough."

"Oh, please, Ma—I would've beat that bitch's ass." Molly giggled again. "Besides, Mike would have pounced on him, too."

"And Clay!" said Molly.

"And Clay," Emmy repeated. "Everything turned out okay, didn't it? So see, Ma—we've got each other. Ga-*doo*-gi."

"Nevertheless . . . have you ever thought about hanging up the gloves and just becoming, oh, I don't know—a doctor or lawyer or something?" Molly glanced at Emmy.

"Ma, I thought you knew me before I knew me and shit . . ."

Sandra and Molly laughed. "Point taken," said Sandra. "Again, I'm sorry for my behavior. Just feel like a genuine rat, so you both know." She swigged her juice again and patted the top of her aching head with the ice. Molly looked at Emmy, then looked down at the floor.

Emmy closed the recliner and slid over to the sofa, resting on one knee in front of her mother like a football player. She looked Sandra directly in the eye. "Bullshit," she whispered. "You're a *fucking* golden eagle, soaring in on the wind over the Arkansas River on a warm spring day, ever watching, ever present. A Cherokee warrior woman if there ever was one." She took the juice from her mother's hand and set the glass on the coffee table. Then she lifted Sandra's hand, brought it to her face, and kissed it. "I got your back, Ma, always."

Molly nodded. "Me, too," she said, unable to say more, a lump in her throat. Sandra turned away, her face to the wall behind the sofa. A tear rolled down her lovely, medium-complected face. She squeezed Emmy's hand, then felt Molly's on top of theirs, her youthful warm hand closing the matriarchal gap with certainty and sincerity.

Clay Blackfox's Duplex
Muskogee, Oklahoma

Clay and Molly had some alone time. His roommate was out of town and they were able to relax. Molly was excited, talking about graduation—they had received their caps and gowns, and Molly tried hers on, Clay taking pictures and selfies and reminiscing about his own graduation. After she changed back into her street clothes, he told her he had a surprise for her.

"What is it?" she asked with wide eyes and a curious smile.

"Damn, girl," he said. "If I told you, it wouldn't be a surprise now, would it? Wait here. I'll be back." He disappeared into his bedroom. She relaxed on the couch, which was definitely a college guy's couch: crumbs on the floor in front, his dirty sock stuck in the corner under the cushion. She smiled and shook her head.

This is gonna be cool.

"What?"

"What?" yelled Clay from the bedroom.

"Nothing," Molly hollered back. She smiled and looked around, just in case.

"Hey, Black Fox," she called, "when are you guys gonna clean up this pigpen?"

"I know, I know," he yelled from the back. "Sorry about that."

"Emmy would say, 'You need a woman's touch, bitch!'" Molly yelled with a laugh.

"And Emmy would be right," he said, coming back into the living room holding what appeared to be a large sketchbook. He smiled at her, sitting next to her on the couch. He leaned over and kissed her. "I can't believe we've actually been out on a date," he said as he pulled away.

"Why would you say that?" she asked. He grinned at her like a little boy.

"Let's face it," he confessed, "I've just always had a thing for you. I'd be lying otherwise." He smiled again and she kissed him back, gently. "Okay," he said, excited. "Ready for this?" She nodded, feeding off his excitement. She knew he had some talent with art, but they hadn't discussed it much since they had been together.

He grinned and opened the book to the first page. At the top, it read:

Retracing the Trail of Tears: Bell Route

The Journey of Her Ancestors

Molly Martha McNair

Clay's artwork was evident on the page. Below the attribution he had drawn a beautiful doe. Next to the deer, highlighted by trees in a forest, were the words *Ani-Kawi*, meaning "Deer Clan." Molly's mom was of the Deer Clan. Clay leaned over and whispered, "This was a real pleasure, Fawn," and gently kissed her.

Molly slowly pulled away from his lips and stared down at the page. She was stunned. She glanced up at Clay, then back down to the page, moving her hand over it. "This is *beautiful*,

Clay, my God." She quickly skimmed through the thick book, shocked at the detail. He had drawn rivers, lakes, and towns. Talking leaves.

Told ya.

"Hey, how did . . . how did you know my middle name? I never told you."

"Emmy."

"What?"

"Yeah. We had coffee one day at Sacred Grounds."

"What? Hey, you tryin' to move in on my sis?" she said, playfully elbowing him in the ribs.

"Yeah, right! God, can you imagine? After the story you've told me about her and Devon, and what she did at Tammy's, can't you just see her hanging me from a set of those pole wires like a pair of tennis shoes—only after beating me to a pulp!" Molly laughed. "Actually, it wasn't just Em. Tara and Rebecca met us there."

"What? They were in on this, too? Omigod!"

"Yeah—your mom knew, too." Molly sat stunned again. "I wanted to catch up—with your background information—you know—from the people who love you. If you look closely, you'll see certain pages that say something special about you." He turned some of the pages for her. "For example, here you'll see a little cameo sketch of you when you were ten—before your dad passed—reciting a poem for him. Emmy said you did that once. Rebecca remembered it, too." She glanced down at a likeness of herself on page seven, her mouth open, hair already down to her shoulders, her right index finger raised as if in mid-verse. Molly put her hands to her face, looked at Clay, and started crying.

"Omigod, Clay, that is so cool." She wept as she rested her head on his shoulder. She let go of the book and latched on to him, turning her head into him and releasing her feelings, remembering her father. He smiled and kissed her head.

"Like it?"

"It's awesome is what," she mumbled into his shirt. He laughed and hugged her. After a minute or so, she recovered and smiled sweetly at him. "Wado, Clay." She exhaled and picked up the book again, marveling at his attention to detail and care for her as a person. He had mapped out the entire trip for her.

"If you decide to do this, I would be happy to go with you. Of course, it would have to be over the summer or Christmas break, or something like that." She stared at him, mouth open.

St. Bernard never mind.

"Oh . . . oh, wow, Clay. My gosh!" She was otherwise tongue-tied, but managed to close her mouth.

"Unless, of course, you don't want me to go. That kind of thing *is* pretty darn sacred. You might prefer going by yourself."

Oh hell no I'm not going without you and I definitely wanna see you without your shirt on so we should go in the summertime and camp out in the same tent and shit . . .

"Um . . . oh, gosh, no. I mean, why wouldn't I want you to go with me? After all, you've mapped this out for me and everything."

Uh-huh. Nice recovery. By the way, you should see him without any clothes at all . . .

Molly's eyes widened. "What!"

"I didn't say anything."

"Yeah, I know; I mean, I was just thinking out loud, I guess. I just don't know what to say . . . this is so special! You know, when Pastor Claire first mentioned this, I didn't really know what to make of it. I mean, all the other guys going on the annual ride and everything—and that event is such a big deal in our community—I guess I just thought it was that or nothing, ya know? I mean, I would still like to make that ride eventually, but with the past few months being the way they've been—I guess I thought it was the ride or nothing at all. Seeing what you did here—this is *so* amazing. Thank you."

"You're welcome. I actually enjoyed it a lot. Just thinking about you, like when you were a girl, then a teenager, how you've grown and developed—it all seemed pretty cool. Tara and Rebecca were a big help—you know, giving me some perspective on things. Helping me see how despite your dad passing and your mom working so hard and Emmy being away at college you did really well for yourself. I think you're pretty amazing." He grinned and played with her ponytail.

Molly stared at Clay. She was on fire. She carefully put the sketchbook on the coffee table in front of the couch. Turning to him and seizing his T-shirt, she planted her lips on his. He kissed her back, and she started yanking at the shirt.

"Take it off," she demanded.

"What?" he said, holding her back slightly.

"Take it *off*," she insisted. "I wanna see you without your shirt. Just do it," she ordered, kissing him heavily again. She reached back, yanked her ponytail holder off, and shook her head, straddling him from the front, her flowing hair falling into her eyes.

"Molly," he said, balking.

She leaned in and kissed his neck violently, trying to suck on it. He pushed her back. She pulled on his shirt and breathed on his neck until he gave in and took it off.

"God, you make me so horny," she whispered, holding his head in her hands and kissing him as passionately as she could. She pulled away and examined his upper body, her hormones trying to rocket through the ceiling of the apartment.

"Molly—"

"I want you," she said, her hands plastered to his chest.

"Molly—"

"I *want* you," she whispered, kissing his neck again. "You and your damn blowgun and your sketchbook and your sexy jaw never mind . . ." She rubbed her hand over his chest, running her fingers across his chest hairs. She nibbled on his earlobe.

"Whoa, Molly!" he said, finally standing and holding onto her hands. "Let's slow down, okay?"

She pulled back and looked at him. "Are you serious? Really, Clay?" She pushed his hands away.

"Molly, wait a minute—"

"Jesus, Clay! I'm throwing myself at you, in case you hadn't noticed! I mean, damn—months ago I get hijacked by one old friend in a goddamned movie theater and now when I'm ready I'm rejected by another one—in his own apartment, for Pete's sake! Like, like, I'm ready to sit on your face, Injun Joe, ya know? Shit!"

Clay reached out and, turning her, hugged her from behind. "Hey," he said quietly into her ear, "you think I *don't* want you? Are you crazy? Look, you're not even eighteen yet. Can we just wait a couple of months before we 'do' anything? Like it or not, I'd feel better if we waited—made it a special occasion. I was thinking that the sketchbook and Trail of Tears plan could be like—you know, a celebration of your eighteenth. I want you—*bad*. I'm just trying to do the right thing here is all." Molly seemed to consider this.

"Yeah?" she said in her best bedroom voice, leaning back into him, resting her head on his chest.

"Yeah," he responded, trying to regain his composure and control his own urges. He could smell her intoxicating shampoo and was doing his dead level best to be as neutral as he could be in the moment. She turned back into him and sighed, kissing his chest and hugging him. She looked up at him and he brushed her hair back. "I think you're beautiful, totally hot. I just . . ."

"Just what?" she asked, staring up at him, admiring that jawline and priming his chin with her thumb.

"I promised your sister I'd be good to you, that's all."

"You *what*? Are you *insane*?"

"No."

"You promised my sister—whose business this *isn't*—that you would be what—a eunuch? Some kind of freaking monk?"

"Come on, now . . ."

"No, for God's sake, Clay. She needs to mind her own fucking business! Just what *did* you and my highly-desirable sister talk about, anyway? Like, when you were *by yourselves*?" Molly's jealousy flared, then settled. She arched her left eyebrow. "Bet she can't get you as caffeinated as I can," she said in a breathy voice, going for his neck again like a vampire.

"She didn't say anything to me, Molly. I brought it up," he responded, resisting her. She just stared blankly at him. "I told *her* at Sacred Grounds—before Tara and Rebecca showed up— that I would not mistreat you, that I wouldn't do to you what Devon did."

"Well, hell, Clay, I know that," she said, nodding. "There's a big difference between you two." She started playing with his chest hair. "You would never do to me what he did," she purred, rubbing her forehead into his chest, teasing him with her hair.

"Yeah, but Emmy doesn't know that. That chick is *scary*. Intense!"

"I wish everyone would stop saying that! Did she threaten you, too? I mean, she damn near scared Devon to death. Hell, for all I know, poor guy's had a heart attack by now."

"No, she didn't. We had a great chat, actually. She loves you, Molly."

"So let me get this straight: You won't snag me because you're pretending to be all moral and stuff, but you're really scared shitless that my overprotective MMA sister will beat you to death, aren't you? Worried she'll bitch-slap you in front of your aikido buddies? Don't be such a pussy—least not while I'm tryin' to give you some." She went for his neck again and moaned.

"Molly, damn it! It's not just that—I've got a lot of respect for your mom, too. She's a respected auntie in this community, a real boss. The three of you have been through a lot lately. It's not my place to bulldoze in here and spread you out on the mattress just because it suits me, ya know? What the hell happened to all this 'stay sacred' stuff anyway?" She looked up at him again, considering that, too, and clicked her teeth with her chin pressing into his chest. She grinned in a sexy way.

"So . . . what mattress were you talking about, Black Fox?" She peeked over his shoulder. "Is it in there?" she whispered, reaching down and kissing his right nipple.

"Molly."

She huffed, then looked up once more and sighed in resignation. "Kay-den. You owe me, bitch," she said, imitating her sister and winking at him. He turned her around again and kissed her ear.

"You got it," he said. "That's a promise. Just a little more time, that's all. You should be legal, Molly, for real. Society is like, out of control these days and I can't afford to be seen as a shit-ass just looking to hump underage Native girls. We've both got too much going for us. I don't want to be disbarred before I ever even *get* to law school." She laughed at that. He bear-hugged and held her. She could feel his wand stiffening behind her, so she knew he was turned on, too.

Don't be stupid, Pretty Feet. Tell him.

Molly patted his outer hand as she leaned back into him a final time. "Wado for respecting me." She felt him nodding and he kissed her head again.

"How can I not? You're special, Molly. I always knew it, somehow."

She looked back and up at him and smiled. "Sorry to come on so strong. Thanks for being the responsible one. You've just got me all stoked and lathered up with that sketchbook and everything. Dang." They separated and he patted her rump. She fanned herself with her hand. "Jesus," she said, shaking her head, "I'm sweating here."

"Tell me about it," he said, feeling the blood drain from his thighs. He quickly put his shirt back on and nearly ran to the fridge to get a soda. He held it to his forehead, then offered her one. She shook her head, telling him she was trying to quit the sugar because of Emmy.

"I *would* like to look at my gift some more, though," she said, arms behind her back and twisting her body. "Will you at least sit with me while I do?" she said with sincerity.

"Of course," he said, grabbing a can of peanuts as well.

Molly sat on the couch and leaned forward, rocking and shaking her head.

"What?" asked Clay, resting his soda and the peanut can on the table and opening them.

"It's weird, isn't it?"

"What do you mean?"

"Well, what makes me any better than Devon?"

"What the hell are you talking about?"

"Earlier this year, a friend I've known since kindergarten assaults me and winds up getting arrested and doing community service shit and here I am in your place—another childhood friend—I mean, technically, right? And what do *I* do? Basically try to rape *you* in your own house. So what does that make me?"

He laughed. "Normal. Look," he said, holding up a hand to interrupt her next comment, "this is not that."

"Really? How so? I mean, Jesus, Clay, the more I think about it, the creepier it all seems."

"Chill, chill," he said, holding his hand up again, then reaching for his soda. "First, women have rights—and protection under the law. Assault on a female—that's a legit charge, and it originated for a reason. Aside from some Amazonian like Emmy—with those amazing kick-ass skills—you all are generally weaker physically and should be afforded certain protections. In our case, I'm older and should take the lead—especially since you're not eighteen yet. Look, Dad once told me that if he ever caught me abusing a woman he would give me the beating of my life. And he was always good to Mom.

I've got kind of an asshole uncle who's an abuser, and, as you can imagine, he and Dad don't get along."

"Oh," said Molly, sitting back now and gazing up at Clay.

"But the laws for women are there for reasons of inequity and should be in place for decency and order in any society, don't you think? And you know—as Christians, supposedly our ideal is to wait for marriage, but most of us don't seem to reach that ideal. I still think it's a good one to have. Something to aim for." He shrugged. "We're only human, I guess."

She stared up at him, narrowing her eyes and crossing her arms over her chest. She leaned up and whispered, "You're stoking me again, talking like that. If I promise not to bend you to my will, will you take your shirt off again?" and snickered, nuzzling his neck with her nose. They both laughed.

They sat for the next forty-five minutes, Clay keeping his shirt on and Molly agreeing to behave, and talked about what a trip to retrace the Bell route might look like, how much it would cost, their ancestors, and so on. As they cuddled on the college guy couch, Molly put her head on his shoulder while she examined the book, like a little girl being read to. As she slowly turned to page three, she exhaled, then confessed.

"I think I'm in love with you."

43

Glorious Things

December 14, 1838
Bell Detachment
Little Rock, Arkansas

As the Bell Detachment moved through Little Rock, there advanced a change in collective mood. A quietness, a cadence of resolve, and a resignation to the destination characterized the Cherokees as the procession moved through the cold December air on the cusp of the new winter. Though Nick could never quite put his finger on it, he knew something had transpired to change his wife's mood from proud and robust to something other than. Despite the perpetual sores on her feet, she developed a singleness of focus, one of just getting to the next place alive. Each day she ensured that she saw to her children—born and unborn—and little else. The woman who passionately seduced him along the trail had long since disappeared. A shell of that young, vibrant, and alluring example of womanhood now made her way west in a rigid, emotionless bent toward mere survival.

Sergeant Thomas and several other soldiers pointed the detachment in the direction of a group of warehouses north of the city along the Arkansas River. As in other communities, even those not nearly as large as Little Rock, townspeople watched the procession of sad, resigned, and exhausted travelers. Little boys and girls stopped playing to pick their noses and stare at the brown-skinned Cherokees. No one—

adult or child—was sure what to make of these strangers from a faraway land.

Despite the hesitation and wonderment, the people of Little Rock seemed somehow more receptive, maybe because they were closer to the Indian Territory. Little Rock, as a city, had been established only three years earlier, and the people were a hearty lot, industrious, trying to create a working environment in this part of the Arkansas Territory. A little girl, munching on a carrot, spotted Enoch and Annabelle's son, Thad. Perhaps thinking he was cute, she smiled, handed him the vegetable, giggled, then ran.

Mary had walked most of the past fifty miles with her head down, concentrating on the goal—living long enough to collapse at journey's end. Nick seemed wearier than before, his backside pounding from being on the buckboard so much. He had developed a headache that wouldn't go away, even after Doc Arbogast examined him. His eyes, shoulders, and hips all ached. He stared straight ahead, oblivious to the surrounding township. Augustine, beside him on the buckboard, yawned and lowered his head. Nick managed a weak smile and rubbed the dog's mighty head briefly.

When they reached the warehouse district, the wagons and animals slowed, the walkers following suit. The Bell Detachment had, somewhere along the line, become mechanistic, slow to embrace hope. Nick knew that he would once again be treating the blisters on his family's feet, including Augustine's. Damage to the feet seemed to be the universal battle scar of the Cherokees, if one didn't count the emotional scars. Families lay about at most stops, treating one another's feet with everything from black walnut to taheebo to tobacco to creek water. Even footwear, be it boots, shoes, or moccasins, was no real barrier against the elements and rugged terrain. Many who had some type of foot covering suffered as much as those who were making the journey barefoot. One could see traces of bloody footprints in the dirt leading to the warehouse openings, which were wide and inviting.

The frigid air brought with it sustained winds which punished the travelers as they prepared for rest within the warehouse walls. The Cherokees struggled to lay down proper pallets because most faltered on their feet. Some of the soldiers helped speed the process of settling in. Though mutual animosity would always exist, both parties managed more patience, if not understanding. Mary propped herself up against the interior warehouse wall. Martha sat between her legs and let her mother brush her hair with her fingers.

Ten days prior, the army had paid Benjamin Ragsdale fifty-one dollars for materials and labor for coffins. Benjamin and his wife, Rebecca, had in essence been serving as traveling morticians for the detachment. Benjamin had overseen the burial of all of the Cherokees since the detachment left Fort Cass. The Ragsdales were Rogers family friends from Georgia. Benjamin, after settling his family in the warehouse, located Mary and Nick. He slid up to Mary and knelt beside her. Nick noticed her jump when Benjamin made his appearance, the way she held Martha tightly. He had not failed to notice his wife's nervousness—but from what?

"Oh," said Benjamin, tipping his hat, "forgive me for startling you, Mary." She nodded, resuming her preoccupation with Martha's hair. "Looks like we've made it most of the way, Nick," he said, watching Nick prepare the area for sleeping. Nick grunted. It was obvious to Nick that Benjamin could see the fatigue taking its toll on the McNairs, just as with all concerned. "Hello, pretty girl," he said to Martha, smiling and gripping her hand. She grinned back, but Mary pulled her closer, avoiding eye contact. Benjamin stood and approached Nick. Nick had just thrown his blanket to the ground when he turned to face Ragsdale.

Without saying a word, the two men embraced. Nick did not want his wife and child to see him cry, but no hiding place existed. He wept on Benjamin's shoulder. "What the hell happened to us?" he asked, not looking up, staring at the multitude of Cherokees now filling the warehouse. Ragsdale patted his back.

"I honestly don't know, cousin-nephew. I just don't know. But we are strong. We are the Principal People. We will go on."

"I'm not so sure."

"You must be."

"I'm not," said Nick, shoulders trembling. Mary just sat, raking her hand through Martha's hair, staring straight ahead. Enoch and Annabelle, across the way with another family of slaves, busied themselves with their own children. Deborah sat on the ground and waved at Martha, who managed a smile for her favorite babysitter.

"Nicholas, it will be up to young people like you and Mary to lead the way in the new territory. You must not lose faith."

"They won, Ben," Nick lamented, pulling away but keeping his hands on Benjamin's shoulders. "They got what they wanted. They defeated us from the beginning. Send the trash to the west . . ."

Benjamin slapped Nick in front of his family.

"Never say that again, nephew. Ever. Do you understand me?" He took Nick by the shoulders and looked him in the eye. It wasn't a vicious slap, merely enough to get his friend's attention. Nick looked down, nodding.

"You are absolutely right," he replied. "That was careless of me. I don't know if I can make it, Ben." He shook his head. Augustine, glued to Mary's side, whined.

"You will. We're practically there, my friend. Just outside the Indian Territory. You will make it. And you will thrive. No other choice is yours, cousin." He nodded with authority. Nick nodded in agreement, looking down at his family. Sergeant Thomas approached.

"Ragsdale, we have another dead Cherokee. Your services are required."

After Nick returned from helping Benjamin prepare another coffin, he took Martha from Mary, cleaned her up, and prepared her for the night. He helped Mary move about, holding her as she dodged the blisters on her soles. Doc Arbogast looked in on Mary to determine the state of her health in relation to the pregnancy. He had her sit again, back up against the wall. Nick observed as Mary pushed the doctor away from her once or twice as he examined her belly. At one point, Doc Arbogast stopped and eyed Mary. They exchanged an intense look, as if communicating telepathically. After an awkward moment, Mary averted her eyes. When he was done, the doctor stood and motioned to Nick for a private conversation.

"She's healthy, Nick, but somethin' ain't right. Now, I don't presume to know more than I know, but maybe you should have a long chat with your wife."

"It's like she's hiding something, Doc. I noticed it a while back—when we were looking for the Fields girl. Just don't know. Like she had a scare of some sort, but she says she's fine." Arbogast glanced back at Mary, leaning passively against the wall. He grunted and shook his head, then patted Nick on the shoulder. "In any case, stay with her. Could just be this unyielding exhaustion we're all so dampened with. But there's a fear in there, somewhere. Don't know. Wish I could be of more help."

"You've done well, Doc, plenty. Thank you for being here." Doc Arbogast nodded and made his way to the next family.

Nick knelt and examined Mary's feet. He went outside to the wagon to retrieve their medicine pouch. Collecting several herbs, he repeated the treatment from earlier in the journey. He dampened the material and applied a poultice to the larger sores. Mary closed her eyes and slept for a brief time as Nick doctored her blisters. He later tended to himself, then reexamined Martha to head off any danger to which he might not have been alert the first time. The Indians were crowded into two warehouses. Looking around, it reminded Nick of a cattle auction.

The next few days in Little Rock were bitter and raw. The air became colder and even the warehouses were no match for the conditions. Captain Ambrose bought more corn and fodder from a Mr. George King outside of Little Rock. By December 18, the Bell Detachment began its trek through the foothills of the Ozarks.

Christmastime
Bell Detachment
Arkansas River Valley
Foot of the Ozark Mountains
State of Arkansas

On Christmas Eve the skies grew dim with the kind of gray that encompassed everything. Nick could feel snow coming. When he mentioned it to Mary, she bucked at the idea, thinking it too early and entirely unfair to their situation. He noticed that she had come around, locking eyes with him more than in previous weeks. She seemed to be returning to her old self and communicating again.

Captain Ambrose, like the leaders of many other detachments, told the Cherokees that "Christmas will come and go without notice" in an effort to keep the party moving. As Methodists, the McNairs found this insulting and evil. Two of Mary's friends, Walela, a woman whose name meant "hummingbird" in Cherokee, and Betsy Simons, began singing "Amazing Grace" as the dingy skies gave way to darkness. At first, some of the soldiers voiced annoyance with the singing, but they gave in after a few miles. Initially, the people sang in Cherokee, but as others joined in, the English language became the dominant voice, though some Cherokee kept to their native tongue. It was harmonious, despite the dual languages and bitter conditions. Now and then, a snowflake fell.

The overnight camp was brutal, unmanageable for most, and heartbreaking to record for the missionaries who, as usual, were faring little better in soul and spirit. Late that evening, Christmas Eve, Tobacco Bill urinated on his last boot. Tame since the beating he received earlier from Sergeant Hollingsworth, he rallied near the end and peed on the boot of a private who had pushed Ida Bird for moving too slow. The private just laughed, refusing to let Tobacco Bill get under his skin. Though much of the sickness in this detachment had run its course, a strange cough had seized Tobacco Bill the preceding week, and he was wrecked with it. He went to some nearby trees in the camp and vomited, passed out, and died.

Benjamin Ragsdale was summoned, and he, Nick, and a few others buried Tobacco Bill on a hillside at the foot of the great Ozark Mountains. Later that evening, not long before midnight, Nick led Mary, Martha, Enoch and family, Augustine, and a few friends in the reading of Jesus's birth in the Gospel of Luke by torchlight. Afterward, Mary hugged her man, thanking him for holding fast to their faith, wondering if this could be her last hug, cold and unmerciful as it was getting.

On Tuesday, Christmas Day, the detachment pulled up stakes and headed northwest. It had become apparent to all that Mary had a gift for singing. She, Betsy, and Walela led many in song, at one point even getting some of the soldiers to join in "Hark! The Herald Angels Sing" as they moved along, winds picking up and the threat of snow in the air. The trail winded around farms and small towns that were sleepy and lonely and not elaborate. Nick noticed that, curiously, Mary became more of her old self the more she sang. He knew she had an amazing voice for church, but to hear it out in the elements amid this heartbreaking distress was other-worldly.

Wednesday, December 26, had the detachment on the march, trying to make up time. Nick was sullen, thinking of home, switching control of the wagon back and forth with Enoch as snow came to the foothills. A couple of inches fell quickly. He took time on foot to monitor Mary, each of them taking turns carrying Martha or putting her on the buckboard next to Augustine. Nick slowed so that he could observe his family from behind, ever mindful of those that might falter. Sometime after the noon hour, several of the women suggested Mary lead a hymn again. When she resisted, they pestered her to the point where she felt she might be neglecting her people.

"'Glorious things', Mary," said Walela, who secretly envied Mary's beauty and voice. She had passed Nick and was coming up behind Mary.

"Oh, I don't know," said Mary, her breath steaming upward in the icy air.

"Yes, Mary," added Betsy, "uh-uh, *uh-uh*." She grunted in Cherokee. "Glorious things—*uh-uh*!" Mary contemplated as she walked, roughly six months into her pregnancy. Relenting, she managed a smile and started, slowly, deliberately:

Glo-rious things of thee are spoken, Zi-on city of our God;

he whose word can-not be bro-ken

formed thee for his own a-bode . . .

The silent snow fell faster. The other women, including Annabelle, joined in. Mary moved in rhythm with the lyrics, kicking snow about as her worn, thin shoes moved through the powder. Nick raised his head, noting that the nearby soldiers, Indians, animals, and even the dreaded white wagon masters had begun to settle, as if hypnotized. Mary's voice rose with each line.

. . . on the Rock of A-ges found-ed,

what can shake thy sure re-pose?

With sal-vation's walls sur-rounded,

thou may'st smile at all thy foes!

Nick wept. He could not get over the hold his wife's voice had on the whole of creation. His weeping increased when he turned his gaze to her once more and saw her bloody footprints in the snow. Back on the wagon, Augustine stared, transfixed.

He and his fellow four-leggeds were snared in the beauty of his mistress's angelic tone. Sergeant Thomas, who silently followed the words, bowed his head as his horse trotted along the path. Coming upon a bend in the trail, Mary led the cadence as the McNair portion of the detachment followed the long and winding curve, her voice reverberating off the trees and a nearby freezing lake as she hit the third verse.

> Round each ha-bi-ta-tion hovering,
>
> see the cloud and fire ap-pear . . .

Enoch rubbed Augustine's massive head to keep from screaming out to the valley, watching his own wife and children stagger through snowflakes which dropped rapidly. Nick did his best to control himself as they marched around the bend. As Mary concluded the third verse, the people, horses, mules, crows, field mice, and other ground-dwelling creatures all fell silent in one great hush of wonderment.

> Thus de-riving from their ban-ner,
>
> light by night, and shade by day,
>
> safe! they feed up-on the man-na
>
> which he gives them when they pray . . .

Nick bowed his head in awe of his wife as they rounded the bend and marched on, covering his face with his shirt against the elements. The Cherokees made their way toward the end of 1838 with a solemn air of dignity and peace that came from the knowledge that no government, subfreezing temperatures, or other humans could eliminate those who called themselves the Principal People. The bloodstained footprints were the evidence, the verdict certain.

44

Who Will Be Privileged to Hear It?

Then come, my Sister! come I pray,
With speed put on your woodland dress;
—And bring no book: for this one day
We'll give to idleness.
—William Wordsworth

Present Day
Saturday Morning, Early June
Emmy's Bungalow
Muskogee, Oklahoma

The small flower bed on Emmy's front porch contained pansies.

She loved playing in the dirt, always had. She needed some alone time and playing in the flower bed was like therapy for her. Planting flowers, Marie, fighting, pistol shooting, making love to Mike, it was all therapeutic. She reached for her favorite garden gloves—her Tuff Chix. It was the only pink thing she was willing to put on. She laughed at herself as she slipped the left one on her hand, pulling it all the way with her teeth, just like her sparring gloves. Old habits, she thought with a smile.

She was intuitive enough to know that Mike might propose to her down the road, and she needed time to think about that one. Should she finish her master's degree before making such a commitment if he did pop the question? Would it be worth being married to a cop—someone who one day might not make it home from work? Did she want to be a mother someday? Would being married keep her from earning a doctorate? And what was it about Cherokee women marrying white guys through the centuries, anyway? Whose fucking idea was *that*? And tragedy of tragedies—what if she *did* get pregnant? Would she have to stop her beloved habit of putting Mike in one of her spur-of-the-moment hip throws in the middle of the living room? He was, after all, the ultimate boy toy. The look on his face as he hit the floor and stared up at her was forever worth the price of admission.

"So *cute!*" she mumbled, giggling to herself. Molly drove up in Clay's red 2015 Chevrolet Malibu. She got out and shut the door. Emmy shook her head.

"Is that a Chevy that you have the audacity to park in front of my place? The hell's wrong with you, Snow White?"

"Clay let me have it for the day. Like it?"

"Do I *look* like I like it?"

"Seriously, Em?"

"Tell that young stud to get a pony car, Jesus Christ. I'd rather drive that shit-pink convertible that postcolonial Barbie-bitch huffs around in than that thing."

"Hey, now, be nice. He's a second-degree black belt, ya know. He'll put some of that Yonkyo wrist stuff or whatever they call it on you," she said, dreaming of Clay and swaying like a dancer on the short sidewalk leading to Emmy's stoop, moving her arms in a flowing motion and adding sound effects.

"Uh-huh," said Emmy, patting down some dirt. "And I'll wrap that second-degree black belt around his balls and hang him up at ThunderClap like a speed bag and let all the bitches have their way with him." She snickered. Molly sat on the steps beside the stoop and watched her sister play in the dirt. "Hey, it was *so* good to see you graduate, Nine-Speed. You, Tara, the Chief—awesome! Well, how do you feel?"

"Dunno. Not really any different," Molly replied, shrugging.

"Are you *sure* you don't want to go somewhere? You know, cut loose? I'll pay for it, kiddo. Now I can't pay for yours, Tara's, and Rebecca's, but I got *your* back." Molly hopped up and hugged her sister.

"Thanks, Em," she said, letting go and shaking her head. "Nah, we actually talked about it and we're okay; none of us are really going anywhere. Tara, at least, is dead set on getting into OSU and is wanting to work as much as she can to save up. Becks is still trying to figure things out. Things being so tight all the way around and all that, we're all just hangin' for now. Plus, there's the trip I wanna take back east for the Trail of Tears at some point. That's *really* important to me."

"I know," said Emmy with a smile, resuming her gardening. "I'm glad."

"Can't explain it, really. Just something I feel like I have to do, 'specially since the ride didn't work out. I feel like I should do something for our people."

"You better, or I'll beat your little butt," said Emmy with a laugh. "Clay still going, too?" she asked, flicking off some dirt that had splattered her cheek.

"I sure hope so. Crazy how it all came about. It was Claire's idea, ya know."

Emmy nodded.

"I think the Remember the Removal ride is one of the absolute coolest things the Nation does," said Emmy as she poured in some fresh dirt from a Sunshine Nursery Too bag. "That's some badass shit. And I understand why they retrace the Northern Route. But, you know, Nine-Speed, not much gets said about the other routes, particularly Bell. I think it will be *extremely* interesting what you discover and what you journal about, sexy little writer that you are. Funny, right? Clay sketches and you write. That should make for a fascinating story."

Molly reflected on that. She studied her sister's face.

"Do you like Clay?"

"Yes."

"What about him do you like?"

"He's polite, he's good to you, and he cares about people—especially *our* people. And he comes from a good family. Always liked his mom. Contessa is a good woman. And he's serious . . . serious about who he is and who he wants to become."

"Are those the things you like about Mike?"

"I suppose. Mike's not Cherokee, of course, but he cares about our people, too. And you already know he's good to me. He's had some trouble in his family—what there is of it, but he's done well. My man."

"When did you know you were in love with Mike?"

"When I realized he loved me for who I am," she said, not looking up, but focusing on her pansies. "All my flaws, my bullshit, my past, my cancer. When I understood that he's courageous enough to tell me like it is to my face—that he only wants what's best for me." She slapped the dirt, flattening it with both hands, her pink Tuff Chix gloves turning black.

"I'm in love with Clay."

"I know."

"How did you know?" said Molly, eyes wide and surprised.

"I could see it coming at Tammy's Tavern, but I really saw it after he did that sketchbook for you. Should have seen him at Sacred Grounds, Nine-Speed. He was like a little boy—all excited about the project, drawing a couple of things for me to get my opinion, all happy and shit." She smiled at Molly and winked. "He's a babe."

"Yeah, I know," said Molly, giggling and rubbing her left arm. "He said he told you he would treat me right," she said, scanning Emmy's face for affirmation. "Why do you think he did that?"

"Cause I told him if he didn't, I'd shove his head so far up his ass he'd have to use a whole can of WD-40 and an impact wrench to get it out." She pounded the dirt as she inwardly grinned.

"You *what*? You didn't, Em! Did you?" she said with trepidation.

Emmy busted out laughing and said no, she was just kidding. "You are such an easy mark sometimes, honestly."

"I know I can be naive," she said, sitting on the stoop and swinging her legs in the Oklahoma heat. "Guess that's why I'm nervous, sorta." Emmy focused on pulling enough dirt away to plant the pansies, listening for the spirit. "Clay came along after that horrible experience with Devon, and I've been feeling kinda weird, lightheaded. It all seems like a blur. Keep getting a crazy feeling that maybe it's not real, like maybe Devon hired him or something to mess with me." Emmy glanced at her. "Pastor Claire says I should trust my heart, but I dunno. Like, what am I supposed to do—how am I supposed to be? You know, like we were just saying—the whole Trail of Tears thing and all—Clay seems too good to be true, almost like somethin' to get ripped away again . . . like Dad."

Emmy looked over at her little sister. "Come over here," she said, motioning with her Tuff Chix. "Help me out here." She asked Molly to hand her two small pots holding pansies. Emmy removed them and placed the flowers in the dirt. Molly tried to avoid getting dirty. "Put your hands in there, princess," Emmy teased, forcing her little sister's hands into the dirt. She smiled and walked behind Molly, turning her toward the flower bed. She removed her gloves, handed them to Molly, and told her to put them on. She told her exactly how to plant and care for the flowers. "Our McNair ancestors in Scotland called these the "stepmother flowers," she said in a Scottish brogue, hugging her sister from behind and playfully digging her chin into Molly's shoulder and causing her to giggle.

"Wow," said Molly, "didn't know that."

"See, thing is," said Emmy, "when you plant something—a seed, a flower, a relationship, do it with conviction. Whether it's a seed, a flower, or a man, be clear about your intentions.

Show that you mean business and plant things with the faith that, with enough love and care, they will grow. Without that faith, you won't make it, and the flower will wilt and die. Believing in yourself, in the idea that you will grow together—that relationships are mutual and reciprocal—that's what it's all about. I think Nancy Ward and Wilma Mankiller would have agreed with me. Those were two Cherokee women who knew a thing or two about cultivating something. Part of being a true warrior is having faith that things will work out, understand?"

"Yeah, actually, I think I do."

"Osda," said Emmy, kissing her sister's cheek.

"Hey," said Molly, leaning back into her big sis, "when are you going to the rock pile again? I wanna learn to shoot." Emmy considered this.

"Hmm. Well, let's have some lunch, and we can drive out there today. Been awhile for me, anyway. But, um, you gonna tell Mom?" she queried, pushing her sister forward with a quizzical look.

"Oh, hell no! Course not!"

"Then we'll go. Seriously, I just don't wanna hear it from her."

"Deal. Hey, we could start a YouTube thing—like a lotta gun people do!"

"Yeah, sure. 'Cherokee Bitches Who Don't Miss,'" said Emmy, holding up her hands as if presenting a banner. "Subscribe if you like our videos!" Molly laughed.

"I'll be lucky if I can hit anything," she said apprehensively.

"Don't worry. When I'm done with you, you'll be able to shave a skinny white guy in the dark at twenty-five yards," Emmy bragged. "We'll take my car. You can park that Malibu Barbie thing in the driveway." She giggled as Molly gave her the finger. "Yeah, tell *Clay*-ton that if he insists on playing with Barbie things to at least get himself a Wilma Mankiller Barbie. I mean, Jesus, have some respect already!" Emmy snorted and laughed, poking Molly's dimple.

"You're *such* a bitch sometimes, seriously!" exclaimed Molly, slapping Emmy's hand away.

2:30 pm
Rock Pile
District One, Cherokee Nation

Emmy carried her range bag and Molly toted a small folding table. Much to Emmy's joy, they had the area to themselves—unusual for a Saturday afternoon. Emmy was also carrying a Rubber Dummies target that Molly kept staring at on the drive out. Emmy had placed it in the backseat, and it probably looked to other drivers like two hot women and a bald guy had been going well over the speed limit in a cool Mustang. She caught Molly occasionally glancing back with uncertainty at the target that Emmy had named Cletus, as if he were talking to her, which amused Emmy to no end.

"Set that up over here," said Emmy, referring to the folding table. "Stay here. Gonna take Cletus downrange." She walked about ten yards out, dropped Cletus in the middle, and walked back.

"Cletus? Seriously? Why Cletus?" asked Molly, shielding her eyes from the sun even though she was wearing shades. It was just one of those Oklahoma days.

Emmy shrugged. "Just looked like a Cletus to me." Molly giggled. "Actually, he's my second one. You can replace them on that little stand they're on—not too hard. After Norbert got all shot up, I took his ass to ThunderClap and hung him. Tina and I beat him to death one afternoon. We had a bet going: first one to cut him in half with either our hands or our tac knives got a nice dinner out of it."

"Who won?"

"Tina. She's a tough chick. Plus, I think she was highly motivated by the idea of trying to seduce me over dinner and taking me home to her place drunk."

Molly roared with laughter.

"So it was Norbert before Cletus?"

"Yeah. He whined a lot. Didn't like being shot in the face so much, the little bitch, so we pounded him with our bare hands, then knifed his ass. Eddie was *pissed*. We had Norbert bits and pieces all over the gym and Eddie yells, '*Bitches*! Clean that shit up or lose your lockers!'" Emmy laughed and shook her head.

She blew Molly's mind when she opened her range bag and began unloading it. Two sets of ear protectors, two sets of eye protectors, numerous boxes of ammo, oil, rags, lead remover in a bottle, etc. Then the guns came out. One after another. Molly started to freak.

"God*dang*, Em. How many guns do you *have*?"

"None of your business, grandma."

Molly cupped her hands together over her face and laughed nervously. "Omigod," she said, "you're scaring the shit out of me, sis."

"Don't get your panties in a twist, Snow White," said Emmy with a sigh.

"Where the hell do you keep all these guns, Emmy? Seriously!"

"Well, since Mike came along, he keeps some of them for me. I have a safe you don't know about. A couple of revolvers, pistolas, a 12-gauge pump shotgun, an M1 carbine, a flamethrower, and a set of tactical knives." Molly just stared at Emmy, mouth open.

St. Bernard again, but this stuff is *damn* funny.

"Are you *serious*?"

Emmy nodded.

"A freaking flamethrower, Em, really? For *what*? A small rebel force?"

"You never know."

"You're not kidding about the flamethrower, are you?" She stared at Emmy.

"No, I'm not. Never joke with white folk."

"Oh, stop it."

Emmy laughed. "Yeah, I'll bring her out here one day. You can fire that little slut. Her name's 'Graciella.' She's a bad girl," said Emmy, flexing her triceps as she spread the guns out on the table. "Always have to bring two fire extinguishers, though. One day Eddie was pissed at the world and he set that stand of trees over there on fire, then he set his own dummy target on fire, some cheap generic-brand dummy that Eddie had named 'Andy' after Andrew Jackson because of the way Jackson screwed our people. Yeah, he was grouchy that day and roasted Andy like a hog on a spit after I asked how his ex-wife was doing. She's that rich bitch that lives in California now. Yeah, Ole Standingcloud fried Andy extra crispy like a catfish."

"Omigod, this is *so* freaked out!"

"Oh, mar-god, this is SO fa-reeked art!" Emmy mimicked. "Here, hold this, my little skirt," she said, handing Molly a Ruger SR .22 semi-automatic pistol. "Keep your forefinger away from the trigger and point it toward the ground and not at me, for God's sake." Molly held the gun out and away from her like it had a disease, pointing it downward as instructed.

"Now," said Emmy, "what are you going to do with it?"

"I dunno. Shoot it, I guess?"

"Wrong."

"Okay," said Molly, looking upset.

"First, sis, relax. Keep it pointed downward. Now, see that button on the grip?" Molly nodded. "Hold your left hand under the handle—that's where the clip—the magazine—will eject. Be confident with your grip—you don't want to drop it. Press that button with your right thumb." Molly did, and the clip fell into her hand. "Good. Is it loaded?"

"Um, no?"

"How do you know?"

"Well, I don't see any bullets, right?"

"Okay. Give me the mag." Molly handed it to her. "Now point the weapon downrange—toward Cletus." Molly did. "Nice. Now, turn the gun sideways, like this," said Emmy, showing her how. "With your right hand on the grip, you're going to 'slingshot' it, as we sometimes say. You grasp the serrations on the slide between your left thumb and forefinger and let it fly—like this," Emmy instructed, mimicking the motion. Molly did, the slide locking the hammer back. "Anything fly out?"

"Nope."

"Good. Now, check it again—twice." Molly did, ensuring no round was in the chamber. "Well done, cutie! That's the first part of your lesson. Every gun should *always* be considered loaded. On a semi-auto, you always drop the clip, mag, or magazine—whatever you choose to call it—first before checking the slide because if the gun is loaded, you run the risk of accidentally loading a live round into the chamber, which, with automatics like this, can lead to multiple shots being fired inadvertently. Got it?"

"Yeah! That makes sense. Have you ever had a shot go off you didn't want?"

"That's called an accidental discharge, or AD, and no, I haven't, because Eddie taught me well. I've never told you this, but Standingcloud is one *dangerous* son of a bitch. He is, to put it mildly, a badass mofo." She shook her head out of respect for her trainer. "Once, a couple of years ago in Oklahoma City, we were coming back from a fight—remember when I beat Chastain? Dropped her with a spinning back kick and she never got up. I felt kind of bad for her, actually. Anyway, we stopped to eat before leaving town and some knucklehead—like that mope at Tammy's—just wouldn't leave Eddie alone. I think he recognized me and wanted to test Eddie. Big mistake. Molly, I never saw someone hit another human being so hard. He beat that guy's head in. The cops came, but we were lucky because all the witnesses stood up for Eddie. I knew then what kind of tiger had selected me and trained me; mad respect. Standingcloud isn't someone you want to cross."

"Yeah. Ya know, I kinda figured that. He's the one who told me how to speed-shift a guy's pecker if he got nasty with me, remember? Just like what happened with Devon." They laughed and Emmy high-fived her sister, leaning in to kiss her cheek.

"And there ya go," said Emmy with a smile. "All right," she said, "let me show you a couple of things. One, I brought some dummy rounds—snap caps—for each weapon I want you to fire today. Then we'll do some actual shooting, but I want you to have your fundamentals down before you start using live ammo. You are going to start with a .22. When you feel comfortable with that, you can shoot the Bodyguard .380. I love .380s. Great round with lower recoil." She separated some of the pistols on the table. "See this one? This is a Smith & Wesson Shield in 9mm, a more powerful round than the .380. This one? This is the Bersa Thunder in .380. The next one is a Glock 17 in 9mm. You should see Eddie's collection; it is a force with which to be reckoned, believe me. I've fired every caliber of handgun— mostly from his collection. I stick mostly with the .380 and 9mm because they're easier to control under stress. This one here? A Ruger EC9 9mm. Mind blown?"

"Pretty much."

Emmy laughed. "One baby step at a time. Six months with me or Eddie out here and you'll be known as 'The Unsinkable Molly McNair.' Just know that, any time you pull a weapon on anyone, there's always a chance they might take it from you. If you ever have to pull a handgun in self-defense, keep at least six feet between you and your target if possible."

"Like you did at the Archway, right?"

"You got it, sista."

"I can't buy one until I'm twenty-one, right?"

"True, but if there happened to be one, let's say, in the house—and you had to use it—well, it's Ma's house, now isn't it? Besides, these laws are mostly for control purposes, half-assed attempts to regulate human behavior. If you have one and feel you have to use it, *do it*. That's what Mom's lawyers are for."

"Yeah—but she'd freak out, for sure. You know, I think Dad's old shotgun is still in their closet."

"Probably not even loaded. Remind me next time I'm there and I'll check it out. Can bring you some shells. Trust me, you'll be twenty-one before you know it. Besides, you can always come shoot with me because it's target shooting and training. It's just good therapy for me. Something to blow off a little steam when I'm not pounding on other women," she said with a grin.

Emmy went through the fundamentals with Molly and Molly had a blast shooting the Ruger .22. Emmy took strips of masking tape and stuck them on Cletus's chest so Molly could see where her hits were. Like most new shooters, Molly was tentative. But she was a quick study. She got seven out of ten rounds in the chest area where Emmy had taped, with a fairly large grouping, but acceptable enough for a kill.

"Ha!" said Molly proudly. "How about *that*?"

"Not bad, Nine-Speed, not bad at all," said Emmy as they walked down to Cletus to examine him more closely. Emmy pulled Molly's tape away and put up her own. She laid three large strips across his chest, plus two smaller ones on his face— across both eyes and over his lips. They walked back.

"Does that mean I'm a pretty good shot?" asked Molly as they turned to face the target again.

"Dunno, are you?" Emmy responded with a suspicious grin. After Molly slipped her hearing protection back on, Emmy glanced at her with a wink and in a millisecond was down on her right knee. She drew and fired the Shield 9mm in a blur and put four rapid-fire shots in Cletus's chest and three in his face.

Molly's jaw dropped. They walked down to get a closer look. Poor Cletus had four marks on his rubbery chest that were all within an inch of one another, and the three in his face were even more impressive. One round entered his left eye, another his mouth, and the third was slightly off, hitting the bridge of his nose just beneath his right eye. Emmy's shooting was as scary as her fighting. She took one look at her results and walked away, saying, "Bet that blonde Malibu Barbie bitch can't do that . . ."

Molly stared at Cletus and mumbled, "Holy *shit!*"

Sunday, 5 pm
Come to the Circle
Muskogee, Oklahoma

Molly was into Pastor Claire's sermon. Like usual when she listened to sermons, though, good or bad, she found herself slipping in and out of Claire's message. The curse of twenty-first-century attention spans.

"Bang!" shouted Claire, making Molly jump. Molly offered a stunned expression as Claire stared at the members within the circle. Claire preferred "church in the round," an atmosphere where the members all get a good look at one another's faces, instead of the traditional front-facing pews or seats. "And just like that I'm on my way to the hospital emergency room in the meat wagon." The small congregation was silent, hanging on Claire's every word. "He beat me so bad I went into cardiac arrest just as the ambulance was pulling into the ER. For those who don't know, I'm Cherokee by descent. My Indian ancestors were a family known as Sanders. So there I am, in that Betadine-smelling environment of the ER, doctors and nurses and techs and whatnot working on me like crazy to keep me alive, 'cept I don't know it, of course.

"And sure enough, next thing I know I'm not in the ER at all. I'm on the Trail of Tears back in 1838. My fourth great-grandfather, Robert—Ole Bob—he's sittin' there on the back of a beat-up old wagon with a fifth of straight corn whiskey and he says, 'Girl, you got shit to do. You might think I'm crazy, but you're gonna be preachin' God's word. I can't help ya with that man—you gots to decide for yourself about him. But I've been authorized to tell you that you can come on with me now, or go back where you came from. If you go back, your life won't ne'er be the same. You gonna set Saint Paul's titties on fire 'cause women will be runnin' churches by then . . .'" Most of the congregation giggled. One woman, Trina Mae, who was Claire's first congregant, howled with laughter. "So . . . I just *had* to come back, didn't I?" she said with a grin. The church members laughed again.

Claire weaved her story into the greater message of the day: understanding of others. Molly perked up when Claire referenced Will Rogers, a distant relative of Molly's. She said, "Will Rogers was a Cherokee Nation citizen. My favorite Rogers quote is 'The successful don't work any harder than the failures. They get what's called in baseball the breaks.' See, not everyone, regardless of effort, can be lucky or successful, regardless of what many Americans today will tell you.

"It just ain't so. *But* your faith can take you places the braggarts in their high-paying jobs with their three houses and offshore accounts can't. It can lead you to peace. Peace within yourself. We've all seen it. Jesus gave you the authority and power to make that happen. As you know, I always commend Matthew 7:12 to you—what we've come to call 'The Golden Rule.' Be as kind to others as you can be. Treat them how you wish to be treated and the rest will take care of itself. Thus, peace be unto you, peace be with you. Amen."

"Amen," Molly found herself responding.

More often than not, Come to the Circle had an eclectic music mix. Much of it was contemporary. The Unitarian church hosting Come to the Circle had a nice pipe organ and Claire contracted with Ruth, the organist, to help with worship services for the Circle, which were usually Sundays at five or Wednesdays at seven in the evening. Claire had asked Ruth for some traditional hymns as of late, and today's closing hymn was "Glorious Things of Thee Are Spoken," which Molly recalled from childhood. Molly had a strong sense of Mary's presence at the service, as if Mary had been speaking through Claire. She felt a lump in her throat, but smiled as they all sang the last part of the last verse of the hymn in harmony.

'Tis' his love his peo-ple rais-es o-ver self, to reign as kings:

and as priests, his sol-emn prais-es each for a thank of-fering brings . . .

After the service, Molly helped Claire gather bulletins left behind by congregants. "Do you think the ancestors speak to us through the hymns?" she asked Claire.

"Yes," said Claire without hesitation. "Next question."

Molly snickered. "Just seemed like it for a minute is all," she said with a shrug.

"Depend on it," said Claire, gathering the last three leftover service announcements.

"That was a *great* sermon, Claire. It was really amazing to hear your story."

"Wado, Molly. Hope people can take something from it. We've all got our stories, just like you. Question is, what are you going to do with it? You have a powerful story to tell. You're a powerful advocate for a lot of people—people like Rebecca and Tara, and dozens of people you've yet to meet." As they straightened a few of the chairs in the circle, Claire added, "Your story is waiting to be told someday, Molly. What are you going to do with it? And who will be privileged to hear it?"

45

Too Cold

December 30, 1838
Bell Detachment
Mulberry, Arkansas
Ozark Mountains

"Sir," said Sergeant Thomas, "according to a messenger from Fort Smith, temperature mercury thermometers between here and there registered six degrees in the wee hours this morning!"

"I have no doubt, Sergeant, none whatsoever. It's so damn cold out here I saw two squirrels engaging in carnal knowledge with the lieutenant's wool socks," Captain Ambrose responded through chapped lips.

"Yes, sir!"

"Carry on, Sergeant, assuming you're able!"

"Sir, yes, sir!" Thomas responded, teeth chattering.

Three Cherokees—two elders, Polly Old Field and Ustah, as well as a nine-year-old girl, Nan Miller—froze to death overnight. The ground was too hard for burial. Ragsdale said they would have to be buried down the trail when things warmed up, but Nick told Mary he doubted the reality of that statement. Mary was so cold it felt like her eyeballs were frozen. Captain Ambrose had stopped the march, trying to find the best shelter he could. Two old barns in the Mulberry area were empty and the army merely took them over. No landowner appeared for a challenge. The hills and mountains were deathly quiet.

The McNairs, along with Enoch, Annabelle, Deborah, and Thad—formed a small huddle to feed off one another's body heat. Thad was shivering so severely his teeth rattled. He coughed up mucus and blood, Deborah cleaning him as best she could. Augustine, however, seemed to manage quite well, snuggling up to his pack as if trying to keep them warm. Most of the other families within Mary and Nick's line of vision had the same idea about group huddles to retain as much body heat as possible. Even the soldiers were bunched close in order to keep their hands and feet from freezing.

"Now I know it *is* possible to be too cold," said Nick as he wrapped his wife and daughter in a human cocoon.

Doc Arbogast made his rounds, looking like a sixty- or seventy-year-old man, hunched over and shivering as he tried his best to attend to others. The missionaries Diana and Simon could be seen spooning in a corner of the barn, unable to develop the energy to minister to anyone. The necessities of managing daily living in the extreme weather conditions preoccupied Mary to the point that she could barely remember the assault, let alone her life before the journey. She felt old.

Someone in the McNair barn struggling to cope with the cold managed to start a fire. It quickly got out of hand and caught the side of the barn on fire. It spread and, out of control, burned eleven people. It forced that part of the detachment outside, where the travelers watched the barn burn down. Most stayed nearby, hoping to absorb the extreme heat to stay warm. Those who were burned lay on the ground moaning, with some of the uninjured tending to them as best they could with frozen hands and fingers. Chaos abounded. Nick and Mary struggled to protect Martha and stay warm, and Nick and the other men relocated their wagons farther out to avoid the flames.

At one point, as Cherokees and army personnel ran about—the soldiers trying to maintain some semblance of order—Mary looked over at the base of a stand of trees. Enoch, Annabelle, and Deborah wept as they surrounded a small body on the ground, burning embers and smoke swirling about. Mary walked closer, waving her arm in front of her face to combat the searing smoke that singed her eyes and throat. The body they encircled was Thad, dead from the cold and forced relocation.

January 5, 1839
Bell Detachment
Frog Bayou, Arkansas
Ozark Mountains

Consistent movement through the upper highlands and rising temperatures brought much-needed relief to the Bell party throughout the following week. Thad's body was one of several being hauled until they could find softer ground for burial. Universal fatigue had once again overtaken the travelers. Though some of the streams in and around Frog Bayou were frozen, they spotted running water in several places and the soldiers and Cherokees attempted to make use of the frigid waterways.

Captain Ambrose, Lieutenant Whitworth, Sergeant Thomas, and others were going up and down the line, informing the Indians that sometime during the next forty-eight hours they would be reaching their destination. The Cherokees looked at one another as if to say, "Really, around here? Is *this* supposed to be where we put down roots?" Wagons creaked along, animals moaned and panted. The burn victims were managing, but barely. Doc Arbogast taught others how to apply salves drenched in linseed oil, willow bark, and melted butter that had cooled.

The detachment continued its way northwest toward what Captain Ambrose called the Vineyard Township. There was a United States Post Office there, he said, where the long train of weary Cherokees would be dropped off. From there, he said, it was up to each family as to where they wanted to settle. The land would be, he said, "magnificently spread out." He told the McNairs and others to count their blessings and that they were "lucky" to have a choice of land for the taking.

"We'll see how lucky *that* is," Nick said as he glanced over at Mary, who was back on the buckboard at nearly seven months pregnant.

46

Weighing the Options

Present Day
Gadugi Center for the Healing Arts
Tulsa, Oklahoma

"How've you been?" said Paisley.

"Pretty good overall, I guess. The plant-based lifestyle is hard, takes commitment." Paisley nodded. "Interesting thing, though, is that I'm trimmer, but have maintained my strength. In fact, I might actually be stronger. I definitely recover faster from my workouts."

"Pretty common thing to hear," said Paisley.

"The protein shakes and those damn avocado sandwiches help me keep my fighting weight. If I'm not careful, though, I can drop too much."

"We can work on that. It's far easier to gain than to lose, as any American woman will tell you!" They laughed together. "So, Dr. Prescott's office sent me her latest recommendation. How do you feel about what she's saying?"

"Damn, Paisley, I don't *want* surgery, that's for sure. I was really hoping to avoid being cut on."

"Well, of course you were. Who would want it?"

"I guess I was hoping all these things we're doing would curtail that."

"Listen, Emmy, cancer is tricky. Whether it's a solid tumor like this one or liquid tumors like one might find in leukemia, malignant disease—that is, cancer, and benign disease or anything else non-cancerous, can be quite different. First, I think the Carcinosin is actually working. This particular homeopathic is derived specifically from breast tissue."

"I know—I researched it."

"I have no doubt. You're a beast."

"Wado!"

"Oh hush. My goal is to treat you as safely as possible. After that, the underlying objectives are to present options to cutting, burning, and poisoning. In my experience with cancer, sometimes cutting can't be avoided."

"Why the fuck didn't you tell me this earlier?" Paisley tilted her head, looking offended. "Okay, sorry. But I guess I thought we could avoid all of it."

"I don't make predictions because my fortune-telling license expired last year."

Busted, Emmy looked down and smiled, shaking her head.

"Okay, okay, I get it."

"I don't say one way or the other because no doctor can determine exactly how a patient will respond to treatment. You have, from everything I can see, a high-performing immune system. According to this last scan report from Dr. Prescott, your tumor has not grown significantly. Usually, by now—in my experience anyway—there's more growth. Thus, I think the diet, herbs, and the homeopathic have harnessed your immune system and slowed down the cancer. With this tumor you run the risk of metastasis whether you're doing chemo or what we're doing. Depends on the person's genetic genome makeup and their habits. Your habits are what we have changed, and that can alter the outcome."

"Right. I feel damn *good*, Doc. Most of the time, anyway. I mean, aside from the initial fatigue and realizing that something was wrong with me, you'd never know I was sick, ya know?"

"I know. And it has to be frustrating. Do you think you will go through with the lumpectomy? Remember, it's Dr. Prescott's strong opinion, but it's only her opinion. You can always seek out another one."

"Yeah, she said she was fine with me doing that." Paisley nodded with appreciation. "Do you think I should get another oncologist's opinion?"

"It's about what *you're* comfortable with, Emmy. It's your decision. It never hurts to get another, but then again, if you are happy with her—which you seem to be—and you respect her clinical judgment, you can forego a second opinion."

"What do *you* think, Paisley? I came to you for a reason."

"Well, if you opt to have it removed, it's out, right? Bye-bye. And we can continue to treat you as we have been. I'm guessing you're still opposed to chemo, even adjuvant chemo?"

"Hell yes."

"Kay-den. Again, up to you. If you choose not to have it removed, the downside is that you are watching and waiting within the realm of high risk, given this type of tumor. It may or may not spread. That can take a tremendous toll psychologically. I've seen it. And I believe extreme stress can not only cause cancer, but advance it. Right now, this isn't an advanced stage neoplasm. I would be more pressing in my comments if it were. But you're in spectacular shape. The recovery would be minimal. The choice is yours, Emmy. Be thankful you have one."

"Right. Well, new question, then?"

"Shoot."

"Are you familiar with fenbendazole and cancer?"

"Yes. That is, from what I've heard and read. It's a veterinary drug, of course, not approved for human use. But there are numerous anecdotal reports of success with certain cancers in people, others not so much. That's about the extent of my knowledge of it."

"Well . . ." said Emmy with evident anxiety. Paisley tilted her head again, this time with an inquisitive expression.

"Well, what?" she asked.

"I've been on it—for about a month." Emmy looked guilty, as if about to have her knuckles rapped.

"Okay."

"Yeah?"

"Look, it helps if I know everything you're taking, right? But it's your body, your life. If you start doing really crazy things like trying battery acid or drinking drain cleaner, I'm gonna refer you out, got it? But from what I gather, the fenben is a big up-in-the-air experiment right now. For some cancer patients, it has evidently worked, and there's documentation to back that up. For others, not so much. Thus, it's not that different than chemo or immunotherapy in that respect. The great advantage seems to be no side effects and the possibility of clearing the cancer. So, what can I really say?"

"Well, the reason I went ahead and told you is that I have felt *much* better since I started it. And it's readily available."

"That's great, Emmy. Better in what ways?"

"More energy. Better attitude. It's clearly doing *something*, I just don't know what, exactly."

"Okay. Well, I say go with that and see where it leads. We'll keep an eye on your liver enzymes. Even if you do the surgery and the tumor is out, I've seen suggestions that the fenben could possibly be used as a preventative measure. And from what little I've read, it seems to help with generating more of the P53 gene—the tumor-removing gene, if you will—thereby intercepting cancerous cells and, hopefully, preventing metastasis. So, keep me informed."

"Will do. I think, after processing this with you, I'm probably going to do the surgery. I just need a little time to think on it."

"Understood. Let me know what you decide. You can call and leave a message or send me a note through the portal."

"Will do," said Emmy, standing and thanking Paisley again.

Early Evening
McNair House
Muskogee, Oklahoma
District Four, Cherokee Nation

Emmy, Sandra, Molly, and Mike sat in the living room and discussed Emmy's options. Mike was quiet and reflective, as he often was. He and Emmy sat on the sofa, his arm around her considerable shoulders. She leaned into him and sighed. Sandra sat in the recliner, Molly on the family heirloom straight-backed chair.

"I think you should get that thing out, Em," said Molly, hands in her lap, legs crossed.

Mike winked at her with a silent "Thank you!"

"Hey, bitch," said Emmy, "I saw that. It's not like I'm refusing to do it, ya know," she added, eyeing her man.

"I know, I know," said Mike.

"Mom?" said Molly.

Sandra chose her words carefully, as usual. "Well, I would prefer you have it removed, Emmy. But it is, of course, your life. It just seems to me that the watching and waiting would be torturous." Emmy thought about this. "Are you going to get a second opinion from another cancer specialist?"

"Maybe, but I really like Dr. Prescott and it does seem to be something that's very straightforward. That is, a fairly simple surgery. She's probably done hundreds, if not thousands."

Mike nodded.

"She was checking you out, by the way, when you went with me for the follow-up," Emmy said to Mike, raising her eyebrows. "Scoping you with those green eyes of hers." Emmy narrowed her eyes at her beau.

"Of course she was," he joked. Sandra and Molly laughed. He winked at Sandra. "Always had a thing for blondes with dark eyebrows—what can I say?" Molly snickered again.

"Uh-huh," said Emmy. "And I'll snap that pretty woman's right arm off and wrap it around your neck and you can wear it as an ascot, Mr. PO-liceman!" Everyone laughed once more. Then Mike took Emmy's hand.

"I want you for life, not as a maybe-maybe for possibly a few years. Please have the surgery."

Molly leaned forward in her chair and cupped her hands over her face. "Omigod," she said. "That is so damn sweet." Sandra smiled and nodded.

Emmy smiled and looked adoringly at Mike. "Hmm. Watch what you wish for, Mikey-Mike. You might be stuck with me." She leaned in and kissed him.

Emmy pulled away from Mike with the same flare in her eyes that Molly had seen when she met Mike.

"Okay," she said softly, resting her head on his shoulder, "I'll do it."

Everyone looked relieved. Sandra reiterated her sincere feeling that Emmy's decisions were hers to make as she thought best. But she couldn't hide how relieved she was that Emmy was willing to undergo a surgery that would likely rid her of the cancer lurking within. She got up and walked to the sofa, holding out her arms. Emmy stood and hugged her.

"Thanks, baby. I'm glad you made this choice. I think it's one you won't regret."

Emmy held on to her mom, patting her back.

When they sat down, Emmy looked at Molly. "So . . . any news on college?"

"Had a follow-up meeting with Dean Adams. Talked about different scholarship possibilities."

"Yeah? Cool."

"Yeah, of course there's the American Indian College Fund, but we're looking into some things that look promising, so . . ." Molly shrugged.

"Still gonna go to school with *Clay*-ton?" Emmy teased.

"I don't know. I like the school, but I wonder if I should explore my options. I know it's late in the year to be deciding, so I'll have to go with whoever will consider me this year."

"Yes," chimed Mike, "I think you should consider your options, but nobody asked me."

"I'm asking, Mike. Why should I consider other places?"

"'Cause you don't know what you're missing otherwise, for one." He glanced sideways at Emmy. "For example, take this thing with Dr. Prescott. Suppose she *hadn't* whisked me off to Hawaii, how would she ever have known what she was missing?" he said with a grin. Molly cackled as she watched Emmy apply a nerve hold to Mike's shoulder. "Ahhhhhhh! Kidding, kidding, kidding, kidding," he said as she forced him to the floor in front of the sofa, patting his head like a dog.

"Yeah, you just stay put, my little bitch," she said as Sandra laughed, shaking her head.

"No, seriously," said Mike, rubbing his neck and shoulder, "by checking out other places, you're freeing up your mind to think in terms of possibilities. Examine things from all four corners of the window—it's an investigator thing."

"Ooooh, nice recovery," teased Emmy. "Good point, though," she added.

"Also," he continued, "wherever you decide to apply, everyone here wants you to have the safest experience possible. I can look further into wherever you decide to go if you want me to—you know, in terms of crime stats, assault cases, and so forth." Emmy rubbed his neck.

"Wow, thanks, Mike, that'd be cool," said Molly.

"Yes," said Sandra. "Thanks for offering that, Mike."

"You going to check out NSU?" asked Emmy. "The one in Broken Arrow has the undergrad ed major. Plus, I know Standingcloud would let you stay at his other place anytime. He's hardly ever there."

"Yeah, I was thinking NSU for sure, especially since that's where you're getting your master's."

"Oh, darn," said Emmy, snapping her fingers.

"What?" asked Molly with a look of concern.

"You've got to be a hot bitch to go there. Think you're up to the task?" Emmy teased.

"Oh eat shit, Em, really," said Molly with a roll of her eyes. Emmy laughed.

"I definitely think she's up for it," said Mike with another sly grin. "Okay! Kidding, kidding," he repeated after Emmy crabbed his shoulder again. Everyone laughed.

"Molly, have you thought much about out-of-state schools?" asked Sandra.

Molly glanced at Emmy. "Nah, Mom, not really."

"I don't want you to be thinking of the cost difference right now," her mom said. "We have options, like Mike has been saying."

"Yeah, I know, Mom. But I'd like to see what's offered around here first. Unless . . . you tryin' to get rid of me?"

"Well, if you must know—yes. I mean, pretty much since birth never mind . . ."

Emmy snorted.

"Hey now," said Molly proudly, "just for that, I'm never leaving! Gonna be here and spinster you out, grandma!"

"The hell you are," Sandra retorted. "I'll have Emmy hang you out the upstairs window again, have her sell you to Joey Littlejohn so he can trade you out at the airport." Emmy roared at that. Mike looked confused and Sandra told him the story of when Emmy was fifteen and Molly eight. Despite being picked on, Molly was happy to see Emmy laughing and having a good time relaxing.

"We're Cherokees, Nine-Speed. Wherever you decide to go—near or far, you'll be back eventually. That, my dear, is an Indian thing," Emmy said with a smile.

Molly smiled and nodded.

47

Not What We Painted Them to Be

January 6, 1839
Bell Detachment
Vineyard Township
State of Arkansas

"I must say, sir," said Sergeant Thomas, speaking to his lieutenant, "I'll be glad when this nightmare is over."

"I echo your sentiments, Sergeant. Not the type of duty that is particularly helpful or attractive. You've done well, Sergeant; your leadership is appreciated. Any idea what you will do upon completion of this removal?"

"Haven't given it much thought, sir. After this, I can confess, sir, that maybe the army life isn't for me—"

"Just hold it right there, Sergeant. I can tell you this: When the time comes for America to make more stringent decisions about what its soldiers are to do and where they are to perform, our country will need good men like yourself to step up and take the reins. Don't shortchange yourself, Sergeant."

"Yes, sir. Begging the Lieutenant's pardon, sir, this just wasn't what I had in mind, sir, regarding the Indians. Not at all. When our motherland has a clear and bitter enemy, I'm all in, sir. But this, sir . . . let's just say that I followed orders 'cause that's my job. The rest I could have done without. I'm loyal to the flag, sir, always will be. It's just that—well, the Cherokee— they're not quite what we painted them out to be, in my view. You can count on me, sir, should our paths cross again and I'm under your command—I want you to know that. I just hope that if I'm called to—as you say—step up in the future, that I'll have a clean conscience, as it were."

"Understood, Sergeant. I have to agree that it's been quite the experience. To tell you that I have no reservations about our role in this affair would be, well, let's just say, untoward in my best thinking and truth-telling. Perhaps you and I will have—at our next posting—the luxury of clarity and God's blessings."

"Here's to that day, sir, here's to that day," said Sergeant Thomas, raising his coffee cup to the lieutenant's.

Nick and Mary combined their blankets once again in a makeshift covering between two maple trees, tucking an exhausted Martha beneath in the best cocoon they could muster from available material. Despite Mary's emotional and physical distance during the recent nights, Nick felt a closeness that he couldn't quite articulate. It seemed to spring from the things they had all seen, heard, felt, and done. From his perspective, it had brought them closer as a family.

"Enoch," he said as Enoch prepared his own family for the evening, "Make sure there's enough bacon and coffee for the morning, hear me?"

"Yezzir," Enoch replied. "I'll head over to the food wagon now, sir."

"Do that."

"Good night, Annabelle," said Mary as she passed.

"Yess'm. Good night, Mizz. Mary." Annabelle glanced at Nick, then turned to Deborah and worked with her to lay out their sleeping blankets.

Enoch's family had been managing as well as could be expected since Thad's passing. Benjamin Ragsdale had managed to find softer ground for a burial later in the week after Thad died. Deborah seemed to accept her brother's death as a fact of life on the trail and had said little or nothing about it. Much like Pretty Water in the Morning transferring her emotional care to Old Nancy upon losing her baby, Deborah had spent more time taking care of Martha. Nick had also seen Mary talking more to Deborah, teaching her some of the intricacies of child care.

Captain Ambrose paid Mr. John B. Carns for a final run of supplies and delivered them to the Cherokees.

Nick lay in the cold night under the bright stars and wondered what tomorrow would bring.

48

He Belongs to Us

Oh, who am I who tower beside this goddess of the twilight air?
—George William Russell, on Aphrodite

Present Day
Dunham's Sports
Muskogee, Oklahoma

E mmy examined the market's latest sparring gloves with interest.

"These things are popular now, Storm," said Evan, the assistant store manager. "The wear is supposed to be a lot better than the older ones." He handed a pair to Emmy. She handled them with care, as she always did, seeing them as almost sacred. She slipped the right one on. She flexed her hand, simulated an uppercut, then tested the weight by holding her hand out, palm down.

"Hmm, I'll keep these in mind, Ev," she said, handing it back.

"Yeah, you just let me know, Emmy. Can always get a pair quick-like in here for you," he said with a flirty smile. She nodded, then retrieved her phone, which was vibrating in the back pocket of her Levis. It was Mike.

"Excuse me, gotta take this," she said, walking away and finding a quiet spot. "What's up, blue eyes?"

Bryan D. Jackson

"Hey, listen, can't talk long 'cause I'm booking somebody at the jail. Just talked to a sergeant I know with the PD. He was telling me that one of his guys filed an assault report about Devon."

"Dammit," said Emmy, "that little roid humper—"

"No-no, babe, that's not what I meant. Apparently, Devon's been doing really well. Robert, his program manager, says he's been trying hard and meeting his community service hours."

"Then what the hell is the—"

"Devon got assaulted, Em. Robert says the supervisor at the food bank told him a couple of Hispanic guys are bullying Devon. They wait for him on the back dock or nearby and one of them kicked Devon's ass the other day."

"But *why*?"

"Robert thinks they're trying to recruit him—maybe as a mule or something else, I don't know. When I get a chance, I'll look into it, okay? T.K. Harvey is a detective friend of mine and I'll ask him if he knows anything about these guys. Just kinda busy right now, Em, but I'll look into it, I promise."

"Okay. Thanks, Mike. And thanks for letting me know." Emmy had that tone in her voice. Mike was all too familiar with it. It was that little girl "I just shit in your gas tank, but I ain't tellin' you" tone.

"Em, you stay out of this, understand? I don't know if these guys are cartel or what. So until I know, just let me deal with it, okay?"

"Of course. We still on for Thai tonight?"

"I *mean* it, Goddess. Stay clear!"

"You didn't answer my question, you hunky special agent, you."

Mike sighed. "Yeah," he said, "Thai it is. I *love* you, Storm, ya know?"

"Love you too, my little blue-eyed, badge-toting sex kitten." She made a kissing sound, hanging up before he could respond.

Mike hung up, and commenced a second search of the arson suspect he and Leon just brought into the sally port.

A woman carrying a bag of groceries and holding hands with her little boy walked down the sidewalk past *Ned Christie* as Emmy shifted into park just outside the food bank. She sat for a moment, thinking. Just gonna check on him, that's all, she told herself. She glanced at her to-go bag, opened it, pulled out her Smith & Wesson Shield 9mm and its holster, strapped it to her belt at four o'clock, and sat back, thinking again. She reached around to the back seat for one of the plaid cotton button-down shirts she always had on hand. She put it on, buttoning it just a few slots from the bottom, then got out of her car. She walked down the street to the food bank entrance and pulled open the door.

"May I help you, ma'am?" a woman asked as Emmy came down the hall.

"Yes, I'm looking for Devon Farmer," said Emmy.

"I think he's in the canned goods room. Are you a relative?"

"You could say that," Emmy replied. The woman took her back, but Devon wasn't there.

"Well," said the woman politely, "I know he's here. Just saw him. He could be in the basement. I'll go check." Just then Emmy thought she heard Devon's voice and a shout out back. She headed that way. "Ma'am! You can't go back there," the woman said, as Emmy started down the hallway. "Mr. Jennings!" she called. Mr. Jennings appeared from his office down the hall. He was about forty, a tall, lanky gentleman with glasses and a bow tie.

"I'm Mr. Jennings. May I help you, Miss?" He was blocking the way, looking down at Emmy.

"No, I'm good," said Emmy. "Just looking for Devon, but I hear him now. Thanks." She started moving again. The man stopped Emmy by placing both hands on her shoulders.

"I'm afraid you'll have to leave, ma'am. No one is permitted beyond this point."

"Move, Jenny," said Emmy, plastering Mr. Jennings to the wall like a paper doll with her own hands and a look that seemed to scare him.

Emmy stepped out on the back loading dock. Sure enough, two Hispanic men were intimidating Devon. As she approached, she could hear one of them say, "Pene *pequena!*" inferring that Devon was a little dick. He seized Devon by his shirt and shook him, then slapped him. Devon looked scared. "You comin' work for *us*, chico!" the second one said, leaning hard on Devon's shoulder.

"Nephew-cousin!" shouted Emmy as she approached the men. She moved in quickly and hugged Devon, patting his back.

As she pulled away, Devon looked confused, but stammered, "Uh, hi . . . Auntie?" The two men, who appeared to be in their early twenties, looked at each other before undressing Emmy with their eyes. One of them instantly recognized her.

"Que pasa?" Emmy inquired with a nod, giving the men one chance, and one chance only, at civility.

"Ahhh," said the larger one, pointing to Emmy. "I seen her, Paco, ona tee-vee!" They both grinned. "Es Cherokee tormenta!" he shouted, eyeing her boobs. "Umm . . . sabrosa! Apuesto que ella es buena, amigo!" Oh, Emmy thought, you *really* shouldn't have said that.

"Si, si!" said the other one. "La bonita boxeador! Umm, yum-yum!" he continued with a leer. He was sizing her up, nodding confidently and rolling his shoulders.

"Oh, si," said the larger one as he reached over and, disturbingly, brushed back Emmy's braid. "Her*mosa* mujer," he went on, "tetas calientes!" fondling his crotch and laughing with his friend.

Emmy employed her favorite starter switch—her right inverted punch to the solar plexus, this one sounding like Rocky Balboa pounding a slab of meat.

"AYEYYYE!" the man yelled as he bent double, as if he might also vomit. Before Devon could register what was happening, Emmy stepped in and seized the man by the right arm with her left, her right arm behind his back, and hurled him violently to the ground with her signature hip throw. "Mi madre!" the thug screamed as his left shoulder hit the cement like a cinder block. Emmy turned to the other man who, though his eyes were wide with shock, charged her.

"*Puta!*" he yelled as he lunged at her.

Emmy did a rapid cross-step side kick, a kick which generated enormous power. She booted the man back a good eight feet and he crashed into a stack of empty milk crates and spent boxes of things like Vanilla Wafers, Quaker Oats, Fruit Loops, Pampers, and Planters Peanuts cans.

"Hijo de puta!" he moaned as he rolled over in the trash. "Ah, *sheet!*" He clutched his abdomen and groaned.

As the larger man struggled to get up, nursing his bruised shoulder, Emmy noticed the crowd gathering at the door of the loading dock. Devon stood there, dumbfounded. Emmy was done playing around. She turned toward the larger guy, pulling up her shirt to reveal the Shield 9mm, draping it around the pistol for easy access. Devon looked as if he might shit his pants again. Emmy kept her hand affixed to the weapon as she heard gasps from the doorway.

"Listen," she demanded of the two men, "¡ban*didos*! I have a relationship—*relationship*, she emphasized, "con la policia! You leave this man alone. He belongs to us, comprende?" When the big one saw the gun he raised his left hand, still holding his injured shoulder.

"Si, si," he said, backing away. He scurried to help his friend, who probably had a broken rib or two, based on the fact that he couldn't stand up all the way. Both men were hunched over.

"You two motherfuckers go back to your goddamn bosses or whoever the hell it is and tell them this chico is hands off, you got it?" They nodded. "You mess with him again and the 'hermosa boxeador' is gonna fuck you up *gran momento*! Now get the fuck out of here," she roared, drawing the Shield, but pointing it downward in a two-handed professional manner. "¡A*hora*!" she shouted with fire in her eyes. They ran.

Emmy holstered the weapon immediately and turned to the staff. "Where the hell is your Mr. Jennings?"

"Right here," the man squeaked. He'd been hiding behind some women, mortified by Emmy's athletics. Emmy shook her head. She turned to Devon and gently touched his jaw, turning his head to get a good look at the black eye the men had given him earlier in the week. She patted his cheek.

"Understand something, Mr. Jennings. Hey! Put that damn phone down," she said, pointing to a woman trying to record everything. The woman lowered it. "Dig this shit, *Mr. Jennings*. I am the one who recommended to the judge that Devon do this work. You, with your dork-ass bow tie, are responsible for creating a safe environment here. You failed to do that, and I'm gonna be talking to Judge Boyer about it. Maybe even a reporter or two. You *knew* these men had assaulted Devon, but you still didn't do shit, you pencil-pushing unicorn!

"I know you called the cops already, so here's what you're gonna do when they roll up. You're going to tell them everything here is fine. Also, for any of you who got this on video, tell your Mr. skirt-hiding-Jennings here for me that if I see it anywhere—social media or TV or in your mother's damn underwear, I will bring a lawsuit against this food bank and the only food you'll be handing out anytime soon will be to the damn rats and raccoons who've taken over the place after we're done with you, you following me?" She motioned to Devon to come with her.

"Well," said Mr. Jennings, holding up his hands defensively, "we have no intention of broadcasting anything, right ladies?" They all looked shocked and just nodded. "I didn't know. You can certainly understand—"

"Just get out of the way!" Emmy barked, escorting Devon back through the building. An officer showed up as Emmy was walking Devon to her car. She turned around and stared at Mr. Jennings, standing in the doorway. She could hear him telling the officer it was merely a false alarm, that he had been worried about thieves.

"Get in the car," she said to Devon. He seemed tentative.

"I thought . . . thought you didn't want me in the car with you," he said meekly.

"I don't. Now get in the car, bitch."

Once on the road, Emmy smiled at Devon through her shades as she drove. "Relax, chebon," she said. Devon exhaled. "As you know," she began, "I'm not happy with you. But you didn't deserve any of that shit. Who are those assholes?"

"The Latinos?"

"Yeah, not that numb nuts pantry boss."

"I don't know, Emmy, I swear. They just fucking showed up one day. It's like, like they could smell it on me or something. I didn't do anything wrong, Emmy. I've been complying with the court conditions. Look, I know you and Marshal Callie cut me a big break, and I appreciate it. I'm clean, too, Em, honest. I don't know *why* those guys are hounding me. I didn't wanna say anything about them beating on me because I figured no one would believe me. It's all so fucked up."

Emmy focused on the road.

"How's Molly doing?" He seemed sincere.

"She's actually doing well, Devon. She asked about you the other day."

"Yeah?"

"I told her I didn't know, that I thought you needed to be left alone while you do your time, so to speak. Told her I thought you probably need a lot of time to think."

"Yeah, I guess that's true," he said, fingering his black eye. "I heard she's seeing some college guy."

She glanced over at him, studying him behind her shades. "Careful there, Dev."

"What? No, I'm glad for her, really."

"*Really?*" she said, not buying any of it.

"No, for real, Em. This program's been good. The whole restoration piece is important—I know it's serious business. I just hope she'll forgive me someday is all."

"Well, she's the forgiving type, remember—kind heart?" He smiled and nodded.

"It's that Blackfox guy, isn't it?"

"*Dev . . .*"

"No, it's just what I heard is all."

"Heard from whom?"

"I dunno. Some guy at a stomp dance, I think."

"Easy there, Dev. Just focus on what you're supposed to be doing. Just stay—"

"I am! Seriously, just something somebody—"

"And don't fucking interrupt me, you little squirrel."

"Sorry." He slid down in the seat.

"Just remember what you did, Devon, just keep that uppermost in your mind. Don't lose sight of the sin you committed. Also, know that Clay is nobody to mess with. He can fuck you up, too, just so you know."

"Yeah, I heard," he sighed. "Black belt, right?"

She glanced his way again and smiled, shaking her head. "So you've been spying, have you?"

"Oh, come on, Em, nah! Have you forgotten what a small, chickenshit town this is?"

"Well, you've got a point there, I must say," she said, zooming past a fat Choctaw man in a 1990s Mercedes. She looked over at Devon to catch his eye.

"What?" he whined.

"You keep focused, Devon. You stay the hell *away* from Molly, and you work on how you can be a real guy to the next girl—like we talked about. Right?"

"Yeah," he said with what looked like a truly sincere expression and smile. "I'll try."

"Kay-den." She studied him. "You know, you're gonna do a lot better for yourself if you stay clean until you finish this program and get some time behind you."

"Yeah, I know. I've been clean three months now, easy."

"No, I mean clean with women. I don't know and I don't *wanna* know what you guys talk about in those meetings, or what suggestions they offer, but you best leave it to jacking off until you get some serious time behind you." He slid down in the seat again, feeling self-conscious. "Look at it this way—at least you eliminate the possibility of any STDs until they decide that your head is on right. Don't go mucking things up even by doing legit sex. It's not worth it, kid."

"Yeah, I guess that makes sense," he admitted.

"Don't mess this up, Devon. It's the only chance you're gonna get. Can't help you any more after this."

"Hey, Emmy," he said, waiting for her to look at him. She slowed to a stop at a traffic light not far from his place, then looked his way.

"Yeah?"

"*Wado* for what you did back there, really. I'm grateful. I know it wasn't just for me that you did it, but I appreciate it anyway."

"You're welcome, Devon."

"That was actually pretty fucking awesome!" he said, laughing and shaking his head.

"Well," she said, turning the corner and pulling up to his house, "I don't like that shit happening in my community. We'll find out who those guys are and keep them off your back. As much as I've despised you for what you did to Molly, you're still one of us, Devon, still Cherokee. Live up to it; don't be a shit-ass."

He nodded appreciatively, then unfastened his seat belt. "I'll keep trying, Em, I promise."

"Okay, Dev, good to hear. I'll talk to Mike—see about getting you another project. I don't want you back at the food bank. They'll find something else. But whatever it is, Dev, *finish* it."

"Yes, ma'am. I mean, uh, Emmy," he said with a smile, then he got out of the Mustang and went into his house. Emmy drove away.

49

End of the Line

January 6, 1839
Bell Detachment
Vineyard Post Office
State of Arkansas

The Treaty Party of Cherokees arrived short of their destination.

Captain Ambrose had since dismounted on the grounds of the local post office, informing as many of the Cherokees as he was able that this was it: all army assistance stopped here and now. Ambrose seemed pleased with himself that he had managed to escort the Treaty Party all this way without encountering any detachments under Chief Ross's supervision, despite stopping short of Indian Territory.

"This is it, people!" he kept yelling as he and others went up and down the line, spreading what was in their mind the best possible news. "The end of the line!"

Nick and George Welch stood and stared out at the landscape. "This is *what*?" said Welch. "Talk about the end of the goddamn line," he added. They scratched their heads as they looked out at the barren countryside, dotted with a few elm trees and post oaks, with the wagons, horses, and people seeming like an unnatural invasion. He and Nick just shook their heads and began preparing for disbandment. Most of the Cherokees wandered about in a haze, fatigued, torn, bitter, and grief-stricken. Augustine bounded from the wagon and surveyed his surroundings. Unimpressed, he dropped the biggest load he could muster center stage. Kicking his feet, he walked several yards and rolled in what appeared to be grass, christening his new home, before standing again and shaking.

Mary looked around the grounds of the Vineyard Post Office and realized she was too tired to cry.

50

Over My Dead Body

There is no mercy in slavery. The kind master is a tyrant and a usurper.

—Rev. Daniel Butrick on the Trail of Tears, Friday, August 24, 1838

Friday, January 18, 1839
Da-li-gwa (Tahlequah)
Thirty Miles Northwest of Disbandment
Indian Territory

Nick, Mary, Martha, Enoch, Annabelle, Deborah, and Augustine rolled into Da-li-gwa on a late sunny afternoon. The area was bustling with activity, and a large sign, hastily hammered into the ground on a feeble stake, read:

Negro Auction

T'marr Aft'noon, Jan 19th 1839

Bring yor best niggers

"Looks like we might wanna take advantage of that," said Nick, nodding at the sign and addressing Mary. "Come a long way with these people. Might need some new stock for this new territory." Mary said nothing. Enoch and Annabelle, obviously within hearing distance, stared off into the dry, dusty wasteland that was the Indian Territory for which the government had promised the Indians five million dollars. Deborah held Martha in her lap. Augustine, exhausted and panting, put his head down and sighed.

A U.S. Marshal for the Indian Territory approached on horseback.

"Creek, Cherokee, or Choctaw?"

"Cherokee," replied Nick.

"Good enough then. You're gonna be down there, on the south end of town. Some trees on the west end of that. They should do ya until you can get proper housing set up. As you can see, things are busy here. I got all I can keep up with. Any trouble, you get arrested. Anything more, I shoot to kill. Understood?"

Nick nodded.

"I presume these niggers are yours?" the marshal said.

"Indeed they are."

"Well, you probably saw the sign coming in. You might see fit to sell out. They're lookin' pretty ragged after your journey." Enoch held his head high.

"Appreciate it, Marshal," said Nick with a tip of his hat. The lawman nodded in return, and rode on.

The McNairs stopped off for supplies. Mary noticed a sign in a hardware store window that advertised a "Lady's Special." She knew what that meant. After surveying the surroundings and the many aggressive-minded people hustling about, some shoving others out of their way as they scurried down the main street, she left Martha with Deborah while Nick was two doors down, buying dried beef and corn. She entered the store.

A man who appeared to be in his early forties stood behind the counter. No one else was around. He took one look at Mary and tipped the bill of his visor to her.

"Why, good afternoon, Madam."

"Good afternoon."

He examined her in a curious but respectful way.

"Cherokee, I presume?"

"Yes."

"And just when might your baby be ready to grace our presence, if I may ask?"

"Not soon enough, if the concern be mine," she said, her fatigue obvious. He let out a good-natured, hearty laugh.

"Well," he said kindly, "awfully pretty, ma'am, if you'll permit me. Sad to say, we don't get many like you 'round here." He smiled and nodded.

"Thank you. Above all, I am a Christian woman. Now show me that gun."

He smiled again, pleased his marketing technique with the sign was working. He retrieved one from underneath his counter.

"This here is a Queen Anne Toby, ma'am. Fine as they come." He handed it to her. Familiar with firearms since childhood, she examined the piece. Mary realized then and there she was tired of not getting what she wanted. She decided that she wasn't above using her considerable physical attributes to get what she needed to make it to the next hour of her life. The store owner explained the particular flint-locking mechanism of the pistol, how to keep the powder dry, etc. She handed it back to him and seized him with her dark eyes. She threw some bills on the counter that more than covered the expense.

"You'll load it for me, then."

"Yes, of course," he said.

"You'll make it right for me, won't you," she said, in more of a statement than a question. She lightly caressed his hand with a sultry look, slowly opening and closing her eyes.

"Why, yes ma'am!" the man said sincerely. Mary was a twenty-four-year-old pregnant woman at the height of her femininity.

"Good," she said kindly. "Do it now."

"Yes, ma'am. Holster-pouch as well, I presume?" He thought for a second. "If you'll forgive me, ma'am, being with child, we might have to consider an adjustment of some sort."

Appearing anxious, he dropped the box the gun came in. Then he dropped the bills she splayed on the counter for him. "Um," he asked nervously, "where, ah, how—that is—what would be your preferred method of carry, ma'am?"

"Hmm," she began, "what about . . . here?" She pulled back her saddle dress, exposing her upper thigh.

"That m-m-might just w-work," he jabbered. "I would hafta—hafta, um, well my goodness!" he said with a head scratch. "Yes, yes. You know, I think I have just the thing," he said happily. He disappeared into a small room and returned with a box. "Another lady's special," he said with a conspiratorial wink. Inside was a garter-type strap made to encircle the thigh and hold a small money pouch, but he said he could most likely alter it to hold the Toby.

"Fine!" she said brightly. "You'll adjust it then, to suit me."

"Um, uh, why of course. I have a Chesterman spring tape measure here somewhere," he said, looking around hurriedly. "Ah yes! Here it is." He held it up, then seemed to panic. "Uh, I, oh dear," he said, thinking about his limited options. She smiled at him, holding out her hand.

"I'll do the measuring," she said softly.

"Why yes thank God," he squeaked in one breath. "I mean, yes, that seems most appropriate." The man furiously fingered his wedding ring as Mary turned toward the hammers and nails to measure her upper leg.

Within ten minutes, Mary had made her first purchase in the new territory. She thanked the man and left, her new Toby strapped and secure.

Saturday Afternoon, January 20, 1839
Da-li-gwa (Tahlequah)
North End, Slave Auction
Indian Territory

"Folks," said the conductor, "this here's a 'highest bidder wins' auction. May the luckiest man win his best workers, am I right?" The crowd buzzed with chatter, laughter, and the occasional nasty comment regarding the various Negros on display.

"We should get in on this," said Nick, looking things over. He and Mary stood just outside the auction block on the edge of the town district. Nick noticed the marshal off to the side, keeping an eye on things. Mary stood there, noncommittal. "What's the matter?" he asked.

Silence.

"Bring your niggers forward, people! Don't be shy!" the conductor shouted. "Here's some fine Negroes here—from the Lower Carolina, as I understand it. Take note of the fine features and hard muscles of this lad, yessir!" He fingered the arm of a teen who looked to be about sixteen. A burly man who appeared to be Creek approached. He motioned with his arm.

"Turn," he said, talking to the young man. "Go on, boy, turn around." The young man did as he was told. "Uh-huh," said the Creek. "Bend over, nigger, lemme get a look at yer backside." The young man bent shyly at the waist. When he didn't bend far enough, the burly Creek struck his back, forcing him over. "Uh-huh, I see," the man grunted. "Four dollars and not a goddamn penny more!" he yelled to the conductor.

"Going once . . ." said the conductor. "Going twice . . ." One white woman looked interested, but changed her mind. "Sold to the gentleman with the earring!" yelled the conductor. The Creek reached up and grabbed the young black man and dragged him away by the arm.

The McNairs brought Enoch, Annabelle, and Deborah, and to Mary it was if they each took on a different, almost foreign, persona. They became detached, staring at the auction block with what appeared to be no emotion whatsoever. Nick seemed unmoved by the entire affair. He was used to participating in auctions and it had never occurred to him to consider the situation from a slave's point of view. Augustine had tagged along, and he whined each time someone manhandled a slave.

The conductor presented a new group of slaves, a family similar to Enoch's. The man stood in the center of the platform. "Gotcha a prime Negro here—appears to be about thirty-five years of age. Seems strong, no scars or blemishes. Feel free to check his teeth now!" The man sold rapidly for seven dollars and twenty-five cents. The next slave to be presented was a pretty girl the same age as Deborah. She stood front and center, her arms instinctively protecting her chest until the conductor slapped them down with a pointing rod.

"Yes indeed, my friends," he hollered. "Now we're talking, am I right, gentlemen?" The crowd, mostly men, hooted with laughter. The girl was told to turn, show her teeth, bend over, speak, and then to remove her dress. A number of people—men and women—stepped up to handle the girl, roughly turning her and using vulgar language to tell her what to do.

Mary heard one man in the audience say, "She's a good one. Get her now and you can get some decent mulatto children out of her. Staff that farm of yours, Harry, in another ten years." Another one said, "I'd bring her home with me, but my wife is already jealous; she's all yours, boys!" Mary closed her eyes and recalled the night in the barn.

"Well," said Nick, spitting out a wad of tobacco, "looks like we should throw our hats in there before people start leaving. Enoch, step on up and get ready."

"No," said Mary, staring at the next group of Negros about to be sold. Augustine whined.

"Whad'ya mean, no? I'm saying we gotta put these folks up on the auction block 'fore too many people scatter." He motioned for Enoch to move forward. Annabelle looked deep into Nick's eyes, no doubt hoping to find an ounce of understanding. She found none. She looked at Mary. To Mary, it seemed in that moment that she was looking into the eyes of the Mary who stood beside the empty tomb and was the first to announce the resurrection of Christ. Annabelle and Mary locked eyes in what could only have been a spiritual relationship. Deborah looked scared, watching the conductor and some other men examine the penis of one Negro boy, pulling on it and then slapping the boy when he resisted.

"I would prefer not to," Mary replied.

"Prefer not to? What the hell are you talking about?"

"It's not a necessary exchange at this time," she replied, trying to appeal to her husband's sense of business. Annabelle looked on, catching Mary's gaze with each opportunity.

"Oh, it's definitely necessary, Mary. The amount of work we're gonna have to do to rebuild is unimaginable right now. We're gonna need some new blood." Turning to Enoch, he said, "Nothing personal, Enoch—just business."

"Yezzir," was all Enoch could say, his face filled with the loss of all hope.

"All right, now, y'all go on—move up to the line now," said Nick, trying to ease the blow. He gently guided Deborah forward. Augustine lay down and whimpered.

"I said no," Mary insisted, and she walked over and stood near Annabelle without even realizing she did it.

"And I'm sayin' *yes,* woman," Nick insisted. He moved to Mary and grabbed her arm, pulling her back. "Over here, out of the horse path," he said, keeping her out of the way of passing horses and riders. "Listen," he said quietly. Enoch and family were still close. "I don't know what's gotten into you the latter portion of this trip, but we got niggers here that need to be passed on, understand?"

"Negros, please."

"What?"

"I don't like that word. Never did. You know that. Father taught me it was wrong. They're properly Negros."

"Yeah, yeah—all right then! But they've been *our* Negros for a bit too long now, Mary. They need to move on, understand?"

"Like us? That what you're saying?"

"Huh?"

"*Removed* I believe is the word the government used for us, was it not?"

"What the hell?"

"I'm saying I would prefer not to, Nicholas, not at this time," she said, glancing over at Annabelle, who had a pleading yet almost radiant look about her.

"I don't understand you!" he said in a quiet but aggravated tone. *"That family is being sold—today."*

"Over my dead body," asserted Mary, challenging her husband in a way she never had before and flanking Enoch's family. Annabelle inhaled, putting her hand to her breast. Enoch glanced at his wife, looking afraid. Augustine raised his head.

"*What* the hell did you just say to me, woman?" said Nick, seizing Mary's upper arm. He glared down at her, the passing townsfolk taking notice.

"Please let go of me, Nick," she said, looking down at his grip on her. Augustine stood and growled.

"I'm the man in this family, Mary," he blurted, "and what I say about *Negro* workers goes, you understand me?" He spoke as if she were a child, yanking on her arm until it hurt. He gave the dog a hard look, then turned back to Mary. "Being an impertinent *bitch* ain't helpin' your cause none." He glowered at her, looming, trying to intimidate.

Contemptuous, fed up with the entire removal experience to date, and void of anything further resembling patience, Mary decreed, "*Unhand* me, Nicholas McNair, or you are going to have a mighty hard time facilitating your water flow in your old age as you hobble about the new Indian Territory."

Nick glanced down and there, shoved flush against his scrotum, was the Queen Anne Toby derringer. He swallowed air as he slowly looked back up at his wife. Her left hand was over her unborn child, as if to protect it, her right hand hidden within his trousers, she was pressing so hard. She calmly blinked her lovely eyes twice. Ears upright, Augustine sat back on his haunches and cocked his head to the left.

Enoch and Annabelle's eyes widened and Deborah refocused her attention on the adults long enough to drop her jaw in shock. She was holding Martha and abruptly turned her in the other direction so the child would not witness this bizarre interaction. Nick gritted his teeth and looked down at his wife.

"*Think* about what you're doing here," he said, trying to bluff her with his eyes. Augustine cocked his head to the right.

"I *have* thought about it," she insisted, repositioning the little pistol to rest on his penis. "And you'd better pray that I don't sneeze, or you call me a bitch again anytime soon, lest you find yourself bowlegged and wearing that little fellow as a necktie the rest of your natural-born life."

"Oh, *Lort Jesus* at the river Jordan!" said Annabelle before she slapped her hand over her own mouth.

"Now unhand me, Nick. Do it *now*." Augustine poked his head forward with an inquisitive look, eyes moving from Mary to Nick and back again, as if intensely curious as to which of his masters would emerge victorious.

Nick smiled uneasily, raising his hands above his head momentarily. "Okay, *okay*," he said, his voice no louder than a prayer. Mary looked up at him with disappointment.

"Delilah Vann McNair would be ashamed of you," she said with a brief shake of her head, pulling Nick's mother into the argument. Nick sighed and looked down, abashed. Augustine stuck his tongue out and panted, as if smiling.

"Yeah, I suppose you're right. I'm sorry." He shook his head in frustration. "Mary, just what in the hell do you propose we do with them?"

"They're coming with us." Mary looked over at the family and nodded. "You're coming with us," she said with authority. Nick swallowed hard as he watched the love of his life glide back her saddle dress and insert the Toby in its little holster. Mary smiled inwardly, knowing that he couldn't figure out how the hell she had gotten that gun. He threw up his hands.

"Uh, well shit, I guess you're comin' with us," said Nick to Enoch.

"Why thank ya, sir, thank ya much," said Enoch, taking his wife's hand and eyeing Mary with awe. Enoch wore an amused smile as he moved along behind Nick. "C'mon, girl," he said to Deborah, now with Martha riding piggyback, taking her hand as the family shadowed their enslavers back toward the south end of town. Augustine padded along at the rear, tail wagging.

51

Cherokee Afternoon

I saw heaven standing open
and there before me was a white horse,
whose rider is called Faithful and True . . .
—Revelation 19:11, NIV

Present Day
Mid-July
Community Medical Center
Operating Room Recovery Waiting Room
Tulsa County, Oklahoma
District Thirteen, Cherokee Nation

Molly, Mike, and Sandra waited as all families do. It wasn't a busy afternoon and only one other family was present. The staff got them acclimated, and soon the TV was boring Molly to death. Mike kept checking his phone for work. Molly placed her hand over his and said, "Please don't, okay? You're making me nervous, Mike." He smiled, putting the phone away, and kissed her cheek.

"She's *everything* to me, sis, you know that, right?" She nodded nervously. He hugged her. Sandra smiled and picked up a *Woman's Day*. A long waiting table—serving as some sort of pseudo-coffee table—rested in front of them. On one corner sat a yellow bag that could only have been Bananagrams.

"Wanna play?" asked Molly after listening to one more commercial about medication that could give a guy a hard-on for four hours and were that the case he should surely panic and head for the emergency room. Mike nodded and they played while Sandra read and Emmy slept.

Community Medical Center
Operating Room #2

Emmy closed her eyes and counted backward from ten as requested, the anesthesia doing its thing.

"Greetings, all," said Dr. Prescott, leaning over to look at Emmy as she fell into the typical deep sleep.

"Afternoon, Doc," said Rice Meadows, the surgical technician.

A nurse anesthetist named Louisa shouted, "Hello, Dr. Prescott!" from the other side of the room.

"Linda," said Cathy Sixkiller, the primary OR nurse, with a smile of acknowledgment.

"Dr. Prescott, how you be?" smiled Dr. Stan Howard, the anesthesiologist.

"Bright-eyed and bushy-tailed," Dr. Prescott replied.

"Want these yet?" asked Dr. Feathers, scrubbing in as her assistant. Dr. Prescott shook her head at the instruments.

"Okay, team, let's go over it," she said. "Should be short and sweet." They briefly discussed Emmy, the surgery, the reason for it, and, for the record, who was doing what.

"Wow, what a beautiful woman," Rice said as she stared at Emmy's face beneath the oxygen mask.

"She is that," Dr. Prescott agreed. "A lovely patient overall. Master's degree candidate. Keeps me on my toes, I must say."

"How so?" asked Dr. Feathers.

"You should see this babe, sitting in my office, flexing her biceps, asking me these graduate-level trick-ass questions just to see if I know what the hell I'm talking about," she said, a smile behind her surgical mask. Everyone laughed and Dr. Prescott requested a scalpel as things got underway.

"Ah," said Dr. Howard, "one of *those*." He grinned, leaning over Emmy and adjusting her medication slightly as the music in the background was switched to Diana Krall. Krall's version of "Just the Way You Are" pulsed through the speakers.

"Oh, yeah, trust me," Dr. Prescott responded. "She's *intimidating*, and I don't say that lightly. Whoever crosses this chick had better own a good pair of running shoes." The group laughed again. Dr. Prescott made a perfect incision, and the operation proceeded as the group discussed their families, pets, and other aspects of their lives, eventually returning to Emmy.

"Anybody see that fight?" asked Dr. Howard. The women shook their heads. Carlos, a young assistant circulating nurse, was assisting Cathy. He was new and had been quiet during the introductions.

"I did," he said shyly.

"You're among friends here, chebon," said Cathy with a wink. Carlos smiled.

"Whad'ya think?" asked Dr. Howard.

"She's somethin'!" said Carlos.

Dr. Howard nodded. "She beat the hell out of LaToya Ortiz, a ranked contender. Ortiz was trash-talking the whole time—even at the weigh-in. She's the UFC bad girl at the moment." Carlos smiled and nodded.

Fully animated, Dr. Howard went on. "She hit that woman three times in the space of four seconds, straddled her neck like a rabid squirrel, then *flipped* that girl with her feet by her head after doing this crazy carnival stunt by bending backward like one of those flex-action Marvel characters for kids. Never saw anything like it in my life!" The women were laughing, and Cathy told Dr. Howard to calm down because they couldn't have *his* elevated blood pressure affecting Emmy's. "Just sayin'!" he added.

"That's my girl," said Dr. Prescott, smiling and leaning in toward Emmy to get a better view of an area where she needed more light.

"People went insane, especially the Natives," Dr. Howard added. "The women were cheering their—Cathy, do your thing—you know what I'm talking about." Cathy smiled as she wiped some blood from Emmy's torso and quickly stepped back from the table.

"Ley-ley-ley-ley-ley-ley!" she sang, her mask vibrating, the high-pitched yelp competing with Diana Krall. The group laughed again as Cathy stepped back to the table.

"Yeah yeah yeah!" said Dr. Howard, smiling at the patient again and shaking his head.

"Easy does it, Stan the Man," teased Dr. Prescott as she fished the tumor from where she had snipped it. "No bird-dogging my patient." She smiled and shook her head as she examined the specimen. She pointed to the edges and addressed Dr. Feathers, an intern. "See this? This part is what I was telling you about earlier," she said, handing it off to Carlos to take to pathology. "You can close, if you want," she added. Dr. Feathers nodded.

"Omigod," said Rice, a short woman in her mid-twenties, dropping the last of the instruments in the dirty surgical tray. "What *is* it with men and hot women who can fight?" She shook her head.

"Big-time fantasy," said Cathy. "Just ask my damn husband," she intoned with a sigh. More laughter. She glanced over at Dr. Howard. "What's wrong, Stan?" He looked concerned.

"Probably nothing. Seemed for a second like she was going into V-fib. Looking better, though." Dr. Prescott frowned. "I think it's okay, Linda. Have no fear," he said in a mock announcer's tone, raising his right hand as if speaking at a UFC fight, "The Cherokee Storm is, and will remain, undefeated!"

Monitors chimed and Emmy's blood pressure dropped like a rock.

"Goddammit," said Dr. Howard. The heart monitor began its ugly, vertical zigzag. "She's in shutdown mode."

"Rachel, let me finish," said Dr. Prescott to Dr. Feathers. She speed-sutured, yelling, "Cathy!" Cathy nodded and ripped off her gloves, picking up the OR phone and stating, "Code Blue, OR Two, Code Blue, OR Two!" She turned to the team and announced, "Retrieving crash cart!" and sped away.

"Beginning CPR!" Dr. Feathers shouted.

Community Medical Center
OR Recovery Waiting Room

Molly smiled at Mike as she chirped, "Bananas!"

"Did they just say something about OR Two?" said Mike, after thinking about it. Sandra put her magazine in her lap and looked back as a team of men and women in scrubs ran down the hallway. The automatic doors swung open and they raced toward the operating rooms suite. Mike and Sandra looked at each other. "Don't worry, Sandra, I'll go check. Be right back."

Molly sat with her mouth open, she and her mom locking eyes. Sandra soon turned, though, seeing if she could spot Mike. He was talking to a nurse or tech at the desk.

Get on your knees.

Molly stood and caught the eye of Mike, who was on his way back. "They said she did fine with the surgery, but something about her blood pressure at the end. They're saying not to worry, so . . ."

Sandra stood. "Is she out of surgery?" Mike shrugged. A woman in a scrub shirt with baby animals on it approached.

"Mrs. McNair?"

"Yes?"

"They said that Emmy did well with the tumor—it's out."

"Oh, thank heavens," said Sandra. Mike knew better.

"What's *wrong*, though? What happened in there?" he demanded in his cop voice. This frightened Molly.

Get on your knees.

"Please," said the nurse, "sit down."

Now, Pretty Feet.

Molly dropped to her knees in front of the chair she had been sitting in. Molly leaned into the chair, crossed her hands, and closed her eyes. This caused Sandra to panic. "Oh, my God, what's wrong? Please tell us," said Sandra, turning to the nurse.

"Emmy may have thrown a clot; we're not sure." Mike sat, leaned forward, and squeezed the sides of his head. Molly moaned. "Her blood pressure dropped without explanation and they had to call a code. That's all I know right now, but I promise to keep you informed." As Sandra started asking the typical family questions to which no answers existed, Molly went deep within her mind to another world.

It's about what you bring to the table, Pretty Feet. Always has been, always will be.

Community Medical Center
Operating Room #2

The medical emergency team arrived. Dr. Stanford, head of the team, attempted to take charge.

"I'm Dr. Stanford," he said, "I'll take it from here." But Dr. Prescott stood her ground.

"I'm good here," said Dr. Prescott. "I wanna take this code, Dr. Stanford. I'll take admin responsibility." Dr. Stanford could see the determination in Dr. Prescott's eyes. He glanced at Dr. Howard, who nodded knowingly.

"Very well," yelled Dr. Stanford for the recording. "Dr. Prescott is lead, Dr. Howard is second, and I'll run the room. Let's get in order, folks!"

Dr. Howard gave a rapid rundown of what had taken place as everyone assumed their roles. As the team worked away,

Cathy Sixkiller seemed to be the only person in the operating room noticing an odd, glimmering light. She kept moving her shoulders as if to try to look around it. "What's with the damn light?" she asked to no response, everyone's hands busy and focused.

"I got nothing," said a MET tech, squeezing the rescue breather between compressions.

"C'mon, Emmy," cried Dr. Prescott, then ordered another 1 mg IV injection of epinephrine.

"She's flatlining," said another MET tech.

"Dammit!" yelled Dr. Prescott. "Hang in there, Emmy, talk to me!" The team worked furiously for the next two minutes, Dr. Prescott switching out with Dr. Feathers for the CPR. Dr. Prescott felt one of Emmy's ribs give way. She shook her head and prayed for her patient.

Cathy turned to the crash cart and, at Dr. Prescott's orders, charged the defibrillator to two hundred joules. "Charging to two hundred joules," she recorded. The defib machine's alarm rose to its apex. "I'm clear, you're clear, we're all clear!" said Cathy, as the team backed away. "Shocking at two hundred joules," Cathy said. The team waited while Emmy's athletic body jolted.

"Resuming compressions," said Dr. Prescott as a male MET member pounded away on Emmy's chest, taking care to avoid her incision. The group continued their vigil.

"Hold compressions and check for pulse, please," said Dr. Prescott. "No pulse. Still in VFib. Continuing compressions. Charge to three hundred and sixty joules!"

Cathy charged the defibrillator again to prescribed strength, Carlos making a written record of each step in the process. The machine whined again as the pitch rose to its apex once more.

"Charging to three hundred and sixty joules!" shouted Cathy. "I'm clear, you're clear, we're all clear!" Another electric jolt seared Emmy's body. The team waited as Emmy went rigid, then they resumed compressions.

"She's gone, Doc," said a longtime MET tech who had seen more of these than he cared to remember. He glanced down at the patient, her once bronze skin turning a pasty white.

Indeed, Emily "The Cherokee Storm" McNair died in OR Two on a sultry, sunny day in the modern territory known as Indian Country from an air embolism. To Dr. Linda Prescott, nothing seemed more absurd. This woman was a machine, a powerful example of good health and robustness. It made no scientific sense.

"Epi push!" she bellowed. Dr. Howard administered the epinephrine.

"Doc," said the tech, shaking his head.

"Keep at it!" ordered Dr. Prescott. The tech nodded to his team and continued, the others looking sad and resigned.

"Linda," said Dr. Feathers, putting a hand on her shoulder. "It's okay."

"No," said Dr. Prescott, resisting Dr. Feathers. "It's over when I say it's over."

"Yes, ma'am."

"Damn this light!" Cathy shouted.

"What *light*?" yelled Dr. Prescott, annoyed at Cathy and trying to focus. "There's no light, Cathy!" Dr. Howard glanced up at that moment, thinking something had caught his eye, then resumed his own focus of medication and airway management until the declaration of death.

Community Medical Center
OR Recovery Waiting Room

Mike sat on a wide seat with Sandra, so no armrest would be between them. He held her as she cried, and he soon found himself joining her, something he never did in public.

Molly was in another world, and she somehow knew that Emmy was gone. She had entered a world she had never inhabited. Tears flowing, she squeezed her eyes as hard as she could—calling forth every plea she could think of. She held a necklace and cross her father had given her for her eleventh birthday. Wrapped around the necklace was the ponytail holder that Emmy had given Molly to hold for her. It smelled of Emmy's perfume, reminding her of her sister's contagious grin. Molly's tears soaked the holder as she continued deeper into this adjacent world, crying to the elders for her sister. Suddenly, she felt a presence. Through the squint of her eyelids she saw a shadow and felt something next to her.

Claire Sanders appeared. Without saying a word, she knelt beside Molly. Molly looked up, her eyes red and her war paint melting onto her forearms.

"You *came*," said Molly, with a look of wonderment.

"You *called*," Claire responded, smiling and handing her a tissue.

"No," said Molly, shaking her head, "sorry, I didn't."

"If you say so," said Claire, who bowed her head, took Molly's hand, leaned in, and prayed with her. Molly shook, shoulders trembling, heart torn in two, knowing that everything was now horribly wrong.

Community Medical Center
Operating Room #2

That Emmy would die on such a gorgeous but unseasonably hot day was depressing enough, given her flair and fiery personality. The hospital trauma community is never happy with another loss. The Cherokee Nation itself had, in that moment, lost a great fighting warrior and the UFC lost what was likely the greatest woman fighter to date. The McNair family had suffered yet another tragedy: Sandra lost her oldest child, Molly lost her big sister, her protector, her idol. The further pain that would be Mike's alone to carry, the pain of losing his Helen of Troy, his rock, the woman that he never got around to telling how safe *she* made *him* feel, could only be described as unholy. The engagement stone stored in his safe he knew had now turned to sand, eternally slipping through his fingers.

Yet, the cosmic calculus being what it is, one could argue that things happen for a reason. It is often said that those reasons are not for mere mortals to contemplate or attempt to explain. It is a holy mystery. Things are not always what they seem. Reality becomes skewed, the lines blurred. Grieving accompanies the nighttime, and the morning follows it. And afterward is a sunny Cherokee afternoon yet to be explored.

Thus it was, on an early Friday afternoon in the heart of the Cherokee Nation, with an outside temperature scorching the asphalt at 108 degrees, some fifty miles from "The Place of the Huckleberries" where she died more than a hundred and fifty years ago, Mary Rogers McNair arose like a phoenix in the center of OR Two. She was facing east, arms outstretched, hair shimmering to her waist. As she inhaled deeply, a powerful wind of all that is good cycled through the room, radiating the weary staff. An apparent explosion that blinded only those who could see—enveloped the room. Summoning all that she had to give, Mary felt her mother's hand in her left, her grandmother's in her right, and exhaled with a matriarchal force that rivaled the sun exploding. Pointing her face to the heavens and closing her eyes, she squeezed the hands within hers and expanded her chest, exhaling in a vortex of vigor and luminosity. The light bounced from the floor to the ceiling, passing through the operating table on its way, and disappeared into a fireball that exited through the top of the room, pulling Mary along with it.

"Got normal sinus rhythm here!" Dr. Howard shouted.

The heart monitor began to register a normal rhythm.

"Atta girl, Emmy!" shouted Dr. Prescott, ordering a dose of lidocaine. "Good job, people!" she exclaimed as she and the team performed the obligatory measures to bring The Cherokee Storm safely back to status.

"I'll be *damned*," said the lead MET tech, staring down at Emmy as color streamed back to her face.

Community Medical Center
OR Recovery Waiting Room

Molly leaned her head on Claire's shoulder. She was spent. Done. She wiped her tears and said, "I can't lose her, Claire. Just fucking can't." Claire patted her hand. Just then, the nurse approached the family. She smiled.

"Emmy's going to be fine," she said. Molly screamed, Sandra wept, and Mike leaned forward on his elbows, closed his eyes, and put his hands to his head. Sandra leaned over and wrapped her arms around him. Molly leaped to her feet and into Claire's arms.

Community Medical Center
Patio Break Area

Dr. Stan Howard found Cathy Sixkiller alone at the small picnic table outside the cafeteria. She looked up at him wearily as he approached. She had just lit a cigarette.

"You okay?" he asked, placing his right foot next to her on the bench. She gave him a sarcastic look.

"You can't be serious."

"What? We did good in there, Cathy! That girl is gonna be okay. We celebrate The Cherokee Storm, right?" Cathy stared at him, inhaling the smoke.

"You know there's no smoking, right? I mean, c'mon, Cath, really?"

"Irony is I quit four years ago, right here at this table. Damn." She puffed away, despite state law and the hospital rules.

Dr. Howard looked down at her again after staring off into the rear section of the hospital property. "Cathy, what's the problem? Talk to me."

"Are you honestly gonna stand there and tell me you didn't see it?"

"See what?" he responded, turning from her and gazing at the trees.

"The woman, Stan, the goddamn woman!"

"Don't know what you're talking about, Cath."

"Bullshit. The obviously Native woman standing, no—hell—I don't know—suspended, for Christ's sake—in the middle of that OR."

"We were all pretty busy in there, Cathy. Hard to say when the adrenaline gets going like that. You saying you saw something that wasn't there?" He gave her a questioning look.

Cathy had known Stan a long time. She hated it when he pulled this kind of crap. "What I'm saying, *Stanley,* is that you and I both know there was a tall woman with long dark hair and she did some kind of Wizard of Oz shit in there. Period. Please don't piss in my ear and tell me it's raining." She rubbed her temples.

"I'm not," he said, raising his hands defensively. "I'm saying we don't know for sure *what* we saw in there. It's stress, Cathy, just stress. All of us have been going hard since the pandemic and weird stuff can happen, that's all."

She stared at him again. "What the hell is it with men? Especially white men? Jesus Christ!" She shook her head and rose from the bench, sighing and heading for the glass door after stamping out her cigarette butt with her shoe.

"Cathy, maybe you need a vacation, ya know? You and Steve—take some time together."

Cathy halted before opening the door. "Stan," she huffed, shaking her head, "oh, just . . . go . . . go fix yourself a *dick* sandwich! One other thing, buster," she said as she flung open the door and pointed her finger at him, "you ever kindergarten-talk like that to me again and *you're* gonna be the one laid out on that OR table. You'll need the *fucking* chaplain to save your ass, you pompous knucklehead!" She blew through the door, talking to herself as she passed other staff members who turned to watch her go by.

Dr. Howard looked down, then out to the trees again, wondering just what it was that he *had* seen in OR Two that morning. After taking a few deep breaths and closing his eyes, he opened them, sighed, and went back into the hospital.

Emmy lay on her right side. Her broken rib was sore. The room was quiet, the television on mute. She had a morphine drip hanging from the pole next to her bed. She was in pain. Yet pain was something with which Emmy had great familiarity. She focused on her breathing, as she often did. The family had been at her bedside constantly, but they had decided to give her some much-needed rest. The last thing she remembered before falling asleep again was a kiss from Mike so passionate that, had she not just been to hell and back, she would've jumped him right then and there. She smiled and closed her eyes.

Psst.

Emmy opened her eyes again. She looked up and focused, forcing a slight smile. She remembered past occurrences, mostly pleasant, some not so much, yet all in balance. Groggy, she mumbled, "You did it again, didn't you? Saved my ass."

So sue me. [shrugging]

"Nah, I'll pass." Emmy managed a more animated smile, blinking her eyes. "Wado."

No problem. Listen, I came back to tell you something. You did good, Pretty Eyes—you know, with Molly. You think you've failed her over the years. You haven't. You did well, girl. We're proud of you.

"I did the best I could. I'm a pretty fucked-up person, ya know?"

Who amongst us isn't? You should know that Molly brought you back. Her prayers—they floored the house up there. That was some serious Viking shit. Girl's got skills.

"Wow. Don't know what to say. She's a warrior, that much I knew. I'll be sure to give her an extra hug and kiss for that one. So . . . I'm never gonna fight again, am I?"

Mike is going to need you. He will need you in his corner. Oh, you weren't kidding, by the way—about his caboose—*nice!*

Emmy smiled.

And don't forget to check in on your mom from time to time.

"I won't. Won't tap out on you, promise."

Don't I know it? Jesus Christ, girl!

"So . . . fight game over?"

Be sweet.

Emmy chuckled, shaking her head. "I'll try."

I *know* you will.

"You'll try what, Ms. McNair?" said a nurse, coming in to check her IV.

"I'll try to take a shit, but making no promises here."

The nurse laughed.

Community Medical Center
Hospital Chapel

Sandra sat, leaning forward with her elbows on the pew in front of her. The exhaustion had long since taken its toll. Tears streamed down her face, and she intercepted as many as she could with her tissue. The chapel was quiet, a place of solace and respite from chaos within the hearts of family members in fear of losing someone. She glanced upward. "Wado, truly, for saving my baby girl," she whispered. She wiped her eyes again, noticing a woman standing in front of the pew that supported Sandra's elbows.

All in a century's work, as we like to say. [curtsying]

The woman was adorned in a burgundy tear dress, her dark hair in an exquisite bun that reminded Sandra of Molly's hair when she put it up. She sat in the pew, placing her left elbow—an elegant brown arm that matched the pigmentation of her face—on the back of the pew and turning to look at Sandra. Sandra laughed, waving her hands as if to say, "My God, grandma, you are just too much!"

I know you've had your doubts these past years, but you've done well, Pretty Hair. Those girls are kind and courageous and you helped make them that way. Well done.

"I've tried, really," Sandra whispered. "I know I have no business saying this to you, but it hasn't been easy. Just not as strong as you. Wish I were."

That's a load of crap. You're a golden eagle, soaring across Indian Country, ever present, ever watching. I knew you before you knew you, or have you forgotten? Just keep being you. And go get yourself a man, *ah-gay-ya*. Emmy was right—you're still a fox.

Sandra laughed again. "Oh, God, girl, please . . ." she said, waving a hand again just as she realized another patient's family member had arrived and was giving her an odd look. Sandra just smiled, rising from her seat. She turned to leave.

Stay sweet!

Sandra waved in acknowledgment as she walked toward the chapel door. She chuckled, recalling the good and the not-so-good, being grateful for both.

52

The Trail Where We All Cried

Monday, February 4, 1839
Salina Township
Twenty-Eight Miles Northwest
Indian Territory

"Well," said Nick, looking around. "This isn't as bad as I thought. Lots of open country. Not quite what we had in Tennessee, but better than some we've seen in our search." Mary nodded as she helped Martha down from the wagon. Augustine hopped off and accompanied them as they explored and scrutinized the countryside. They noticed several streams and creeks branching off from somewhere near the Neosho River. "Whad'ya think, somewhere between here and that Huckleberry place they were sayin' is up the trail a ways?" He politely awaited Mary's response. She could sense his newfound respect for her knew no bounds since finding himself pressed against a loaded Queen Anne Toby.

"I suppose," she said. Her exhaustion had reached new heights, and she felt as if she was seven months pregnant with a baby bison. Most of the Cherokees with whom the McNairs had made the difficult journey chose to settle closer to Da-li-gwa, many in surrounding areas that were being discussed as future "districts." The Salina area, later called the Saline District, was farther north and far less populated. A handful of full-bloods—Drowning Bear, Pigeon, Robin, Sarah, and Walela—decided to travel with the McNairs farther into Indian

Territory. Just as Mary was about to add to her thoughts, she wobbled. Nick caught her in the middle of a dead faint.

"It's the trail, Mizz. Mary," said Annabelle as she held Mary's head in her lap and patted her with the wet part of an old shirt. "It's the trail where we all cried," she said, softly wiping Mary's head with water from the nearest stream. Nick and the others had walked about the open range in order to give Mary some rest while Annabelle tended to her. "Too much ask any human, let alone a pregnant one for heaven's sake. You just relax now, ma'am." Mary smiled up at Annabelle, touching her chin with two fingers and nodding. "I've been wrong not to make mention of it enough over the years, Mizz. Mary, but you sho is a pretty thang. Not a woman anywheres more beautiful, most specially when you're with child."

"You're a kind person, Annabelle," said Mary, patting the woman's cheek.

Annabelle looked around with a conspiratorial glance—as if keeping a lookout for Nick—then stared down at her master. "I'za righteous nigger, Mizz. Mary. Yes, ma'am," she said in a musical tone, "I'za righteous, quarrelsome nigger with fire in my drawers and *lightning* between my legs!" she added with poetic resonance and cackled, which made Mary laugh, patting Annabelle's cheek again. "You gives me hope, Mizz. Mary, you gives me hope that maybe someday things will change fo' us black folk." She carefully rubbed Mary's eyes with the wet rag, patting her head. "You jest relax now, ma'am, you relax and lemme hold you here fo' a bit. And don't you worry none," she said, "when you haves that baby, I'll be a right here by yo' side, hear me?" Mary smiled and nodded. Annabelle wrung out the rag, changing the water from a small wooden bowl.

Mary drifted off to sleep and dreamed of her childhood home in Georgia, once upon a time in the old Cherokee Nation.

53

A Gift to Your People

Present Day
Emmy's Hospital Room
Community Medical Center
Tulsa County, Oklahoma
District Thirteen, Cherokee Nation

Emmy hated hospital gowns. She once said she wouldn't be caught dead in one.

Sandra, Mike, Molly, and Eddie Standingcloud surrounded Emmy in her room. Eddie leaned against the large windowsill with his arms crossed, giving others the chairs, one of which Mike swiped from the hallway. Mike sat closest, holding Emmy's hand and rubbing her left thigh, which was tightening up on her now and then. Sandra sat on the opposite side, having moved Emmy's tray table out of the way and holding a large Styrofoam cup of iced green tea with a straw for her, giving it to her to sip from on occasion. Molly was in her chair on Sandra's side of the bed near the foot, studying her sister.

Mike looked at Emmy. "How's your pain level, Goddess?"

"I'm okay," said Emmy. "The rubbing is helping. Wado."

"Some flowers over there from Elias Pumpkin, Emmy," said Standingcloud.

"Yeah, Mom said," Emmy responded with a smile. She looked down at Molly. "How's *Ned*?"

"He's good," Molly replied with a grin. "I could get used to that guy!"

"*Don't*," said Emmy, showing Molly her fist. Everyone laughed.

Just then, Tina Gallager stuck her head in. "Osiyo, girlfriend," she said with a smile.

"Hey, Tina," said Emmy and smiled back, genuinely happy to see her friend.

"Did I say that right?" said Tina. "Don't wanna butcher your mother tongue, now." Emmy nodded and Tina walked in. "I won't stay too long. My sister's down the hall with Edgar, keepin' him entertained." She walked over and hugged Standingcloud, then greeted the others. She stood at the foot of the bed. "How ya feelin'?"

"Oh, pretty good, I guess. Takes more than cancer and a clot to take this girl down," said Emmy.

"Don't I know it, sweet thing." She looked at Sandra. "Girl can *hit*, mama bear!"

"So I've heard," said Sandra, winking at Emmy.

Eddie asked Tina about her upcoming fight with Paula "The Pirate's Treasure" Patterson.

"Ready as I can be, big guy," said Tina. "Been waitin' a while for this one. She's a good fighter; I like her style. She's gonna be begging for my phone number after I arm bar that little hottie."

"There ya go," encouraged Emmy, holding up the iced green tea that Sandra had just handed her. Sandra looked back at Emmy, reflecting on their lunch conversation, and Emmy winked at her mom. Tina held a small gift bag, and she leaned over the bed and handed it to Emmy.

"From me and Edgar," she said with a warm smile.

"Oh, how sweet!" said Emmy, untying the bow from around the medium-sized white box that she pulled from the bag. Emmy opened the box and shrieked. "How unbelievably awesome!" She pulled a small bobblehead figure in Emmy's likeness from the wrapping paper inside. It had black hair in a fighter's bun, a white tank top, and her signature orange and green fighter trunks. The figure had long, dark legs attached to a beige stand, the front of which was inscribed "The Cherokee Storm." She put it in her lap and held out her arms to Tina, who walked over for a hug. "Wado, girlfriend, really! That is simply too much!" She patted Tina's face. "Thank you, Tina." She handed the bobblehead to her mom. Sandra laughed and poked at it.

"Omigod how freaking cool is that!" shouted Molly. "I love it!"

"Glad you like it," said Tina, moving away and winking at Eddie, who gave her a thumb's up.

Before anyone could say anything else, The Black Mamba stood in the doorway, flanked by her trainer, an assistant, and her bodyguard. She sauntered in without asking. Emmy handed her gift off to Mike, who looked concerned. Eddie moved from his relaxed position at the window and stood erect, surprised. Ortiz's trainer nodded and waved his right hand from side to side in an "It's all good" signal. He stepped over and shook Eddie's hand, then stood by him. Ortiz, always a snappy dresser, wore a leopard-spotted shirt that must have cost two thousand dollars, and beautiful slacks. She was a stunning figure, ripped yet feminine. Tina immediately bucked up to Ortiz and blocked her from coming any closer.

"The *fuck* you want?" she said, challenging Ortiz. Molly looked nervous. Sandra glanced at Mike, who had his eye on the entire group.

LaToya held her hands up and said, "I come in peace, I come in peace. But you," she looked at Tina, "step aside, formaldehyde." She gave a shooing motion with her hands, clearly trying to agitate Tina. "Don't make me sweep you under the rug, little girl."

"Bitch, I ain't scared'a you!" Tina huffed, refusing to let Ortiz by, looking her over and rolling her shoulders.

"Formaldehyde my backside! Take you *out*side and beat your ass all over that pretty front lawn, you ass clown."

"*Tina* . . ." said Eddie.

"Hmmph," grunted Ortiz. She waved Tina away as if acknowledging a peasant.

"It's okay, Tina," said Emmy, "it's all right." Tina stepped away as Ortiz sneered at her.

Ortiz nodded to the family and stood at the foot of the bed, no closer. "Just wanted to come by and wish you well, Storm." Eddie arched his eyebrows, Mike watched her hands like most cops do, Molly's jaw dropped, and Emmy just stared at Ortiz. "I also wanted to apologize for my behavior in the ring. You didn't deserve that."

Emmy nodded. "No, I didn't," she agreed. She softened and smiled. "Thanks, LaToya. I appreciate it."

"I'm really sorry to hear about everything, Storm. I wish you well. 'Sides," she added, "I want my rematch!" and smiled at Emmy.

Emmy smiled back and said, "I'll see what I can do."

"All right, then, be well," said Ortiz, then she turned to leave, nodding to the others. Except Tina. She held up her fist to her and said, "You next on my list, Paradise Lost. Oh yeah, you *definitely* scared'a me!" and rolled her own shoulders and faked a move toward Tina, who didn't even blink.

Tina spewed, "Bitch, *I will lay your grungy ass out as soon as look at ya,* you half-past-a-monkey's-ass has-been!" She took a step toward Ortiz and Eddie lunged and grabbed her as Ortiz's bodyguard kept her at bay.

Ortiz turned her back on Tina and laughed as she exited, snapping the fingers on both hands and warning, "Been told, crawdad!"

"Eddie," Tina growled after they were gone, "I want that bitch on my card after Patterson, hear me?"

"Okay, okay, settle down, child," said Eddie, holding up his hands and trying to keep Tina calm. Tina turned back toward the family.

"Sorry about that," she said, shaking her head. "Now I gotta go shower—get that lice offa me." She looked at Molly. "*Hate* that ass clown," she hissed with a wink. Molly snickered. Tina looked at Emmy. "Well, girlfriend, I should get. Sorry to get all lathered up while you're tryin' to heal."

"That's okay," said Emmy. "So glad you came by." Tina cocked her head, studying Emmy. She began moving toward her, walking around behind Molly and Sandra. She playfully put her fist up at Mike.

"Don't you move, boy," she said. "Don't you move a muscle."

Mike held up his hands as if to say, "What did *I* do?"

Tina tiptoed over to Emmy, bending down and looking into her eyes. She winked and then gently kissed Emmy on the lips, closing her eyes, as if putting her soul into it. She then pulled away and looked down at Emmy. "I always wanted to do that," she whispered.

"I *know* that!" Emmy whispered back. The two women laughed and Tina put her forehead to Emmy's.

"Love you, girlfriend," she said, patting the side of Emmy's head. "You get well soon, hear me?"

"I love you, too, Tina. I will," she replied, patting Tina's hand. Whatever Sandra had to say about Emmy's profession, Emmy knew that her mom could not deny the deep bonds that sometimes formed, for which she knew that Sandra was grateful. She once said that she knew a lot of people were in her daughter's corner.

"Okay," said Tina with a deep breath, "I'm outta here."

Suddenly, a small figure appeared in the doorway. It was Edgar, grinning from ear to ear. Tina smiled. "Ready, champ?" she asked him. Edgar gazed at Emmy, then pointed at her.

"Hey, you! Pretty lady over there!" he yelled, putting up his fists. Emmy grinned at him, holding up her own fists. Edgar giggled. Everyone laughed.

"*Ed-gar*," said Emmy, "thank you for my gift, handsome." He giggled again. "Come here," she said, pointing to her cheek. "Come over here and give me a kiss!" She winked at him.

"No!" he roared, beaming and clearly charmed.

"Yes," she said, making kissing sounds and pointing to her chin this time. "Come on! Put one right here!"

"NO!" he yelled, grabbing his fanny with both hands, sticking out his chest, and cackling at the top of his lungs. He turned and ran back down the hall, narrowly missing a nurse carrying an IV bag to the room next door. She just laughed and shook her head before knocking on the door.

Molly turned to Emmy and Tina and, wide-eyed, said, "Omigod, he is *adorable!*"

"You want him?" said Tina. "He's up for grabs," she teased, the typical weary mother expression taking over. Sandra looked at Molly.

"Girl, you need to hit Tina up for some babysitting time. Bring him over for your next date night," she said to Tina. "We can just sit him on the couch and love up on him. What a cutie!"

Molly nodded. "For sure," she agreed.

"I'll definitely keep that in mind," said Tina with a grin. "Guess I should probably keep him, huh?" Everyone laughed again. Tina waved, heading for the door. Then she stopped, as if thinking deeply. She turned and faced Emmy, her powerful body reflecting consistent time at the gym.

"Everything okay, sista?" said Emmy with an inquisitive expression. Tina glanced at Standingcloud and took a step forward.

"I'm so glad you made it, Storm."

Emmy smiled and nodded.

"All right, girlfriend. I'm just gonna say it: You're the best goddamn fighter I've ever seen. We can't have you sick like this," she preached, a tear rolling down her cheek. "You got a gift, Storm, somethin' the rest of us just stand in front of the damn mirror and dream about. You got that serious fast twitch muscle fiber that few people are born with. I'm good at this thing, right? But I ain't *great*, like you. That's some crazy genetic shit you're carrying."

Emmy shook her head. "Tina—"

But Trouble in Paradise would not be moved. "Took Edgar to see his great-grandpa last weekend—my Gramps. Had some alone time with Gramps while Moms watched Edgar. Had a long chat while we snapped green beans together. Know what he said, Emmy? Said he remembers when Muhammad Ali was still Cassius Clay. He said you got that kinda star power." Emmy managed a weak smile despite her rapidly reddening eyes. "Said he used to watch films of Sugar Ray Robinson when he was growing up." She looked at the others with a nostalgic smile. Then, addressing Emmy again, she added, "Gramps was Golden Gloves. Really good amateur in his day. He likes to call you 'Sugar Shack' 'cause you remind him of Sugar Ray. Says you gots sugar in your heart. He said youza gift to your people— to the world."

Emmy was weeping now. Mike smiled—proud of his lady— and squeezed her hand.

"Tina . . ." Emmy gurgled.

"Nah, shut up; lemme get this out. Gramps said talent like that only comes along once every fifty years or so at best. He said you could stop a FedEx truck with that right hand of yours. Said what you did to Ortiz was some crazy acrobatic circus shit. Know what else he told me, Storm? He said, 'Girl, I love you more than anything, right? You and that little boy of yours. So I'm gonna tell you this for your own good. Don't get in the cage with that woman. Don't do it. Yeah, you gots talent and you're a great fighter, but that Cherokee woman is in a whole other league, little girl. Don't let her put that kinda hurtin' on you. You my grand-baby.'"

Wiping her eyes now, Emmy begged, "Tina, please . . ."

"I said shut up already," said Tina calmly. Emmy cried the way she had in Dr. Prescott's office, making the chipmunk sound, shoulders trembling. Molly grabbed tissues from Emmy's tray table for herself, and Sandra just sat with her eyes closed. Standingcloud stared at the ceiling, trying not to become emotional, and Mike put his head down. Tina continued. "Ali, Sugar Ray, Amanda Nunes, Floyd Mayweather, Beyoncé, the Beatles, Rolling Stones, fucking Elvis . . . girl, you got serious chops. I know being Native is seen as a handicap in promotions, but that shit's changing, and you're helping change it. You just *gots* to get well, understand? You goin' places, like I always say. Yeah, that grad school stuff is important and you got plenty of time for that. But you got bitches need spanking before you hang up the gloves, you read me, girlfriend? Every wannabe bitch out there needs to know the Sugar Shack is comin' for 'em. You got to promise me you gonna get better. I don't wanna prove my Gramps wrong over some kinda foul like cancer. Just ain't right. So you get better, bitch. Love you girl!" With that, she turned on a dime and almost ran out the door.

"Oh, *shit*," said Emmy, massaging her temples as Molly gave her the tissue box.

"Tina's awesome," said Molly. Emmy nodded and blew her nose.

"She's right, ya know," said Eddie, walking around to the foot of the bed. "Let's get you well and get you back out there. It'll take some time, but I think we can pull this off!"

"Really, Standingcloud? The guy who's always on my ass about taking care of *me*?" she said, smiling and cleaning her face, then snuggling her bobblehead again.

"Well, we can't have those women thinking you're scared, now can we?" he said with a grin.

"My *ass*," Emmy retorted. Everyone laughed. Eddie moved to the side of the bed beside Mike and took Emmy's left hand and brought it to his lips. He kissed it and patted her wrist.

"Love you, bitch."

She smiled up at him. "Love you, too, asshole."

"Take care of her, son," he said to Mike, hand on his shoulder.

"Will do," said Mike.

"Oh, listen," Eddie added, "some people found out—knew you were sick. It ain't like it's all over the country or anything, but word *did* get out. You got some fan mail back at my place. When you're ready, I'll bring it by—or Mike can swing by and get it. Just lemme know."

Mike nodded.

"Bill Stoddard sent you a gift as well, and it's on the floor beside my desk with the box of fan letters."

"Okay," said Emmy. "Thanks, Standingcloud—wado for looking after me, as usual." He smiled and headed for the door.

"Thanks, Eddie," said Sandra with a smile. He winked back, then glanced at Emmy.

"See you later, bitch," he said with a grin and blew her a kiss.

"Not if I see you first, asshole."

They could hear Eddie laughing as he headed down the hallway.

54

The Place of the Huckleberries

April 2, 1839
Guwaya ("Place of the Huckleberries")
Indian Territory

S pring had sprung.

Mary lay in a makeshift birthing bed that Nick and Enoch had created. Despite her circumstances, she was grateful for warmer weather. During the forty-five days or so since the family left Salina Township, the men had managed to build two rough drafts of a simple one-level house. Between the Union Mission to the south and the small hardware store erected in Guwaya, they gathered enough supplies for Nick, Enoch, Pigeon, and Drowning Bear to generate passable roofs for the respective dwellings. It was a small community effort, though one which still saw Indian quarters and slave quarters as distinct.

The men made themselves scarce, using the time to hunt turkey and wild boar. Annabelle, Walela, Robin, Sarah, and even Deborah were left to tend to Mary's birthing needs. The faint smell of honeysuckle was in the air as Annabelle made Mary as comfortable as she could when Mary's labor pains grew severe.

"Now you just breathe in, Mizz. Mary, and then you just breathe out." Mary obeyed. "That's it, that's it, girl, that's my girl—you jest let the Lort guide you as always and let this here child come when's he's a ready."

"He?" moaned Mary as she looked upward, blowing air in brief and rapid gusts.

"It's a feelin', Mizz. Mary, strong feelin'. But we let the Lort decide that one, won't we?" she added with a chuckle. Annabelle and Walela provided the primary support and encouragement through a difficult morning. Mary's rhythms gained in frequency and intensity. The women guided Mary faithfully through her final contraction until a Cherokee child introduced itself to the world. It was, no surprise to Annabelle, a boy. Though just as much Caucasian, he was in fact Cherokee because Mary was, and Cherokee children claimed that birthright from their mother.

When the men returned from the hunt, Mary was rested. She and Annabelle presented the child to their father.

"I have a son," said Nick with a grin. "Well I'll be damned." As he held the boy, looking down at his face, he asked, "Whad'ya wanna name him?"

"Let's call him John," she said, "John Ross McNair."

"You sure about that?" he said, surprised. She nodded.

"Nick, I know we've had our differences with Chief Ross, particularly in the past year or two. But I think most will admit he's been a great leader. The child should have a strong name, don't you think?"

Nick nodded and ruminated. "You know, we could say that he's named for both your father and Ross. He'll always be able to say that he was named John for your father and Ross for a Cherokee chief. I suppose that's fitting. Is that a proper idea?"

Mary nodded and smiled. "I think that's more than appropriate. We've come so far, fought so hard for our place. I want all of our children—even those down through the ages—seven generations and even seven times seven, to understand they came from strong folks. I want them to know they came from the Principal People." Nick nodded as he cradled the baby in his arms.

They looked out at the breaking sunset and gave thanks for another Cherokee afternoon—one filled with joy and new birth.

55

Sounds Like a Plan

Present Day
Early August
Marina Del Rey Resort
Grand Lake O' the Cherokees
District Ten, Cherokee Nation

M olly and Emmy sat in the sunshine.
The *Ned Christie*, parked not far from the cabin,
soaked in the sun's rays. Emmy sat in the rocker, feet
up on a table, her Adonis legs roasting in the summer heat.
Sandra and Mike were on call for the weekend, so the girls had
opted for some sister time. Molly got up from her rocker and
wiped the seat with her beach towel. Emmy snickered.

"While you're up, grab me a Prairie Bomb, my little
princess," she said with a grin. In typical fashion, Molly flipped
her off as she went in. "Grab one for yourself, if you want it,"
Emmy hollered.

"You serious?"

"I won't tell if you won't!"

Molly returned with two. "Never had one of these," she
said, examining the bottle. They popped the caps and Molly
looked at her sister.

"Cheers, Em," she said as they clanked the bottles together.

"I love you, Nine-Speed," said Emmy, with a thoughtful
and appreciative expression.

"Love you, too, Em."

They sat in silence for a couple of minutes.

"A little birdie told me you did some serious praying for me."

"What little birdie?" said Molly, surprised. Emmy smiled at her behind her shades. "Well—me and Claire. She just showed up out of nowhere, Em, kinda like she did when I first met her. I mean, seriously, what were the odds of her showing up at Sacred Grounds exactly when she did?"

Emmy shrugged.

"I'm so glad you made it, Em. It's a true miracle, you know that?"

"That's what they tell me," said Emmy, leaning back in the rocker, turning her face toward the sun.

"I was told, Emmy; I was told to get on my knees and pray for you. It was like, like, like I didn't have any choice. Like I was compelled to."

Emmy took a long swig of her beer. "Well," she said finally, "I'm glad you were so compelled." She held up her bottle in salute.

Molly shifted in her rocker, looking as if she wanted to say something, then sighed. She shifted again. "Do you believe . . . do you believe our ancestors speak to us?" Emmy looked at her again, studying her sister through her sunglasses. She smiled, then downed some more beer.

"Have you ever thought about the fact that all of this—the lake, the trees as we know them now—weren't here during the Trail of Tears?" Emmy said, deflecting the question. Molly reflected.

"Not really, I guess. That's pretty wild."

"Well, I mean, all of this that we enjoy—this damn beer, for one, my car, your hairbrush, air conditioning, refrigeration, birth control, that nice sketchbook that *Clay*-ton gave you, the amazing music from the past hundred years or so—things like that. They had none of that. It was a rough, rough, time. And people really didn't live that long. We're lucky, Molly. We need to cherish the time—and the people—we have now."

They sat for a while without talking.

"So," Molly inquired, unable to stand it any longer, "*do* you think our ancestors communicate with us?"

"Of course."

"In what way? I mean, like, how so?"

"How do *you* think they communicate with us?"

"What the fuck, Em?"

"What?"

"*What?*"

"What-what?"

"Screw it. Forget I asked."

Emmy snickered. "My, raggie today, aren't we?" Another middle finger from the baby of the family. Emmy chuckled again.

"I also hear that you're making serious plans for this Trail of Tears trip. How are you gonna do this? Bike? Car? Horse and buggy?"

"We'll drive it. He wants to go—you know—to help with the project and all."

"Uh-huh," teased Emmy with a wide grin.

"It's not like that!" said Molly, dimples vibrating.

"Uh-huh."

"It's *not!*"

"If you say so. I just hate that you're gonna be humping all that way in a Malibu Barbie plastic car from Toys "R" Us."

"You are *so* infuriating!" Molly said, slapping her armrest.

"You are SO, in-*furry*-ating!" Emmy mocked. "Get me another beer, bitch."

"Up yours!"

Emmy laughed and got up and got her own beer.

The sisters lay on a blanket in front of the cabin, watching the stars and listening to the frogs. A coyote howled in the distance.

"Remember when we used to do this?" said Emmy, reaching over and holding her little sister's hand. Molly smiled in the dark. "I was about thirteen or fourteen and you were six or seven. We would camp out in the backyard sometimes on Friday nights."

"Yeah, I remember. You would tell me ghost stories—scare the shit out of me." Emmy snorted. "I'm so glad you've been in my life, sis, really." She felt Emmy squeeze her hand. "Like, remember when I was about ten and you were about my age now, and Stevie Christopher lived two streets over?"

"God, girl, how can I forget?"

"Yeah—he was always bragging about being white, for heaven's sake. He was like fourteen or so. And he kept calling me 'half-breed' and kicked me real hard in the butt. God, that hurt."

"Yeah, I walked all the way over there and told him to come outside and then beat his ass right there in his front yard."

"Yeah! And a bunch of the neighborhood kids and I were following you down there, wondering what you were gonna do, and the whole neighborhood saw it, practically. Man, you really bloodied that guy's nose!"

"I think that's when we knew I had a pretty mean right! Yeah, I'm yelling for him to come outside and he comes storming out the front door and shoves me back a few feet. I just launched at him—hit him twice with a right and the second one turned his face into hamburger. His mom's running around the front yard freaking out and ole Stevie is lying there, crying like a bitch, and his nose draining blood like a fire hose. That was fun!"

"Wonder what ever happened to that guy?"

"Little fucker's probably doing time somewhere."

"Yeah, he probably saw that fight with Ortiz and is hiding in a manhole in Tulsa or somewhere just waiting for you to jump out at him!" Molly giggled uncontrollably, partly due to two Prairie Bombs. The sky seemed to be spinning. She belched loudly and they lay there in the grass, giggling like children.

After more quiet time together, Emmy lightly squeezed Molly's hand again.

"Hey," she said in a serious tone.

"Yeah?"

"If something happens and Clay can't go with you for some reason, I'll go with you."

"Really?" Molly could see Emmy nodding in the darkness. "You'd do that?"

"Yes."

"That's sweet. Wado."

"Well, they are, after all, *our* ancestors, not just yours."

Molly reflected on that.

"Do you wanna come anyway?"

"Well, let's just see what happens. You two should go. I just don't want you going alone. And I trust Clay. Plus, he knows I'll kill him if anything happens to you."

Molly giggled again.

"You know, Em, this whole learning experience about the Trail of Tears—it's been a real eye-opener. So sad and frustrating. And then I see somebody like you—a fighting warrior—making it right for our preople," she added, slurring her speech. Emmy gripped Molly's hand again, then patted her wrist.

"You're a warrior, too, sister, a *prayer* warrior. That trumps the UFC any day. I might be dead if it weren't for you."

"You keep saying that," said Molly, raising up on her elbows. "I was just doing what—I don't know—what I was told, I guess."

"I know."

"What? How?"

"A little bird, that's all."

"You said *that* too already! Wutta you mrean? What bird?"

Emmy laughed softly. "Just a pretty little bird. It doesn't matter. You just keep being you—doing what you do. That's your gift, Molly. A kind heart. And *serious* prayer and smoke, apparently."

"Yours is being a protector. Between you and Mom, I got two mama bears lookin' after me."

"And then some, no doubt."

"Make a deal with ya?"

Emmy nodded.

"You look after me with that mean right hand you got, and I'll look after you with prayer. How's that?"

"Deal," said Emmy, her infectious smile glowing in the dark.

Sounds like a plan.

Both women smiled at their own understanding of the woman in the dress as they held hands and felt the gentleness of the cool Cherokee evening breeze.

Author Commentary

In 2012, I returned to postgraduate student status as a chaplain resident at Johnson City Medical Center in Johnson City, Tennessee. I was struggling with whether to continue in the crisis ministry that embodies hospital chaplaincy. A nurse called me at exactly three o'clock in the morning one day to tell me that the parents of a ten-year-old child were expecting me. The child had just died. It was an on-call weekend, and I was exhausted. I approached the elevator, wondering what I could possibly say to these grieving parents. I pushed the button, said a prayer, and awaited the elevator.

The chime sounded, the doors opened, and I entered. What happened next is a little fuzzy. A semicircle of mostly faceless people formed in front of me in what was one of the longest elevator rides of my life. I went somewhere. It was distant, but not unpleasant. The only face I could see was Mary Rogers McNair's. Mary was my third great (great, great, great) aunt. She said something to the effect of "I walked in freezing weather in my bare feet," symbolizing the Cherokees' brutal journey on the Trail of Tears.

When I said I wasn't sure if I could do this anymore, she affirmed my difficult history as a young cancer patient and heart attack survivor. She told me I was needed downstairs, and that I would say the right things, reminding me that I had done this dozens if not hundreds of times. She would be with me, she assured me. The other faceless individuals nodded, embracing me. I remember that it was warm. The chime sounded again, the doors opened, and I got out. I checked the time. I had been in the elevator for no more than twenty seconds, earth time. I don't recall what I said to those parents, but whatever it was, it was sent by the Great Spirit through Mary and was of some comfort.

Ancestral transmutation, as I like to call it, is the reaping of benefits through a space-time relationship with one's ancestors. This is common among Cherokee and other indigenous persons, provided one believes that such a thing is in fact natural and possible. When the idea for this story developed, I wanted to give the reader a realistic picture of the harshness of the Cherokee Trail of Tears while presenting a reminder of some of the great challenges of modern life— challenges such as breast cancer. I also wanted to paint a conversational portrait between a contemporary Cherokee and her ancestor.

As a cancer survivor, I wanted to encourage those who have cancer, those who have had it, and those who might one day develop it. This story was written for an older audience than most of my tales. I hope the overall message is the same regardless of the reader's age: We can overcome seemingly insurmountable difficulties, especially with help from those around us. The graphic accounts of sexual assault in this book are meant to provide a window into the truth of what happened to indigenous women then, as well as what happens today. Above all else, it is the author's duty to tell the truth whenever possible, however unpleasant that truth might be.

Mary Rogers McNair and her family can be found on the Cherokee Drennen Roll, the census of Cherokees in Indian Territory (now Oklahoma and Arkansas) who were forcibly removed from eastern states such as Georgia, North Carolina, South Carolina, and Tennessee. The family settled in the Saline District, Indian Territory. My paternal grandmother told me about Mary many years ago. Mary's journey to the west had survived family oral tradition, and I later confirmed it through the good work of my friend and researcher, the late Don L. Shadburn.

Molly, Emmy, and their mother are products of my imagination, but they are meant to represent some Native American women of today. Likewise, the specific parallel story about Mary and her family, though fictitious, embodies truths of real events that occurred on the Trail of Tears, supported by written accounts of eyewitnesses later in their lives. The story is fiction; some of the events and people are real. The Nicholas McNair family provided wagons for use in transport for what was known as the Bell Detachment, which departed Fort Cass in the old Cherokee Nation on October 11, 1838, and arrived at the Vineyard Post Office near today's Evansville, Arkansas—in the new Indian Territory—on January 7, 1839. The party navigated one of the coldest and harshest winters on record.

Lieutenant Edward Deas of the Fourth Artillery, U.S. Army, was the actual disbursing agent for the Bell Detachment. Captain Ambrose is a literary device, meant to represent the whole of the various detachment leaders and escorts. According to Duane King in his book, *The Cherokee Trail of Tears*, Lieutenant Deas's journal vanished in 1840. He stipulated that the notes Deas took—some of which we still have—might have been the most important of all journal entries on the removal. Deas drowned in the Rio Grande during the Mexican War.

It is generally accepted that three voluntary Treaty Party detachments traveled in 1837, and another voluntary detachment left in the spring of 1838. During the summer of 1838, three forced detachments guided by the military made the journey. Thirteen detachments under Chief John Ross's supervision, but led by others, undertook the journey in the fall of 1838. The one military-led detachment of Treaty Party members, consisting of roughly 660 people, led by Cherokee John Bell and escorted by Lieutenant Deas, left and arrived as described above. Information varies slightly on the number of births, deaths, and desertions within the sundry detachments.

Some Cherokees, such as Sequoyah (credited as the inventor of the Cherokee syllabary) and Will Rogers (humorist, political pundit, and my third cousin, three times removed, who made part of his living poking fun at powerful politicians) are known for their innovation and commitment to new ideas and going against the tide. I viewed Molly's sister, Emmy, in the same light. She had the courage to tackle a dangerous disease with intelligence, humor, and vicissitude. The cancer experience and the fortune of being a survivor are but a part of the larger story of what can, at times, be interpreted as a trail of tears for all of us.

Scientific empirical data, as well as personal success stories (known as "anecdotal evidence"), continue to prove that whole food, plant-based nutrition can halt or reverse certain diseases. Although my Cherokee ancestors occasionally consumed meat, much of their fare consisted of vegetables like corn, wild potato tubers, and squash. They ate fruit that they could grow, such as apples, peaches, and persimmons. They enjoyed nuts like chestnuts and acorns and legumes like beans and peas. Many of these same foods made up Emmy's diet. Her doctors in this story were modeled in part after my own, as well as several other physicians and providers I have known.

The other holistic practices in which Emmy participated, such as meditation and prayer, are now thankfully practiced by millions throughout the world. Cancer will one day no longer be hated and feared, but embraced as an object of love and respect, much like a friend gone awry who needs to be returned to the fold. Nutritional science has already proven this with respect to heart disease.[1]

Mary's story reflects the sad reality of what humans can inflict on each other. The Trail of Tears is the unhappy benchmark of Cherokee history. Most of the horrible events in the 1838 portions of this book are true and taken from eyewitness accounts made available by the "Indian Pioneer History Collection" by Grant Foreman, the Trail of Tears edition (Oklahoma Chapter) of the Rev. Daniel Butrick's journal entries, and the National Archives. The Bell route was a relatively organized affair, with well-educated Cherokee "mixed-bloods" for the most part, but it was not without its tragedies and difficulties. Twenty-one (or twenty-three, depending on the source) deaths were recorded. I tried to paint a picture that, hopefully, captured the overall flavor of the detachments that journeyed during this terrible period of genocide in American history.

---

[1]1. T. Colin Campbell and Thomas M. Campbell, *The China Study: Revised and Expanded Edition* (Bella Books, Inc., 2016), 115-119.

We each have challenges, some worse than others, that confront and threaten us. Fortunately, we have giants who came before us on whom we can call when we are in peril. It's merely a matter of finding the right frequency. For me, it's been "a Cherokee thing," but anyone can harness this energy. The ancestors are waiting for you to summon them.

The ride for which Molly prepares early in this story is based on the annual Remember the Removal Ride, in which both eastern and western Cherokees (usually young persons) participate. It is a great source of pride for those of us who cherish our Cherokee heritage. The riders, escorted by select leaders, including the Cherokee Marshal's Service, receive the cultural experience of a lifetime as they retrace the journey of their ancestors on the Trail of Tears.

It is a matter of speculation and tradition as to why some Native Americans find solace and hope in their ancestors. The idea of an ancestor reaching through time and comforting or awakening a person to something important probably seems strange and unrealistic to many. For some of us, however, the notion isn't odd at all. As Molly's encounters with her ancestor, Mary, grew more frequent, they made more and more sense to her. She eventually found them almost a natural part of the rhythm and flow of her life.

Many of the young people taking part in the Cherokee Nation's Remember the Removal bike ride likely haven't had a chance to think much about the specifics of their ancestors' lives. Reports indicate that often changes by the end of their journey. Some of life's sweetest moments materialize on the heels of great sadness and agony. In Molly's case, it wasn't so much the possibility of the ride itself that made the biggest difference in her life, but her active participation in her family's response to her sister's life-threatening illness.

Emmy's newfound propensity for eating plants instead of animals is based on rapidly growing science that supports the concept that a starch- and plant-centered lifestyle not only slows the progress of some of our most complicated diseases, but can also reverse them.[2] I have tried to stress that this isn't about personal purity; it is about commitment to personal principles that increase one's responsibility for self, particularly when one is facing a deadly disease. I believe this is precisely what Emmy accomplished as a survivor.

In the old days, Cherokee women were consulted as a matter of habit and wisdom regarding not just the everyday affairs of the tribe, but also during times of war; their counsel was usually needed when preparing for battle. I tried to bring some of that "lady wisdom" to the forefront of this story, where it deserves to be. For young women like Emmy and Molly to be productive in today's world, self-reliance (tempered by interdependence) and sister power are necessities. The Cherokee concept of *gadugi* (ga-doo-gee, with a hard "g") means working together toward a common goal or objective.

I reached out to Mary to ask permission to use her, in the context of this story, as a symbol of the brutality forced upon Native American women of her day. The story is a reminder that, unfortunately, that brutality continues in many areas of Indian Country.

As with my middle-grade novella, *Chattahoochee Rain*, it has been incumbent upon me to honor these Cherokee ancestors. It has been my hope and prayer that I have done just that, lest I disgrace those giants on whose shoulders I have proudly stood.

Bryan D. Jackson
Tahlequah Community, Vashon Island, Washington
2024

---

[2]2. T. Colin Campbell, *The Future of Nutrition* (Bella Books Inc., 2020), 205-229.

Elements for Discussion

1. The surname McNair is a Gaelic name that formed in Scotland and eventually found its way into Ireland. It was recorded in the United States during the early 1800s. Many people today have stereotypical ideas of Native American surnames. Did you find the name McNair for modern Cherokee Nation citizens surprising? How do you think Molly and Emmy's surname originally came about?

2. This story portrays brutal yet realistic aspects of Cherokee removal. The true stories of Native Americans having been removed from their homelands are deplorably absent or lacking in today's education system. What, if anything, should be changed about that? How might there be a more thorough educational review and study of the displacement of America's first peoples?

3. The assault and murder of indigenous women is a serious problem in North America. In the author's description of Devon's assault on Molly, Devon is ultimately presented as redeemable; that is, with attention and treatment, he was able to make positive changes in his life and begin to view women differently. How is this redemption characteristic of actual situations of which you might be aware? Do we have the proper procedures and programs in place to truly help men with this problem, and, if so, are these programs helpful? Why or why not?

4. From the story's beginning, Molly finds comfort in the presence of her ancestor. Her ancestor doesn't replace the core guidance of her Christian faith, Jesus Christ, but rather complements that. Mary comes across as a messenger to whom Molly can relate. How does Molly grow as a person as the communication with Mary increases?

5. Emmy uses a number of coping mechanisms to come to terms with her problems, past and present. She is focused on her education and professional development as a graduate student. She prays and meditates for guidance, makes money

through mixed martial arts to support herself, undergoes psychotherapy to increase self-awareness, shoots man-style targets at the pistol range to relieve stress, and utilizes nutrition as medical treatment for a serious disease. How might some of these attributes be helpful or harmful examples to other young American Indian women as they navigate troubling times?

6. Early in the book, Rebecca tells Emmy about Devon's assault on Molly. Emmy, much to Rebecca's frustration, appears detached and disinterested, telling Rebecca that Molly is an adult and should handle her own problems. Later, we witness Devon getting ambushed by Emmy in the dark of the night. What might the author have had in mind by painting the picture in this fashion?

7. Eddie Standingcloud is a pseudo-father figure to Emmy (and Molly). At first, despite knowing how single-minded Emmy can be, he forbids her to fight Ortiz. After she pleads her case, he gives in. What does it say about Eddie and Emmy's relationship that Eddie changed his mind under such potentially dangerous conditions?

8. We know little about Emmy and Molly's father except that he died of a heart attack and that he was likely a good man. During a therapy session, Marie makes reference to Emmy's father in terms of her budding relationship with Mike. She explains that Emmy has an emotional connection to her father even though he's dead. What might Marie have been trying to help Emmy understand about herself in relation to Mike?

9. Because this is a story that alternates between 1838 and the present day, an opportunity exists to consider the difficulty and simplicity of the respective time periods. What are some of the many conveniences of today that would have been unavailable to Nick and Mary in their time? Conversely, based on the technology and many discoveries of the modern era, what are some of the realities of their day that might actually have made their lives simpler?

10. The annual Cherokee Trail of Tears Remember the Removal Ride is a major annual event. Due to Molly's injury, she missed out on that year's journey and had to find other

ways to cope with this loss, all the while knowing that her sister could die of cancer. Identify some of the places that Molly found to shelter from the storms in her own life.

11. Mary chose to give up a significant part of herself to rescue Tulip in the barn. The man gave Mary the chance to leave the situation, and she refused. Why did Mary make the decision she did? In what ways did Mary change after this event?

12. In 1869, General Philip Sheridan supposedly said, "The only good Indians I ever saw were dead." Over the years, this has become "The only good Indian is a dead Indian." We have no proof that Sheridan said this. Even so, colonial actions during the past two hundred years or so would suggest that many felt (and possibly still feel) this way about indigenous peoples. Where can we find examples of this attitude in today's society?

13. In Chapter Fifty, "Over My Dead Body," Mary stands her ground against her husband regarding the selling of their remaining slaves, Annabelle, Enoch, and Deborah. Her decision is based on revelation born out of a personal, tragic experience, to which Nick is not privy. Somewhere along the line in United States history, people of the south had to have felt the same way Mary did, or we would still have enslaved black people today. What could be some of the factors that made white people decide that what they had been doing for centuries was appalling, callous, and irredeemable?

14. Select a female character who effectively defines herself in an often male-dominated world. In what ways does this resonate with you as a reader?

15. The Trail of Tears is often seen as a benchmark in Cherokee history. It exemplified the difficult decisions that had to be made for some between keeping personal property and identifying as a new United States citizen, conforming to colonial policy and procedure, or maintaining tribal sovereignty—thereby relinquishing land but keeping an Indian identity and moving west to Indian Territory as part of the tribe. What might be some contemporary examples of a "trail

of tears" for people today having to make similarly harsh personal decisions?

Suggested Reading

General & Academic

Coates, Julia. *Trail of Tears*. Greenwood, 2014.

Fitzgerald, David and Duane H. King. *The Cherokee Trail of Tears*. Graphic Arts Books, 2008.

Garrison, Tim Alan. *The Legal Ideology of Removal: The Southern Judiciary and the Sovereignty of Native American Nations*. University Of Georgia Press, 2009.

Inskeep, Steve. *Jacksonland*. Penguin Publishing Group, 2015.

Johnston, Carolyn. *Voices of Cherokee Women*. John F. Blair, Publisher, 2013.

Payne, John Howard and Daniel S. Butrick. *The Payne-Butrick Papers, Volumes 1, 2, 3,* edited by William L. Anderson, Jane L. Brown and Anne F. Rogers. University of Nebraska Press, 2010.

Purdue, Theda and Michael D. Green. *The Cherokee Nation and the Trail of Tears*. Penguin Books, 2008.

Rozema, Vicki, ed. *Voices from the Trail of Tears*. J.F. Blair, 2003.

Shadburn, Don. L. *Unhallowed Intrusion: A History of Cherokee Families in Forsyth County, Georgia*. WH Wolfe Associates, 1993.

Smith, Daniel Blake. *An American Betrayal*. Henry Holt and Company, 2011.

For Young Readers

Bealer, Alex W. *Only the Names Remain: The Cherokees and the Trail of Tears*. Little, Brown, 1996.

Bruchac, Joseph. *The Journal of Jesse Smoke: A Cherokee Boy*. Scholastic Inc., 2001. (middle grade fiction)

Bruchac, Joseph. *The Trail of Tears*. Random House, 2003. (for grades 2-4)

Broyles, Anne. *Priscilla and the Hollyhocks*. Charlesbridge Publishing, 2019. (fiction ages 6-9)

Cornelissen, Cornelia. *Soft Rain: A Story of the Cherokee Trail of Tears*. Random House Children's Books, 2009. (middle grade fiction)

Jackson, Bryan D. *Chattahoochee Rain: A Cherokee novella*. Gadugi Media, 2019. (fiction for ages 12 and up)

Lossiah, Lynn King. *The Secrets and Mysteries of the Cherokee Little People, Yuñwi Tsunsdi'*. Book Publishing Company (TN), 1998.

Robinson, Prentice & Willena. *Nature Names in Tsalagi*. Cherokee Language and Culture, 2000.

Roop, Peter and Connie Roop. *If You Lived with the Cherokee*. Scholastic, 1998.

Tapper, Suzanne Cloud. *The Cherokee: A Proud People*. Enslow Publishers, 2005.

Acknowledgments

My wife, Penelope, is always willing to hear the first draft aloud, which stretches the bands of marital commitment to new cosmic heights. *Gvgeyui.*

My editor, Amanda Gibson, converted a pain-inspired tossed salad into a healing medley that made me thankful I survived and followed through. *Wado.*

Paul George (Cherokee Nation), my dear cousin-brother, graciously offered his production skills, best thinking, and compassion, to help make this book a complete Cherokee project.

Doug Sutherland, MD, FACS, Nicole Strickland, MD, and Jack Walter, MD, kept me alive through seven hours of surgery on a cold February day so that I might once again emerge cancer-free and see this book to its publication. Patricia Meyer, ND, helped treat me for the final five years I was able to keep my bladder and was my primary care provider for most of my adulthood. My childhood friend, Doug Austin, helped make *Ned Christie* come alive; that's some boss stuff, Doug! Tom Craighead was kind enough to send me updated photos of the Cherry Mansion area on the banks of the Tennessee River in Savannah during his recent journey; they provided much inspiration. My thanks to my grandmother Aileen, who first made me aware of who Mary was, and to the late Don L. Shadburn for helping me verify the particulars.

To my beta readers, especially Mary Price Boday, Ellis Craig, Paul George, and Joseph Warren, all of the Cherokee Nation, for providing helpful feedback on the draft—wado!

David Fuller, of Australia, has been kind in lending his time, talents, and compassion. MariLou Harveland shared her thoughts and perspective on teen dating and whether or not things are anywhere near what they once were. I was happy to hear that, sometimes, they certainly are. Jan Keny was willing to share her professional observations on whether Devon's character was redeemable, which was greatly appreciated. The same goes for Larry Easterling, another valued beta reader, who also ultimately agreed that this guy had the potential to come around; thanks for the encouragement, Larry! Feather Smith (Cherokee Nation) was kind enough to share her knowledge about white eagle corn. Victoria Harrison (beta reader) of Houston has been a wonderful source of encouragement through the years. My Cherokee Nation communities, Cherokee Community of Puget Sound and the Mt. Hood Cherokees, have been supportive over the years, and I'm grateful for the companionship.

I wish to thank Claire Elise Ary and Paisley Fao for their inspiration. Sometimes writing is just plain fun.

Early on, Alexis Watt (Cherokee Nation), 2015 Cherokee Remember the Removal Ride alumnus, was extremely generous in helping me understand the basic intricacies of preparing for and participating in the annual ride. She helped me realize the sacredness of this journey is such that it is almost impossible to do it justice in writing absent some direct observation. Thus, the story took the path that it did. Wado, Alexis, and we continue to be proud of you and your contemporaries.

And finally, I extend my gratitude again to my adopted "auntie," Mary Price Boday, for her continued encouragement and enduring friendship.

About The Author

BRYAN D. JACKSON descends from a prominent Cherokee family instrumental in Cherokee Nation history. The Rogers family occupied the area of northwest Georgia that served as the gateway to the old Cherokee Nation. His direct ancestors are listed on the Reservation Roll of 1817, the Henderson Roll, Tahlequah, Oklahoma citizenship rolls of 1887, as well as the Siler, Chapman, Hester, and Miller rolls.

Some of Bryan's collateral ancestors journeyed the Trail of Tears in the Bell Detachment from October, 1838 to January, 1839, and his father and grandmother grew up within two miles of Kituwah (*Gidu-hwa*) Mound, considered the mother town of the Cherokee people.

Bryan earned a master's degree in theological studies and a bachelor's degree in criminal justice. He is the author of *Chattahoochee Rain: a Cherokee novella*, and lives on an island in the middle of the Puget Sound, sharing space with his wife, Penelope, and their beloved canine family members. He enjoys communing with the deer, raccoon, bald eagle, osprey, coyote, river otter, and orcas.

His tribal affiliation is extended through his membership in official satellite communities of the Cherokee Nation. His cousins within the Cherokee Nation descend from the Collins, Cordery, Harris, McNair, Rogers, Sanders, Vann, and other families.

Other books by Bryan D. Jackson

12 ½ Wall Street

Chattahoochee Rain: A Cherokee novella